HER TUMULTUOUS LOVES . . .

Charles Ashton—the dashing young Lord who swept her off her feet and taught her love's most dangerous lesson . . .

Galen Le Blanc—the spirited Revolutionary who sparked her desire and exposed the depths of her woman's power . . .

Jonathan Rathrock—the proud sea Captain who would own an island, build an empire, and carry her along on his tempestuous tidal wave of glory . . .

Bryan Rathrock—the prized son whose wild romantic spirit, like Lucy's own, would sire a new generation of Rathrocks . . .

These were the entanglements of Lucy Hamlin's life . . . the men whose strengths, passions and longings stirred her own consuming desires, and whose destinies would never escape the hold of her womanhood. . . .

Hide My Savage Heart

GIMONE HALL

PYRAMID BOOKS NEW YORK

HIDE MY SAVAGE HEART
A PYRAMID BOOK

Copyright © 1977 by Gimone Hall

All rights reserved. No part of this publication may be reproduced or transmitted in any form or by any means, electronic or mechanical, including photocopy, recording, or any information storage and retrieval system, without permission in writing from the publisher.

Pyramid edition published January 1977

Library of Congress Catalog Card Number: 76-55128

Printed in the United States of America

Pyramid Books are published by Pyramid Publications (Harcourt Brace Jovanovich, Inc.). Its trademarks, consisting of the word "Pyramid" and the portrayal of a pyramid, are registered in the United States Patent Office.

PYRAMID PUBLICATIONS (Harcourt Brace Jovanovich, Inc.).
757 Third Avenue, New York, N.Y. 10017

PART I

Lucy — 1847

Chapter 1

Even before darkness had fallen, Lucy Hamlin knew this night would change her life. Restlessly she flung open French doors and, smoothing the rose-colored layers of her silk ball gown over her horsehair crinoline, she stepped onto the front balcony of Callow Hill. Letting her gaze roam across the bare, dusky heaths for which her home was named, she searched for something distinctive to mark the momentous hour.

All along the avenue of carefully tended oaks, carriage lights glowed like fireflies of the just vanished summer. She heard the sigh of dying locusts, the staccato crunch of horses' hooves, the laughter of ladies handed down from broughams. Tonight was the final ball of the season, the last of Lucy's coming-out year.

The breeze, wafting up, had a current of autumn coolness, but if the air held the clue Lucy sought, if it smelled of catastrophe, foretelling that the change in Lucy's life would be other than she envisioned, she could not have noticed. She was enveloped by the aroma of gardenias pinned against her twin clusters of black sausage curls.

The card accompanying the flowers had said only, "Always, Charles." Words did not come easily to Charles Ashton, but tonight he had achieved an unwitting eloquence. In those two words Lucy read the sum of the rest of her existence. Tonight and forever, Charles. A kind and gentle fireside, an adoring husband, and—Grandemas.

Cousin Caroline, joining her on the balcony, could not help murmuring, "Oh, how lucky you are, Lucy!" How often did a suitor who would one day be a lord and inherit an estate like Grandemas speak for the daughter of a country squire—even though she be the granddaughter of a second son of a baronet? How often could a girl restore a title to her family by marrying a man so completely pleasing as Charles?

Lucky—but Caroline would have been astounded and dismayed if she had known that from the events of the night Lucy's life would flame and, as though a spark from the quiet hearth had ignited something very combustible inside her, she would go blazing across continents, where the sweet lamplit evenings of Callow Hill would be lost forever.

"Caroline—" Lucy's voice trailed. There had been some confidence she had wanted to make—something about her peculiar lack of ecstasy at this zenith of her girlhood. But Lucy herself did not understand. She did not know how to explain it.

Lucy's pretty cousin turned her head and smiled fondly. It was to be expected that Lucy forget to complete her sentences tonight. It was natural she be at a loss for words. She thought she saw what had claimed Lucy's attention.

"There he is! Step into the shadows, you brazen goose! Don't let him see you watching for him!" Used to deferring to the younger Caroline in matters of decorum, Lucy jumped back instinctively. "Oh, he *did* see us!" said Caroline. "Charles! Charles, hullo!"

The man in the skirted frock coat looked up, sweeping his hat from his head. In his lapel he had impishly thrust a gardenia matching Lucy's. It was rakish, for Charles Ashton. He was in a rare mood, having come tonight not to dance, but to claim his prize. He had allowed Lucy her season, her admirers, her fun. Indeed, he believed it necessary to a woman's contentment that she have such memories.

It had been trying for him. It had pained him to see her waltzing in other men's arms. But now he was to be rewarded for his patience. Tonight he and Lucy would be betrothed. Charles had jumped lightly from his carriage and his voice was gay as he called out. Obviously no harbingers of tragedy had come to *him*.

"Caroline! Come down at once. I cannot wait!" Laughing, Caroline turned to Lucy, who was blushing in the murk. It was for Lucy the message was intended.

"We're coming, Charles!" Lucy cried, feeling ridiculous at having hidden, wanting to deny the strange wave of emotion that rushed over her at his words. Was this love? If so, she did not care for it. It reminded her of the way she'd felt the first time she'd gone flying over the head of her father's best hunting horse. It was reminiscent of the sensation in her stomach when she'd been sent to Miss Alpin's school where, with great travail, she'd acquitted herself only fairly at music, painting on velvet and embroidery.

Dread. Not fear, which was simpler, purer, but dread, which was more debilitating. Imagine dreading poor, dear Charles! He was a man—was that it? Did she dread the marriage bed? Or was it something else?

He had brought a friend with him—a stranger, looking very military in his frogged jacket. And fierce, she thought with that dark red mustache, as though his very nostrils spewed fire. The stranger gazed up at her shamelessly, and she thought in despair, "I shall be stared at from every quarter tonight. Everyone knows." She turned abruptly to go inside and with a burst of energy, descended the stairs so rapidly that Caroline was left gasping behind.

"Lucy, may I introduce Jonathan Rathrock, a dear friend of mine? He was captain of our rowing team when we were at school together, and we've shared many a dunking. He's captain of more than a racing shell now. He commands his own ship, young as he is—Jonathan could never stay away from water—and he's due to be decorated by Queen Victoria for sending a gang of pirates to the briny depths off Borneo."

"So you're a hero, Captain Rathrock. You may have my first dance, then. I always award it to heroes."

Jonathan Rathrock was taken aback only for an instant before he swept Lucy away into a waltz. Lucy was more astonished at her behavior than he. In fact, she scarcely noticed him at first, so busy was she trying to explain it to herself. She could not excuse herself that she had only been gracious to a friend of Charles. Tonight of all nights he should have had the first dance, and she was stung at the sight of him, waltzing with Caroline, treading on her gown in his confusion.

Then she was aware of the captain's blue eyes boring into her without a flicker of the humor with which other men greeted Lucy's little unconventionalities. She had never danced the waltz quite like this, either. Captain Rathrock did not hold her waist lightly to avoid crushing her dress, as her partners usually did. He guided her as though she were the helm of a ship. She felt as though she were mindless equipment in his hands and, as they skimmed across the floor, the good wind of Jamaica might have filled the sails of her crinoline and petticoats.

She looked up into his face with something akin to awe, struggling now for words, for Lucy was unused to being subject to men. Always it had been she with her looks and her wit, who had subjugated them.

"Allow me a confession, Captain," she said prettily, "I've never danced with a hero before."

He did not laugh as she expected. He only said solemnly, "I am no hero, Miss Hamlin."

"Oh, but the pirates, sir!" she cried with ladylike horror.

"Poor, mangy thieves! I had bigger guns and their junks were no match for my vessel. A victory of the strong over the weak."

"But the queen—"

"That is exactly the sort of victory the crown is always ready to reward," he replied scornfuly. "It's the savings of cargoes of tea that has merit. Twenty pounds a head, the queen offers for pirates in the China seas."

"Oh, do cease this protest, Captain. Enjoy your acclaim. I predict it will not be the last. I predict you will be hung with as many decorations as a Christmas tree before your career is done."

"You're no seer, Miss Hamlin," he said. "It's something of more substance than glory I'm looking for. I intend to petition the crown for it, and when I have it, I shall leave the Navy."

"And what is this thing that attracts you more than glory, sir?"

"Land, Miss Hamlin. I come from a long line of Navy men, not a one of whom ever had a substantial holding of land. A man is incomplete without land."

"You'll become a gentleman farmer, then? Give up the sea? Pardon me, sir, if I tell you I do not believe it will work. You seem to belong so much to the sea, I can almost feel the rocking of the waves."

He smiled then, at last, his blue eyes lighting, the mustache twitching up gaily. She did not know whether his smile was especially wonderful, or if the extreme contrast with his solemnity only made it seem so. To her distinct relief, he seemed more manageable now that she had made him smile.

"Give up the sea! What an idea! I must have the sea

all around me. That is exactly why I shall ask the queen for an island."

Lucy could not help laughing aloud. "An island! And you shall run it like your ship, I suppose. Really, Captain, do you think the queen hands out islands like Cornish pasties to every worthy young ship's master? England is an island, sir. Can't that satisfy you?"

"No, Miss Hamlin, and I am not just any young ship's master. My father was at Nelson's side at Trafalgar, and, as for myself, this is not my first or even my fifth decoration. Well, I've told you my dream. Tell me yours."

"Mine?" But the music ended and the memory of her treatment of Charles was upon her. She looked about frantically to find him.

"Save me another dance, Miss Hamlin—a waltz, I cannot bear the quadrille," Captain Rathrock said as he walked away.

Then he was gone, and Charles was at her side. *He* had known where *she* was. *He* had not been bemused. She danced away with him, as if to say that there was her dream, of course.

"Did you like Jonathan?" Charles asked.

"Oh, dear, I don't know. He has vainglorious ideas, hasn't he? And he did not even thank me for the dance, only said to save him another."

Charles laughed. "Well, you shall not. You will be too busy with me."

She smiled at him and saw the smile breathe happiness into his eyes. How good he was! He had not even been cross with her. She felt warm as a bird returned to its nest. She was only glad he was dancing her toward the veranda door. The dread had vanished. It had been nothing but a case of nerves. Her mother would have told her if she had been alive.

"Lucy," he said as the darkness closed around them, "let's go for a drive in my carriage. We won't be missed."

It was what she had expected. She knew she should protest that the air was chill and let him rush off triumphantly for her cloak. But it was all too ordinary, and Lucy had just come from the arms of Captain Rathrock, who was not at all ordinary. Perhaps it was a desire to prolong the sensation of the dance. Or perhaps it had to do with her earlier feelings that the night must be special, worth remembering to tell her children and their children.

"Charles—I would sooner ride horses than be tugged along behind them. Shall we? There is a moon."

"Ride!" he exclaimed. "You cannot ride in that gown!"

"I'll change and slip out. No one will know. Please, Charles!"

He smiled tenderly. It delighted him to indulge her. He was aware she would give him uncomfortable moments in marriage, but all in all, he liked the surprises she gave him. She would make life at Grandemas interesting. "As you like, Lucy. Only take care you are not seen."

"I will meet you at the stables, Charles." She squeezed his hand and went back inside. Mounting the stairs, she was elated. *This* was how it should feel, she thought. Across the room she saw her father among the guests. Dear Papa. He had tried so hard to be both mother and father to her. She knew he had despaired of her on occasion. Once when she had defied a dictum of Miss Alpin's school, he had wept over her. "I'll make you proud of me tonight, Papa," she vowed. "In an hour I'll be back, and you can make your announcement. I will give you a son who is a lord to make up for the heir my mother couldn't provide, dying giving birth to the likes of me."

In her room she struggled with the many buttons down the back of her gown. She should have brought Caroline to help, but it was too late to think of that. As if in answer to her thought, a knock came on her door.

"Who is it?" Lucy whispered.

"Aunt Madeliene," came the conspiratorial reply.

"Thank goodness!" Lucy opened the door to Caroline's mother. "Come and unfasten me, Aunt."

"Unfasten you!" Aunt Madeliene's stern mouth dropped in astonished horror. "Don't dare pick this moment for a female complaint, Lucy Hamlin! Too much is at stake!"

"Female complaint! I am only going for a ride with Charles."

"Can you never do anything sensibly, Lucy?" Aunt Madeliene said, laying her hand against her bodice, which was still heaving from her having climbed the stairs too rapidly. The gesture, which she had had many an occasion to resort to during the years she had had charge of Lucy, was meant to draw remorse for torment of her poor, rheumatic person. Her injured tone told Lucy she knew whose idea the ride had been.

Lucy gave her aunt an affectionate hug. The torment of the years had been mutual, for since Aunt Madeliene and Caroline had come to live at Callow Hill on the death of Caroline's father, Lucy had endured an endless succession of lectures, rapped fingers, and hairbrushes that pained equally no matter on which end of her body her aunt used them.

Yet, all that time, Lucy had never discerned favoritism for the well-behaved Caroline. Even now, Aunt Madeliene seemed as happy for Lucy as though Charles' attentions had come to her own daughter.

"Aunt Maddie, is it so wrong that I should have a bit of fun with my proposal?"

"Most girls would think it fun enough on the veranda," sniffed her aunt.

Aunt Maddie was sparked to action at last, and the thought of the waiting suitor made her hands tremble on the buttons. Fastened into the blue skirt and velvet jacket of her riding habit, Lucy assessed herself in the pier glass.

There were the bright brown eyes she had used so well to tease and mock, the brows a trifle too thick for style, and the mouth, always a little crooked, with nothing she could do about that. She made the crooked mouth smile to show herself how very pretty she was in spite of her shortcomings.

Aunt Madeliene stood back, lips pursed. "Perhaps it's just as well. In a way that outfit becomes you more than the gown, for all the work and fine silk that went into it. Do take those gardenias out of your hair. They look silly now."

Lucy set about removing the flowers, turning this way and that before the glass to make sure no trace of plumpness had attached itself to her slim figure.

"It's a wonder," said her well-padded aunt, "the way you consume cherry tarts. If only you'd been more careful with your parasol—you've a trace of tan."

"Oh, Aunt—"

"Go on with you, Lucy, you're fit for a lord, indeed! I'll stay and hang the gown. It mustn't be rumpled later when your engagement is announced."

One last hug, and then Lucy ran quietly down the stairs and out through the deserted servants' lodgings. Charles already stood in the stable door, holding the bridles of a gelding and of Gypsy, Lucy's mare. Mounting, they trotted sedately up the lane, out onto the road. Then, breaking away, Lucy called, "I'll race you, Charles!

Gypsy is faster than that beast of yours any day—or night."

She heard him cry her name, heard the thud of hooves behind her. She laughed, knowing he was not concerned for her. She was a fine horsewoman. Gypsy had been a present on her thirteenth birthday, and the two of them had been a team for years. Over a small fence she went, her carefully coiffed curls jouncing loose. So much work with curling rags, all for naught. How would she explain that? On they raced through the moonlight.

"When I catch you, Lucy Hamlin, you'll be caught for good!" Charles shouted, infected with the spirit of the chase. "When I catch you, you'll be Lucy Hamlin no longer!"

Lucy wanted the moment to last forever. She wanted to go on tearing through the night with its scents of rock moss and flowering gorse, forever a hoofbeat out of his ardent reach. But remembering that there was a purpose to all this, she disciplined herself and reigned in suddenly. He was beside her instantly, his horse half rearing at the abruptness of the halt. He seized her bridle as he leaped down.

"I couldn't ford the creek," she cried. "I'd have gotten my shoes damp." And she lifted her skirt to show him a scandalous ankle, still clad in its thin dancing slipper.

The sight broke Charles Ashton's last measure of reserve. Gripping her around the waist with both hands, he pulled her from her saddle and crushed her in an embrace. Her breasts were pressed to his silk cravat and only the voluminousness of her clothing prevented unthinkable contact with his tight white trousers. She had never been in such an intimate situation before, and the sureness of his possession frightened her.

"Charles, stop!" she moaned desperately.

"Stop! Whatever for?" he cried joyfully, "I love you!"

The dread she had felt on the balcony came rushing back a hundred times over. Only now she was reminded of having accidentally shut herself into a small pantry closet. She had forgotten the jar of peppermints she had come for and had screamed and beaten on the door. Now she beat on Charles Ashton's chest. She shoved against him with her knees. It would have been more seemly to faint or to pretend to, but it did not occur to her. As his grasp loosened, she flung herself onto Gypsy's saddle.

"Lucy!" His shout was incredulous. As she urged Gypsy forward, he seized the bridle. The confused animal whinnied and rose on its hind legs. The hoof of a foreleg caught Charles in the temple. Horrified, Lucy saw him crumple, but Gypsy had gone mad and she could do nothing but cling for her life as the mare tore across the heath.

"Gypsy! Easy!" The tone of Lucy's voice was far from calming as she was carried from the spot where Charles lay. Then the mare plunged into a clump of willow near the stream edge and, stumbling, went down among the rocks. Lucy rolled off and ran back to Charles.

He lay perfectly motionless, his face as pale as the moonlight. Blood ran over the hurt expression he still wore. With a cry, she waded into the stream, wetting the front of her skirt with cold water to bathe his face. Charles did not revive, but now her skirt was covered with his blood.

Perhaps he was dead. She hesitated, too frightened to put her hand beneath his waistcoat to feel for a heartbeat. "I must go for a doctor." The thought cleared her mind, and she ran back to the mare. "Gypsy, get up! Get up!" But the animal only floundered. Charles' mount had vanished, so she struck out on foot, flinging aside the wet slippers that dragged her back, lifting her skirts so that her pantalets gleamed as she ran.

Breathless, she gained the road, tripping and falling, adding a thick layer of its dust to her wet, bloody clothes. In the distance on a rise of land, she could barely see the lights of Callow Hill, and, too exhausted to move, she began to shout, sitting there in the road. Oh, no one inside would hear her, but maybe some groom dozing beside a carriage in the drive. . . .

Hoofbeats came toward her. A man on horseback galloped around a curve. "Miss Hamlin! Charles' horse came to the stables alone. I've been looking—"

"Oh, Captain Rathrock—a terrible accident!"

"Where?"

"I'll show you. You don't know the way."

"Tell me," he snapped, "and go on to the house."

"Cut away from the road in the next field. Go until you jump a stone fence, then east until you reach a stream. He is lying beside it."

Somehow his assumption that she would go on for help renewed her strength. Staggering, she ran until at last she reached the drive where she wasted one dear second to catch her breath against a lime tree in the dooryard. The windows had been thrown open to cool the dancers and through them she could see dresses swirling like a field of primroses. Claret sparkled in the family's best Waterford crystal and violins wavered a familiar Strauss waltz.

Into this setting on the night that was to have been her father's proudest, rushed Lucy Hamlin, barefoot, her hair streaming ludicrously from its pinnings, her riding habit torn, wet and covered with blood.

"Where is Dr. Bittle?" she cried above the screams and shouts. And then, remembering where he was, in the graveyard two months since, Lucy did what she should have done in the first place, what would have saved so very much trouble—she fainted.

Chapter 2

"Is he dead?" The words were out of Lucy's mouth almost before her eyes opened. Before she had had the opportunity to find herself lying in her nightdress in her jappaned bedstead, the damask curtains drawn over the windows so that she could not tell if it were night or day. Caroline still in her yellow ball gown, her face pale in the dim glow from the lamp, pushed her cousin's shoulders back against the goosedown pillows.

"He is not dead. He's in a coma, so Captain Rathrock calls it."

"Captain Rathrock! What has he to do with it? He is no doctor!"

"He is the best we have. Your father has sent for help, but we cannot expect a physician before morning. Captain Rathrock is familiar with medicine. He learned it at sea."

"What does that mean—a coma?"

"He remains unconscious and cannot be brought to his senses. What else it means, I don't know."

"Caroline! Do not use that brainless female pose with *me!* You know what else it means. It means he still may die, doesn't it?"

"Lucy—try to rest."

"I must go to him at once!"

"Don't! He won't even know you are there. What good can it do to make another spectacle of yourself dashing through the halls in your nightgown at three A.M.?"

"Three A.M. Is that the time? I shall be a murderess if he dies!"

"Murderess! Not you, Lucy! Charles would never say so. Oh, how could this awful thing have happened! I don't understand at all."

Caroline's sweet face was so baffled, so tragic, that Lucy could not help trying to explain. She took her

17

cousin's hand and held it tightly, as though Caroline were the sufferer instead of she.

"I don't know—I wanted to tell you before. It was a feeling I had first on the balcony when he called to us, and then when he was holding me—"

"Kissing you?" whispered Caroline, her eyes wide.

"Kissing me? Oh—I can't remember. He was—holding me very tightly, and I thought of the pantry where we used to steal candy. Or I did; *you* never would. And I remembered the time I was locked in. You were there to let me out. It was just like that. I was somewhere I shouldn't have been and this time there was no cousin to undo the latch. I was to bear the consequences forever."

Caroline shook her head, struggling vainly to comprehend. Her expression said she thought Lucy might be delirious, suffering some strange aftereffect of the strange evening. "He was holding you, and you thought of a pantry full of peppermint? And you cannot *remember* if he were kissing you? If Charles Ashton had kissed *me* I should have noticed. I should have been rapturous."

"I'm sure you would," said Lucy, giving her cousin a studious glance. "Any woman ought. It must be that something is wrong with me. Something I have known ever since I realized he loved me. Oh, I enjoyed the luring of him, and I was glad that one poor girl child could make her papa so happy. Yes, I enjoyed it until the very last moment, when I showed him my ankle to provoke him. He was so suitable—how could I admit what I must now—that something is left out of my character—that I am less than a woman?"

"Oh, Lucy, don't say such things!" cried the distressed Caroline. "You want a husband and children and a home, which is what any woman wants. And you are fond of Charles."

"Yes, I am fond of him," Lucy said grimly. She propped herself on an elbow and turned up the wick of the oil lamp. In the increased light she noticed for the first time the redness of Caroline's eyes that showed she had been weeping, the crushed satin rosettes on her ball gown that, like Lucy's life, could never be made the same.

"I'm fond of him, but I don't feel what he feels. When he held me, I could feel he was driven by some terrible power, one I could not experience or understand. I was frightened. And yet, I wanted to feel it too. It must be wonderful to be as consumed as he was. Was it love, do you think, Caroline?"

"Love," snorted Caroline. "It was the demon of his sex. If your mother were alive, you would have been more prepared for it. No woman would want to experience *that*. It's to be endured because it's necessary, like corsets and tonics."

"Are you talking about the marriage act, Caroline?" said Lucy, mildly astonished. On the balcony, it had crossed her mind that she dreaded it, but she had only a vague idea what was meant. Caroline, nodding wisely, knew little more. *Her* mother had put the matter off, thinking that the next year, the year of her daughter's coming out, was time enough for such distressing revelations.

Lucy lay back, remembering the power of Charles' arms around her, his seeming consumed with a desire to consume her. No, she would never be able to submit to that, not unless she felt that way, too. She was unlikely to feel it, if Caroline were right, and what did that bode for her?

Unable to endure the thought of life as a spinster, her mind turned again to Charles and she cried out, "Caroline, if only he lives, I shall devote my life to him!" Any contradiction between this and her earlier thought did not bother her, for she thought of Charles now as a dear invalid, to be loved for having had such feelings toward her, to be petted and catered to, since he would be no longer capable of doing anything about them.

"Oh, if only you can!" said Caroline. "Your papa has sent for Charles' father. Lord Ashton may not allow the match, even if Charles recovers. You behaved very badly. Your papa says you are likely ruined. He says you are to go away as soon as he can arrange it."

"Go away! But I don't want to. I want to stay at Callow Hill. I want to stay near Charles."

"Your papa says it is best. But you shan't go alone, cousin. I'll go with you. We'll be together, no matter what."

"You're too good, Caroline! You mustn't suffer for my misdeeds."

"But I want to go. I should worry so terribly about you. I shall always want to be with you."

"Come to bed, Caroline. You've been up all night.

Sleep beside me the way we used to when we were children."

"I *am* tired," sighed Caroline. "I suppose it will do no good to exhaust myself. In the morning we may all need our strength more." She turned for Lucy to unfasten her and, tumbling out of petticoats and corsets, fell into bed in her camisole and drawers, her slight form making a deep indentation in the fine goosedown mattress.

Lucy lay wakeful until her cousin's breathing told her she slept. Then quietly she got up and, taking a candle, crept out into the black halls. She was not certain which room had become Charles Ashton's, but a tiny glow beneath one door guided her way.

Pushing it open, she was aware of nothing but Charles' face, so white she could scarcely tell the skin from the swath of bandages. A candle near the head of the fourposter threw light onto the still face as though it were already that of a corpse. Was it? She sprang forward with a cry and bent over him to search for a sign of breath.

"That's not necessary, Miss Hamlin, I'm watching him." She whirled, making the flame of her own candle gutter, and the form of Jonathan Rathrock wavered into sight. He was sprawled awkwardly into an upholstered chair and looked as though he had been half asleep. There was something unusual about him. For a moment she could not think what; then she realized that his shoes were off, and she could see the straps of his trousers beneath his stockings. Lucy was unused to seeing men even in such a minor state of undress, yet such was her state of mind that seeing him did not remind her that she herself was in her nightclothes.

"Captain Rathrock! How is he?"

"There's no change."

"I'm going to stay, too," Lucy said, blowing out her candle and sitting down in a straight chair close to the bed.

"But there's no need, as I said. Anyway you've hardly the proper attire for the occasion."

She remembered then and flushed, wondering what outlines he might have seen beneath the muslin of her gown. Nonetheless, her chin tilted up and she said, "This is not an occasion, Captain, like a hunt or a tea."

For the second time that night she made him smile, and for the second time felt relief at having done so. His mouth turned in amusement, and he said, "You are right, of course, Miss Hamlin. There is no correct dress for it. Well, you shall stay, and if anyone comes who would not understand the matter as we do, you shall hide in the wardrobe and cause no more talk tonight."

They sat for a while, each occupied with private thoughts until Lucy began to wonder what *his* thoughts were. He kept staring at her, and though she was deep in the shadows, she began to long for at least a quilt to put around her. She could say she was cold, but either she would have to give him a better view by rising to get the cover or he would have to bring it. She was not sure she wanted him closer, for if an ankle had had such effect on Charles, what might a nightdress do to Jonathan Rathrock? Some intuition told her he was not a man of the same niceties as Charles and that what Caroline had called the demon of his sex would be stronger in him than in Charles.

At last he spoke. "I've been thinking, Miss Hamlin, that we might agree as to what happened on the heath last evening. We might say, for example, that you were set upon by a band of thieves who stole the ring Charles was to give you. You see, Charles does not have it."

Reaching into his pocket, he took out a beautiful pear-shaped diamond surrounded by tiny emeralds. Lucy gasped, thinking that even now it should have been on her finger. Captain Rathrock put the ring away. "A report could be filed with the police, and they would receive mysterious information about a London pawnshop where they would find it safe and sound. I could arrange it."

Her heart jumped. Not to be disgraced after all! To have Lord Ashton's blessing, another chance at everything symbolized by the magnificent ring—if only Charles lived and forgave. But even as gratitude welled up, she heard herself say, "You are gallant, Captain Rathrock, but I must tell the truth. It would not do for Charles to recover and find me a liar as well as whatever else I am."

"As you say," he nodded, and went across the room to replace the ring among Charles Ashton's clothing.

"Captain," she said to his back, "I am grateful for all you have done tonight. I had forgotten to thank you."

"It was nothing, Miss Hamlin. I am only sorry I had to shoot the mare."

The mare! Suddenly to Lucy's mind came a picture of her beloved Gypsy floundering among the rocks, legs broken, she realized for the first time. She had gone to death without a thought from her mistress, and suddenly Lucy's tears burst forth. It was her final shame of the evening that Captain Rathrock should see her at Charles' bedside, weeping over a horse.

Morning came somehow. Jonathan Rathrock shook her awake where she slept with her head buried in her arms on the night table. She slipped down the hall to crawl into bed with Caroline. Lord Ashton arrived, so livid with anger that Lucy was told to stay out of his sight. A letter was posted to Mme. Fichaud's school in Paris inquiring about immediate admission for Lucy and Caroline.

"A school!" cried Lucy. "Oh, I cannot bear it. I will not do one more piece of pokerwork or embroider one more homily on a satin pillow!" She had been done with school, done with teachers who discovered her Jane Austen hidden beneath her needlework, who turned her neat-looking embroidery to its underside tangle and, shaking their heads, made her do it all over. Lucy would never be able to bear those empty-minded hours. She wept again, this time in fury.

"I am too old for school, Caroline!"

"It's a great opportunity, Lucy! We never thought we should go to school on the Continent. But now that your papa must get you far away, he doesn't mind the expense. He will even pay my way, so that I may go with you as a good influence. He will do anything to protect your match with Charles. And we shall not do needlework as much as we shall learn French—the language and the music and the fashion—oh the fashion, Lucy! It is a school for English girls to do just that."

Lucy did not see Charles again. He remained unconscious, cared for by the doctors and nurses that Lord Ashton brought in. Now and then one of them would bustle past her in the hall, but Lucy never dared to speak.

At length Lord Ashton himself sent for her. In her bottle green taffeta, judged by Aunt Madeliene to be her most demure dress, she was ushered by that lady to the door of the library, where most reluctantly she relinquished her grip on her aunt's hand.

She had met Lord Ashton only once before, and at that time he had paid her little heed, apparently not believing the seriousness of his son's intentions. He had spent much of his time recently in London, where, according to Charles, he labored in Parliament to prevent the passage of something called the Ten Hours Act, which he declared would wreck the economy. He had given his consent to the match mostly on the strength of Charles persuasion.

Now, in the library, he appeared no larger a man than Lucy remembered, and yet his presence filled up the place, changing it so that this room where she had spent so many pleasant hours belonged to him and not to Callow Hill at all. He paced about her, reminding her of a hound with a rabbit at bay. Her legs shook, and she was glad for the crinoline which hid the trembling.

"I cannot understand it!" he cried at last. "You are pretty, but a dozen girls of Charles' own circle have whiter skins and daintier features. What is it that drives him to you?"

"There is more to a woman that her looks, sir," said Lucy in a faint but steady voice.

"Oh to be sure!" said the frustrated lord impatiently. "There are her manners, her deportment. Surely you do not excell *there*. That leaves only your accomplishments, and I have heard you play a barcarole. In truth, Miss Hamlin, you missed notes!"

"I should have done better had I played Beethoven," said Lucy, her voice stronger. "I much prefer it." Her legs trembled even harder, so that she was afraid they would not hold her. The demon that was always in her had surfaced. She knew better than to say what she had said.

"Beethoven!" The rage within him was released so simply. "Beethoven is not for a young lady! If you come to Grandemas, you shall not play Beethoven! If you come to Grandemas—and that shall not be decided until Charles is well. I don't mind your knowing I shall try to talk him out of this marriage. I may even forbid it. It will depend on you. I myself have chosen Mme. Fichaud's school. All the women of our family have attended it. You will smooth your rough edges, Miss Hamlin, and prepare yourself to be the mother of nobility!"

"Sir, no sons of mine shall ever make you blush in shame," said Lucy, blushing poppy-red herself. Without waiting for his leave, she fled the library, and running down the hall, closed herself behind the doors of the drawing room where she launched into a spirited rendition of a German dance on the piano.

"Oh!" she thought as she poured her anger into the music, "smooth my rough edges! What has French fashion to do with motherhood, anyway?" She told herself she hoped he heard her Beethoven, though she had shut the doors especially to prevent it. "It's almost as though he thinks I did it on purpose! It was only an accident. It could have happened to anyone." But could it? Or was it the flaw in her character? Was misadventure her destiny? The very doubt of herself made her angrier, so that she played even more loudly, while tears ran down her cheeks, and truly she did not care if Lord Ashton heard.

A few days later, answering a knock on her door, she found Jonathan Rathrock in a greatcoat. "I am leaving, Miss Hamlin; I came to say good-bye."

"You are off to London then, in quest on your island?"

"Yes, and I shall have it, even though you laughed."

"I am sorry I laughed, Captain. You said once you were no hero, but you will always be one to me."

"And you, Miss Hamlin, will never be a liar, whatever else you are. And whatever else you are, I would marry you post haste if I were Charles, though I would do it full knowing you are a woman who will cause talk."

His eyes twinkled once again like stars out of the night of his gravity. He turned on his heel and was gone. Watching him from her window as he rode away, she supposed she would never see him again.

Chapter 3

On a cold November morning Lucy herself left Callow Hill. Only a dull line of dawn was in the sky when she awoke chilled with something that had nothing to do with the unlighted fires. The house was still. No servants' footsteps scurried past. There was no scraping of embers in the grates. She tiptoed down to the room where Charles Ashton lay and stealthily pushed open the door. In the chair where Jonathan Rathrock had sat was a florid nurse, snoring. Quietly, Lucy crossed to Charles' bed and stared down into his unknowing face. "Good-bye, Charles. Only get well, and I will love you forever," she whispered and, to mark the promise, she bent and kissed him full on the mouth. She imagined then that his lips responded to hers, that they strained upward to keep contact, as if wherever he was, he knew who kissed him, and knowing made her vow sacred.

There was little else to say good-bye to. She endured stilted farewells to her father among the pile of portmanteaus and basket trunks. Gypsy was dead, Caroline, her only real treasure, was going with her. Good-byes to Aunt Maddie would come later, since she had volunteered to make the trip as chaperone. The house itself was a bleak mound against the gray sky, the avenue of trees a line of gaunt soldiers called for review one last time as the cob pulled the laden carriage down the lane.

"I'm glad to be away," the practical Caroline sighed as the scene passed from sight.

"I wish the sun would shine," Lucy replied. "It seems to be getting darker instead, as if night were coming on instead of day. I feel as if a black angel is traveling with us."

"Don't talk so," reproved Aunt Maddie. "It's only going to rain; my bones are never wrong."

And rain it did—even before they had reached the village inn where they were handed aboard the Dover coach. "We'll outrun it soon," Caroline predicted, but if anything the clouds thickened. Inside the coach the sound of the rain on the roof made talk all but impossible, and dank wind rushing in through the cracks made the girls draw deeply into their cloaks. They were alone, for, although the driver stopped at inns or taverns to cry, "Anyone for Dover," the reply was always, "Not even a fool in this weather!" At least the road was macadamized, Lucy thought. There would be no slipping of horses in the mud, no upsetting of the coach. Sometime past noon, they braved the rain and, aching in every limb, made their way inside an inn for a meal of hot tea, pork pie and boiled damson pudding.

"Well, we have done half of it," Caroline said bravely. "Another five hours and we shall be in Dover."

"Yes," said Lucy glumly. Five hours to Dover. Then the steamship to Calais. After that, the journey to Paris, to the undelightful regimens of Mme. Fichaud's school. Lucy was bored. The coach had been so dark she had not even been able to read the novel she had tucked away in her reticule. Lucy did not think she could bear any more, and she had half a mind to feign a spell of vapors so she might stay here at this inn the rest of the afternoon, tucked into a warm bed, sipping tea and reading.

Suddenly the door blew open and several men in waterproofs came dripping in, talking loudly and making huge puddles on the ringbone floor. Without a glance at Lucy, Caroline or Aunt Maddie, they made their way to the snuggery and called for beer and gin mixed in a Dog's Nose. Their arrival seemed to cause undue commotion. Voices rose; discussions became heated.

"Darby Mill," someone said. "You'll not be thinking of driving the coach through there today, Tom."

"That's my route, of course. What would my gaffer say?"

"Like as not he'll be charging you for a coach burned to a cinder if you go," returned the other. "Oh, it's a disgrace, it is. They ought to hang the blighters what started it."

Aunt Maddie glared as Tom cursed and a string of terrible epithets reached the ladies' ears. He came stomping angrily out, bundling himself into his cloak. "We must leave at once," he said curtly. "We have a detour to make, and we'll have the Devil's time making Dover on schedule."

"Does he mean we may miss the boat?" Caroline cried, "Oh, I do not want to get back into that coach yet! I'm not warmed through, and I haven't finished my pudding." But the driver was already trudging out into the rain, and, climbing onto his box grimly, looked as though he wouldn't mind leaving them over a moment's delay. He had taken a bottle with him, Lucy noticed with misgiving.

Before they turned off the comforting macadamized road, Aunt Maddie, exhausted from the strenuous morning, had fallen asleep. When the horses began to strain in slick brown mud, she only slipped sideways without awakening. The girls could hear the cracking of the whip, the cursing of the driver. The wheels of the carriage slid, and the vehicle swayed. Caroline and Lucy clung to each other, too frightened to voice their fears: Either the carriage would overturn, and they would be killed; or it would become hopelessly stuck, and they would be stranded all night with the drunken Tom.

"Why did we have to make a detour?" Caroline asked. "What do you know of Darby Mill, Lucy?"

"I have never even heard of it. It can only be an insignificant little industrial town. I cannot imagine why we should avoid it. Oh! I shall have a word with Sir Tom's superiors when we reach Dover!"

"If we reach Dover—"

"We shall reach it, Caroline. I am too angry to die!"

But at that moment, as if to contradict her, the coach came to a stop.

For a long moment nothing happened. Then the door opened and a man climbed in. He was soaking, and his boots and trousers were caked in slimy mud. He shook himself, scattering droplets everywhere, glaring about as if he blamed Lucy and Caroline for being comparatively warm and dry.

"Keep your boots on your side, sir," Lucy said, drawing back her tartan skirt. "You are getting mud on me."

"I would not be if you did not take up the space of two people in that crinoline," he returned in a soft, French accent.

"I have no choice being a woman and fashion being what it is," Lucy said, secretly liking him for the audacious way he spoke to her. "But if I were a man, I would not choose to enter a carriage with muddy boots and smear them on a lady." She wanted to know more about him. He intrigued her, coming out of nowhere into the coach with his fine, delicate features that marked him for a gentleman and his clothing, a little too rough and plain, which denied it.

"I had no more choice than you," he said. "My horse threw a shoe and I was obliged to go on foot."

"So you left the poor animal to fend for itself." She was baiting him now, intent on keeping interest in the conversation.

"The horse will find its way," said the stranger. "I might have know your were one of those kind of ladies who value the beast above the man."

He got more of a reaction than he might have hoped for with this, for Lucy, reminded of her tears before Jonathan Rathrock, flushed and fell silent. It had grown dark, and the rain, if anything, had become thicker. Lucy wished for the ordeal of the journey to be over whether they made connection with the steamship or not. She fell to wondering how much of the bottle Tom had drunk to warm himself on the box, and she wished she had not lost the thread of conversation with the Frenchman, who had been diverting her mind from such thoughts.

Suddenly they topped a hill and far away on the horizon a ruddy column of fire rose into the night, tinged with tones of crimson and copper that scraped against the laden clouds. "What on earth is that?" exclaimed Caroline.

"It's Darby Mill, miss," said the Frenchman.

"But I cannot imagine that the smokestack of a mill would produce such a light."

"It's not the mill, it's the town. At least half of it is in flame. It would have been more if a merciful God had not sent this rain."

"Darby Mill," said Lucy. "So that's what the detour is about. Someone at our last stop said they should hang the ones responsible."

"Hang at least," said the Frenchman vehemently, "though some would disagree who it should be. The workers will tell you it was done deliberately by the mill owners to quell the strike, and the owners will say it was started by a striker upsetting a lantern while resisting arrest in some house in the back streets."

"A strike!" said Lucy. "Well, strikes are illegal, and those who break the law deserve what they get. So my father always says."

"You have a lot to learn, young woman! I only wish

you could have seen it—the streams run purple with filth, the children of nine bent over the pottery wheels, those that did not escape younger by dying of damage to their lungs. And the two-room houses, back-to-back, ready to burn like tinder as soon as these people dared to demand a few of their rights as human beings!" The Frenchman did not take his eyes from the red column, and in the dim coach they seemed to glow with reflected fury.

No one could doubt he had just come from Darby Mill or whom he blamed for the fire. "Such scenes will take place all over England if the Ten Hours Bill is not passed," he said. "Mark my word on it."

A sudden jerk of the carriage claimed their attention, reminding them of immediate danger, and Caroline cried in dismay, "We will never reach the steamboat on time!"

"I shall be glad for a stopover," said Lucy, "if only we reach Dover." She thought the Frenchman looked apprehensive at the news that they might miss the connection with the boat. It stood to reason that he would be crossing to France, but she wondered what he had been doing in a place like Darby Mill. One crossed the Channel to see the sights of London or tend to business in Liverpool. But why did one go to Darby Mill?

It was far past time for the boat when they rolled into the quiet, cobbled streets of Dover. "Has the Calais steamship gone?" Tom's unsteady shout from the box was only a formality. And the innkeeper's reply, "Hours ago," was no surprise. What did surprise the women was that when they reached the anteroom of the inn, the Frenchman was no longer with them. "Maybe he has friends in town to stay with," Caroline said. "And maybe he was not bound for Calais after all."

Lucy was too tired to care. She went directly upstairs, and having ordered up a light supper, climbed into bed, wishing for a hot water bottle for her feet, but too exhausted to call for one. She hardly knew what awakened her in the still-rainy dawn. At first she thought it was the sound of the sea. Then she realized that the sussurrant ebb and flow was made up of various sounds—the shuffling of feet, a murmur of voices, the squeak of ungreased wagon wheels. Opening her shutters, she looked out.

Below her window a line of perhaps a hundred persons straggled through a weighty fog. She was struck by the grayness of their bodies, bowed with defeat, covered with ashes and grime that matched the gray day. Some carried sacks of belongings. A boy of eight or ten, without mother or father, clutched a tiny sister as though she might vaporize into the rain.

But most terrible of all was the cart she had heard squeaking. From her second-storey window Lucy looked down through swirls of mist into the disfigured faces of the dead bodies it carried.

She snapped the shutters closed and sank onto the bed trembling. An intense need surged in her to do something for the people of Darby Mill who were seeking refuge in Dover. But what—toss down a few shillings? It certainly was not her affair.

"Lucy, are you ill?" Caroline sat up in bed.

"I'm only cold. The weather has not improved. Please don't open the shutters."

"You've caught a chill," Caroline declared, alarmed. "That awful ride! I'll go and have them send for a doctor. We won't go on to Paris today."

"Yes, we will," said Lucy, wanting nothing more than to be far away from here. "I shall be perfectly all right." She got up and began to wash determinedly in the marble-topped basin.

But quickly it developed that the question was not Lucy's health, but Aunt Madeliene's. "It's my rheumatism," she moaned, "I can hardly move."

"I'll get some camomile tea," said Caroline, "and we will wait here until you're better."

"It's no use. I'll be like this for a week at least."

"Then we'll wait a week," said Lucy.

"We'll lose our places, if we don't arrive on time!" cried Caroline.

"Well, then, we'll just lose them," said Lucy, although she did not relish returning to the gloom of Callow Hill, even to be near Charles.

"No," said Aunt Maddie, pulling up her covers. "You shall go on alone."

"Leave you by yourself! Go without a chaperone!" cried Caroline, shocked.

"Don't worry about leaving me," said Aunt Maddie. "I'm a tough old woman and equal to anything. Would you give up the chance of your life, Caroline? I wager Lucy is not afraid to go, even though she is already set for marriage."

They both looked at Lucy, who said with a shrug of her shoulders, "No, I'm not afraid. It's only the Channel boat and a coach to Paris."

Lucy's aunt eyed her warily. "You will not get into trouble? Your father would never forgive me. I would never forgive myself."

"I promise," said Lucy with a laugh. "It's a very dull ride. I have been before."

Then, after many kisses and admonitions on both sides, there was barely time for the two girls to breakfast before their departure. Downstairs the dining room was crowded. A long sideboard held ham, eggs, tongue, cold fowl, prawns, lampreys and potted char, but Lucy could choke down nothing but muffins and tea. Here too the shutters had been kept closed to keep out the oppressive sights of the streets, but the atmosphere of trouble drifted in, and the gentlemen talked of nothing else.

"Have they caught that madman yet?" Lucy heard someone say.

"Oh, I pray they have!" she exclaimed involuntarily.

"I fear they haven't, miss," another answered. "But they will. He gave them the slip in the night, but they'll catch him yet, even in the fog. The place is full as a tick with police. Every escape route is covered. He'll hang, no doubt."

"And well he should—anyone who would start such a fire!"

The speaker looked at her quizzically. "It's not the one who started the fire they're searching for. It's that agitator —tthe Frenchman, Galen Le Blanc, who spewed such nonsense into people's heads, the one who led the strike, a riot it was, with crazed workers blocking the way to the mill door."

Frenchman! Lucy felt suddenly faint. She knew very well which Frenchman it was.

"Our Frenchman!" Caroline whispered, her hand gripping Lucy's.

"He is far away by now," Lucy said. But she remembered the look in his eyes when he had heard that they would not make the boat. He had wanted to cross to Calais. She was certain of it.

When they stood on the wharf, cloaks held tightly against the blowing rain, they could see police uniforms everywhere. As the boat whistle echoed, vigilant eyes scanned the crowd and two guards stood at the gangplank to check the boarding passengers. "Let's hurry," Lucy said. "The sea will be rough, but at least we shall be out of the weather when we are on the ship."

She never knew quite how it happened, where he came from out of the mist and the crowd, but as she reached for her basket trunk, a man's hand brushed hers from the handle. Close to her ear a French accent whispered urgently, "Say I am your brother."

She did not look at him, and yet she could see that his clothing was more disheveled than the night before. It had been slept in, if sleeping he had done. He had cleaned his boots and combed his hair, but who would believe he was her brother? Everything about him looked French—his coat, his slender Gallic form, even the slightly triangular chin with its tell-tale thrust of purpose.

Her pulse throbbed against her ears, and she could hardly see the way before her as they approached the officers, he was carrying the trunk. She took his arm as they mounted the gangplank. Was it mere female custom that made her do it or was it a decision on her part, a gesture of solidarity?

"Your identification, sir!" Lucy heard the policeman's voice in a daze.

Galen Le Blanc was investigating his pockets earnestly. "What a nuisance. I've misplaced it. Perhaps *you* have it, my dear?"

"I will vouch for him," said Lucy, jolted from her trance. "He is my brother."

"Your brother, miss!" the tone was sneering. "But you are English, and he is French, as anyone with ears would know!"

"Certainly, he is French, if it is any of your business. My father's first wife was French, and when she died he was sent to live with her family."

"A likely story! We shall have you both hauled before the magistrate, and we shall find out!"

"If you delay us one moment longer, Lord Ashton shall hear of it," warned Lucy with sudden inspiration.

The officer wavered, and, seizing the instant, Lucy pushed past him with Galen Le Blanc in her wake. Pressing through the throng of passengers, they found a deserted spot on the railing away from the view of the police. As if by mutual agreement they stopped, and turning to each other laughed jubilantly.

"My word! You are a natural revolutionary!" said Galen Le Blanc.

"You are a good actor yourself. I was almost convinced the way you searched your pockets."

"I've had practice. But you! You were magnificent! It's a rare woman has spunk enough to save a man from the gallows! Who is Lord Ashton?"

"My fiance's father. He is very important in Parliament, I understand."

"Your fiance's father! We had better hope he never hears of this. He would change his mind about the match! There now! What witty thing have I said?"

The thought of Lord Ashton's attitude had sent Lucy into paroxysms of laughter. A release from the memory of his grim presence at Callow Hill, she supposed. Sobering, she knew the Frenchman was right. If her match with Charles weren't already hopeless, it would be if Lord Ashton heard this new tale.

"I don't know why I helped you," she said. "I took a terrible chance, and you are a common criminal."

"I'm sure it was because a person of your gentle upbringing could not bear to see the slightest suffering, even that of riff-raff hanging," he said, mocking her.

Lucy, still thinking of Lord Ashton, hardly noticed. "I hope you won't come back to England," she said. "I would not be on hand to help you again."

"I suppose I must leave England for others now," he said with a sigh. "But there will be plenty of work for me in France. Before a year has passed there will be revolution and I will be in the thick of it."

"I have heard nothing of such a revolution!"

"Not many believe it yet, but it will come. Poets and writers will be on the barricades, and when history is written, books will divide at the year 1848, the year after which France will never be the same."

"And you, sir, are you a poet?"

He laughed. "I am only a student, a sometime journalist. My family has a vineyard in the Champagne region near Paris. I am said to be marking time until I come into it. Now I think it will be safer if we separate, in case that officer should decide to look for us again."

"Yes. I must go and find my cousin. You will hang yet, since you are determined to remain outside the law."

"I'll remember your warning, mademoiselle," he said, mocking again as he turned away.

A stupefied Caroline was seated inside when Lucy finally saw her. "We are at sea, Caroline," Lucy whispered. "All is well. Feel the roll of the waves!"

"They are making me seasick," Caroline answered weakly. "I almost died. I should have, had I been you. Did he have a pistol to make you help him?"

"No," Lucy said.

Caroline shivered uncomprehendingly. "I hope we do not see that dreadful man again!"

"I hope so, too," said Lucy. But she knew that she did not hope it at all. He had turned a dull journey into the adventure of her life. He had called her magnificent, and she had not even told him her name.

The excitement he had awakened in her would not be quieted. During the entire crossing, she was unable to be still and rose continually to pace about.

Chapter 4

Lucy waked as the stagecoach in which she was traveling clattered over a bridge. "Paris!" she thought, shivering in the cold, stale air of the carriage.

Caroline, wrapped tightly in her pelisse, slumbered on, one brown cashmere shoe nestled against the Russian leather boots worn by a snoring Frenchman across the aisle.

Caroline would be aghast if she could see the way she slept, but there was no need to wake her yet. This was only the outskirts of the city. They were still outside the walls. No lady in her right mind would want to gaze on this.

All the same, Lucy, delighting in her solitude, pressed her face to the window, trying to stretch her cramped limbs without jarring the legs of the gentleman. The rain had parted company with the girls at last and an ambitious ruby dawn fired a corner of the horizon as though hoping to warm the gray November world.

But the scene beyond the window seemed hopelessly desolate. Dirt sidewalks ran beside the road. Spindly trees enclosed by protecting laths had branches of an unnaturally dull hue. The rain, instead of washing them clean, had turned the dust to a mud enamel. Chemical factories gave off orange smoke and acrid odors; gates opened onto filthy courtyards.

Gradually the houses drew closer together. They passed a tobacco shop marked by a huge tin cigar. The windows of long, reddish brown taverns were painted with crossed billiard cues inside wreaths of flowers. A midwife's sign depicted a woman holding a baby in a lace gown.

At the gates of Paris the coach stopped while a flock of sheep meandered across the road. Caroline sat up, looked at the snoring passenger distastefully and drew her feet gingerly back beneath her skirts. Then suddenly, she put her face to the window. "We're here! How cold the sentry looks pacing about with his hood down. Oh, I'm freezing, Lucy. Can you see who is ahead of us?"

"Only a poultry vendor and a wagon—and the sheep," her cousin replied from the vantage point of the other window. The coach jolted as the toll collector leaped onto its roof. Then with a blare of coronets and the crack of the whip, it sped down the boulevard.

Smocked workers jumped back to avoid the spewing mud, and women wearing madras kerchiefs paused to watch the coach race past. Shoeblacks were busy setting up their boxes. Grocer's boys shook their coffee roasters and the air grew rich with the aroma.

The girls were rapt beside the windows. Even Lucy, who had not wanted to come, was excited. Something mysteriously important seemed to emanate from these crowds of people. Or was it from the great buildings and monuments—the Arc de Triomphe, the Pantheon, its dome glowing in the sun like a cherry atop a whipped cream confection? An arched bridge took them over the sulphurous waters of the Seine. The coach mixed with laundry carts, phaetons, broughams and landaus. They crossed the river again at Pont-Neuf, passed the Louvre and arrived at a posting house on Rue Coq-Heron.

They were handed down into the wet courtyard, where a coachman got them a cab. When the trunks were loaded aboard, they set off again, pulling back the muslin curtains for the view. The neighborhood became quieter, more elegant.

"Imagine, to be in Paris and yet to be cloistered in a school!" Lucy grumbled.

Caroline had a different thought. "We're arriving too early. No one is awake *here*. It's only the workers who rise with the dawn."

"Don't be silly," returned Lucy. "If we were at Miss Alpin's we should have been roused long ago and set to needlepoint while the rooms were still so cold our fingers would be numb."

By the doorway of the school a gas lamp held by a brass hand still flickered, smug with knowledge of the Parisian night. As they stepped down from the cab a breeze swept along the sidewalk, and the bright awning over the ornate doorway flapped loudly, as if shooing the travel-stained girls away. They rang twice before a maid appeared, yawning in their faces.

The baggage was deposited in the anteroom, the postilion paid and the cab sent off. They were led away into a drawing room with tall windows and a chimney piece on which sat a pair of limoges vases. The carpet was sky blue, patterned with camelias, and a volume of de Musset lay on a gilt and walnut console table.

"Mme. Fichaud cannot be disturbed so early, but I will send for Mademoiselle Pauline," the maid murmured, slipping away through the tapestry door curtains.

Caroline and Lucy stared at each other, nervous and disheveled. It was too grand for a school; this was more like the home of a countess. The only similarity to the loathed Miss Alpin's was the cold. Lucy shivered, more from apprehension than from the temperature. One look had told her her father could not have paid for this. It was Lord Ashton who was footing the bill.

A sudden oppression seized her and the walls with the beautiful Ribera paintings pressed in on her. She was filled with a frantic grief, as she might be at a funeral. And it was after all a kind of funeral, for she was to be changed into a proper wife for Charles, just as death might transform a mortal into an angel. Her old self was all at once a dear old friend from whom she did not want to part, and she wondered senselessly how she could ever get on with the new person she would become. Why did she worry so? She should be glad to perfect herself for Charles.

Caroline would be happy to do such a thing, Lucy thought. She glanced at her cousin, who was absorbed in cataloguing the slender columns, the Egyptian heads, the ormolu mounts of the Empire furnishings. Caroline would say it was a woman's duty—no, her *life's work*—to mold herself into the wife her husband required.

Lucy remembered her confrontation with Lord Ashton, and her legs began to quiver under her crinoline just as they had then. She felt herself still in his grasp, and she wanted to wriggle loose, like a kitten from the rough clutches of a boy.

To distract herself she picked up the book of poetry. "De Musset," she said, "wasn't that peculiar woman, that writer, George Sand, his mistress? Let's see what he has to say of love."

But before she could open the cover, the volume was plucked gently from her fingers. "He says that the only way to know love is for oneself, Miss Hamlin," a voice with only a trace of French accent informed her. There stood Mademoiselle Pauline in a blue merino robe, her hair flowing loose from its chignon, splashing delicate titian waves about her prominent cheekbones. She was tall and thin, pretty in a way, though her nose was a little too narrow and her forehead overly high. Her raisin-black eyes darted, disconcertingly bored one instant, lighting with interest the next.

"It's my book. I left it here carelessly yesterday. Do forgive our informal reception. We were all at the theater last night. A new play, but not a good one, I'm afraid. It's made us all very tired."

"The coach—" Caroline began apologetically.

Pauline waved a tapered hand. "I am glad to greet a dawn from time to time. It reminds me of a part of life I tend to forget. Come along. You have been traveling all night and will want to wash and rest. I am the language instructress, so we will get to know each other better very soon."

She took them down a hall into a courtyard where a big, bare-branched acacia and an arbor of tangled brown vines overhung the mossy, rain-scented paving stones. Through its gate hurried a young man, head bent as he studied where to place his feet to protect the rosettes on his shoes from the puddles.

Becoming aware that he was not alone, he stopped short and smiled winningly. *"Bonjour,* Pauline. I am out for my morning constitutional. There is nothing better for the health."

Lucy thought he smiled as if he knew that smiling were his special talent, all that he needed to get along in the world.

Pauline gazed on him in amusement. "You'll catch pneumonia on a morning like this, Georges. They'll be sending for the doctor with his leeches and blisters."

His handsome face registered genuine horror. "Oh, no, you've got it all wrong. It's sitting about reading as *you* do that does the damage. It settles the blood. And you'll be so blind you can't thread a needle when you're forty."

"Well, then, I shall wear my clothing with rips and be spared the chore," said Pauline. "As for you—"

But Georges did not wait to hear more. He gave a little wave and went on, too worried about his shoes or the doctor's blisters to stay longer in the damp.

Pauline flung open another door and led them inside, up a staircase. "Georges is the music teacher," she said. "He has an apartment at the back of the house." She paused and then, with a sigh, added, "I might as well tell you now, that he is not at all suitable. It will save doing it later on." She turned a knob of flowered porcelain and showed them a room with an apple-green carpet and a canopied rosewood bed. The branches of the acacia were silhouetted on the lace curtains.

"You are lucky. You'll have a view and the air will be sweet in the spring. It's the best room in the house." Pauline gave them a curious look now, for as Lucy quickly understood, the best room had been no accident. It was more of Lord Ashton's bounty. Why was he so generous? She did not believe he cared if she were happy here. Was it so that Charles, if he lived, could not reproach him? Or was it just to satisfy his own pride?

Whatever, Lucy's feeling of gloom lessened. The room was cozy, from the little tapestry chairs to the bronze moon globe lamps. She loved the way it was tucked away in the corner of the house, so that one could step right out of it and down the stairs into the courtyard. She had found a sanctuary.

"I'll send a maid to start the fire and help you unpack. Your bags will be up shortly, and breakfast will be in an hour," said Pauline, and left the cousins alone to share their impressions.

Caroline was most interested in Georges. "Where do you think he had been, Lucy?" she cried with a giggle. "Not on his constitutional—or, if it could be called a constitutional, it was certainly not a walk. Monsieur Georges has been out all night. Who would go for a morning stroll in evening pumps and with a gold chain across his shirt? Where do you think he has been? To his mistress?"

Lucy was more interested in Pauline. "Think of it—she is a spinster—a woman as attractive as that—and she must be well-educated, too, to be an instructor here. What a wonder that no man wants her!"

"Well," sniffed Caroline, "perhaps it's her attitude."

"You mean what she said to Georges about wearing her clothes with rips and tears?" said Lucy, who had found the remark intriguing. Could it be that another woman hated needlework as much as she? It was her first indication that she would find a soulmate in Pauline.

"If Georges is unsuitable for her as well as us, I suppose it doesn't matter what she says to *him*. But if she often makes such comments it must make men cautious. Do not associate with her too closely, Lucy. The influence could be dangerous."

Lucy laughed. "Maids have always mended my dresses, Caroline, and I have never wanted for admirers. I am already betrothed."

"You are *almost* betrothed." The tone of her voice made the words the closest thing to a reproach that was likely to escape her lips. Caroline's sweet round little chin set firmly. She knew she had a duty here in this strange, luxurious place. She meant to perform it. "Take care, Lucy," she said wisely, and then a servant appeared to light the fire, putting an end to such discussions.

The dining room was filled with rich aromas. The china was an old and delicate Sevres, the shade known as rose pompadour, and the silver was heavy and ornate. An antique Dresden chandelier hung over the long table. At the sideboards, about a dozen girls were eagerly filling their plates, pouring themselves *cafe au lait*. All the dresses were unpretentious wool or muslin, but the practiced eye could see they were a better quality, a higher fashion than Lucy's and Caroline's. Only Mme. Fichaud wore silk. Her gray gown, its high neck trimmed with lace, complimented a still-slim figure and accented the occasional thread of white in her auburn hair. What a contrast *she* was to Miss Alpin! Her laugh tinkled everywhere, and two little Havana lap dogs sat at her feet greedily catching the dainty tidbits she tossed them.

But when Lucy and Caroline were brought to her, she reminded them of Miss Alpin after all, looking them up and down with a professional eye, making them blush for the road dust in their hair and their clothes still wrinkled from the trunk.

Quiet streams of speculation flowed about the room. "I hear she is to marry a duke," someone whispered.

"No, an earl."

"No, no, she has been sent to be reformed."

"Do you mean the dark-haired one? But the other is prettier!"

"Is *she* engaged then? Neither has a ring. It must be a peculiar story."

Then Georges appeared, making a grand entrance,

blowing everyone collectively a kiss. They were all delighted to see him. Even Mme. Fichaud's face lighted with pleasure. He was the only male in the house; he was the spoiled darling. The conversation turned to the play they had been to the previous evening, *Pere et Portier* at the Palais-Royal. It had been a comedy and Georges, certain of his audience, began to imitate one of the actors. The performance drew laughter. Breakfast began to seem like a party.

"What luck he isn't suitable," observed Caroline. "What a rush there would be!"

Noting that more than one young lady flushed at Georges' attention, Lucy wasn't sure there was not a rush anyway. "Pauline is not here," she observed.

After breakfast the jollity vanished. The school settled down to the routine which was to be followed each day. Pauline gave private lessons in a small, informal drawing room decorated with a silk-tasseled Japanese screen and canvas-covered chairs. "But you read French beautifully!" she exclaimed to Lucy. "There is only your speaking accent to work on. I shall teach you Italian. It will give us something to do."

Mme. Fichaud herself taught the group lessons in beauty—how to hold one's hands, how to turn one's body to make it look more slender, how to use cinnabar and antimony so discreetly that a gentleman could not tell it.

Standing in front of them, she would make sounds like a turkey. "Gob—ble," she would say, dropping her jaw and showing her dainty white teeth and her little tongue. Then they would all be required to do it with her, like a flock of turkey hens. Afterwards, Mme. Fichaud would slap herself beneath her chin and tell them with satisfaction, "There! Do that twenty times every day of your life, and you will never have wattles or a dewlap. I am forty-seven and have not the smallest sag."

Caroline, who developed a great admiration for Mme. Fichaud, gave close attention to gobbling. "One day your husband will come into your bedroom while you are doing that," Lucy warned.

Caroline's eyes opened in horror. "Goodness, cousin! I will make him knock. I would never let him catch me!"

Lucy, though she never dared ask, felt sure that Pauline did not do gobbling. Coming downstairs one morning especially early, she discovered that Pauline breakfasted before anyone else, her face deep in a book. Lucy sat down beside her, and after that she always breakfasted with Pauline. In spite of Caroline's admonitions, they did become friends. Pauline tolerated Lucy like a patient big sister and from time to time she would read her passages from Lamartine, Hugo, or Balzac.

She knew fascinating tidbits about all the writers. Victor Hugo's mistress was a member of the Orleans family, the royal pretenders. Balzac had a house on Rue Rayouard. The garden had two exits so that he could flee through one when a creditor was waiting at the other.

"They say Balzac understands women as no other writer ever has," she said.

"Do *you* think so?" asked Lucy.

Pauline shrugged. "I think he will be on our side."

"On our side? When?"

Pauline gave her a condescending look. "In the revolution, of course."

"The revolution!" Lucy caught her breath.

Pauline smiled. "Don't tell me it means something to you, *ma petite*."

"I have scarcely heard of it," said Lucy, unable to explain the wave of excitement that rushed over her at the thought of the agitator, Galen Le Blanc.

"You will hear more of it," Pauline predicted. "Afterward women will take their proper place in society. Marriage laws will be reformed; divorce will be reinstated. Women will not only cast their ballots with men, they will help to make the laws as well, like the wives of the Hurons, who sat on the tribal councils. Women shall realize their potential. They shall be free!"

Lucy was astonished. It had never occurred to her that women should be free. Women were to be protected. And what potential did Pauline mean? What possible future could any girl have except to make a good marriage?

"I thought the revolution was to be for the workers," she said tentatively.

"It will be for everyone who is downtrodden," said Pauline. And then, sounding exactly like Galen Le Blanc, she added, "After it, the world will never be the same."

Sometimes Pauline read what Lucy came to know were the left-wing authors—Fourier, Saint-Simon, Louis Blanc. She never read to Lucy from these books, which she bought on her afternoons off when she always visited a cousin.

But if Pauline told Lucy no more about the revolution, she did add to her knowledge of the members of the household. Pauline herself had run away from a suitable marriage to a clergyman at the age of eighteen.

"A clergyman?"

Pauline's eyes twinkled. "What is wrong, Lucy? Can't you imagine me with a clergyman?"

"I supposed you were Catholic, like most French are."

Pauline's long neck arched as she threw her head back in a laugh. "What fun you are to have around, Lucy! I am not a Catholic, and my family has not been for two-hundred and fifty years! Huguenot ancestors of mine died fighting for religious freedom at the Massacre of St. Bartholomew. Ah, I was raised on tales of martyrdom, and at first I was very pleased with the clergyman.

"But it began to come to me that I did not want to pray away my life hoping that God would listen to me and change the world. Sometimes it seemed to me that God must be incredibly stupid. So I decided to change the world myself. I became a secular revolutionary, and I ran away."

Lucy had turned very pale. She had never before heard anyone speak so disrespectfully of God.

Pauline sighed. "There now, little friend. Now that I have told you this, I suppose we shall be friends no longer. I suppose I shall return to breakfasting with only a book."

"Oh, no, Pauline! You have told me something important about yourself. Now we are really friends. Where did you go when you ran away?"

"I hid in the attic of a newly-married schoolmate. She was terrified that her husband would find me, but finally she arranged for me to be recommended to Mme. Fichaud. I have been here ever since."

"But doesn't Mme. Fichaud mind that you are a revolutionary? Doesn't she object to these books you read?"

"Mme. Fichaud does not see further than the end of her powder puff, Lucy. It is easy to keep things from her."

"Tell me about *her*, Pauline."

"Mme. Fichaud was widowed young when her husband was killed in a duel in the Bois de Boulogne. She expected to be wealthy, but the will her husband had supposedly made in her favor was never found. Everything except the house and furnishings went to the child of his dead first wife. Mme. Fichaud was beautiful, accomplished and fashionable, so she did what was natural. She opened a school to impart those characteristics to others. She has made a great success of it, and the school has become famous."

"But why didn't she marry again?"

"Some say she was too much in love with someone who could not marry her. Some say she insisted on a bridegroom as rich as her husband. Love or money—it was one or the other. Do you know why she takes only English girls now? It is because she cannot bear to be schoolmistress to the daughters of her old friends. It is too demeaning."

"Or too sad," said Lucy.

"Ah, or too sad."

Georges had been at the school three years. His father and grandfather had been great supporters of Napoleon. Before the exile of the emperor they had had wealth and title. Now they were lucky to have their lives. They did not feel lucky, of course.

"Georges lives for the return of the Bonapartes. He is a strange bedfellow of the revolution. He would do anything to bring about the fall of Louis Philippe. It is the only thing that might bring the Bonapartes back. Never let him get started on Napoleon, Lucy."

Lucy almost wished Georges *would* talk to her about Napoleon. Her lessons with him were the worst time of her day. While she played, he would pace about the square rosewood grand, the expressions on his fine, mobile features changing from thunderous to beatific with the music. Lucy believed that the purpose of these displays was to convince her of his depth of soul.

She, however, would only be disconcerted, and her distraction would cause her to miss notes. Then Georges would jerk back with a terrible grimace, as though he had been shot; and Lucy, witnessing this for the first time, had leaped up in terror.

Other times his method was to coax the music from his pupil. "Mademoiselle—are you unhappy? Has your lover deserted you? The music is a lover you can trust. *Give* yourself to it!"

And standing behind her, he would reach around her to the keyboard so that in a way he was embracing her. His cambric shirt would brush against the back of her gown, and his warm breath would blow against her cheek. He would whisper "A-flat" and *"pianissimo"* as though they were endearments.

His long, stroking fingers would brush hers on the keys. She would feel him tremble as the ineffable strain of a Chopin waltz drifted into the air. At such times she felt that at the slightest gesture of assent from her, he would sweep her into his arms. She did not want his kisses, and yet these moments had a kind of fascination for her like contemplating the drop at the edge of a precipice.

How many of Mme. Fichaud's girls had succumbed to his persuasions? Perhaps a great many, because Lucy's indifference seemed to annoy Georges. Every day he redoubled his efforts. One day, tensed almost to tears, Lucy did suddenly give herself to the music, launching into her favorite German dance, the one she had played to relieve herself of her anger at Lord Ashton. It was a mistake, for its explosiveness detonated something in Georges himself.

"Oh, Lucy, Lucy! I am impressed! Most girls would not dare to play that! They would be afraid of mussing their hair. See, your curls are falling. Let me fix them for you." He slid down quickly beside her, and his hands fastened over the corkscrew twists of her tresses. "Ah, how soft and plump they are, your curls!"

Lucy shuddered as though she had nerve endings in her hair. In another moment his hand would graze her breast. She knew it in her soul, and for an instant, she felt too frozen to do anything about it. Then, with a hard, swift motion, she struck out with the dance again, almost knocking him from the bench. She played it through in all its variations, horrid discords ringing out beneath her quaking hands.

When she finished, she looked up to see him gazing at her in wonder. "Lucy, there has never been another like you. I have never known any girl with such spirit." He spoke quietly, and Lucy sensed a change—defeat or a switch of tactics.

"You must see more of Paris—a girl like you. It will be your city. I will show you everything—the theaters, the cafés, the museums. You will take it in your heart when you return to England—*if* you return, for Paris may hold you more closely than this mysterious lord of yours."

"Have you gone mad?" cried Lucy. "I cannot go about in public with you!'

He laughed. "I didn't mean alone. We will take your cousin, Caroline. We will take Pauline. She likes that sort of thing. Mme. Fichaud will approve. I have escorted young ladies before. It's all part of their education."

Everyone who heard Lucy's wild rendition of the German dance, and surely that must have been *everyone*, knew that something unusual had happened. Lucy was aware of whispers and studied glances as the girls sat that evening listening to Georges play first Liszt and then a selection of Mendelssohn's *Songs Without Words*. His listeners, including Lucy, were all enchanted.

How could he play like that and still be such a rogue? Lucy had always believed that music would reveal shallowness of spirit. Georges was the exception. Her face burned, and to hide it, she moved far away to a window seat beneath the gold velvet curtains.

"I must be more careful," she told herself. "I must have a good report—for Charles, poor Charles." She looked at Mme. Fichaud, who, with her hair done in ringlets and a kiss curl at the nape of her neck, was leaning over the piano, as she always did when Georges played. Georges was smiling up at her as though his performance were for her alone.

"He knows who puts the honey on his bread," Lucy thought suddenly, and then, "She adores him as much as though she were one of her own pupils."

Somewhere, deep inside, she was warned of just how dangerous Georges could be.

You are a woman who will always cause talk. The words drifted through her mind that night as she sat brushing her hair by the light of the moon globe lamp. For a moment she could not remember who had spoken them. Ah—Jonathan Rathrock. How long since she had thought of him and his island!

She studied her reflection as if it were she, and she some disinterested omnipotence.

"No! Not always! Charles will recover and marry me and it will all be over. I shall be safe. I shall be loved and cared for, and all this will come to an end!"

Her reflection came out of the mirror and joined her again, and the gilded cupids around the mirror's frame mocked her until she climbed into the silk-canopied bed and put out the light.

Even then she lay wakeful and angry. Rathrock's face haunted her, and she wished the sea captain present so that she could challenge his arrogant presumption.

Chapter 5

Georges, good as his word, took Lucy and Caroline to a matinee at the Gymnase the very next day. It was only the beginning, for Georges had been right. Paris was Lucy's city.

She forgot for hours on end the storm clouds she had left across the Channel. Then suddenly they would come swooping back, dimming the Parisian brilliance. Lord Ashton would obscure her soul, calling on her to account for her guilty enjoyment of her exile. Charles' face, wan and wistful, would darken her pleasure.

But the faces would fade, unable to compete with her bursting discovery.

Lucy dragged them again and again to the Louvre, until Caroline complained of swollen feet. They saw Greek and Roman antiquities, the deathbeds and mummy boxes of the Egyptian collection, Babylonian frescos, the *Venus de Milo* and the *Winged Victory of Samothrace*.

Best of all were the galleries of paintings. The da Vinci's, the Titians, the Raphaels and the Rembrandts.

Georges would stand transfixed by David's *Coronation of Napoleon*, and Caroline and Lucy, observing him, would nudge each other and smile. But it was not really funny. Georges had a dream and a dream that certainly was not his alone. It was the thing that kept his music from betraying him, Lucy thought. He had a devotion to something beyond himself.

They saw the last of the chrysanthemums in the Jardin Fleuriste, and when the weather was fair they would take Pauline and walk the quays, breathing in the freshness of the Seine. Their excited talking and laughing would make a white vapory mist about them, and Georges, in his fur pelisse, would stamp his feet impatiently while Pauline dawdled over the wares in the stalls of the *bouquinstes*.

"Pauline, how can you look so long at all those gray covers?" he would say. "Here, buy this one. It is thick and dog-eared. It has been read a great deal, which may be some sort of recommendation."

Lucy was never bored at all, but she left the book-buying to Pauline. Among the crowd she felt adrift in a great Continental stew, and each person, each ingredient that swept past her held her interest. Over the entirety hung a spice, a seasoning unlike any she had ever experienced.

She would listen to the urgent thunder of omnibuses and laundry carts over the arched bridges and watch the bright sails of clean wash flap ferociously above the houseboats. Life sparkled for her in a way she had never expected, glittering like the cold sunlight on the water of the river.

"Pauline! I shall die of hunger on this very spot!" Georges would threaten. She would add her voice to his, for then would come cream tarts purchased over the marble counter of a *patisserie* or a trip to Café Gascard or Vautier's for coffee and *brioche*.

One blustery day Georges suggested a horse race at the Hippodrome. "I shall bet on Royal Hope," he announced as they climbed onto the wooden tier of seats overlooking the oval course.

"Don't be sentimental, Georges," said Pauline. "Royal Hope only reminds you of the Bonapartes. Royal Hope has a pulled tendon."

"Pauline, how little you think of me! My politics do not extend to horse racing. You will see Royal Hope is quite recovered."

'Do put a few francs on Spring's Darling for me," said Caroline. "Lucy, what horse do you choose? Lucy?"

But Lucy was not listening. She had seen someone in the crowd and her heart had almost stopped. She *thought* she had seen him. She stood up, almost tumbling through the rows of the grandstand in her excitement.

"Lucy, do make up your mind or it will be too late!"

Lucy did not answer. She craned her neck to see over the crowd, over the pedlars of race cards and cigars, the rattle-shaking vendors of licorice water.

A red flag dropped, and the horses were off. With a roar everyone rose from their seats, and Lucy's view was blocked. Her cry of frustration was lost in the tumult.

"Pauline, do you see that! Royal Hope is taking the lead!"

"She will never keep up the pace, Georges!"

"The devil, she won't! There, she is still ahead of Spring's Darling on the curve. Lucy, do look! My horse is winning."

But the roaring in Lucy's ears came not from the crowd, but from the tumult within herself. She was peering everywhere frantically. Her eyes sought the pavilion outside the paddock, the stands in front of the royal box. She had lost him. He could be anywhere by now.

Royal Hope had won the race.

"I concede, Georges; you were right," said Pauline. "I will bet with you next time."

"Never mind, Pauline. It's only because I'm an expert on the horses. At least you saw my horse win. Lucy did not even notice. What were you looking for, Lucy?"

They all stared at her quizzically.

"Oh, nothing. I was only looking at people. They are more interesting than horses. It doesn't matter."

It didn't matter; how could it? But Lucy's excitement was replaced by a sense of loss. She had seen a vaguely familiar figure, tall and carelessly kept, and she had been certain it was Galen Le Blanc.

She was distracted for the rest of the afternoon.

Finally it was nearly Christmas. Most of the girls were going home for the holidays, but not Caroline and Lucy, and the season darkened their spirits. Lucy's father had written to say he did not think their return wise, which meant that Lord Ashton did not wish it.

Mme. Fichaud was entertaining with a party for her students, and to their astonishment, Caroline and Lucy were deposited at the famed House of Worth to be fitted with gowns for the occasion. Caroline's was sky blue; Lucy's was magenta, a color that brought out the glow of her cheeks and the darkness of her eyes. The dresses were Christmas presents from Lucy's father, they were told, but the cousins knew that such lavishness was uncharacteristic of him. Perhaps it was more of Lord Ashton's doing.

"He does not hate you, after all, Lucy," Caroline said.

Lucy shook her head. "Perhaps we may be associated with his name and he wants us to look well," she guessed.

Caroline examined the fashionable slitted sleeves of her dress. "Well, it's the most marvelous gown I've ever owned, and I'm going to enjoy it. My mother's pearl necklace with the ruby pendant will suit it perfectly."

"I am trying very hard to hate mine," Lucy said. "Who shall I wear it for, since Charles is not here?"

"You must not languish over Charles, Lucy!"

"Why ever not? He is the man I am to marry. Oh, why is there no more news of him! Every week there comes the letter—he is the same, the very same. And this week, nothing. I am so nervous and upset I could not dance if Louis Philippe himself asked me!"

Caroline looked down, toeing the green carpet with her black satin galosh. "Nothing is ever gained by languishing. You must make yourself have fun; it will be your own fault if you don't."

Lucy groaned. "That is what Aunt Madeliene always told me before every silly tea party I ever went to."

Caroline giggled. "You're right. I remember now. Afterward when you'd been miserable, you were always wracked with guilt. Never mind, Lucy. This is Paris. *This* will not be a silly tea party."

On the night of the entertainment there were footmen in gold lace, and silver vases of roses stood on every table. A jasmine-covered lattice decorated the dining room, where party-goers sampled dishes of potato straws mixed with truffles, a York ham with madiera sauce, shrimp, oysters, pitchers of *vin rosé* and bottles of brandy.

The men wore six-buttoned coats of cashmere, flowered velvet or silk interwoven with gold and silver threads. The ladies' low bodices were trimmed with deep, lacy berthas, and their demi-trained skirts marked them as French. The couples made a panoply of color, twirling together to a quadrille, a waltz, and now and then, a polka.

Lucy, unable to follow Caroline's advice on having fun, was in a black mood. The glittery, vainglorious party had nothing to do with the Paris she had come to love. It had nothing to do with Christmas. She thought back to the great, fragrant trees she had used to decorate at Callow Hill, the quiet singing of carols, the childish gifts she and Caroline used to make each other.

"I should have been a bride, making Christmas for Charles in our own home this year," she thought, "and instead, I am here and he—" She did not finish the thought. Tonight she could not bear to picture Charles white and unknowing. She was chilled to the core and thoroughly glad that none of the young eligibles who had been invited to meet the girls were paying any attention to her.

The word had gotten around, she supposed. She was spoken for by a nobleman and had not a large fortune anyway, more the wonder. Lucy Hamlin was not one to waste one's efforts on and neither did the cousin have title or wealth.

Georges, neglected, too, by girls in pursuit of better game, danced with Caroline, who was radiant in the blue Worth gown. The pearl necklace with its ruby hung down below her collarbone, accentuating the daintiness of her shoulders and neck.

What a shame all this was wasted on Georges! Lucy was moved by a pity for her cousin, who would have no hope of finding a husband until she was back among her own kind.

But Caroline's face shone happily, as though she did not care, as though the fact that it was a ball in Paris was all that mattered, a memory to be kept in spite of the fact that she was ignored. Caroline always made the best of everything.

Lucy's temperament was quite different. She grew tired of walking back and forth to admire her reflection between the heavy linteled frames of the *trumeau* mirrors. She noticed that the rooms were growing too hot, that the smell of Turkish cigarettes was making her ill, that her stays were pinching. She hid yawn after yawn behind her fan.

She began to think of a novel she had to read which Pauline had given her. She decided no one would miss her if she went upstairs. No sooner had the idea taken hold than she put it to action, moving languidly toward the mahogany staircase, taking an orange from a blue faience bowl she passed on her way.

From the top of the stairs she saw Caroline still dancing, again with Georges. She would make a scandal dancing with him so much, Lucy thought, considering going back to warn her cousin. But Lucy had already made good her escape, and Caroline was an unlikely person to create a scandal. Caroline did not need warning.

Gaining her sanctuary, Lucy sighed dejectedly. She hung the magenta dress carefully away, rubbed at the angry red pinch marks on her waist and snuggled into a woolen robe. Stirring the fire with a brass-trimmed rod, she settled against the Aubusson tapestry of the chair and peeled the stolen orange, tossing the rind into the flames.

The novel, which was George Sand's *Lelia,* disturbed her vaguely. Through its pages a woman sought from lover after lover an ecstasy she never found. "Ah! She is nothing but a bit of baggage," Lucy thought, on the point of throwing the book down. And yet there was a cry of outrage, a bitterness that kept her reading.

Lucy's mind wandered back to that dark night on the moor with Charles. She remembered that terrible power that had seemed to drive him. Passion—was that what Lelia wanted? Was it what Lucy wanted? Was she, Lucy, at heart a bit of baggage? Vowing to accept no more of Pauline's literary gifts, she put out the light and tried to sleep.

The party was still going strong. Below in the drawing room young men and women jousted for positions that might determine their entire lives. Shrieks of laughter rose above the strains of the orchestra, which sounded weary and out of tune. Uneasy dreams drifted through Lucy's head.

She was aware of the scrape of footsteps under the bare branches of the acacia. Someone had come into the courtyard beneath her window.

Through the window, cracked to admit fresh air, came the sound of a sigh, the whisper of a man's voice. A pair of lovers was there but Lucy was no gossip. Lucy did not care. Then the woman spoke and something too familiar about that voice brought Lucy upright in bed.

The fire had gone out. The room was frigid as Lucy, shivering, drew her robe over her muslin gown and crept guiltily to the window. Below, in the sallow glow of a gas lamp, were a man and a woman. She with fair hair and a gown of blue beneath her cashmere shawl. He, in a Chesterfield wrap, his curled hair brushed forward from the back. Caroline and Georges!

Murmuring softly the pair drew close together. Georges seemed to embrace Caroline's neck, but the shadows of the tree hid them so that Lucy could not tell if they kissed. She shoved herself away from the window, forcing herself back to bed, where she lay shocked and trembling, all thought of sleep vanished.

What should she say to her cousin? Would it help to let Caroline know that she knew? Should she rant at the impossibility of a marriage between two persons with such lack of fortune? Should she rage that Georges did not intend marriage anyway, that he would likely ruin her? But Caroline was no fool. These things would already be in her mind. How strong her love must be to fly against such obstacles!

Through all their rambles, their drives about Paris, it must have been happening. Lucy had not even noticed! Or had she? Caroline had grown quieter, more subdued with every day. Was that the way an unsuitable love affected a young lady?

The door opened, and Caroline came stealthily in. Lucy had not decided what course to take and seized with confusion, she pretended to be asleep. From under lowered eyelids she watched Caroline undressing in the dimness. The dress and crinoline were put away, and Caroline, in pantaloons and camisole, bent to remove her white satin evening boots. It was then that Lucy noticed something amiss; and without a thought, she burst out, "Caroline, what has happened to your necklace?"

"Why nothing, cousin. I've put it away."

"You haven't!" cried Lucy, stung by the lie. "I've been watching you! Wait! I know! You've given it to that rascal Georges!"

"Georges is no rascal!"

"Oh, Caroline! You did give him the necklace, didn't you?"

"What if I did? It was mine."

"You're in love with him!" Lucy challenged.

"Oh, come, cousin!" Caroline's voice was angry. "I had another reason for giving him the necklace, but I do not want to share it."

"What other reason could there be?" Lucy persisted, upset at not receiving Caroline's confidence as she was accustomed. "If you are not in love with him, why are you quiet so often?"

"So you've noticed! I have tried my best to keep up my spirits. Well, that I *can* explain. You must know sooner or later, but I had hoped to keep it from you until after Christmas." She whirled to the desk and lifting the writing board, took out an envelope. Beneath the English stamps, Caroline's name was written in Aunt Madeliene's round hand.

"She wrote to Caroline and not to me!" thought Lucy, hurt again. Aunt Madeliene's letters were usually addressed to the two of them. But Caroline was grimly offering her the letter to read. Lucy lighted the lamp and spread the pages with quaking hands.

> *"Dear Caroline,"* the letter went, *"I am writing to prepare you for Charles' death. The doctor says he is failing and cannot live much longer. Do not tell Lucy yet. Let her have a few happy memories of Paris to bring home with her. It will end for her soon enough, and what can her future possibly be—"*

"Oh Caroline!" The riff between them was forgotten, along with Georges and the necklace. They held each other tightly. "What shall we do?" Lucy said.

"Do? There is nothing to do. Except pray. I pray every day for Charles—during my lessons, while I am walking down the stairs—any time there is a moment. Don't you?"

Lucy was abashed. She always meant to say a prayer for him before she slept at night. But she would be so exhausted and there would be so much to think of about the day's excursions. "I will pray in just a minute," she would think, and in that minute, she would often fall asleep.

"Let us pray *now*, Caroline!" she cried.

"All right, but in bed, where we will not catch pneumonia," returned Caroline sensibly.

This night it was Caroline who drifted asleep first, her hands still prayerfully clasped over the bodice of her nightgown. Alone in the dark room, Lucy felt abandoned. Keeping her eyes tightly closed, she concentrated with all her strength, as if this might get her message through to God.

"Do not let him die! Do not let me become a murderess!"

She sensed no comfort, no reply. Then suddenly she pictured her parting from her suitor. She remembered how she had bent and kissed him and how he had seemed to respond to her, as if he would hold her beside him with his lips.

Her eyes flicked open. She was astonished at the immediacy of the vision.

"I should never have come here, no matter what Lord Ashton wanted. I should have made them drag me away! It was only because I was made to feel I had done something so horrible that I was intimidated. Well, I shall put the matter to rights this very night. I shall go home at once. It may ruin me, but Charles' life is more important. If he were to hear my voice again and feel my kiss on his lips, it might rouse him from the coma. It is a chance I must take. I cannot live knowing that I remained here while he died!"

Was this vision God's answer or was it only the influence of Pauline? Had Lucy heard God's voice or had she simply become impatient with Him, as her friend had?

No matter. Lucy felt an urgency to do something. She was a person of action, and her mind moved on to practical matters. How was the leaving to be accomplished? For one thing it must be done quickly. She could not see the hands on her watch, but it could not be many hours until dawn.

The watch, a lovely thing with an enameled back and a long, delicate chain, could be pawned in the morning along with other pieces of jewelry to pay for her coach and boat ticket home. She got softly out of bed, and selecting her warmest clothing, began to dress. She put on her crinoline, two flannel petticoats and two cotton ones. Over that went a Grenadine dress with a jacket bodice. She slipped on her heaviest shoes, made of gray stamped kid, her overcoat and her gloves. She packed the jewelry and a few toilet articles into her reticule and crept into the gloom of the hallway. Where would she go to be safe until daylight? She did not have an answer; she knew only that she must leave before a single servant was stirring.

She slipped down the stairs, and holding her breath, lifted the latch of the door. She was outside, the cold slapping at her like a forbidding hand in the darkness. The naked acacia tree rattled and moaned a warning. Lucy hesitated, half-terrified. But what, after all, was there to be afraid of here in the courtyard? She listened, hearing nothing now except the rustling of old wrinkled leaves on the arbor. She had not even had to pass one other room on her way—not at all like Miss Alpin's where such an escape would have aroused the household and its three sheep dogs as well.

It was going to be simple, she thought, gaining confidence. She had only to cross to the gate and let herself out. So simple, except that tonight the courtyard gate was locked. Why had she never noticed the heavy chain and padlock hanging there?

Rage welled in her as she gave the gate an angry shake and stood looking up at the smug gilded spears atop the tall, wrought-iron fence. She willed herself to control the frustrated tears that filled her eyes. "I will not throw myself down and cry like a silly young girl," she told herself. "I set out to do something and I shall do it. Only I must find another way."

She studied the fence again, this time calmly. Was there something she could use for a ladder? Some tree she might try to climb? Some part of the knotted wisteria vines that might hold her?

No.

It would have to be not over, but through. She measured the spaces between the bars with her eye. One space, the one between the gate and the fence, was wider than the rest. Lucy thought she was thin enough. She pushed herself at it. Her head and shoulders passed through, but her skirts bunched, holding her back. Lucy withdrew and considered.

"It will have to be without my crinoline," she decided. Lifting her dress she unfastened it. She placed the crinoline against the fence and rolled up two of her petticoats beside it. Shoving into the space again, she squirmed and grunted as the unyielding metal bit into her hips. She went on all fours, her body twisting, her hands grating against pebbles outside the fence.

Suddenly she realized she was stuck, and in panic, she fought to wriggle backwards. She was securely imprisoned, helpless and freezing. While she was wondering if she would remain so until morning, she heard the heavy footfalls of a man behind her. Her heart turned to stone.

Then a voice said softly, "Ah, Mademoiselle Hamlin, you are a fine pig in a poke. Well, you do have a fondness for eclairs. You see what happens. How much better if you had a fondness for me!"

"Georges! How did you get here?"

The music instructor, still wearing his primrose-colored evening gloves, leaned on the agate head of his bamboo walking stick. "Through the other door, of course," he said. "I might ask you the same question, except that I have been watching you, ever since you removed your crinoline."

Lucy, from her peculiar vantage point, noted his black silk stockings and the little ribbons with which he tied up the slits in the narrow legs of his black kerseymere trousers. "If you have gawked enough, be kind enough to get me out," she said.

"Delighted, mademoiselle." He tipped his hat and laying hold of her thighs, tugged mightily. Lucy came loose, scrambling up and shaking off his intimate grasp. His hand reached out and fingered her dress.

"What an upset you've had, mademoiselle," he said, his eyes twinkling. "You'll need a cup of tea. By coincidence I was just going to my rooms to make some. Come along, then."

"Certainly not!" whispered Lucy, still panting, her face crimson with embarrassment.

"Oh, certainly so," returned Georges. "Should you refuse, I would probably give a shout of disappointment and then the entire household would see you here, limp as a noodle, and with *me* besides. You are mine, now, Lucy! I shall do as I like with you. Come along."

She knew he was right. She gathered up the crinoline and petticoats and followed him meekly through the rooms littered with debris from the party, out another door into an outside passage where the cold air was fragrant with wood smoke. Stone steps led to the entrance of his apartment. He unlocked the door and with a grand flourish, stood aside to let her pass.

The room was cozy and dim, lighted only by a brass-based lamp with a shade of rose-colored glass. Spring blinds and double curtains covered the windows and vases of heather gave the room a scent that made Lucy suddenly wish for home, for the comforting arms of her Aunt Madeliene.

Never had Lucy got herself into a predicament as bad as this! She shuddered as the door closed behind Georges. A debilitating dread had come over her. *I shall do as I like with you.* Her imagination could not picture it—or refused to try. Her fingers were icy inside her gloves. She stepped closer to the fire.

"Excuse me, I will make myself more comfortable," said Georges. He had removed his wrap and his waistcoat and was untying his cravat.

"Oh, pray, do not undress!" she cried in alarm.

"Why not?" he returned saucily. "You did. And in the courtyard, too." He went into the bedroom and returned wearing a brocaded robe, open to show the velvet braces on his trousers.

"Now, we will not need these anymore." He pulled the

crinoline and petticoats from Lucy's still-clutching arms and tossed them carelessly onto a chair. "Ah, Lucy." His hands embraced her neck, and she shivered, feeling dizzy with fear as they stroked down to her shoulders.

"How long I have dreamed of having you here! Don't be afraid, my little one. It will be all right." His hands were working on the tiny covered buttons of her dress. Now it was his mouth that was against her neck, covering her skin with dozens of tiny kisses.

The dress fell away into a heap at her feet. Quickly he pushed the two remaining petticoats after it. His head went down into the cleft between her breasts, kissing, kissing. She gasped, her flesh quivering at the violation. She grabbed his curly hair and tried to pull his head away.

Mistaking her reaction for passion, he let himself be moved, swinging up to press his lips against hers. Her teeth ached with the pressure; the liquor smell of his breath was suffocating. She swayed and, tripping on her dress and petticoats, fell to her knees.

Georges, mindless, fell on top of her, his body incredibly hard and heavy. "Don't faint and spoil it, my pet," his smooth voice whispered. His kisses poured over her; his hands tore at her stays. "It is the first time for you, but you will like it. I have known it ever since the day you played Beethoven. You are the kind of woman for me, Lucy!"

"Never!" Her voice was suddenly strong. She heard the sound of breaking glass. It was the shade of the lamp. She had no idea how she had reached it. The brass base was a torch in her hand.

"You'll set fire to us both, you fool!" cried Georges. "You'll burn down the house!"

"If I must!" she returned. He sat up and tried to wrest the lamp from her. She hung on with all her strength. He took a deep breath and blew the flame away. In the glow from the fireplace she struggled on for possession of the heavy base.

Then the door flung open. A gentleman stood there, arms akimbo. Lucy cowered, hardly knowing whether to be glad at being seen almost naked by another man. Saved but discovered! Now even if Charles lived, Mme. Fichaud would write such a report that Lucy would be disgraced forever.

Who was this gentleman? She could not see him

plainly in the semi-darkness, but he looked somewhat a dandy in his pleated Scotch-plaid trousers. A calico shirt with three rows of frills peeked from under the open paletot that covered him to the knees, and his stick was carried fashionably, with its top plunged into the side pocket of his coat.

The man spoke. "Georges, you are a scum!"

With a cry Lucy threw herself sobbing into the speaker's arms. For the voice had been feminine. The gentleman was not a gentleman at all.

Chapter 6

"Pauline! Pauline! Is it really you?"

The girl laughed and removed her top hat to show the mound of bright hair tucked beneath it. "It is I, Lucy. Am I not the cheese as you would say in England? Put your clothes on at once and we will get out of this place."

She turned on Georges. "As for you, you have gone too far!" Her hand curled about her walking stick, and Lucy thought she would strike him.

The instructor cowered away from her, his ever-present smile curdling on his lips. "Pauline, you have a nerve interferring in my business—"

She cut him short with a gesture. "It is not your business I am interferring in, Georges, only your lecherous pleasure. Come, Lucy. Do you have everything now? Button your coat. It is getting colder."

Dazed, Lucy let Pauline take her arm. Outside the wind had started to blow. A dusting of new snow was falling, swirling about on the sidewalks and in the yellow glow of the gas lamps. The streets were almost deserted. Once in a while a brougham or tilbury clattered past. Tin chimney pipes rattled in the gusts.

Shudders washed over her in waves. "Oh, Pauline! If you had not come!" she whispered finally.

Pauline put a hand on Lucy's elbow to steady her. "If I had not come, you would have bested him, even though you were weaker and ignorant of his low ways."

Lucy still trembled. "Why do you say that, Pauline?"

"Because you would have fought with your entire soul, which is far better a weapon than any of his. You are not the sort to faint away."

"Georges was afraid I *would* faint. 'Don't faint and spoil it,' he said. Do you know what else he said? That I would enjoy it. How could he imagine such a thing?"

"Because he is a conceited fool. But don't sell love

short. There can be pleasure in it, and one day you will have the opportunity to know it."

"Do you mean if Charles recovers? I did not like it when he kissed me either, though it seems disloyal to say."

Pauline laughed. "I did not say with whom. If you marry Charles and do not love him, then someday I think you will take a lover."

"Pauline! Oh!" said Lucy, much shocked. But she was beginning to grow calmer. She looked at the strange figure her friend made and asked the inevitable question. "Why are you dressed like a man?"

"Because I am going out alone, and it is late. Unheard of for a lady. But a man? No one even pays attention. So I become a man when it suits my purpose. I am a free person and the cloister is not for me. I am not the only woman who does it. Now, tell me how it came about with Georges."

Lucy spilled out everything. About Caroline's necklace, Aunt Madeliene's letter, her determination to go home.

"Ah," said Pauline. "It's a method of his, the necklace. He makes Mme. Fichaud's girls fall in love with him. Then he swears he would marry them if only he had a fortune. There is always some scheme—a china factory or a coal mine. The poor, bewitched thing surrenders whatever treasure she has. And the investment is always a failure—usually because it is made at the racetrack or tailor's. The girl never dares to accuse. She would be ruined."

"But Mme. Fichaud—can't she do something about him? Why doesn't she dismiss him? Doesn't she know?"

"Mme. Fichaud is all alone with no husband. Her bed would be so cold without Georges. And if he admires the young girls, if they sometimes give him their jewels and their kisses; all the more reason Georges will be contented and will be meticulous in his duties toward her. No, if I were to go to Mme. Fichaud and tell her the things Georges has done tonight, it would be I, not he, who would be dismissed. But Georges is not to be blamed entirely. He is the product of a rotten age. He may have good qualities buried deep. Someday perhaps we may seem them. Well, here we are."

Lucy's state of mind was such that she had not even wondered where they were going. Pauline opened a door, went up a flight of slightly shabby stairs, and put a key in a lock. "This is my apartment," she said.

"Your apartment! But you live—"

"At the school?" Pauline finished with a smile. "I have a room there, but it's too confining. Here I do as I please. I work for the revolution. I entertain my friends."

"But Mme. Fichaud—"

"Do stop saying 'but Mme. Fichaud,' Lucy! Mme. Fichaud does not know. This is my cousin's—the dear cousin to whom I am so close, and who, of course, does not exist."

Pauline read another question on Lucy's bewildered face. "Yes, men. I do entertain men here. Some come only to talk. Now and then one comes for love. How else should it be? I was not meant for marriage. So now and again, not often, I have made a man happy by loving him instead of miserable by marrying him. Sit down, Lucy. You look pale. I'll go and fix you tea."

Lucy sank onto the tufted bocatelle sofa as Pauline, tossing her hat and stick onto a japanned console, went out to the kitchen. The apartment was smaller than Georges'. It had no bedroom as such, only a pair of screens between which one could see a cast-iron bed done in swirls and lyres and stars. There was no fireplace at all, only a stove. The two oak trees that seemed to grow about it were disguised stovepipes.

The tabletops were littered with copies of *Siécle* and *Revue des Deux Mondes*, and artwork unlike that in the carefully-spaced frames at Mme. Fichaud's hung everywhere, one charcoal sketch or watercolor above another. Lucy's English sensitivities were scandalized at the sight of a nude. She leaned back, closing her eyes, opening them again at the clink of china. Pauline was bringing tea in a Marseilles Ware pot with a monochrome of green flowers.

Sitting beside Lucy, she poured each of them a cup, spooning heaps of sugar into Lucy's without asking. "You need the strength," she explained. "Have you decided what you'll do now?"

Lucy hesitated, confused by her narrow escape.

"I should hate to see you leave Paris. You have great potential as a woman. You will never find it after you are married to Charles Ashton."

Lucy let her head loll wearily against the upholstery. "Do you think I was not meant for marriage, either, Pauline?"

"No. Quite the contrary. You are not like me. But

you are not like most women, either. In the long run, you will give some man more than just your affections. You will give him your entire being. You will need wisdom, Lucy. You need to know what is inside you because eventually you will not be able to suppress it."

Lucy sighed. "Do you know what is inside me, Pauline?"

Her friend laughed. "I only know there is a woman, whom you dare not see or hear. She is there, nonetheless. She is the one who got you stuck in the fence. She is the one who rails at the barriers set for you. You see, I have thought a great deal about you, Lucy. Well, I must leave. I'm late already."

"You are going somewhere?"

"Yes, of course. I was on my way to a meeting when I heard the sounds outside Georges' door."

"At this hour?"

"These are dangerouus times. Stay here and sleep awhile. I'll be back before daybreak and we'll decide what you are to do."

"Sleep! Impossible! Let me come with you."

A smile twisted the corners of Pauline's mouth. She put on the top hat and offered Lucy her arm. "Well, come along then. We shall make a handsome husband and wife this night."

Outside the snow was driving harder. Lucy's feet slipped in the accumulation, and she wished she had had the foresight to wear her India-rubber boots. The snow was getting too deep for carriages; the streets were utterly empty of vehicles. In the morning when the snow had stopped, men would come to shovel it onto huge sleds and take it beyond the city walls. Urchins would scramble to get aboard to ride those strange white mountains and to hurl snowballs at the tall hats of passersby. The hem of Lucy's dress dragged, getting soaked and heavy with snow. She became preoccupied with it, trying to lift it clear, wondering if there would be stains.

Suddenly the gothic heights of St. Eustache soared up, unmistakable with its uncompleted right tower. A man in a smock and ragged list slippers went past, drunk and singing a snatch of song.

"Pauline, we are in Les Halles!" Lucy whispered in alarm.

"So we are. It's a little rough, but good for what we

are doing. Never worry, Lucy. You'll not be bothered. Remember you've a good male protector."

Lucy was not reassured. It did not help when they had to feel their way down a flight of unlighted stone steps to a basement. Pauline knocked, gave a name, and they were admitted.

Perhaps fifty people were in the room. Some wore the smocks of workers. Many, looking like law students, wore waistcoats with Hussar points and buttons of blue steel or horn. Here and there a woman's bavoleted bonnet showed, its crown trimmed in drooping feathers or fly-away bows.

Heavy shades were drawn tightly over all the windows, and the air was hazy with the smoke of cheroots. An excitement as tangible as the smoke followed its curling white trails around the lectern, among the wooden chairs, across the crowded, red-tile floor.

Lucy savored it as though it were a breeze. It had an urgency, an importance entirely missing in the atmosphere of a party or ball or even a fox hunt. It brought to Lucy the heady aromas of idealism and danger, and though she had no way of knowing it, these were kin to her soul.

At the lectern a man was talking about the next reform banquet. Lucy had heard of these. They were given to avoid a law against public assembly. The speaker, his cravat loosened, laughed, took several comments from the floor, and crying, "Who's next?" stepped down. He was relinquishing the lectern to a woman!

"It's Jeanne Derione," whispered Pauline. "She will be a martyr yet."

A hush came over the room. Mademoiselle Derione looked fragile in a brown silk dress and hair plaited in circles over her ears. But when she spoke her voice sang forth with a purpose that had Lucy instantly spellbound.

"*Le Démocratie Pacifique*, which has dared to serialize the novel, *Woman's Share*, has been brought to court for it." She paused for effect. "That makes a thousand, two-hundred and twenty-nine press trials since we last trounced the tyrants in 1830! So has freedom been subverted, sisters and brothers! And this time only because of a story about a woman!"

The audience applauded. There were cries of "Down with Louis Philippe!"

Jeanne Derione's pale cheeks flamed, and her eyes glowed as if from a fire beneath her translucent skin.

"See how frightened the despots are of mere woman!" she cried. "There will never be justice until everyone is free. Brothers, you will never be truly free while your sisters are in chains! Women must vote! Women must take their place in the Assembly! Women must sit on courts of judgment! We must all fight together—"

Suddenly a cry rang through the hall. "Police!" Mademoiselle Derione froze at the lectern. Nobody moved. Nobody spoke. Boots clattered at the basement window. Then a sigh sifted through the gathering. Someone whispered to Mademoiselle Derione. With a nod she stepped down from the podium, earnestly shaking the hand of the man who was to succeed her.

He leaped onto the platform, coattails flapping, and a muted cheer went up. There was the jutting triangular chin, the carelessly-kept clothing—plain-cut trousers and instead of a cravat, a Byron tie, a bit of *mousselaine de laine,* no wider than a broad shoestring.

Lucy gasped and was seized with a trembling. It was Galen Le Blanc.

She noticed things about him that she had not before. That his wavy crop of hair extending into side-whiskers was the color of dandelions in summer. That the strong framework of bones in his lean face was like a definition of character. She noticed that his eyebrows were straight and purposeful and that beneath them his blue eyes could light with mischief, then go dark with a breathtaking suddenness, as if turned in to the depths of his spirit.

"Compatriots, a thousand pardons! It was I who brought on the police. But I have escaped again, you see— as France itself shall escape across this moat of suppression and injustice—"

He was eloquent, but there was something about him that moved the crowd more than his eloquence. He was an outlaw in the cause of the republic; and the fact that he stood before them free gave power to their campaign. Galen Le Blanc was aware of the symbol he was. He stood tall as though daring bullets, and his voice breathed strength into his listeners.

Lucy felt a consolidating of forces. What had been a collection of discontented individuals merged into one mind. An almost audible hum of energy swept among them. Galen thrust his thumbs under his arms in the manner of a dandy and told a joke at the expense of Louis Philippe. His audience howled with approval.

Lucy was as carried away as anyone. The republic, democracy! Suddenly they were important to her. Why should they be to an English girl whose only concern should be that the future Lord Ashton live and marry her?

Was it the memory of Darby Mill—the cart squeaking away into the dawn with its cargo of human debris?

Or was it the taste of freedom she had had this evening, a freedom that she had not even known existed—the promises of Jeanne Derione of liberation of which she had scarcely dreamed?

Lucy became one with the crowd. She sighed with it, murmured with it. Tonight she had found what was amiss with her life. Tonight she had begun to sense all that was held back within her. Lucy's trembling grew stronger. She felt that Galen Le Blanc was speaking to her alone.

To her alone! Did he even notice her? Did he know or care about her presence? He had stopped speaking and had leaped from the platform, all of him but the smooth crown of his head lost from sight as he was pummeled by well-wishers.

Pauline, having exchanged greetings with her friends, was nudging her. The crowd was dispersing cautiously by two's and three's. When it was their turn at the door, Pauline again gave Lucy her arm so they would look a proper pair as they strolled out into the crisp air. The snow had stopped. Far away the towers of Notre Dame rose blackly against a line of pink dawn.

The snow had changed everything. The streets were gone, indistinguishable from the sidewalks. Snow was plastered against the houses and wine shops on the windward side, making them look as if they had a new coat of paint. But it was not the snow that made the world look strange and different to Lucy.

"Are you still determined to go back to England?" asked Pauline. "I will help you get aboard the coach."

Lucy shook herself out of a trance. If she went home, she would come back to Paris someday, but it would never again be like this. She would be the proper wife of Charles Ashton; or, if he were dead, the wife of someone else. The things she felt now would be forgotten, and she would walk these streets with her husband, remembering vaguely a thwarted dream.

But what of the vision that had seemed the answer to her prayers?

She considered the matter thoughtfully. If it had been the answer, she would not have got stuck in the fence. Georges would not have caught her without her crinoline. Going home had been her own idea, not God's. God, after all, demanded that young women obey their fathers. God, to Lucy's mind, was much like her old teacher, Miss Alpin.

She trembled at the thought of herself half-naked in Georges' apartment. How close she had come to ravishment! And if the flare of the lamp had touched her clothing—then she would have been in her grave before Charles, whom she had been hoping to save.

Such was the price of disobedience, which she had barely missed paying. No, she had been foolish to think of returning to England. She was powerless to aid Charles.

In Paris she might at least help Caroline, who was as dear to her as a sister and who was likely to be ruined by Georges.

"My duty is here, Pauline," Lucy answered at last.

Pauline smiled knowingly. She saw relief seep through Lucy as she made her choice. She saw the excitement that followed quickly on its heels. Pauline guessed easily enough that the meeting in the basement had help to mold Lucy's decision.

But even Pauline had no idea that in Galen Le Blanc, standing free and defiant, answering to nothing but the light within himself, Lucy had realized for the first time all that a man should be. And his face with the eyes that drew her in after him, was still swirling in her mind.

Chapter 7

Lucy's life was changed from that moment on. The milestone had been passed even before Pauline had let Lucy back into the school with her own secret key to a side door. Lucy tiptoed through the still-quiet house, past the remains of a turban of rabbits in the dining room and stained linen napkins flung here and there on the backs of chairs. How long ago that party from which she had crept away in boredom!

Caroline still slumbered peacefully as she must have through all that had happened to Lucy. Lucy, thinking of the episode with Georges, wondered how she could look so serene.

"*My* face will betray everything I have felt tonight—all my secrets! And what secrets I have—unlike any I have had in my life!" She slept at once, exhausted, and her face, had anyone seen it, might truly have betrayed secrets—secrets she kept even from herself.

Christmas came and went. Lucy gave Caroline a gray silk umbrella with an ivory handle. Caroline's gift to Lucy was a beautiful Syrian scarf. Lucy and Pauline exchanged books, and Lucy, forgetful of her pledge about reading any more of Pauline's literary beneficences, spent a long Christmas afternoon reading Alexandre Dumas in front of her fireplace.

Pauline's book was a leather-bound volume of the poetry of Lamartine, who would head the new government when it came, Pauline said. "Poets will lead France," she declared, and Lucy was reminded again of Galen Le Blanc.

The cousins waited each arrival of mail with trepidation. Lucy's heart would pound as the names were called, and she would seek Caroline's hand, finding it cold with fear. But the dreaded news of Charles did not come.

The rift between the two girls, begun with the incident of Caroline's necklace, deepened. Caroline, slipping out alone in the afternoons, would deny Lucy's requests to accompany her. "Oh, you will only want to go to some museum, while I want to shop. Let me go by myself today." And Lucy, hurt to the quick, would be sure that Caroline was meeting Georges.

The gray umbrella disappeared. Caroline professed to be worried to distraction about it. "Do you remember last Tuesday when it was raining so in the morning, and then the sun came out? I stopped to rest in the Tuilieries, and I must have left it—"

Lucy, passing a pawn shop in the Rue de la Paix, saw the umbrella in the window. She was certain that Caroline had given it to Georges. What were the signs of an impossible love? A wan solemnity, absentmindedness, preoccupation? Caroline had all these. Lucy was pained that her cousin did not confide.

On the other hand, Lucy did not tell Caroline about her new activities. She could not. Caroline disapproved vehemently of Lucy's friendship with Pauline. Just once, Lucy chanced on the subject of women's suffrage.

"Women vote! It would be unnatural!" cried Caroline, rolling her eyes in such horror that Lucy never ventured any related subject again.

"It is Pauline who gives you these ideas," Caroline said. "Take care, Lucy. She will lead you into trouble yet!'

"I am a grown woman, Caroline. I will be nineteen on the fifteenth of January." Lucy smiled to think how astounded Caroline would be at where Pauline had already led her.

She often went to the political meetings with Pauline now. She had learned about unions and right-to-work laws. She had heard complaints about the cost of the royal coach on the Northern Railway, satires on the king's costume at the St. Ferdinand's Day Ball, debates on freedom of the press. A banquet in the Twelfth Arrondissement was forbidden by the police, arousing the anger of the reformers. Faces grew tighter, speeches more inflammatory.

"Soon," said Pauline. "It's coming."

"Yes," said Lucy and felt a marvelous surge of excitement.

When the meeting was late or distant, Pauline would lend Lucy a second-hand frock coat with a Prussian collar, trousers with canvas braces and a calico shirt. Over all would go the greatcoat and the tall hat to hide her hair. The transformation complete, they would venture out together like a pair of young men-of-the-town. Unable to resist using their disguises simply for fun, they would explore Montmarte or the Ile de la Cite; or best of all, they would go to the Latin Quarter to sit in the cafés and listen to the talk of the students from the nearby Sorbonne.

Lucy never went without Pauline. "It's safer that way, Lucy," Pauline would say. "You are naive yet about the ways of Paris."

Lucy did not feel naive at all. She knew more about Paris than women twice her age. She began to chafe at Pauline's restrictions. One evening when Pauline was ill, Lucy went out alone. Jeanne Derione was to speak, and Lucy didn't want to miss hearing her.

In her male garb she slipped out into a frosty night and, breathing deeply, stretched her legs into the free stride of a man. Excitement rushed up as it always did, rich and golden as the glow of the gibbous moon which cast her unfamiliar shadow on the paving stones. Lucy thrust her hands into her pockets and began to whistle. "I can go anywhere, do anything I like," she thought, wishing every woman might have this experience at least once.

> *Whistling girls and crowing hens*
> *Always come to some bad end.*

The rhyme wafted through her head and vanished. It had been one of Miss Alpin's little dictums, but it had not the power to spoil her enjoyment now. She was feeling very bold as she took her place in the meeting.

Then came the sentry's signal. Police!

The silence fell. Everyone stiffened. The boots clattered. There seemed so many of them! And then the clattering stopped. Lucy felt relief for an instant before she realized it was not a good sign. A pounding came on the door. A cry to open immediately.

After that everything happened at once. Windows broke, the lectern, quickly shoved against the door as a barricade, was splintered as rifle butts broke through. Chairs flew about in the air; some, wielded like clubs, connected with uniformed heads.

The room was emptying. Some of the revolutionaries had escaped up a stairway to another floor. Without quite knowing how she had gotten there, Lucy found herself outside, crouching on a sidewalk. Someone must have pushed her through a window. Shards of glass were on her clothing.

Scrambling up, she started to run on shaking legs. *"Arrêtez!"* came the cry of a policeman behind her.

What disaster if she were to obey! The idea lent speed to her feet. She ducked instinctively and turned down an alley. The policeman, not fooled, followed. He would catch her, of course. She was only a girl. She had had no practice running since a long-ago time on the heaths of Callow Hill, when she had been too young for the prison of petticoats and crinoline. Lucy's lungs ached. A sob burst from her throat, and she cursed it as a waste of breath.

The policeman's footsteps came closer; he ran faster as he scented victory. Lucy's feet faltered. She stumbled. An arm grabbed her hard about the waist. She started to scream, but a hand clamped itself over her mouth so tightly she was almost strangled.

"Quiet! I'm on your side!"

She was dragged into a small passage between two buildings. The night glow, several stories above, was blocked by the walls, so she was prevented from seeing the man with whom she shared the dank, narrow, gravelike space. The policeman's boots echoed, going on past.

"We're safe," she whispered.

"Not at all," said her rescuer. "He'll be back in a minute. Come this way."

"I can't." Lucy's legs trembled, too weak to hold her. He hesitated an instant; then with a sigh, he picked her up and slung her over his shoulder, his hand clasping her buttocks.

Lucy gasped, and feeling her hat slipping away, clutched it with both hands to preserve her disguise. He carried her up a metal ladder, out onto a sloping rooftop. She felt his feet wobble on the spiked, iron footholds and closed her eyes in terror. She was helpless; she was going to die. Protests rose to her lips, which were too tightly clenched to allow her to speak. As she waited to fall, the accusing faces of everyone she had failed passed one after another before her—Aunt Madeliene, Caroline, her father, Lord Ashton, Charles.

Somehow they were no longer on the rooftops, and she began to breathe again. Then she was falling, falling after all, gripping the hat as if even in death she might not be discovered.

Her body sank against something soft. Startled, Lucy opened her eyes and let go of her hat. She was lying on a bed.

A man was looking down at her, his eyes astonished. "You're a woman!" he cried.

"And you," she said softly, her voice quivering with something that was not quite fear, "are Galen Le Blanc."

He went off into a sudden diatribe, pacing about on a small tapestry carpet, his arms flailing in Gaelic gestures. "How can you be such an idiot as to go about in men's clothing? Do you know what might happen to you? You will be treated like a man! Or worse! I could not imagine what was wrong with you. I thought you had been injured. I thought I would have to send for a doctor. And it is only that you are a woman!"

"There is nothing wrong with being a woman!" Her voice was strong and angry. "I thought you would kill us both!"

"I must be agile in my work," he said, looking at her closely for the first time. "Wait! I have seen you before. You are the one who saved me from prison on the Dover ferry! And now I have saved *you!* What are you doing here, and what has become of the lord you were to marry? Did they find out what you did that day?"

"No. I am still to marry him."

He backed off, sat down in a chair and put his chin in his hands. "I don't understand you; I don't know what to do with you. There are police everywhere, and yet you will have to go home. Why do you take such chances? Were you slumming? I will have to risk my neck for you again."

"I wanted to hear Jeanne Derione," said Lucy foolishly.

He relaxed and smiled at her. He had a beautiful smile. The quick warmth in his eyes made Lucy feel comforted. "So! I did say you were a natural revolutionary, didn't I? And I was glad enough when you took a chance that morning at Dover. I was going to offer you a grog. But I suppose since you are a woman I must offer you tea instead. Meanwhile, you will have to remove what an English gentleman would call his inexpressibles. There is a rip—"

She glanced down and saw her pale thigh exposed

beneath the tear in her trousers. Galen Le Blanc handed her a blanket and went wordlessly into another room. Lucy stripped off the pants, looking around her as she wrapped herself in the blanket. The wallpaper was flowered with grime-obscured roses, and here and there it hung in tatters. The bureau was as pockmarked as though it had survived a dread disease, and the mattress of the iron bed had a hammocky sag. A musty aroma of rot emanated from the sill of the dormer where dark, decaying wood testified to years of leakage. A step down into the next room was hollowed from many decades of feet. Somewhere a mouse began to chew, the busy sound racketing into the silence.

"How very far I have come from Callow Hill!" Lucy thought, more intrigued than horrified. Curiously she stepped across the warped floor and peered into the next room. She had expected an ordinary sitting room, but here instead were glassed-in bookcases filled to overflowing and a big, leather-topped desk littered with papers. Wooden crates everywhere brimmed with more materials.

"Give me the trousers," said Galen Le Blanc, turning from setting a tea tray beside a pressed-glass lamp on the desk.

"Oh, but I—" He took them from her hand and motioned her to a velvet armchair. She sat clutching her blanket, balancing a teacup and watching him sew with a neatness that would have been applauded at Miss Alpin's school.

"What are you staring at?" he said.

"I have never seen a man sew before."

"It's a necessity. Torn pants are one of the hazards of my work. And it's obvious I have no woman about." He waved a hand at the disorder of the room.

"Is this place your lodging?"

"Yes, but more important, it is the office of *Le Revue Démocratie*. Isn't it grand? You are privileged to be speaking to its editor. We do not always make our publication date. We are too busy running from the police. It has not endeared us to Louis Philippe that we have called for dumping him, crown and all, into the Seine. Since moving to these quarters a week ago, we have not even swept, but at least only the rats have found us.

'There! Go and put these on, and we will have another cup of tea to warm us before we pit ourselves again at the cold hearts of the police."

Through back alleys in which the blackness itself seemed made of strange scents and exotic sounds, Galen Le Blanc took her home. She strolled at last beside him up the elm-lined street that led to Mme. Fichaud's.

"You're a schoolgirl!' he said. "I should have known. Well, promise me you'll be good and do your lessons. And promise you'll not wear trousers again."

He turned to go.

Suddenly pride welled out of Lucy's humiliation. She was overcome with a need to explain herself. "Monsieur Le Blanc!"

He stopped and came back.

"I am not only a schoolgirl! I am—I am—" Something there was about her that made her different, that made her more, but Lucy Hamlin did not yet know what it was.

"You are magnificent, as I once said before," he finished for her. "Tell me your name this time."

She told him, and her heart sang.

Chapter 8

She could think of nothing else. She thought of being lifted and carried like a doll over the shoulders of Galen Le Blanc. She remembered with more pleasure than embarrassment the feel of his hand on her hips. She would think of the vitality of his eyes, of his glance on the bare skin of her thigh. She had never known a man of such purpose. He was not one who accepted the world or who merely grappled with it. He was of the rare sort who could change it. She wanted to be near him, to hear his voice, even if it were saying only that she was a silly schoolgirl.

In her dreams Galen Le Blanc kissed her hand. He stroked her cheek and made shudders run to her toes. Twisting one of her curls around his long fingers, he drew it to him and laid his lips against it. And he called her magnificent, magnificent!

She would awake, hot and flushed in the January night. The bare branches of the acacia would rattle against the window, and she would leap up, still half in her dream, thinking he had come to her. She would be filled with a peculiar longing, an inexplicable, almost physical need. In the morning she would be wan for lack of sleep.

Caroline, attributing her condition to worry over Charles, petted her, while Lucy, not trusting herself to go out, frantically filled her leisure hours with any task she could think of. She poured olive oil on her head and wrapped it in hot towels to make her hair shine. She sat with her elbows in lemon halves to make them white; and unable to concentrate on a book, she even did needlework.

Was it love? How could it be? But she had never had such feelings about Charles Ashton.

Lucy stood it for less than a week. Then one afternoon when her lessons were finished, she walked several blocks from the school and hailed a cab. She had no idea how to get where she wanted to go, but she had memorized the address. The driver looked startled when she gave it. "Are you sure that's right, mademoiselle?"

"Quite sure." And they drove across Pont-Royal to the narrow streets of the Left Bank and on and on, until there were beggars in the streets, urchins spilling from doorways, and the windows of the houses were stuffed with newspaper against the cold. The cab stopped; and Lucy, dismissing it, went inside, trying to hold the braided hem of her dress off the thick dust of the stairs. Heart thumping she made her way up three flights to the top and knocked on the door.

No answer. Lucy was almost relieved. Then she was only frustrated. Going down again she roused the concierge. "I am the sister of the gentleman at the top. I have arrived earlier than expected, and he is not home to let me in."

The old woman looked Lucy up and down, amused. She took in the veiled bonnet with tuffs of tulle sewn inside its brim. Her eyes studied Lucy's fur-trimmed coat and her cashmere boots. She did not believe that Lucy was Galen's sister. She thought, rather, of a different relationship. But her day had been dull, and something interesting might occur if she let Lucy in. She would have to climb all the way up, but Lucy looked as though she would be good for a sou. The concierge gazed at the stairs and rubbed her poor back meaningfully. Lucy took money from her pocket and a moment later she was in Galen's rooms.

Nothing looked changed. Sunlight sifted through a dirty skylight, making the dust in the air sparkle. The skylight must suit Galen well. She supposed he had descended through it from carrying her over the rooftops of Paris.

Lucy had not thought what she would do once she was in, but, having removed her bonnet and coat, she spied a broom and by instinct gave the place its much-needed sweeping. Then she decided to make order of the scrambled heaps of papers on the desk. Before she knew it, she was reading. Her work slowed. She hardly knew when the pen came into her hand, when she began to put the thoughts in her head onto the papers, scratching out words in one place, adding others.

Time passed, unnoticed. Then the door swung open, hitting the wooden door stop with a loud whack. A familiar voice said, "Lucy Hamlin! Are you a spy of Louis Philippe's come to take over my paper?" She started up guiltily, fearful of anger in the face she had so longed for.

He looked only amazed to see her. "How you've improved this place! You yourself might be mistaken for a chimney sweep, of course."

Lucy, clapping her hands to her face in horror, brought them away covered with grime.

"But my papers, Miss Hamlin! Those are sacred! Go and wash while I see what harm you've done." He looked at her in amusement. Lucy would almost sooner have had him furious.

Chafing at his condescending manner, she went into the bedroom. "What a fool I am," she told herself. "I got the rooms clean and myself dirty and I dabbled in his private things. I have done everything to make him despise me!" Caroline would simply have sat and been beautiful behind her fan. Tears mixed with the water Lucy splashed onto her cheeks from the washbowl. She wanted to run away, but certainly she could not go through a skylight in a crinoline. She would have to face him.

When she returned, he was sitting with his boots on the desk and a bemused expression on his face. Before she had a chance to wonder what it meant, he said, "Lucy, you've a talent. Would you like to be my assistant?"

He had not said, "It will be dangerous. The police might come and throw you into jail. And your reputation, at very least—" He knew that Lucy understood these things. She had made her decision already in coming here, and had taken herself and her china reputation out of cotton batting.

She came almost every day after that, dismissing her cab a block or so away and making her way to his door through streets filled with urchins, kerchiefed housewives and ragpickers' carts. Hurrying up the stairs, her heart would lighten with each step, as she floated up to his heady world, leaving mundanity below on the street. Since he was sometimes not even home when she arrived, he gave her a key to the place. She kept it tied to a long ribbon on her camisole, where she could easily draw it out and where she could feel it warm against her heart.

Lucy would sort through and edit all the articles Galen had left for her. When he was present he would work, too, writing away in the big, upholstered chair that accompanied the desk, while she drew up a smaller chair at the side.

How Lucy loved those hours! The lamp would be between them, and she would glance from under her lashes to watch him secretly, to see the wonderful light that came into his eyes as he wrote. Sometimes he would solicit her opinion of some paper he had just received. "Lucy, should I use this? Do you think it is too irresponsible in tone?" And she noticed that more and more he depended on what she told him.

Best of all were the times he would call a halt and bring out bread and sausages and wine. Sometimes he would talk to her about politics, but more often about his boyhood in the Champagne Region vineyards or his days at the University. It was because he needed a release from the tension that grew stronger every day over all of Paris, Lucy thought.

"Growing grapes is a timeless thing, a thing of serenity," he would tell her, "and I am neither timeless or serene." He would ask her about Callow Hill and listen to tales of her childhood that she had forgotten for years.

One day she argued with him over some matter for print. How did she dare? She had never put forth her views so strongly to any man before. In truth she had never had strong views.

Half-flustered, he fought back, crying out at last, "Lucy, you make good points, and you speak well. Write it up yourself, and I will print it."

"I?" she said, astonished.

"Yes, certainly. It is your idea; you can express it best."

Lucy took her papers home with her and worked far into the night. When Caroline, wakening, asked what she did, she said simply that she was writing a letter. The article, which she signed, *La Flamme*, was only the first of many she wrote during the next weeks.

She was an instant success. Even Pauline spoke of *La Flamme*, and visitors to Galen's office would ask in her presence who the mysterious new writer was.

"I cannot tell," Galen would say, and his eyes would sparkle.

Lucy would be in ecstasy. "He is proud of me!" she would think.

Proud of her! Was that to be all? It was not enough! She had admitted to herself that she loved him. But he seemed to feel nothing. Never while they worked together did their fingers so much as touch. Never did he make her a pretty compliment of the kind a man makes a girl. Only in her feverish dreams did his kiss caress her, and only there did he swear to love her to the death and beyond. She knew she could never love anyone but him; and knowing it, she put the terrible future from her mind, living each day as though she would die at dusk.

One day Caroline stood before her in great agitation. "Oh, Lucy!" she cried.

Lucy's heart gave a queer turn. "Charles!" What else could be so dreadful?

"No, no. It's not Charles. Mme. Fichaud has found out about Georges and me. She has found the necklace!"

"What has she said?"

"She called me to her rooms and lectured me. She said I must give him up at once."

"What did you say?"

"I said I would. I don't love Georges."

"But why did you give him the necklace—and the umbrella?"

"For the revolution. He said he would give the money to the revolution."

"You! A revolutionary!"

Caroline's eyes burned. "Do you think you are the only one of us capable of high ideals? I saw the refugees from Darby Mill as well as you! That was England but justice in France is no better. Wait—you have not heard the worst of it! Georges has told Mme. Fichaud that he kept the necklace because he loves me. I thought I was only one of his flirtations, but *he* will not give *me* up! Mme. Fichaud is livid!

"She will send us both home with a bad report, she says. It is because she must be rid of me, since she loves Georges so herself. She says you go out too often in the afternoon and never bring back any parcels. She says you are meeting a man. You would never do that, of course, but she will not need proof! She will say so and Lord Ashton will believe her!"

"Caroline," said Lucy softly, "even if you don't love Georges, you are in love with someone."

Caroline cast her eyes down at the rug. "Yes, but I can never tell who."

Two impossible loves! This had been the fate Paris had held for the cousins. In a panic Lucy fled without even putting on her bonnet. She ran all the way to Pont Royal with no thought of hailing a cab. Then, not seeing any, she stumbled on, her side aching, her lungs bursting, the February wind biting at her ears and tumbling her hair. She pounded with both fists on Galen's door. It swung open immediately as though he had been expecting her. He was wearing his greatcoat.

"Galen! I am to be sent—"

"Lucy, go back to the school at once. Stay there, and I will send you a message."

There was such a look in his eyes that she said not another word. She obeyed him.

She did not sleep at all that night. In the morning, without a thought for lessons, she went out again. He might be angry with her for coming, but she must risk it.

Something was odd about the atmosphere of the city, but Lucy did not understand what. There were such crowds, such noisy crowds. She turned a corner and caught sight of smocked workmen tearing up paving stones to make barricades. She knew *then* what was wrong with Paris!

Clutching her bonnet, she began to run, her feet weighted by fear. Galen did not answer her knock. She had not expected him to. She pulled her key from next to her bursting heart and flung open the door. Whirling about the room she looked for something, anything to confirm the meaning of the expression she had seen on his face the night before.

A copy of Galen's paper lay on the desk, and Lucy saw for the first time the manifesto that it, like all the reform papers, had carried the day before. It called for everyone to attend the reformist banquet that the government had forbidden. It asked students, citizens, the sympathetic National Guard.

The National Guard! If they responded it meant revolution!

A letter lay carelessly beside the paper: "Le Blanc," it read, "The pear is ripe. Place de Panthéon at dawn." The pear was Louis Philippe. The shape of his head had given him the nickname.

Lucy sank down atremble. Then leaping up, she ran out again into the street. It did not occur to her to go back to the school where she would be safe. In fact no danger could have seemed greater to her than that which waited for her at the school, where she might be shipped away forever from Galen.

It did not occur to her either that she was a mere woman and could be no help to Galen. Lucy was past such thoughts, though there might be truth in them. She did not think how she might protect him; she only knew she must be near him.

Men jostled her along the sidewalks. Many seemed drunk, whether with liquor or with a wild realization of power. Lucy had to lift her skirts to clamber over the growing barricades. Trees were overturned, urinals lay on their sides, and coils of wire were being spread to stop the cavalry. Lucy heard the *Marseillaise* being sung in the Madeleine. Hurrying into the square, she saw a column of University students going past, marching two-by-two. They would be going where the action was, she thought, changing her course to follow them.

They marched to the Place de la Concorde, into a flood of people, swaying and flowing, washing the square with the turbulent currents of revolt. To one side of the church Royal Regulars tried futilely to push the people back. Lucy saw a group of Municipal Guards flailing about them with the flats of their sabers. A fine, cold rain was falling onto their helmets, onto the crowd.

She did not see Galen anywhere. Now and then she would glimpse someone she recognized from the meetings. She would elbow her way through to him and shout out her question. Someone had seen Galen at the Café Halbourt. Another said he was heading a group on the Champs-Élysées. Lucy followed every lead. She lost her bonnet. The trimming ripped from the sleeve of her coat as she was pushed against a balustrade. Shots rang out. She saw men fall and ran with the scattering mob.

"It is official now," she thought. "Men are dying for the republic."

A block away a *patisserie* was open, doing a furious business. Becoming aware that she was weak from hunger, Lucy bought three and stuffing one into the deep, inset pocket of her skirt, forced herself to eat the others as she walked. The liquor shops were open, too. Men were crowding in to fortify themselves with wine and a smoke before returning to the fray.

Lucy noticed the passing hours only in her growing exhaustion. The gray day grew darker; dusk came early, even for February, and the crowds began to call, "Lights! Lights!"

It was an old Paris custom which meant for everyone inside the houses to put lights in their windows to show agreement with the insurgents. Soon almost every window glowed. The crowds hurled rocks at the windows that remained dark. The wind whipped a fury of echoing voices from block to block along the dark streets, and the shatter of glass excited insurgent hearts. Red caps dotted the flow of people everywhere now as members of the National Guard entered Paris from outlying districts.

In the icy rain Lucy felt the exultation of the throngs. The world was going to change, just as Galen had said. History books would divide at the year 1848— But Lucy's strength failed her. Without willing it, she found herself at the gates of the school. Everything was locked tight. She went around to the side and let herself in with the key that matched Pauline's.

Sympathy lamps shone in all the windows, but the hallways were oddly dim. Without any idea what she would say to Mme. Fichaud, Lucy went softly across the carpets.

But something was wrong. The house was too quiet, and the rooms were all dark, save for the window lamps. A dark shape rose to one side of her as she crossed a doorway. She screamed and ducked. Her scream echoed in the emptiness.

"Lucy! Is it you?" Caroline, running out of the shadows, threw aside the brass andiron she had been brandishing and fell hysterically into Lucy's arms. "I am here all alone!"

"Alone!"

"Mme. Fichaud has taken all the other girls and fled the city. I could not go without you. I could not leave you in Paris. Oh, Lucy, what has happened to you? You are all torn and soaked through. You will catch pneumonia! You must have a hot bath and a meal. I will fix them myself. All the maids are gone."

Having thought what must be done, Caroline became calmer. "Lucy, whatever were you doing out there? You weren't near the shooting, were you? You might have been killed!"

Lucy, naked in the porcelain tub, absorbing the caress of hot water over her weary body, let the lock on her heart open at last. "I have been out looking for the man that I love," she said. "Tomorrow I will look for him again. He has never said he loves me, but he is all that matters. I have a dreadful fear that he will die out there, for he would be a special prize at the end of a bayonet. But I must be beside him, Caroline, so long as he is alive." The spirit of revolution gripped her; she could be suppressed no more.

Caroline, unnerved, spilled half a kettle of boiling water onto her dress of silk pekin. Brushing at it distractedly, she cried out, "Lucy, this is insanity! Who is ths man?" And hearing his name, she swayed, on the verge of fainting.

"Lucy! You are engaged to Charles Ashton!"

"I am *almost* engaged, as you have pointed out to me yourself. I have made no promise to Charles. There was a moment when I should have done it, and something stopped me. I was frightened then, and I am frightened now. But that was a different kind of fear from the fear I feel in loving Galen Le Blanc."

"But—"

"Charles will not recover," said Lucy in a choked voice. "Most likely he is already dead." Indeed he was as unreal as a ghost to Lucy.

And he belonged to a world that was dead for her.

Chapter 9

They left the sympathy lamps burning all night. Lucy would fall into a tortured sleep only to be jerked to consciousness by a far-off burst of gunfire. In that instant between sleeping and waking, she would imagine that every bullet pierced Galen's heart; and so doing, killed her as well.

She died twenty deaths before dawn tinted the sky outside her window, and then, leaving Caroline sleeping with the covers clutched over her fair head, she went downstairs. She put out all the lights and ate cold stew that she found in the kitchen. Then wrapping herself into her coat, a boa, and a velvet muff and clipping up her skirt with a metal page to make walking easier, she went out into the frigid morning.

The rain water had turned to ice overnight, making the cobblestones slippery. The sun began to shine, and the coated tree limbs and fences sparkled. All Paris glittered, and the light refracted into prisms of red and gold and blue.

She heard the beat of drums, then the singing of the "Marseillaise," and from another direction that of "Girondins." There was distant cheering. Lucy began to run. A National Guardsman came into the street, carrying a musket, a bloody bandage around his shoulder.

"What has happened?" Lucy cried.

"The government has fallen."

"Then it's over!" A wonderful joy filled her.

"No. It's not enough." The soldier gestured in the direction of the palace. "Down with tyrants, mademoiselle!"

"Of course. Down with tyrants. The pear is ripe! Have you seen Galen Le Blanc?"

"Have I seen him! Behind the barricades, on the rooftops! Last midnight in a charge on the Hotel de Ville. And everywhere he goes, men follow him. Everywhere he is, men find a courage they did not know they possessed."

"But now?"

"They are fighting at the Porte Saint-Martin. Perhaps he is there. Do not go! It would be very dangerous!"

But she went, pushing her way through the celebrating crowds toward the sound of gunfire. A bullet whined through the air and thudded into a wooden post near her. She saw a man dig it out with his knife.

"It is one of those new pointed bullets that can kill at fifteen hundred meters," he mused, heading off in the direction of the fighting. Lucy followed until she almost stumbled over a dead guardsman whose life's blood had drained into the gutter and frozen.

Reeling with nausea, she withdrew her foot from the soldier's uncaring flesh and retreated back to Galen's room. Galen would come sometime, she thought. She would wait. But the afternoon passed, and as darkness approached, she thought of Caroline alone at the school. "I must go back. She will be terrified; she will be imagining I am dead."

The streets were gay. Along the boulevards the houses glowed with the light of Venetian lanterns. But the crowd was too thick. Somewhere came the noise of a fusillade. Lucy could not make her way. She was driven back and felt herself lucky to regain the safety of Galen's apartment. She unhooked her crinoline and stays, and, lying on Galen's bed, tried to sleep.

Hours slid into dawn again. And then somehow she knew that something important had begun to happen. It was as if Galen's winds of change had seeped through the drafty windows with the cold night air. She leaped up, hearing nothing but the twittering of pigeons beneath the eaves. Yet she knew—

"To the Tuileries!" came a shout in the street. Snatching on her clothes, Lucy obeyed as though the summons had been for her alone. A church bell rang the tocsin; the bells of other churches joined it.

The morning was foggy. Or what was fog and what the smoke of guns, it was impossible to tell. As she came closer to the Rue Saint Thomas, the drums beat louder and louder. They seemed to pound against her very ears, but that was only her heart hammering there, bursting with her effort.

She did not doubt that she would find Galen now. She

might find him as she had the soldier, dead in a gutter, but she would find him. The Rue Fromanteau was full of regulars. Her way was blocked. With a cry of despair she ran toward the Rue de Valois. That was blocked, too, by a towering barricade of paving stones. A soldier ran atop it, outlined for a moment against clouds of smoke. Galen? He would be cut down! But the man scrambled to safety. And it had not been Galen.

The guard post at Château d'Eau, angered by such bravado, let forth a round of shot through the loopholes of its oak shutters. Lucy was thrust back against a wall. Now and then a man, struggling forward with his musket, gave her a glance of disbelief. It was all dream-like, but Lucy did not fit into anyone's dream. She was out of kilter—a woman here.

Men charged up the steps of the guard post and beat at the door with iron bars. A barouche, stuffed with burning hay, was dragged along the wall. A barrel of brandy was up-ended for igniting fluid over straw and wood.

Now she could see the palace itself, dull and somnolent in the February light, sitting like a stupid, inert monster near the edge of the open ground that led off to the open-air stalls. She glimpsed the Hotel de Nantes, the dome of the Louvre.

A roar, an explosion of voices rippled the throng. It seemed to Lucy that the ground trembled. "The king is gone! Louis Philippe has abdicated!"

In the frenzy she was almost more frightened than she had been in the shooting. But suddenly her fear vanished. She saw Galen high on the steps of the palace, lifted on the shoulders of his compatriots. Somehow she was pushing forward as the crowd surged toward the open palace doors.

With every breath she cried out, "Let me through to Galen Le Blanc!" And as though the name worked miracles, she moved closer. There were other women in the throng now, women in kerchiefs, prostitutes. But the sight of the elegant Lucy caused men to give way instinctively. She was swept to the very steps, calling out to him, "Galen! Galen!"

She must have been one of dozens shouting his name, and yet he heard her, as though praise from her voice had been what he was listening for. He leaped to the ground, seized her around the waist and lifted her into the fresh breeze beside him.

His trousers were black with powder. His coat was torn away at the shoulder, and there was blood on its silesia lining. He was injured, and yet she did not say, "You are wounded."

Her eyes burned with tears, and her throat ached with pride as he put his hand in hers. She gripped it hard. "Long live the Republic!" she murmured.

The triumph that charged his eyes passed to her like a current. *"You* have helped to make France free," he said. "Let us go and see the palace that belongs to the people from this day forward."

Foregoing coffee on the first floor, they went upstairs where the portraits of the marshals' gallery looked on impassively as the victors destroyed chandeliers and curtains and tossed tables and sconces from the windows. People were rolling on the beds, rummaging in drawers, dumping the contents of cupboards onto the floors. They wore laces and ostrich-feather hats and sashes of the Legion of Honor.

"Galen, it's so senseless! Can't you stop it?"

He shook his head. "It is destructive, but it is not senseless. It is retribution and better taken on the palace than on the person of Louis Philippe. Ah, I'm like you. I find it disgusting. But there's one thing we must tend to. Come quickly."

He led the way, shoving among the crowd, until they came to a room with a red canopy stretched over its ceiling. There dirty soldiers were taking turns sitting on the throne. Someone recognized Galen.

"There's Le Blanc!" A clamor went up. "Vive Le Blanc! Le Blanc must sit on it." Lucy with a sense of panic held tight to his arm.

He waved his admirers back with the arm that was free. "It shall never be said of me that I sat on *any* throne! Perish the throne!"

They took it up as a chant. "Perish the throne! Reform forever!" Some of them lifted the throne and passed it from hand to hand over their heads. At last they threw it from a window to those in the streets below. A huge cheer went up.

"To the Bastille! Burn it!" And the throne was borne away.

Galen watched with satisfaction. "There. That is what I wanted to see. Should I die now, my life would be complete."

Die. The word on his lips made her frightened again. "You are hurt," she ventured to say. "Can we not go home now?"

He smiled at her gently. "Yes. Why not? The job is done, Lucy. Let us go."

She could feel how weary he was as they entered the attic apartment, he leaning against her shoulder. But suddenly he grew tense. He was staring at the bed.

"What is it, Galen?" she asked fearfully.

"Someone slept here. I did not leave the bed rumpled. Perhaps the police, waiting."

She laughed. "It was only I who slept here waiting."

"You! Did you care so much what happened to me?" He turned and looked at her. His eyes, red-rimmed with battle smoke, lighted with a different sort of fire. She had not the leisure to make sense of it before he had seized her in his arms and was kissing her.

"You shall sleep here tonight, too, Lucy Hamlin! Oh what a marvel you are! What a struggle I have had to keep myself from you! One embrace and I would have been lost—lost as the throne of Louis Philippe! But, Lucy, the world has turned about more than once this day. It has seen the dark of the moon a dozen times, and you are not to marry your lord! There is not another woman like you! You shall not be wasted on him!"

She did not question how it was to be or what would happen to her. She gave herself up to him, trusting him entirely. She trembled in delight as his kisses moved ravenously over her lips and against the warmth of her throat. Her eyes went shut so that the lids could share the rain of his love.

"Lucy," he murmured joyfully, "you love me, too. Don't be afraid to love me back."

As though his words released her, she flung herself against him, and with a little cry of rapture, put her mouth against his. It was the first time she had ever kissed a man, but she spared only a moment's wonder at the flood of unlady-like feeling that welled in her. It was nothing like the time Charles had tried to kiss her on the heath. She took his face in her hands and kissed it all over as he had kissed hers. Then, as though she could not bear an inch of space between their bodies, she pulled him close again.

She felt his fingers on the tiny pewter buttons of her dress. "Galen, what are you doing?" she whispered.

"I must see you as you are, without these trappings!"

She did not resist. She knew vaguely that this had to do with love. The dress fell away. He jerked impatiently on the strings of her corset. She turned her back to make his task easier. Reaching behind her to help him, she drew a strange, shuddering breath as the stays parted.

Her crinoline, her petticoats followed each other to the floor. She stood in only her pantaloons and camisole. She had not quite thought of discarding these, and she gasped with surprise as he jerked the camisole over her head and her white breasts fell free. Dazed, she looked down at her firm, round bosom.

Did she please him? She was suddenly afraid to meet his gaze, and, blushing hotly, noticed the small brown mole adrift on one breast like a speck in cream. Did he mind that?

He answered her question by taking her breasts gently in his hands and lowering his lips to them reverently. A moan escaped her.

"The pantaloons," he breathed. She fought for a moment to hold them up. He sank to his knees and rested his head against her smooth stomach. Her flesh quivered, and she too pushed at the pantaloons. His hands ran over her, exploring her hips, her thighs. Deep sighs came one after another from his lips.

She began to ache oddly and, starting to quiver, wondered if she were ill. Perhaps she was, for she felt overwhelmed by a need to lie down. She was on the point of saying something to him, but he understood her weakness, and lifting her, carried her to the bed and put her there with care.

"Your poor, hurt shoulder," she murmured in his arms.

"I am not too injured for this. I would not be, were I on my deathbed!"

He began to strip away his own clothes. Lucy watched in fascination, loving him, loving all that she saw. But still she did not understand what was to happen, why she felt as she did.

He got into bed beside her and suddenly she knew. There was ecstasy in the pain, for suffering for his sake was only a part of her joy. She welcomed him into her body, glorying that this should be possible, that she could hold him, comfort and caress him in the depths of her being. She felt herself dissolve in the power that emanated from his beautiful soul, and her body, not needing her to direct it, lifted to his, to her destiny.

Lucy twisted her fingers in Galen's hair as the wonderful sensations washed over her in great waves. Then came one wave larger than the rest. Its great explosive force seemed to wrest them from each other. It tore from Lucy an astonished moan. Galen loosened his hold.

"Lucy," he whispered, as she still cradled soft and naked beside him, "I was wrong this afternoon at Tuileries. My life was not complete then. It has never been complete until now."

His breathing grew deep and regular. She realized that he slept, and stroking his hair tenderly, she thought fiercely, "I am his. I shall love him forever. I can love no other man."

Chapter 10

Night had fallen. Lucy had gone out and brought back bread and cheese and wine. The stove, filled from the coal supply over the firebox, gave off a rosy heat. Galen, in a clean shirt, his bandages freshly changed, lay with his head in Lucy's lap.

"They are still cheering in the streets," he said.

"Yes, and dancing in all the squares, when I went out."

"Are they? I will get dressed and take you. We have never danced together."

She pushed him back. "No. Your shoulder might start to bleed again. We will have another celebration soon. We will save our dancing for that."

He smiled at her fondly. "What celebration will that be?"

"Why our wedding, of course."

His brow darkened and he sat up. "Our wedding! We are not to be married!"

"But I am not to marry Charles Ashton!" she protested in bewilderment. "You said so yourself!"

"No. You are not to marry Charles Ashton. You are not to marry anyone. Can you not see what slaves marriage makes of women, Lucy? You yourself have almost had the experience of it."

"But it is different when one is not forced into it. I want to marry you!"

"Has it occurred to you that I am not at all suitable?" he said with sarcasm. "Your family will lose the Ashton title. Your dear papa will disown you; I am a wanted man in England. Your dowry will be nothing, perhaps not even a grave in the family plot. Such are the fruits of marriage, Lucy."

"But in France you will have position now! Oh, even had you not, I love you, and I must do what my heart says is right."

"Yes, yes. You will always do what your heart says is

right. It will not matter what other people say. That is why I love you so!" His voice was eager. "That is why you must understand what we must do. I am a revolutionary and will always be one, and you are a woman who can lead other women. You have shown that quality already as *La Flamme*. You showed your mettle again when you came to look for me at Tuileries. What a team we will make, Lucy!

"When at last there is no marriage, men and women will stand equal. Then no government, no shame will stand in the way of love, and in such a world, the rank and title that sets men above each other shall crumble. You can help to bring it about; you are a true revolutionary, as I am. Do not think that today all the battles are won.

"Lucy, I respect you too much to subjugate you beneath the weight of marriage conventions. Flaunt yourself with me, and a hundred years from now all womankind will call you saint!"

She did not want to be a saint. She wanted to be his wife. Yet even more than this, she wanted to be what he wanted her to be. And she did understand. It would be weak of her to marry him. She would have to struggle all her life, but she would struggle beside *him*.

In the morning she went down to the street and calling to an urchin, paid him to take a note to Caroline.

> "*Dearest cousin,*" she had written, "*I am not coming back. I am staying with him always. Tell Mme. Fichaud I have fled to friends in the country for fear of the revolution, and pack my things and send them to me. Do not weep over me, for I am happier than I ever dreamed.*"

Her trunks arrived the following afternoon, carried upstairs by a panting postilion. Below in the street, Caroline herself alighted from the cab. She had indeed been weeping. Their embrace wrung from her one last moan of misery.

"Lucy, what does this mean? You cannot stay here!" She gazed around at the decaying rooms.

"It is better than a palace with him, Caroline."

"Oh, cousin, what have you—"

"I have given myself to him!" cried Lucy, her face

glowing. "Yes, yes, utterly! Caroline, you cannot imagine what love is! It cannot be described!"

Caroline's eyes were round with horror. "I know what sort of love this is! It is disaster! What of Charles?"

"I cannot marry him, that is all."

Caroline grew thoughtful. Lucy was amused to watch her brain begin to turn, never despairing, seeking to salvage the situation. "This Galen. Is he at all suitable?"

"He says he is not. But he comes from a fine family in the Champagne Region. It is irrelevant whether he has title, for if he has, he disclaims it. In England he is a hunted man, and until yesterday in France, too. But he will be important in the new government. I am sure of that."

"Perhaps your papa will relent."

"You are dreaming, Caroline. Papa will never forgive me for not marrying Charles."

"But if he is dead—" They were both silent, thinking that the city had been disorganized, the mail service interrupted for nearly a week.

For a moment Lucy saw Charles lying as she had left him. Her vow to love him forever weighed upon her, choking her. But she was no longer the person who had made that promise. It did not bind her. It could not! She shook free of the vision and said calmly to her cousin, "It is no matter whether Papa accepts Galen or not. He says we shall live as equals. We are not to be married."

"Not to be married! Lucy! Forget this madness!"

"It is not madness. It is one of the finest ideas the world has ever seen. What will you do, Caroline? Will you go home to England, now?"

"No, I will stay. Mme. Fichaud has no need to be rid of me now. Georges has gone. He has resigned his position. Imagine—he gave up his soft berth over me. I suppose she does not enjoy seeing me about, but she cannot send me home until she finds you. I will stay in Paris where you are as long as I can. Your alibi cannot last long, cousin, and you will be destroyed. Think about what I have said." And kissing Lucy's cheek, she hurried down the stairs before tears overcame her again.

The days passed and became weeks. Galen was pressured to become a minister of the Cabinet. He refused, to Lucy's surprise. He wanted to write, he said, and since they were no longer hounded by the police, they moved the office of *Le Revue Démocratie* to a pleasant townhouse.

The drawing room was hung in chintz, and there were ottomans with fringes. The furniture was soft and tufted, and flower stands of ivy geranium and asparagus fern sat in every window. The sun streamed in all morning while Lucy wrote at the beautiful rosewood desk he had bought for her, and in the afternoon he would always tumble her deliciously in bed. She would rise, still naked and stretching her fine young body shamelessly for him to see, would declare herself happy that he had not taken the cabinet post. It meant he was here to love her the more. And he, laughing that she was indeed the reason that he could not drag himself from the house, would leap up equally naked and pull her back to take her again.

On days when he became too preoccupied to suggest the bedroom, Lucy would remind him herself, sometimes with a teasing kiss while he worked. Sometimes she would come to him more dramatically in only a chemise and sit on his lap as she gayly pulled away his clothes. Those times they rarely made it to the bedroom at all, but would slide to the floor, and he, parting her willing thighs, would love her in the ribbons of sunshine on the carpet.

In the evenings they would go out to dine. Paris had a holiday atmosphere. Flags hung in all the windows along with posters of Louis Philippe as a pastry cook or a leech, and everyone wore rosettes in their buttonholes. Galen and Lucy would shop for bric-a-brac for their house—paintings, screens, little ivory statues and Dresden bowls. They would select each piece carefully, buying only what was beautiful to both. They would buy eclairs running over with gooey icing and eat them while they watched churchmen blessing the planting of a Tree of Liberty.

Galen's paper drew a wider circulation. Galen himself was often recognized. Lucy, who had abandoned her curls for a more mature swooping of her dark, rich hair into a chignon, would be noticed as well.

"She is the one who was with him at the sacking of Tuileries."

"Can it be she is *La Flamme?*"

"Yes, and she lives as she writes. They are lovers—can anyone doubt it who sees them? She flaunts every law of decency. She should be miserable and yet—"

Lucy heard no more from Caroline. Pauline, herself

dissociated from the school, came often, her only confidant. At Galen's urging Lucy began to speak at rallies. Her speech was as eloquent as her pen, and woman stood as spellbound before her as she herself before Jeanne Derione, a few months ago, in her girlhood, a lifetime away.

Spring came. The lime trees leafed. Daffodils and tulips bloomed, then azaleas. Children sailed their toy boats in the fountains of Tuileries Gardens. The city was beautiful, Galen said, as it had never been before.

"Is it because Paris is free," he wondered, smiling at Lucy, "or because I see it through the eyes of love?"

The first day they saw blossoms he took Lucy to a jewelers' and bought her a round gold locket with an emerald set. The set symbolized the eternal greenness of his love, he told her; and inside he had their names engraved along with the place and the date, Paris, 1848. She wore it always, discarding those dresses with which it did not harmonize.

They were in love; yet all was not well. The government was beginning to go awry. Galen spent more and more time away, returning tense and worried.

"There will be more trouble, Lucy," he warned when the elections returned a conservative Assembly. "We will have to fight again."

"But it was a free election, Galen. It was the people's will!" Her stomach tightened at the thought of more violence. She could not have bullets whizzing again about Galen. She could not bear it!

He sat at his desk, looking down, his face drawn. "A free election cannot be valid if the voters do not understand the issues, Lucy. The ignorant people from the provinces voted against us, and because of it, there will still be suffering and starvation, injustice, inequality."

"But the king is gone. We have a republic. We will educate the people and work within the system."

He shook his head tiredly. "The workers of Paris will not see it that way, if the government does not respond to their needs. Hunger will not wait a generation or even for new elections. There is a basic difference between us, I see. You, with your English background, are more parliamentarian; while I am a revolutionary, who gets things accomplished. Remember Darby Mill, Lucy. There we did not go armed. We chose only to strike, to petition.

I feel responsible for the disaster of Darby Mill. It is a mistake I will not make again."

"But if a second revolution fails, the monarchists may come to power again."

"Yes, most likely."

"And you will be—"

"Executed. Thrown into prison, at least."

"Oh Galen," she cried, unthinking. "Let us leave Paris! Let us leave France!"

He stiffened. "That is unworthy of you, Lucy. Our place is here. I could not live with a coward, nor could you."

He was right. He must do what he had to, and she said no more.

She began to live in fear. Was it fear that made her feel so unwell? A wave of dizziness came over her one morning as she worked on an article for Galen's paper. The next morning the dizziness overpowered her as she tried to rise from bed. Day after day her willpower dragged her back to her work. Not wanting to bother Galen, she made herself smile for him, while her appetite evaporated and flesh melted from her body.

"I have some terrible disease," she thought. "I will die of it. I must find a doctor." But she languished, feeling too weak to venture out alone.

Still in her pelisse robe one afternoon, she answered a knock and found Caroline there. Her slim figure in a flounced barege dress swam before Lucy's eyes.

"Lucy! What has happened to you?" cried Caroline, seeing at once what the distracted Galen had not noticed.

"Oh Caroline! I don't know. I am ill. I am so glad you've come. You'll help me—"

"Yes, yes, of course. I'll take you away at once. I knew it could not last. See what I've brought!" and beaming, she held out a letter.

Lucy reeled, feeling in the grip of an hallucination. The envelope was addressed to her in Charles Ashton's own hand. She gazed a question at her cousin.

"He has recovered!" breathed Caroline. "It came in the post this very morning. Open it and see what he says."

Lucy broke the seal and ripped open the envelope. Words in the hand she had never expected to see again spun before her.

My love—only an accident, nothing you are to be blamed for. It can only have been my love for you that saved me, when I had been all but given up. I lived for you. Come home and marry me at once. It has been postponed too long already. I wait impatiently.

Lucy passed the letter to Caroline and sank down, her clouded, bewildered mind trying to make sense of it. "How can this be? Doesn't he know about Galen? Hasn't Papa disowned me?"

"Your Papa knows nothing, and neither does Charles," declared Caroline triumphantly. "I arranged it."

"Arranged it! How?"

"I threatened Mme. Fichaud with Georges. I knew about him and her, you see, and I said I would destroy her reputation if she destroyed yours. I said I would see that all the English gentry knew, and no one would send their daughters anymore."

"I did not ask you to save me!" cried Lucy tearfully, surprised at this display of mettle by her gentle cousin. "I will not go home!"

It was somehow depressing to find her burned bridges still so solid as though nothing she could do had power to free her from the lot society had appointed her. After Caroline had gone, Lucy, too stunned to rejoice over Charles' recovery, wept for hours. Thus Galen found her, face down on the bed, her clothing rumpled, her cambric handkerchief soaked through with tears.

"My angel! What is wrong?" He lifted her up, and she clung to him, pouring out her story.

He did not mind her display of weakness. He held her and smoothed her hair. "Lucy, there is nothing to cry about. Only be happy that Charles is alive and well again. Now you need worry over him no longer. Simply send him a letter and tell him you cannot marry him."

"Yes, you are right," and she tried to smile.

But he was looking at her a different way. He was seeing her thinness, her pallor, all that he should have seen before. "There is something else—"

And so encouraged, she told him.

He questioned her closely. Then at last he began to smile again. "You are pregnant, Lucy. It can be nothing else. Now you are mine as you have never been before. There is not a chance now that duty can force you to marry Charles."

He took off her clothing and putting her into a gown,

tucked her between the covers. "You must rest, and you will not write any more for a while. You have been working too hard."

He drew the curtains and left the room. She lay in the dimness as the enormity of it washed over her. "I am to bear a child, and I am not married!"

And deep inside she wished she could change herself into a pampered little wife.

Within a week the working class and the middle class had left their houses in numbers and were living under arms in the public squares. Working frantically for compromise that would prevent violence, Gallen went daily to the Hotel de Ville. Lucy, still weak, unable to help him with the paper, railed at her sex, the limitations of which had been unknown to her. She berated the baby that so surprisingly had come inside her, and just as quickly she blessed it.

How privileged she was to carry it! If woman's only duty were, as some thought, to bear children, it was enough for her, since it was Galen she would re-create. It was not a sentiment that Pauline or Jeanne Derione would have entertained, but then, they had never been in love like this. Someday all women must be free to love and be loved as she, Lucy would think. And lying abed, she would plan articles she would write when the sickness had passed.

Galent, fearful for her health, wanted to cease their lovemaking, but she would not have it. She pulled him to her every night, crushing him against her naked breasts, loving him as though every time must last forever.

"The doctors all advise against it," he would protest, helplessly.

"They know little about preserving life, then. I would die without loving you!"

Then one morning she awoke to the sound of gunfire. Beside her the bed was empty. The nightmare of her life had begun.

Chapter 11

She ran into the streets, toward the Hotel de Ville, the city offices where she hoped Galen might be. The barricades had been built again from paving stones and assemblymen, wearing their sashes, hurried past. Seeing one who had been a part of the winter revolution, she stopped him to ask, "Is Galen inside?"

"No. There has been terrible fighting at Saint Denis Gate. Most likely that is where he is."

Should she go after him? She felt the same drive to be with him she had in the February fighting. But it was different now. She knew he loved her. Might he be careless, protecting her? And there was their child whose safety must be thought of. But she must do something! She could not go back to lie in bed and wait.

While she was considering, a storm came up. The sky darkened and thunder drowned out the sound of the guns. The rain fell like millions of piercing silver bullets. Lightning spit from the heavens like the armament of God. Drenched, she took shelter in a café.

"This will put an end to the fighting for today," she heard someone say. "It will give one more chance for compromise to be reached."

But the rain stopped, and as the sun shone again, the sound of guns grew nearer. Lucy's heart leaped. The insurgents were gaining. Drums were beating the call to arms. Trumpets blared a wild discordant music. Lucy wandered out and found herself on the Rue Notre Dame des Champs.

Suddenly she noticed something different from the February Revolution. Women were behind the barricades, loading weapons for the men. Close to Lucy a young girl was struggling with her brother's carbine. Lucy, seeing the urgency of the matter, seized it. She had never touched a gun before, but her father had always been an avid huntsman. She had watch him a thousand times at Callow Hill.

Hours passed as she loaded and reloaded the rifle. She was unaware of the illness of her pregnancy, of her aching back, her empty stomach. Then as she handed the weapon to the workman, he was no longer there. With a cry, she looked down into his dead face.

She glimpsed a uniform topping the barricade. Raising the gun instinctively, she fired at the figure above her. The solder fell backward. Had it been her shot that had hit him? Had she killed him? An awful horror filled her; she felt faint. But at the same time, she was automatically reloading.

Later she would have no clear recollection of all that happened during the next few days. She would remember eating bread, its crust black from gunpowder on her fingers, and tortured sleep beside a bivouac fire.

Then came the slow realization that the rebels were losing. At last she was at the Faubourg Saint Antoine, the last bastion of the revolution. She had thought to find Galen here, fighting to the end, but she did not.

It was over, and she knew he must be among the dead. She went to the Place du Pantheon, where black patches of dried blood darkened every barricade like a fungus growth, and the houses were as speckled as bird's eggs where gunfire had flaked the plaster. The Pantheon itself was being used as a morgue, and there Lucy wandered like a sleepwalker among the corpses on the floor.

Someone touched her shoulder. It was Pauline, who had been working as a nurse. "Lucy, you must leave Paris at once!"

"I cannot find Galen."

"But you are on their list! They know you are Galen's woman! They know you are *La Flamme!* Think how they will enjoy showing their wives what comes of a woman like you! Think how they may use you to torment Galen, to try to flush him out of hiding! They will have both you and his child!"

"I must tell Caroline," Lucy murmured, dazed.

"Very well, we will send a messenger, then."

Half an hour later the cousins met at Pauline's apartment. "But where will you go?" said Caroline. She thought a moment, then ever-hopeful, asked, "What did you write to Charles?"

"I wrote nothing. I was ill."

"Then he waits for you. You will marry him now, after all. And you will make him happy at last. He loves you so."

Lucy began to laugh hysterically. "Dear, forgiving Charles! Even he cannot long overlook the child I carry."

"I know of a convent in Belgium," Pauline said. "There are nursing sisters, and you would be safe."

Caroline took the announcement of Lucy's pregnancy matter-of-factly, without tears. She sighed, knowing that the child put the seal on the course Lucy had already set. "If you are to have a baby, there is nothing else to do," she said. "We will go to the convent."

"We? But, Caroline—"

"I will stay with you, always," said Caroline.

Lucy put her head into her cousin's lap and wept.

She let them do as they would with her. A landau appeared from somewhere, already loaded with her things from Galen's house and Caroline's from Mme. Fichaud's. Pauline proffered false identification papers naming Lucy as a Mademoiselle Girard.

"You will have to get past the city gates," she said. "They are checking everyone."

Just as the carriage was pulling away in the darkness, a man jumped in beside them. He was impeccably dressed in a saxony frock coat and gray trousers, and his shirt buttons were voguish, tiny rubies set in narrow circles of gold. In this torn, battered city, he was freakishly untouched, like a china vase after a fire or explosion. He might have been on his way to a party.

"Georges!"

"Good evening, Caroline, Mademoiselle Girard." He smiled impishly and tipped his low-crowned Brimmer hat. "It is a nice summer evening for a ride. A trifle warm, perhaps, but it will be cooler in more ways than one, when we are outside the city walls. I myself am in need of a little fresh air, so I have volunteered to be your sentry." And he patted the bulge of a revolver beneath his coat.

The horses' hooves echoed on the cobblestones. Streets that would have been filled on ordinary June nights, were empty. Once there was a spate of gunfire, and the horses whinnied and made the carriage lurch. Lucy saw the lights of the gates, the sentry box. The papers were handed over.

A face evil with suspicion peered in at a window. A lantern held so close she could feel its warmth made her blink. "Mademoiselle Girard, throw back your veil, please."

She hesitated, but she had no choice. She pushed away the veil.

"Mademoiselle, would you be so kind as to step down—"

Her heart seemed to stop.

She had no time to think what she would do. Georges, rising from his seat, leaned over her, yelling wildly at the horses. The landau jumped forward. She saw the revolver in Georges' hand. The smoke from its discharge filled the carriage and choked off her breath. She heard the crack of rifles.

Georges fell across her lap. Blood spread over her dress. She caught him with her arms, and he gazed up at her. He seemed in that moment like a small frightened boy who had been hurt at play, and she wanted to comfort him as a mother would.

"The dress will wash, I think," he murmured. "Caroline will be safe. Caroline—" The childish look in his eyes was replaced by something more profound, then by emptiness. He became suddenly heavy in her lap and slid away, hitting against the door, which flew open with the pressure.

Both girls clutched at him as he rolled away to the road. "We must stop the carriage!" Caroline screamed.

Lucy pushed Caroline roughly back into her seat, reaching for the door and pulling it shut. "There's no use. It would only give anyone pursuing us a chance to catch up. He is dead." She had seen enough of dying now to be sure.

Caroline's slender frame was wrenched by a sob.

"Don't cry for him. There is no better fate than to die for love. He found what was fine in him because of you."

The carriage rumbled on into the night. After a while it seemed impossible that Georges had ever been with them in the coach. Only the stain of his life's blood on Lucy's dress and his hat, lying on the floor between there, were reminders. Paris itself seemed unreal.

Finally Lucy took the hat and threw it out the window. Then, exhausted from days of holocaust and lulled by the country air and the swaying of the coach, she slept.

Chapter 12

The convent was high in the Ardennes Mountains near the Luxembourg border. Winds smelling of pine caressed its blank, unresponding walls, and the only sounds in the forest silence were those of mourning doves; the lonely, tolling bell; and chanting which merged dirge-like into the whisper of a swift stream.

From her cell-like room, Lucy wrote at last to Charles Ashton, taking more pain with the letter than with any of the articles she had written for Galen's paper.

Dearest Charles,
I have not written before because I have been ill, and because there has been another bloody revolution in Paris, as you will have heard. Do not worry about me. I am safely away in a convent, and I am better. My heart overflows with joy that you are well.

My kind, wonderful Charles, when I left you so death-like, I made a vow to love you forever. It is a vow I cannot keep, for I did not know then what love was. I fell in love in Paris, and now I can never love another.

I can never marry you, Charles, for you are too good to suffer a marriage without love. I grieve that I make you unhappy, but I do not make you as unhappy as you would be if we were wed.

She mailed the letter as well as one to her father explaining that she and Caroline had fled to the convent from the turmoil of the revolution and that, as she was unwell, they wished to remain awhile. Then, thinking she had done the right thing, she was at peace.

She gave her attention over to the baby, which, as though responding to her thoughts, fluttered with the first amazing stirrings of life.

Winter came early and snow stood to the sill of her small, high window. Inside it was as cold and colorless as out. Crusts of ice formed overnight in the pitcher of her washstand, and her feet stung with cold when she put them to the stone floor to search for her slippers.

Dark-habited nuns flitted silently from the shadows like ghosts of the dead, and the cheerless atmosphere did nothing to alleviate her fear for Galen.

Below the convent was a village, and looking down, Lucy would see splashes of color and hear the distant tinkle of sleigh bells. How she longed to be there, to speak to people, to be a part of that life! But she could not. It was one of the conditions of her stay that she not make a "show" of herself in her condition. She was as isolated from humankind as though she had been on the moon.

Caroline went often to the village, always returning with fragrant pastries wafting warmly of life. Lucy ate them greedily, though they only whetted her appetite for all she had once had.

"Do you remember how we used to buy these at a *patisserie* after we had walked along the quays in Paris?" she would ask Caroline.

"Yes, I remember."

"How beautiful those days were! Don't you long for them?"

"This place has a charm, too."

"Ah, easy for you to say! *You* are not a prisoner here!" And then when Caroline looked downcast, she would seize her hand and cry, "Do forgive me! You are here for my sake. You could be in England, and I am grateful you are with me instead. I should certainly die without you!"

And for Caroline's sake she would exclaim over the lightness of the crust and the juiciness of the filling, and she would fight against the desolation of the bleak, barren convent.

Her body swelled out into a crescent. The nuns helped her make skirts with great plackets, and she went without stays, eating all the pastries she wanted. She was treating her child as well as herself.

Then came a time when her greatness seemed to overpower her. She could not sleep, and she ached when she drove her weight from bed.

Before dawn one morning she cried out with a terrible pain. "It is beginning," said Caroline, coming to her, and they clasped hands, helpless with fear. Then the pain blotted away Caroline's face, and Lucy was aware only of the pressure of her hand.

She knew vaguely that the sun came up and went down again. She thought that Caroline went away, that a nun replaced her. But when she could look, it was Caroline; and light was coming again through the window.

She screamed for Galen, feeling betrayed that he did not come. She wept. She beat at the unseen enemy, the pain that had become her existence.

"Poor thing, it is often this way with a first birth," she heard someone murmur. And Caroline's voice, strangled, asked, "Will she die?"

She began to long for death. She pleaded aloud for it to come to her. She knew that firm hands took her flailing arms and tied them to the bed with leather thongs. Suddenly her body seemed to be coming asunder. She fought against it with all her might, trying to hold her being together.

A nun with a stern face stood over her. "Let go!" she said. "Let go!"

It seemed like a command from God himself. She obeyed and felt herself disintegrate into a thousand pieces.

The pain was gone. Far away she heard a baby cry. "What day is it?" she whispered. Somehow that was important, to mark the time, the day that this rending thing had happened.

"Why, Christmas Day. You have a fine gift, too. A pretty little girl."

The baby was christened Alyce. It was a name that Galen had once said he liked. She nursed her through the winter, getting up to re-tuck the covers around her in the cold night, even when there had been no cry. The nuns spoke to her gently, urging her to give the baby up. "Let her have both a mother and a father as God intended," they said.

"She has a mother and a father," Lucy would reply fiercely, holding the child closer. She would never be parted from her little daughter.

The nuns said that the baby did not gain enough weight, and to Lucy's distress, they insisted on weaning her to goat's milk. Lucy knew they meant the weaning as the first step toward separation. She would have to do something—soon!

Caroline still bore about her the sadness she had had

in Paris, and Lucy, worrying over her, suggested regretfully that she returned to England. "It's spring. You would be in time for the season."

Caroline shook her head. "I don't want to go back. There is nothing for me there. I would like to stay here forever, if I could. If I were Catholic, I would take the vows of the order. I am thinking of becoming a convert."

Caroline, a nun! She was still in love then, hopelessly, as she had been Paris. Lucy tried to talk to her about it, but she was as uncommunicative as ever. Could it have been Georges, after all?

She almost wished the nunnery could be a solution for her, too. She wished she found it peaceful, as Caroline did, instead of only bleak and desolate. But Lucy hadn't the spirit for such a quiet place, for the meditative life or for obedience.

She had a child, and her heart screamed constantly for the man who would make the family complete. She did not even know if he were living or dead.

If he is alive, he will find you. She thought of Pauline's words every day. But at last she could not stand it any longer. "I am going back to Paris," she told Caroline. "I must try to find Galen."

"It is too dangerous!" said Caroline.

"They will not be looking for me now, and I will be careful."

"I'll come, too. I may be of some help," said Caroline.

Before they left, Lucy removed the locket with the emerald set from around her neck and gave it to the nuns. Only death could prevent her returning, but if it did, the locket was the only inheritance she had for Alyce. Her other less meaningful jewelry she took with her, in case she should need it to pawn.

It was June when they returned to Paris, exactly a year since they had left. Scarcely any sign of the revolution remained. Here and there was a house with a corner of plaster shot away. On the back streets paving stones had never been replaced. Napoleon III sat on the throne.

"Poor Georges. How happy he would have been, now that the Bonapartes are back!" said Lucy and immediately wished she had not said it.

They went to Pauline's apartment. She had opened a small bookshop to support herself. It was well-patronized, for Paris's intellectuals had soon learned how knowledgeable Pauline was, how she could ferret out any edition, no matter how old or rare.

Pauline had heard nothing of Galen. "He may be in prison," she said, "but many have died there." And she told of the nine hundred men who had been incarcerated beneath the riverside terrace of the Tuileries. Disease had broken out, and the authorities, afraid to investigate for fear of an epidemic, had left corpses among the living. The stench had been beyond belief; and whenever the prisoners had approached the ventilation holes, the guardsmen had thrust at them with bayonets to keep them from shaking loose the bars.

But most of the prisoners were at Belle-Isle, now. Jeanne Derione, who had run for the Assembly in the election of the ill-fated Republic, was in a Paris prison.

Pauline promised to put out feelers about Galen. "Many of the Republic's sympathizers come to my bookshop," she told them. Lucy herself began to visit old haunts discreetly, speaking to people they had known. She found nothing. Not a trace.

Then one afternoon wearily climbing the stairs to Pauline's apartment, she saw a man's luggage outside on the landing. Her step quickened. She flung open the door, ready to fall into Galen's arms.

"Charles!"

He stood there as hale and handsome as the night of her ball, this ghost from her past who would not rest. He took her hand and raised it to his lips. She felt him quiver. "My love!"

"You must not call me that! I wrote to you—"

He did not release her hand. "Yes. I know. You were in love with someone else. But it must have ended badly or you would not have stayed at the convent. You have spent a year there. Isn't your heart healed? I do not mind that you have loved someone else if only you love *me* now."

"It has not ended badly, Charles. It has not ended at all."

He said nothing. It seemed that he could not speak. He dropped her hand and turned to the door. Even when she had seen men dying, she had never seen such pain in a human face.

After he had gone, she paced about, distraught, and when Caroline came in, she flew at her. "It was you! You sent for him! You told him I was in Paris. You told him to come to this house!"

Caroline's face flushed. "Yes! Yes, I sent for him. Forget Galen! He is dead, or he has forgotten you! Leave Alyce to the nuns. If you are married to Charles, you will always have plenty of money to send her. It is the very best you can do for her. You are a fool, a fool, not to marry him!"

Lucy rushed from the place, betrayed by the one she had always held most dear. Could Caroline be right? Was this the only solution? Was she wronging Alyce by not marrying Charles?

But she could not give up looking for Galen before the search was exhausted. And she had not even really begun—there had been nowhere to start, no clue. She could not doom herself to a life without Galen or Alyce to a convent childhood.

If only there could be some word!

A boy blocked her way on the stairs. "Mademoiselle Girard?"

"Yes," she said, automatically taking the note he held out. Brushing away tears to see, she broke the seal. The message came from Pauline at the bookshop.

> *Lucy—a customer tells me that a friend of his in Marseilles has word of Galen from a sailor off a boat from Africa. He was exiled to Algeria with a shipload of revolutionaries, and now he has escaped to Tangier. If you leave tonight you can make connections with the Kumrah, which is sailing for Tangier. It is not a passenger ship, but her captain is bribable. Good luck, my friend, for all your life, for I do not doubt that you will go. I know we may never meet again.*

Africa! Lucy was stunned. She could not go to Africa, a woman alone! Oh, she had dared to step outside her woman's niche before, but that had been in Europe. On that savage, primitive continent, who knew what might wait!

But Pauline was right. It must be done. She must find Galen, and no risk was too great, no plan too unworkable, if it might bring them together. "If I die, Alyce will fare little worse," she thought. "The nuns will take care of her."

She gave herself to joy as she ran back up the stairs, through shafts of dusty sunlight and burst in on Caroline. "He is alive and I am going to him!" she cried.

"Alive! Where!"

"Africa!" I must leave at once and get aboard a coach to Marseilles!"

Caroline, her features rigid, watched Lucy rush about tossing garments into a portmanteau. "You will surely die in Africa, Lucy. It is unthinkable!"

Lucy smiled. "I hope I shall be safe. But if I die, it will be while being true to my heart. It will be a noble death."

"Like George's death?" said Caroline bitterly.

"Something like that. Won't you wish me godspeed, cousin?"

"No!" Caroline chocked back a sob. Then her voice hardened. "I have come as far as I can, Lucy. You have broken Charles's heart, and now you will risk leaving an innocent child an orphan. I am determined not to care any more what happens to you!"

"I suppose I do not blame you, Caroline. You will go back to the convent, now?"

"Yes, I think so."

Suddenly tears streamed down Lucy's cheeks. "When you go back, you will kiss the baby for me, Caroline, and you will rock her to sleep—no one but you. You will not let the nuns give her away!"

"Yes, I will do all that, Lucy," said Caroline, trembling with emotion.

"And—and—if I do not return, you will tell her about me when she is older. You will explain how I loved Galen. You will make her understand the sort of man who fathered her. You will make her proud of him."

"Yes. I will try."

Lucy could not trust herself to speak further. There were things that she wanted to say, but she could not find the words. She picked up her case and kissed her cousin's cheek.

Behind her a tear-smothered voice whispered, "Godspeed, Lucy!"

Chapter 13

The *Kumrah* flew a French flag, and the gangplank was down. She rushed up it, mindless of the astonished glances of sailors who, stripped to the waist, were loading wooden crates into its hold. An officer, all aflutter, came rushing forward to meet her. "Mademoiselle—"

"I must see the captain!"

"But—"

"At once!" She let her voice ring with command. It was part of her heritage of aristocracy. Galen, with his republican views, might not have approved, but it was useful. Her clothes, her bearing, her voice all marked her for a lady, not to be denied. She was ushered into a cabin. A door slammed behind her.

The captain, his jacket unbuttoned in the heat, brought his feet crashing down from his desk. A half-eaten peach dropped from his hand and, catapulting away, rolled across to the edge of Lucy's skirt. She sized him up. He was graying and paunchy, with the look of loving to pamper himself. But his hands were gnarled, as though they had spent many years pulling lines at sea. The captain had not come by his command easily, and she doubted that he was a man of delicate scruple. He could be bought, as Pauline had said.

"Captain, you are bound for Tangier tonight. I have come to book passage."

"Mademoiselle! This is not a passenger ship. We are hauling laces and carriage parts."

"No matter. Find me suitable accommodations. I must go to Tangier immediately." She unfastened the long gold chain that held her watch to her waist, and taking the fine timepiece from her watch pocket, laid it on the desk.

The captain gave a long, wistful sigh.

"There will be a ring, too, when I return." And without giving him a moment to consider, she sealed the bargain by departing.

It was dusk when she boarded the ship again. The tiny cabin assigned her was airless and sweltering. She was afraid she would be seasick before they left the quay. But it was better than being on deck with all those lustful sailors' eyes peering out of the murk. The latch on her door did not seem very strong, so she pushed her trunk against it and atop that she put all the furniture that was not bolted to the floor.

Before dawn she felt by the motion of the vessel that all the sails were set, and that they had caught a good wind. Cool, salty air blew in through the porthole, and though the boat was not fast, she felt it was flying as it bucked awkwardly over the swells.

"Africa!" she thought. She was truly on her way. She would bring Alyce to share Galen's exile with them, and they would build a life. And though she was unsure what Africa was like, she knew her life there would be far different from the one she would have had on the dank moors of Charles Ashton's Grandemas.

She stayed in her cabin most of the next day. Then, unable to bear the cramped quarters any longer, she went on deck. They were far at sea; not a gull was in sight. Lucy stood at the rail for hours, hypnotized by the smooth, green waves. The boat that had at first seemed a pair of wings to carry her to her lover now seemed incredibly slow and indifferent.

When she saw land birds again, her heart gave a leap before she realized it was only Mallorca.

At Ibiza a boatload of sailors went hunting and brought back fresh duck. Lucy accepted the captain's invitation to join him at dinner in his cabin. The smell of roasting duck, the lack of human contact made her reckless. She had been completely without companionship since leaving Paris.

The dinner was sumptuous. The captain had brought out a good vintage of *lip fraoli* wine, and the table was graced by a delicious shellfish soup, fragrant breads and new potatoes drenched in sauce. Lucy, who had been existing on sailor's rations of Dutch cheese, dried fish and hard biscuit, made a glutton of herself.

Then the sea air and the rocking waves made her drowsy. She was so sleepy she hardly heard what her host was saying. She made polite sounds and longed to lay her head down somewhere, even on the walnut table.

"It is a shame about your pretty watch and ring," he said solicitously. "You must hate to lose them."

"Yes, indeed I do. The watch was a gift from my Aunt Madeliene, who was like a mother to me."

"A gift. That makes me feel a cad. I should like to return it."

"You are too kind. I could not ask it."

"Ask nothing, my sweet." She became aware that he had risen and come around to her side of the table.

"You look uncomfortable," he said. "Why don't you loosen your stays? The *Kumrah* is such a slow boat, as slow as the African beast of burden it is named for. Time lies heavy. We are friends, aren't we? We needn't stand on formality at sea."

Sudden sickness was in her stomach as she felt his hands on her shoulders. "Captain," she said warningly.

"Come now, mademoiselle. When a woman travels as you are, she is not worrying about her virtue. Certainly you will not keep it long in Tangier, alone with no protector."

"I will not be alone in Tangier, Captain. A man is waiting for me—my—husband."

He laughed. "You are amusing. No husband in the world would allow his wife to make such a journey unchaperoned. The man is not your husband. He is, perhaps, someone you love desperately, who does not love you in return. You are following him hopelessly, and your reputation, of course, is ruined already. Why not give me a little of the love he despises? I will treasure it." His hand slid smoothly into her bodice.

Just before he could clasp her breast, she lifted the wine bottle, and with a great blow, broke it over his arm. Wine sloshed onto her dress. The captain screamed in pain, as she fled, her step unsteady on the rolling ship.

"Oh how could I be so naive! I who am twenty and a mother! I, who have undertaken to be responsible for myself! I behaved like the child I was the night Georges took me to his apartment! Well, I have learned something. I will be harder, more vigilant. No one shall have an easy chance at me again!"

Fearing the captain's vengeance, she stayed in her cabin the rest of the voyage. Lying sleepless during the lightless ocean nights, her nerves were jarred by every sound on deck. She would imagine that the captain had loosed his crew to have their way with her.

Toward dark one evening she saw a sea swallow, and before daylight she felt that the ship was anchored, tossed gently by the sea. From a distance she heard the cries of wild animals, roaring, grunting, and screeching. There was the almost human echo of hyenas. Through the blackness she saw the lights of fires along a shore and knew they must mark the camps of Arabs, which by day would be hidden in the scrubby fringes of the mountains.

Daybreak turned the bay silver. The mountains remained an ominous black, silhouetted by the sun, rising behind them. She saw the tower that crowned Cape Malabata and the chalk-white buildings of Tangier, melding into a golden shore. Plover and snipe flew about the *Kumrah*, and above the rooftop gardens of the city, she saw the towers of the mosque and the Casbah, the palace of the Sultan.

A great ramp led from the shore to the pointed arch of the city gate. Lucy, put aground there with her luggage, knew a moment of panic. All around her surged masses of strange people in burnooses, tunics and haiks. She had not a friend on the entire continent, and everyone looked dangerous.

She felt a tug at her sleeve. She started, looking in horror. The person who had accosted her had a curved scar on one cheek, carried a cudgel, and wore a jeweled knife at his belt. When he spoke, his gold front teeth shone in the hot African sun.

"Pardon, Madame. I am a jannissary. Would you like to retain my services?"

She was certain she would not.

"But, madame, Europeans always need a jannissary. Do you doubt my qualifications? No one will dare to fight with me. I am the executioner. You cannot get a better bodyguard."

Bodyguard! She had been trying to move away from him, but now she whirled around and hired him on the spot. He grinned widely, showing more missing teeth and picked up her portmanteau.

"My name is Hassen," he said, waxing talkative in a garbled French. "Whenever a ship docks, I come to see if I can find business. I shall enjoy guarding you, madame. I shall need to be especially ferocious to guard such a beautiful lady, but my fee is only four sous. I will be your guide for two sous more." Lucy accepted the bargain, and they passed beneath the city gate, which was guarded by a soldier with a musket with a gold chased barrel and a butt inlaid with ivory.

"Where do you wish to go?" Hassen asked.

"The consulate."

"Which one? Oh, no matter. They are all together. Except for the mosque and the Casbah, they are the only two-storey buildings in Tangier. Remember that if you ever become lost."

The cobbled streets were filled with vendors of poultry and charcoal and wood. Their wives, beside them, wore hats of plaited rushes. Camels, laden with dates or figs, stretched their necks to scream. Moorish women in blue and white blankets crouched on the rooftops and Lucy saw one climb from one roof to another to visit.

Then she caught sight of a top hat among the crowd, and giving a little cry, stood on tiptoe. It was not Galen.

"Did you think it was your husband? A pity he is not here to meet you."

"I have no husband, Hassen."

"No husband!" The jannissary looked thunderstruck, and the scar on his cheek went almost straight as his jaw dropped. "Unmarried ladies do not come to Tangier! Only the wives of diplomats. Ah, wait. You are to be a bride. You are to be wed!"

He smiled with relief at having fit her into the pattern of things, and she thought it best to answer, "Yes, Hassen. I am to be married."

Lucy was stared at from all sides. Arab women, their eyebrows lined in Chinese ink, studied her mysterious crinoline from behind their veils. Shopkeepers, lying in the doorways of their cave-like establishments, paused in telling their prayer beads, or drew pipes of sweet-smelling hashish away from their lips, as if believing her a vision of the smoke. Fountains splashed into the air and trickled onto the cobbles. An arid wind tossed out cool sprays, and rainbows shimmered in the white glare.

Lucy was glad when they reached the green-shuttered buildings of the consulates. Hesitating in front of the British Consulate, she decided that the French would serve better and turned in beneath the tri-colored flag. After the brightness of the streets her eyes struggled to adjust to the shadowy interior of the building. She felt she had been tossed into a cave or lair, and she wished Hassen had not stayed behind outside.

Her eyes focused, and a portrait of Napoleon III frowned down from the wall behind the reception desk. Lucy stepped back involuntarily, as though she had accidentally ventured into the presence of the King himself.

And the King *was* here, in a way. His power extended across the ocean vested in these authorities. She had not been thinking of that; she had been feeling safe, away from French soil.

She reeled, a roaring came to her ears, and she stood again with Galen in the throne room of Tuileries. She saw the throne lifted and carried away—that throne that would not stay vanquished. She heard Galen saying, "If I were to die now, my life would be complete."

But it was not Galen's voice at all. It was too dry and light, as if the heat of Africa had parched away its substance. "Mademoiselle? Are you ill?" a clerk was saying.

She thought of Galen and exerted her will. If they had heard of *La Flamme* here, if somewhere in those piles of brittle yellow papers on the mahogany desk a communication bore her name, then a display of nerves would only help them recognize her.

She was *La Flamme*, Galen Le Blanc's woman, and she must ask for him here in the jaws of the enemy. But they would not be expecting such daring. That would be on her side.

She drew herself up and smiled at the clerk. "I am all right. It's the change in climate, I suppose. I have just come from France. I am looking for someone in Tangier. A French citizen."

The clerk smiled back, charmed. "Indeed we try to keep track of them. What name, please?"

She drew a deep breath and forbade herself to tremble. "Galen Le Blanc."

The clerk's smile vanished, wiped away by astonishment. "One moment, mademoiselle." He rose from his desk and went into another room. He scuttered away, Lucy thought, as though her notoriety had leaped out and frightened him. Did he suspect she was *La Flamme?*

The clerk returned and motioned her to follow him. "You must see the consul," he said, ushering her to an office.

Here at least was no portrait of the King. Behind the desk was a map of North Africa. The walls were lined with varnished cabinets, and the floors were covered with mats of woven rushes. Sunlight sprayed through the slits in the shutters and lay in prison bars across the gleaming desk top with its onyx inkwell and its silver candlestick for sealing.

The consul looked at her with eyes as sharp and penetrating as the sunlight. She winced as they seemed to illuminate every hidden corner of her soul. She had not been looked at so since the guard at the Paris gate had commanded, "Mademoiselle Girard, throw back your veil!"

"What do you want with Galen Le Blanc, mademoiselle? He is a dangerous person. He is wanted by the police."

Lucy considered a long moment. Then, fluttering her hand to her forehead, she burst out, "Oh, monsieur, it is embarrassing to tell you! My father is dead; my mother is old and sick. And my brother, Galen Le Blanc, has taken the family jewels—"

Why was it she so often had to own him as a brother? Her mind flipped back to that first time at the gates of the Dover ferry. And there had been the time that she had gained admittance to his rooms. Would it work again?

The consul's expression had changed. They were on the same side of the thing after all. "He has been in Tangier. Perhaps under the circumstances the police may give you information. I will make inquiries. In the meantime, you must have somewhere to stay. Please accept our hospitality. There is no other suitable place."

Her room on the second floor of the consulate had pinewood floors and a canopied bed. French landscapes hung from the papered walls, and all the furniture, except for a Syrian rug, was Louis VX. She spent the rest of the day with the consul's wife, watching her do a piece of embroidery, as compulsive with the thread as a drunkard with his bottle. The woman was pathetic in her need for company, her desire to hear news of Paris.

"It has been so long since I was there," she sighed. "Tell me, it is true that the Princess robe is coming into high style? And do women use these new bust improvers instead of cotton wool? There was an advertisement I saw in an old paper—"

A faint odor of hashish clung about her private sitting room, and Lucy did not think it blew in from outside.

"What shall I be like when I live here with Galen?" she wondered. "Will it be like this for me? Away from the culture of Paris, the writing that once was so much a part of me? No, no, it will not be that way. I will have Galen and the child. We will have more children."

She daydreamed away, wondering how many petticoats she dared remove in the heat, and keeping watch through the windows on her faithful jannissary, who dozed, cudgel across his knees, beneath a fig tree.

In the morning the consul told her there was no record on Galen's whereabouts. Lucy thought he was holding back. Someone higher had decreed it. Not liking the man, Lucy did not blame his wife for her misery.

"It's a pity you've come so far for nothing," he said. "I will book you a passage on the first decent ship that sails for Paris. I will arrange for a chaperone."

"But I am not leaving."

"You will find nothing here," he said, his face a mask.

They were hiding whatever they knew of Galen. At least it must mean he was still alive. The sailor's report had been no mistake; she had learned that much. She put on her coolest dress with a deep lace bertha, and taking a hinged parasol went out to the fig tree, where Hassen sat as though he had not moved all night.

"Hassen, this man I am to marry cannot be found. Will you help me find him? He is a French exile, and his name is Galen Le Blanc. I will pay you thirty francs if you find him."

The name did not faze Hassen. His eyes gleamed at the thought of so much money, and his hand touched his dagger as if to pledge he would use it in the quest, if necessary. "It will be done. Wait for me, mademoiselle."

She waited all day, sitting by her window, watching the empty spot beneath the fig tree. At mid-afternoon he returned and waved a cudgel above his head in greeting. The gold teeth flashed in pleasure. She ran downstairs, lifting her summery gingham skirts.

"Hassen! Have you found him?" She was unable to contain her elation.

"Not quite. I have found where he is likely to be. Tonight there will be a wedding celebration. One of the exiles is to marry a Moorish woman. Numbers of exiles will attend, even from outlying districts. Do you have a miniature, so that I may recognize him?"

Lucy shook her head. "No. I have a better idea. I will go with you."

"But—"

"Do not argue with me. Remember the thirty francs. Now take me to the bazaar at once."

She had learned one lesson well in Paris. If one is to go about freely, one must blend with those who do so already. But this time she did not choose to use a frock coat or even a man's clothing of any description. The garments of the Moorish women were tantalizing in their beauty, and with a touch of vanity, she thought of the impression she would make on Galen, should she find him while she was dressed so.

Among the wares of silver coffers, tortoise shell, turquoise, sashes, burnooses and coral-studded guns, Lucy chose a blouse, a transparent chemise, red trousers with gold embroidery, velvet slippers and a camel's hair haik. For finishing touches, she bought veils, orange blossoms to thread in her hair, and a vial of kohl, a cosmetic which Hassen said was made of wood ash and mother-of-pearl burned with brightly colored beetles.

She took her purchases back to the consulate and with some delight made her toilette before the pier glass. The kohl behind her lids made her eyes shine. She was a new person—not Lucy Hamlin or Mademoiselle Girard or even Galen's sister. It was after dark when Hassen signaled with a lantern. Looking carefully to see that no one was about, she left her room and crept down a back stair, out into the breezeless night.

The chalky buildings, reflecting the shine of the moon, made the town white and glowing to be a moonscape itself. Shadows made the narrow streets dark, treacherous craters. Lucy was glad for Hassen's light, and even gladder for his cudgel and knife. Soon she heard music—bells, tambourines and drums melding in strange Moroccan harmonies.

They came out into a crowded courtyard surrounded by houses with roof gardens. Beneath its ancient fig tree, a woman, holding a kerchief twisted like a rope, was dancing to a monotonous cadence. Hassen drew Lucy's attention to a room where a young girl sat, her veil thrown back, her cheeks red with cochineal. "The bride, mademoiselle."

Lucy looked. "Why are her eyes closed?"

"It is part of the ceremony. She has not opened them since it began seven days ago. This is the last day, the day of Hennah. She will be taken to her new home, and there she will open her eyes."

Lucy shuddered. It occurred to her that Galen, with his ideas of freedom for women, would avoid such a gathering even if friends of his were here. Still, she began to pick out European features under native headgear, and she forgot about the wedding as she became caught up in searching each new face.

The Basque drums beat louder. Torches were being lighted, throwing shadows like monstrous spiders onto the walls. "The wedding procession," Hassen whispered. "They are taking the bride to the home of her husband. Come."

They fell into the line, which was led by the bride, her eyes still closed. A terrible despair filled Lucy, for now every rooftop, every foot of wall was lined with onlookers. How could she ever hope to find Galen in this mob?

The French bridegroom waited by the door of a house. He looked sheepish, Lucy thought. Needing someone to sleep with, he had bought the girl, Lucy guessed. The bride's relatives certainly considered the physical the crux of the matter, for Lucy saw them carry the bride to a bed and draw its curtains around her.

"Poor child! It will not be the way it was for Galen and me," she thought. "He will want only her body. It will be more like Georges." She trembled violently, seized with an almost overwhelming urge to go and jerk the girl to safety.

Suddenly she saw a face she knew. It was that of a man who had often come to Galen's office. Grabbing his arm, she pulled him into the deep shadows between two houses.

She pushed aside her veil. "Paul! I am Lucy Hamlin. Do you know where Galen is?"

"Lucy Hamlin!" he whispered agape. "You were *La Flamme*—"

"Yes, a hundred years ago, it seems. Have you seen Galen?"

"Galen! He is not in Tangier. You must not try to find him."

"I must. Where is he?"

"No one can say, exactly. He fled here from Algeria, where he led a group of exiles in commandeering a felucca to sail home to France. The captain of the ship was killed during the attempt, and the ship itself was blown to pieces by a French corvette. Most of the exiles were drowned, but Galen escaped. He was here in Tangier, but the authorities were close on his trail. If he is caught, he will be shot, of course. I heard he had started for Tunis. That is all I know."

"Then I will go to Tunis."

"No! They will follow you! Have you been to the consulate? They would tell you nothing, of course. Because they know nothing. But how they would like to know!"

"They will not know. Find me a spot on a boat for Tunis. I will send my man, over there, to you each day to see if it has been done."

"Lucy, are you sure you were not recognized? They may have you followed."

"I will be careful. You will do this for me, won't you, Paul, for old times' sake?"

He gave her an address. Lucy waited three impatient days at the consulate, doing nervous embroidery herself to pass the time. She went again to the bazaar and purchased a large pouch into which she could stuff some of her clothing. When the time came, she did not want to alert anyone by removing her luggage.

Each evening she paced before the window waiting for Hassen to return from his errand. Doubt assailed her heart. Was she putting Galen in more danger by what she was doing? But if she gave up now, she left him forever. She could not bear that. She believed Galen would think her weak to turn back. As always, she did what she thought Galen wanted.

On the third evening, Hassen gave her the signal. Disguising herself again as a Moorish woman, she crept away.

"Can't you come with me, Hassen?" she said at the quay.

"No, mademoiselle."

"I'd pay you well."

"But who would take care of the executions?"

She sighed, wondering that she should feel such a sense of loss at parting with a hangman.

Chapter 14

In the morning she awoke to the blue waters of the Mediterranean once more. The ship, a beautiful, low-slung felucca with three masts, skimmed over the swells with incredible speed. It was nothing at all like the *Kumrah*. Lucy sat beneath the awning that replaced the foredeck and sipped Malaga with the captain. His boat was carrying a load of embroidered silks to Tunis, he told her.

The exile, Paul, had done his job well. The captain was a wealthy but sympathetic Venetian. He could be trusted, Paul said. She could stay at the Venetian's house in Tunis, and an invitation to the palace of the Bey would be arranged for her.

"The Bey does not like the French, and neither do the Arab chieftains he entertains at Bardo. If your Frenchman has succeeded in escaping across the desert, they will know him," the captain said.

The days aboard the felucca were a balm to Lucy. She slept well for the first time since leaving the convent, and she spent her time watching fish jump, basking in the sea wind, studying the changes in the vividly colored currents of water. Then they approached Tunis, and as the ship entered the channel that led to the Lake of Tunis, Lucy had to leave the bright ocean behind.

The atmosphere, even in the channel, was ominous. The still, red-brown water reeked and on every post sat a funereal cormorant waiting to prey on fish beneath the foul waters.

"The water is poisonous," the captain told Lucy. "A man would die if he ate one of those fish."

They passed small boats being poled toward the sea, and once a flock of flamingoes flapped from the shore, displaying red diamond markings on their bellies.

The moon rose over the weird waterscape as Lucy and the captain were rowed to shore. A coach with an Arab coachman was waiting to take them to the town, half-a-mile away. They could not walk, for great ugly dogs came howling around, hackles risen, standing away only because of the sight of guns.

They entered Tunis through a dark, vaulted gateway. The Venetian pointed out the British Consulate with its green shutters and the Moorish residence of the French consul. Throughout the ghostly town, Lucy caught glimpses of shadowy derelicts of houses, crumbled by the heat of the sun and left untended with fig trees twining through the windows.

The captain's house was Moorish, too. He rented it, he said. Europeans were not allowed to own houses in Tunis. He handed Lucy into the care of his wife, who saw that she had a bath and that her crumpled European clothes were freshened. It was important that she should look her best. The Bey was giving a ball the next evening.

Lucy saw little more of Tunis, and she was not sorry. Nothing was between the town and Bardo, the residence of the Bey, except a barren landscape scattered with old olive trees. Riding in a carriage with the captain and his wife, Lucy caught sight of its minarets almost as soon as they left Tunis.

They were received in the French Chamber. Sofas lined the walls, and a profusion of Turkish cushions were spread on the porcelain-tiled floor. Lamps shaped like ostrich eggs hung from the ceiling. The Bey, sitting crosslegged, wearing his insignia in diamonds, greeted the captain. The two women were not worthy of his glance. The men filled ther pipes and drank rose-perfumed coffee. Seated on a sofa, Lucy watched native girls dance, one after another, for at a Tunisian ball, guests were not expected to do the dancing.

The room filled with Arab chieftains, all flourishing their robes self-importantly. There were other diplomats and their wives. Lucy's stomach tightened as she realized the captain had mentioned Galen to one of the Arabs.

"Galen Le Blanc, the exile who caused such an outcry in Algiers. Have you heard of him?"

"Do not speak ill to me of Galen Le Blanc. He is a hero if Allah ever made one."

"You've seen him then?"

The Arab shrugged. "He lives in the desert and leads raids against the French, who oppress us. The tribes all protect him. I would not tell you where he hides if Sid, the lion, took hold of my tongue."

The Basque drums were beating loudly, and Lucy's heart pounded with them in a wild rhythm. The Venetian had pointed her out to the Arab. He seemed to be explaining, persuading, cajoling. The two stood up, and she knew that a bargain had been struck.

"You are to disguise yourself again as a native," the Venetian told her, "and ride in his caravan as one of his wives. He will send a messenger ahead to arrange a rendezvous. Have you a jewel you can give him?"

Lucy unfastened her shell cameo necklace, the last of her riches, and gave it to the captain to put in the Arab's hand.

The next day she found herself in the desert, her body subjected to the rolling gait of a camel, the heat made more stifling by the atouche in which she rode. The little tent guarded her identity the more. It kept others from staring at her, and she was glad at least for that.

By night the heat had changed to a dreadful chill. When they stopped to make camp, Lucy was shivering even with blankets over her camel's hair haik. She shared a tent of black and white skins with other women, and though she could not understand their language, they communicated with some universal empathy of their sex. Lucy would long remember the sisterhood they seemed to feel for her, even though they did not know why she was among them. Seeming to sense the tiredness of her body, the fear in her soul, they brought her a bowl of fragrant *coucousou*, made of millet, meat and leaves of the baobab tree. Smiling and gesturing, they showed her how to make her bed, but Lucy, listening to the howl of hyenas beyond the camp, lay wakeful and trembling.

At daylight she saw a cloud of brown dust coming toward their camp. A horseman galloped up, his burnoose swirling as he leaped down. For one heart-stopping moment she thought it was Galen. The horseman spoke rapidly to the chieftain. Another horse, with a sidesaddle, was brought forward. The chieftain spoke in French to Lucy. "Go with him. He will take you to your husband."

So that was what the Venetian had told him—her husband! She rode away, glad for her English horsemanship that kept her seated on the spirited beast.

They rode for what seemed several hours. Lucy tried to speak to her guide. She tried French, English, even the

Italian Pauline had begun to teach her. At last they reined up beside a stone hut with a round roof. The Arab handed her down and ushered her inside. He tethered her horse and brought in a flask of water and a loaf of bread. Then he astounded her by speaking in French.

"Wait here. It is a *marabout*, a place of sanctuary."

"But—" Lucy began as he rode swiftly away. No matter, he would not have understood her. Someone had taught him those few words to say to her.

Hoping there were no scorpions about, she arranged her haik as a blanket and sat on the sand floor, leaving the door open so she could see to the shimmering horizon. She was aware that the sun passed in zenith. She ate some of the bread to keep up her strength and sipped at the water. More hours passed. The hut threw a long shadow. She would be left to spend the night here, she thought. The door might be protection against the hyenas, but what other dangers might lurk?

Worse, what if Galen did not come at all? She had no idea where she was, no way of knowing which way she should ride to civilization. She would be at the mercy of the desert. Then, just before evening, came another cloud of dust.

At first she was not certain she saw it. Then she thought it must be a whirlwind. Finally she was sure it was a horseman. She stood in the doorway trembling in every fibre. Tears of relief and joy burned her eyes.

"Galen, oh Galen!"

The horseman came closer and again she saw that it was not Galen. But as he reined up he spoke something in Arabic that included Galen's name, and he motioned her to her horse.

The desert air was cooling for the night. She felt her heart lift; the burdens of a year slipped away as she rode. Soon she would be in his arms again, where all would always be well.

They approached a town, its walls rimmed with rusting cannon. Beyond was a bay with gulls and plovers flying above it. That would be their destination.

But the Arab did not lead her into the town. He turned suddenly and urged his horse up a hillside. What sort of place was this they were passing through? A Turkish cemetery, where each man's turban rested at the head of his grave.

They were not passing through at all. One grave was

different from the rest. It was fresh, not covered with sharp grasses like the others. It lay a bit apart as if in a place of honor and a small cross marked it for a Christian's.

The Arab reined in and pointed. Lucy read her lover's name carved into the cross.

Her memory blurred after that. She heard a scream so primal it must have come from some desert animal, not from her own throat. She tasted sandy earth in her mouth as she lay sobbing on the fresh mound. She wanted to die too, and in her delirium, she believed the ground opened and swallowed her with him into a desert grave.

It was dark, and the darkness was not that of the grave, but that of night. She was no longer in the cemetery, but inside the walls of the village she had seen. How had she come here?

She remembered that the Arab horseman had lifted her from the grave. She had fought him as though he were the enemy, even after he had succeeded in throwing her over his saddle in front of him. The blood had rushed to her head. The desert had careened past under galloping hooves, and she had kicked and clawed—

She had got free from him at last. In this village? Had he brought her here, perhaps to turn her over to his women? Or had some base, unworthy instinct for survival driven her in, away from the vipers and jackals of the desert night? She heard the wailing of wild dogs like those at Tunis and thought that she would rush outside to throw herself to them, so that her body might be shredded along with her soul.

It was not only that Galen was dead; she knew she had killed him. He had been alive when she had started from Tunis; the meeting had been arranged. She had been followed somehow, in spite of how clever she had thought herself. If only she had behaved as a woman ought! If only she had trusted him to do the finding! He would have found her, but now he never could in this world.

He was not the first man to look at death because of Lucy. Only a miracle had saved Charles Ashton. "It is a curse I have that I cannot let men arrange my life," she thought. "That must truly be nature's plan if my life is an example."

She could not seem to locate the town gate. The streets

were a ghostly maze. The inhabitants, in their robes and burnooses, were equally spectral. Perhaps after all, she had died, and this was the after-life. A new panic seized her. This was not the other world she had been seeking! Here was no Galen, no surcease of grief. Here were only shadows, indifference, coldness. Her limbs were numb, as if indeed her heart had stopped with sorrow, unable to pump blood about her body.

Exhausted with her search, she sank down next to a fountain, almost fainting against its rim. From near oblivion, she heard voices above her, Arabic mutterings, low and excited. A hand touched her veil and then jerked it away.

Something deep and fundamental stirred in Lucy, warning her of an impending violation that bore none of the comforts of death. Roused suddenly from her swoon, she must have wandered into the worst section of town, for their clothes were dirty and full of fleas; and the air was oppressive with the odor of unwashed bodies. One of them had hold of each of her arms. Another grabbed her hair, and loosening it from its pinnings, wrapped his filthy hands in it. They tore at her clothing, not bothering with fastenings, and they laughed and gestured and seemed to boast to each other.

Lucy did not need to understand the language to know of what they spoke. She did not need Arabic to interpret the obscene gestures. She knew what they intended to do to her, each of them in turn. It would kill her at last; she would be dead as she had wished. There was something fitting in this death. She would be killed for her womanhood, just as Charles had suffered and Galen had died because of it.

Yet an anger surged in her; a pride sprang up and would not let it happen. She began to scream, and striking out with a slippered foot, landed one Arab a blow to his stomach that sent him sprawling backwards in the street.

She heard footsteps running. Her screams had attracted someone. Then incredibly, English voices rang with a warmth and resonance that reminded her of home.

"Let go of that woman, you blighters!"

"Run or be run through, you bloody Arabs!"

Lucy felt herself fall free as her attackers turned to meet the new threat. British sailors! But there were only two of them, and daggers were being drawn everywhere.

"Tom! Edward! Don't mix in native troubles. I'll have you court martialed! Oh hell fire!"

An officer leaped into the fray. She saw him disarm one Arab and send him fleeing into the night. He pulled out his sabre to deal with another. Lucy saw a glint in the shadow behind him. With a cry she jumped at the dagger aimed for his back. He whirled and helped her wrestle the Arab to the ground. Squirming loose the Arab fled, leaving Lucy on the cobbles with the officer.

His hand over hers on the knife, he looked into her face. "My god! I am dreaming! You cannot be Lucy Hamlin!"

"Captain Rathrock! You were right. I do always cause talk," said Lucy and fainted.

Chapter 15

She did not know quite how he took her away from Africa. She remembered nothing of leaving the village, nothing of a voyage. She lay with a fever. Images floated above her; starched English nurses made crisp, efficient movements about her bed. Once, coming momentarily out of her delirium, she asked where she was.

"This is Gibraltar," came the answer. "Rest easy; you are on British soil."

Lucy did not rest. Hideous nightmares came into her illness. She saw the desolation of Galen's grave among the pagans. Jackals and hyenas howled about it and dug into the sand in hopes of opening the coffin to feast on his flesh. When her mind had taken all that it could, she would sink into strange stupors.

"She must be sent to a madhouse," she heard someone say, during one of her quieter moments.

"No. She has a strength within her that will make her recover." Lucy did not know how she knew that the voice was Jonathan Rathrock's.

Somehow the faith he had in her gave her courage. She became aware that he was often at her bedside, that he fought for her in a way, that he willed her to get better. She felt it through the fog of her grief, and she began to make an effort.

She thought for the first time of Alyce and knew that her child needed her. She must not have a mother who was mad, as well as a father who was dead. A sense of purpose grew in her and she became calm.

Jonathan Rathrock was delighted. He moved her from the hospital to a discreet hotel, and the first day she was able to be out, he took her for a drive beyond the garrison walls to see the Barbary apes chasing each other up and down the mountain.

"They are weather oracles," he told her. "When the British first came to Gibraltar, they found their barometers would not function in the heavy fogs. Then they discovered that when the monkeys played on the west side of Calpe, the weather would be fair. If they played on the east, it would be stormy. There are serious penalties for killing one of them."

"If there were such oracles in the lives of people, they would always play on the stormy side for me," Lucy sighed.

"No, no. It shall be sunny west for you," he said.

She did not see how that could be, but, not wanting to spoil the outing, she flashed him a brave smile.

He brought her presents of clothing—dresses, chemises, slippers, a crinoline; and when she protested that it was scandalous of her to accept them, he laughed aloud. "Ah, Lucy, you will be more scandalous without them."

He brought her an evening gown of terry velvet and took her to a dinner of beefsteak. She felt at home immediately in Gibraltar. Everything about the town was English. Wooden signs swung from over doorways, creaking in the breeze, and the flowers in the gardens, transplanted from their native sod, wafted familiar scents. It was difficult for her to believe that she was so far from England, and more difficult still to believe the destruction she had made of her life.

At first she enjoyed the company of Jonathan Rathrock without question. His mission was to survey the coast of Africa and he was bored at the duty. That alone was reason enough for him to seek her company when he returned to the rock. But gradually she came to understand that it was more than that. He was as eager for her company as she was for his.

What did he think of her, she who had sent Charles Ashton plunging from his horse on the night of their engagement, she whom he had rescued from a pack of Arabs, continents away from where she had any right to be?

He did not think she lacked scruple, for he treated her as a lady. He made no advance, no suggestion. He asked her little about how she had come to be where he had found her, as if fearing the subject might again destroy her reason.

"Was there a man, Lucy?" he asked gently.

"Yes. A French exile. I was in love with him."

"Were in love? You are not, now?"

"I will always love him, but he is dead."

Finding it a relief to think of something besides her own problems, she asked him about himself. "You have not gotten your island yet, Jonathan?"

"No. But I shall." He said it with the certainty of a man who could never be satisfied with only a dream. She had laughed at him once, as an ignorant girl, but now she saw the beauty of it, and along with the beauty of the plan, the beauty of the man himself, the depth of longing that had created the idea.

He was a man of the sea; he could not let go of it. The sea was his birthright, but it was not enough. He was more than the adventurer his forefathers had been; he was a builder. He longed for roots, for a place shaped and molded according to his lights. Lucy saw a certain similarity between herself and him. Neither of them was satisfied with what life had intended them to be.

"He will have it to suit himself," Lucy thought, watching him as he talked, his eyes burning with command that never left him. "The Queen will not dare to reject his petition. He would exact his island even from God himself."

How different he was from Galen! His dreams were for himself and for a family that did not yet exist, but whom he already loved better than all mankind. He did not care for the world, only for his place in it. He would hone one small spot to perfection, and he would found a dynasty to inherit it. There his seed would grow, ripe and perfect as corn in a field for season and season again, until the world dissolved.

These things he told her only after some urging, for he had a deep reticence about him. Unlike Galen, who had been always ready to expound his vision, whose medium had been the printed word, Jonathan Rathrock seemed to have no need of an audience. What he did concerned him and his, no more.

Or perhaps it was only a shyness, unexpected in a man of such confidence. Once he opened himself to Lucy, he talked on and on.

"There is a place I have been that is more beautiful than any other I have ever seen. Cliffs drop two hundred feet to the ocean and virgin forests grow into the sky, ready to be cut for the masts of ships. In the spring there are wild strawberries, meadows of columbine and creeping juniper, and goldfinches to sing for you. Great tides rush about, and there are harbors no man has dared to make."

"And you will make them," Lucy smiled. "Where is this fabled place?"

"Off Canada. In the great Bay of Fundy. They call it Hazard Island. It must belong to no one but me!"

Encouraged, he drew her maps of the island, showing her the north with its unscaleable cliffs, the sphagnum bogs, the pebble beaches and gentler land of the south.

"The south end shall hold the town of Hazard, where my sailors and their families shall live, and over here on this rise shall be my house, facing to the sea. I shall call it Rathrock, of course."

Lucy frowned and shook her head. "I do not like that name, Jonathan."

"You do not think I should give my name to my house? Why not?"

"Rathrock. It sounds angry and hard. A home must not be those things."

He laughed. "And do you think *I* am angry and hard? What name do you suggest?"

She thought the matter over for several days. It took her mind from her dilemma. Finally she told him a name she liked. It was warm, and homelike. "Call it South Cottage," she said.

He looked astonished. It would not fit the house, he told her, and drew for her his castle, to be built of stone hauled to the island by his ships. She looked at the turrets and towers and shook her head again. "It won't do. Anyone would think it just another of the cliffs."

For a moment she thought he was going to be angry. Then his face changed, and he asked with interest, "It is a house most women would think magnificent. Show me the house you would like, if you were to live in it."

Eagerly she took his pencil and began to draw a roomy house of native timbers, adorned with a single cupola. She drew a simple, elegant sweep of stairway and rows of tall windows. She landscaped the house with a sweep of curving drive, lined in birches, white and black trunks matching the white house with its long black shutters.

He studied the drawing and put it in his pocket. "I will have to think about it, Lucy. Ah, you have upset all my careful ideas."

She did not learn what decision he made. He never

spoke of it again. Perhaps he had not made up his mind.
He was thorough, not to be rushed.

He told her of his plans for a great fleet of ships that
would haul herring to the West Indies and return with
rum and salt. "There is a group of fisherfolk already on
the island," he said. "I will take their catch, and we will
prosper together."

"But have you money for all this, Jonathan? For a
fleet of ships and sailors?"

"No. But I shall form a company. A dozen English
lords will subscribe and line their pockets along with
mine."

Lucy smiled a secret, wistful smile that puzzled him.
"Why are you smiling," he asked.

"Oh, it is nothing. You reminded me of someone." He
had a light in his eyes when he spoke of his dreams, that
made him not unlike Galen after all. And he had a sureness, too, that was the same.

The summer air began to hint of the coolness of
autumn, and Jonathan, in spite of his preoccupation with
his own ventures, would turn the conversation to Lucy.
"You must let your family know where you are," he
would say.

"It will be a blow to my father. He must be hoping I
am dead and will not come back to disgrace him further."

"And your Aunt Madeliene? Is she so unfeeling?"

"No. I hope she loves me still."

"And Caroline?"

Caroline. She felt certain of her cousin, though they
had quarreled before parting. A guilt weighed on her that
she had not written to Caroline, that she had been unable
to put on paper the words that would tell the horror of
Africa; the words, "He is dead, and my life is over."

If only it could be true that her life were over! If only
she did not have this responsibility of her child, Alyce!
And yet her one joy, her one solace was that Alyce
existed, a lasting memorial to the moment of their love.
How was she to provide for their daughter?

If she had money, she might return to France and
open a shop—but she had sold away all her jewels. Would
her papa give her that much money to be done with her
forever? She thought of searching for Galen's family, but
decided they would not be likely to own the child. She
had no proof that Alyce was Galen's. Galen had drawn
up a will in her favor those last months in Paris, but that

was no help either. Even if the government had not confiscated his holdings, she could not present herself to the authorities to claim her inheritance.

Each day she awoke hoping that during the night some new idea had come to her, but every day was as blank as the one before. There were only memories of dreams in which she held her child, laughing with her, marveling at her baby smile.

"I am missing so much!" she would think, and calculating the baby's age would wonder, "Has she a tooth yet? Does she crawl?" She wished she might make a little dress to send her but someone might see and guess.

The nuns would take good care of Alyce. And Caroline would be there, poor Caroline, with her blighted love for a man whose identity Lucy did not even know. Had Caroline become a Catholic by now? Was she among the novices, angelic in her white veil? The image fit, and Lucy was comforted to think of Caroline in the convent with the baby.

She thought again about taking vows herself. It would never work, she decided. "I could never keep a covenant with God, because, if I were sent away from Alyce, as I well might be, I would feel God had broken a covenant with me."

But she could not remain forever on Gibraltar at the expense of Jonathan Rathrock, who was paying for her food and lodging.

"You must present a bill to my father," she told him one day, "and if he does not honor it, you must give it to me. I will repay you one day, somehow."

He laughed and took her hand in his. "There can be no bill, for if anything I am in your debt, I who have had you to welcome me home from the empty sea and to stand on the shore when I cast off again. How I shall miss you when it is over!"

His hand was rough, unlike that of Galen or Charles Ashton, and it gave her a sense of protection, when it clasped hers. "I am sailing for England next week," he said. "Do you want to come?"

She felt cast rudely from her sanctuary.

She went, of course. She could do nothing else. He took her aboard his man of war, and his tars treated her as though she were royalty. It was an outgrowth of the feeling they had for their captain, she discovered.

Wrapped warmly in her cape, her hair plaited in circles

about her ears to keep the wind from blowing it, she stood on the deck and let stories about him wash over her with the salt spray. Tales of how the Captain had sunk an enemy ship in battle though he had but one gun left, how he had risked his vessel to turn back into a storm to look for a sailor who had gone overboard in the night.

The tars had a pride in him, as though he were theirs, and as she heard the stories, she thought, without surprise, "Yes, that's right, he would do that!" And she felt the pride, too, though she had no claim to him at all. She wondered if the sailors thought there was romance between them, that someday she would be his wife.

"Will you marry Charles Ashton now?" Captain Rathrock asked her.

"Perhaps," she answered. If it were possible, she would. She remembered the pain in his face, a pain that surely could not be erased in the several months that had passed. She would marry him and try to make everything up to him. It would be the saving of her, and she would manage to send money to Alyce. It was the best thing she could do, just as Caroline had said.

She saw the coast of England and thought she would be parted from Jonathan Rathrock then. But as they debarked, he said, "I will take you to Callow Hill."

"Please. Don't trouble yourself. I have been too much a burden already."

"I should not be able to answer to myself if I allowed a woman to go unescorted," he said, and she, thinking of her many excursions in Paris and Africa, could only laugh inside.

They reached Callow Hill at dusk on an Ocotber night. The trees were bright with color, and lights glowed from the windows. On just such a night as this, it had all begun, two years ago at her fateful ball. If only it could be that night again, would she do it differently, exchanging all her agony for never knowing Galen's love?

But suddenly, as she stepped trembling from the coach, it did seem to be that night. The door of the house opened, and Charles came running out, seizing her hands in his and crying out with joy because she had come home.

"Oh Charles! Can you ever forgive me? Oh, how I regret the pain I have caused you!"

"You could not help it, Lucy. I understand."

"My dearest! I will never do anything to hurt you

again!" He was so kind her heart filled to bursting with feeling for him.

Her Aunt Madeliene came swooping down the stairs and caught her to her soft bosoms, cooing exclamations of happiness. Lucy sank against her billowy warmth, rapturous as a child who had been lost on the heath. She had come full circle; it was ending well. She was home.

Then, in the entrance to the drawing room a shadowy figure appeared. Caroline, not in the pale white of a novice, but in a silk dress with a sleeved chemisette and a triangle of flounces from the waist. A jeweled comb was in her hair, and she was no longer the forlorn girl of the convent. She was transformed with radiance, and on her finger was a ring—a pear-shaped diamond surrounded by emeralds. Charles Ashton's ring!

Chapter 16

The magnificent ring sparkled in the lamplight, more beautiful than it had ever been before, as though reflecting the happiness of the wearer. Caroline, seeing her cousin, stopped short, an alloy of shame, defiance and fear welding her features. It was the last that affected Lucy the most—that Caroline should fear her.

She saw clearly now that the man Caroline had longed for in France had been Charles Ashton. And yet Caroline had done everything possible to see Lucy marry him! She had cajoled, covered Lucy's bad conduct, brought them together at Pauline's, and finally called Lucy a fool. Loving Charles, she had wanted him to have what he so desired; and loving Lucy, she had wished her the best of worlds, which was the only thing marrying Charles could be.

"Lucy!" whispered Caroline.

Lucy rushed to hug her cousin.

"Dear Caroline, I am so glad for you! You deserve him and he you. You will make him so much better a wife than I!"

A question formed in Caroline's eyes. Expertly she separated Lucy from everyone else and whisked her upstairs to her old room. She pushed a door shut and stood with her back against it while she locked it.

"There! Now tell me!"

"Tell you!" said Lucy in a faraway voice.

A breeze smelling of woodsmoke blew in through a small opening in the mullioned windows, swirling the damask curtains in a ghostly dance. Her japanned bedstead was still there, but the hangings had been changed to a heavy brocade that Lucy did not like. Except for that the room was as she had left it. A fresh linen towel hung from the towel rail as though Lucy had been expected, and on her satinwood dresser sat a doll with a bisque head.

The same place, but not the same. Now the curtains that had once reminded her of whirling skirts were hideous, burnoose-clad Arabs. The doll, which had been a sweet reminder of childhood, made her heart convulse with thoughts of Alyce.

"I do not think I can ever tell you, Caroline!"

"Did you find him, Lucy?"

"I found him."

"He no longer loves you?"

"He will love me forever and I him, but he is dead and I cannot follow him. I must take care of Alyce."

"Oh, Lucy. What will you do?"

"I don't know. Before anything I will help you celebrate your wedding. When is it to be?"

"On the first day of the new year. It is Charles' fancy. And there is so much to do! We are to have a smaller house until Grandemas is ours, and it must be cleaned and decorated and new rugs bought—and oh there is the cook to hire and my wedding dress to be made—and your dress, too, Lucy. You will be my attendant as we always planned." She paused, breathless, and they both laughed.

"I'm frightened, Lucy," said Caroline, sobering suddenly.

"Frightened? You? You shall be Lady Ashton someday and have your own carriage and the latest bonnets and a dozen fine children. Whatever are you frightened of?"

"I am frightened that I shall not please him."

"That is silly. He would not have asked you if you did not please him."

"I mean—I know nothing of how to please a man in a marriage way, as you did Galen. Tell me what to do, Lucy. So many women seem to fail their husbands. I don't want to fail Charles. I could not bear it."

Lucy smiled. "Don't worry. You love him, and you shall know what to do when he takes you to his bed, just as I did with Galen."

"I am frightened that he will not forget you, Lucy."

"What nonsense."

She knew it was not nonsense. She saw the way Charles looked at her still. And the way he had greeted her had been the way of a lover, before he had remembered his commitment to Caroline.

Jonathan Rathrock left Callow Hill the next day, so much in a hurry to be on with his life that he did not even seek her out to say good-bye. At first she was unaware he had gone; then, sensing an emptiness, a hollowness replacing a vitality to which she had grown accustomed, she went to the stables and saw that his hired landau was missing.

The air was all at once too chill, and going back into the house, she pulled a spoon-backed chair close to the fire in the drawing room. Aunt Madeliene was there with Charles and Caroline, whose head was bent over trousseau embroidery in the lamplight.

"Captain Rathrock is gone," Lucy said, hoping vaguely that they would feel as bereft as she.

"Yes, off to London again with his head full of schemes," said Charles. "Do you know what he asked me to do?" He paused and Caroline looked up, ready to exclaim prettily.

"He wanted me to buy shares in a company he is forming. It has something to do with an island he does not yet own, and it is to be called the Hazard Company, appropriately, I'm sure."

"It will be a good investment, Charles, mark my word," said Lucy.

He marked it indeed. His laugh broke off; his eyes smoldered. "Then I will make it, Lucy, if you are so certain." Caroline jumped up and fled the room.

"Whatever is wrong with her?" Charles asked.

"You are stupid if you do not know," Lucy said. "You must be careful not to be attentive to me since you and Caroline are engaged."

"Attentive! When we are talking of investments in shipping?" He rose and paced the floor with uncharacteristic agitation. "I have promised to marry Caroline, and that is what I shall do," he said suddenly. "But my word! I cannot live so boxed in!"

She was glad she had spoken as she had about the Hazard Company. Jonathan would have a powerful ally in the Ashton fortune. But she knew she would have to get away from Callow Hill. If she remained so near after Charles and Caroline were married, she would only mar their relationship. She must out-distance Charles' love.

"Oh, why must I always be a blight on those I love?" she wondered. "Better that I had never come back. Better I had let the Arabs have me!" She had no idea where she would go.

She endured a terrible scene with her father when she

asked him for the money for the shop. He called her names she could only guess were applicable to a woman of her situation, and he declared he would spend not one more farthing on her, except for a ticket to send her away.

"A shop! You shall not disgrace me further by becoming a shopkeeper! You shall not be free to live whatever wild life you had in Paris again! You shall become a governess, since you were always good at books; and it will cost me nothing. That is, if anyone can be found fool enough to have you!"

She felt cold and lost. So that was his plan for her! She could not be with Alyce or help her as a governess. She would have barely enough money for herself.

On Christmas Day, the anniversary of the birth of her child, Lucy stayed in her room and wept, her agony greater than on the day she had brought the baby forth. She thought then that she reached the pinnacle of human grief, but that was still to come.

The letter from Belgium arrived on New Year's Eve. The round, scholastic handwriting of a nun told Lucy that her last hold on life was gone. The baby had vanished. One night she had been in her cradle; the next morning there had been no trace of her. She and her possessions had been neatly taken away. It could not have been an easy job, because whoever had done it must have climbed to the child's window up the stone heights of the nunnery. The doors had remained bolted, and footprints had been hidden in a new fall of snow.

Though the kidnapping had occurred weeks before, the nuns had not wanted to alarm her before the search was exhausted. Now the police had all but given up. It was thought that the kidnappers had been gypsies who had heard of the child's existence in the village below.

> *"If she is sold, it may well be to parents who will love her,"* the nun wrote. *"Consider that she had no name, that you could not provide for her. Perhaps God in his wisdom has arranged it. Forgive those responsible. Take care of your own soul."*

Lucy thrust the paper from her. Forgive indeed! She was beyond tears. Even her numbed fingertips gripping her chair seemed unreal, and sounds of gaiety in the rooms downstairs seemed a thousand miles away.

The evening brought a party, larger than the usual end-of-the-year gathering, since it was to celebrate the next day's wedding as well. Caroline, wearing Charles' wedding present of a jasper cameo with matching pendant earrings, was pale below the bright stain of blushes on her cheeks. Her lips remained devoid of color, no matter how many times she went to her mirror to bite them.

"She will faint at the altar tomorrow," Lucy prophesied, and dancing a waltz with Charles, dismissed him with a mechanical smile. Feelng heavy and languid, she sat at a zebrawood loo table, and running her slipper absently over the smooth curves of its pedestal foot, played whist until midnight.

When she heard the bells ring out the year 1849, she lifted her glass with the others and toasted the end of the world in champagne.

She was up early the next morning. No one wondered that she looked strange, that she did not eat her breakfast. That could be laid to excitement. After breakfast, their toilettes made, the cousins were wrapped like delicate crystal in velvet mantles and taken to the church by Aunt Madeliene. Once there they were put into their finery and not allowed to sit down until after the ceremony.

"There must not be a crease; it would be a scandal," said Aunt Madeliene, bustling about, slapping at the skirts with her hand. Lucy sighed, feeling weak. Caroline's fair curls trembled like buttercups in a breeze.

"Marriage shall not separate us, Lucy," she said. But Caroline's azure eyes were already as distant as though they had been the sky. Lucy studied her cousin fearfully, wondering at her remoteness, and though she clasped Caroline's icy hand, it was as though Caroline had already gone.

The organ filled up the chambers with its great reverberating music. Lucy felt the floor quiver beneath her blue broche slippers as she began her walk down the aisle. She felt Charles Ashton's eyes on her, admiring her in her pale blue satin gown and her white bonnet, and she looked away to the great banks of lilies before the altar. The music grew even fuller, and Caroline in white gros de naples, her veil falling from a wreath of blossoms, swept down like a cloud from heaven, billowing in all her flow of Honiton lace and silk.

They spoke their vows. Charles, forthrightly, his eyes

fixed on his bride; Caroline in a voice limp with wonder. It was done, and the wedding party moved back up the aisle. Caroline, though she swayed on Charles' arm, had not fainted. Suddenly the figure of the bride and groom blurred. Lucy had been holding herself tight until it was over, and now, in horror, she realized she was the one who would swoon.

Pride rushed up to help her. Whatever might become of her, she would not have it said that she had fainted, as though of a broken heart, at Charles Ashton's wedding. She broke from the group at the foyer and tried blindly to find an open door.

A man's arm went around her, steering her into a small empty room. The door slammed behind them. Baffled, she heard it lock. "Lucy, do not faint. It would be inconvenient," he said. And then she was being kissed. It was warm and deep, tasting of some distant clime, pungent and fresh as the sea wind with unknown excitement. It was a kiss for her tired soul to meld into. A kiss that could not be denied. And even before she opened her eyes, she knew who kissed her with such mastery.

"Jonathan!" she whispered. "Why are you always near when I need you most?"

"Oh, Lucy! Lucy! I have my island, and you shall be its mistress. No one but you shall be its queen, the mother of my dynasty. Say you will marry me!"

She gasped, but her head cleared, and she was no longer in danger of fainting. "But Jonathan—surely you must know the sort of woman I am!"

"Indeed I do!" He put a finger over her lips. "I think I have been in love with you ever since that first night when you came to Charles' bedside in your nightgown. And after that back street in Africa, after Gibraltar, I knew I could have no other. You are a woman of grit and resource, a woman whose devotions consume her and make her daring. You are a woman who can make commitments to which no persuasion, no hardship can ever make her false."

"But I may not even have a dowry, Jonathan," she said.

He waved that revelation aside. "You have in yourself a dowry no other woman can offer. I will give you a new commitment, Lucy Hamlin, a new passion to fill up all your days on earth. My island, my dream, my children. Marry me, Lucy!"

A new commitment, a new passion. A world that had not yet even been built. A shared dream and children to obliterate the pain of Alyce. Oh, how she had missed him. And now that he was beside her, she wanted never to be parted from his strong, friendly arms again.

"Yes, Jonathan, yes," said Lucy, and gave herself with joy to her new purpose.

Chapter 17

She did not love him in the same way she had loved Galen, yet there was something that made her want to cling to him and merge her life with his. There was a hope and confidence that she wanted to embrace as her own.

He knew about her, he said, but he knew only that she had loved a French revolutionary and had followed him to exile. At night Lucy lay wakeful, wondering if she must tell him the entire truth—that she had given herself to Galen as to a husband, that she had had a child.

"I must tell him, that is the only honest thing to do," she would think, and then, "It is all part of something gone. It will only make us both unhappy."

She valued him far too much to risk it. Over and over she thought of the things he had said about her, and she began to feel good about herself. She was no longer a misfit, but an exceptional woman, the woman Jonathan Rathrock needed at his side to build his empire. She had not felt so pleased with herself since she had heard the praises of Galen Le Blanc.

The betrothal was sealed with a diamond ring, much more modest than the one she would have had from Charles, but beautiful, nontheless. Once it was on her finger Jonathan seemed to change. He became more formal, and to her disappointment did not kiss her again with the verve that he had at Caroline's wedding.

The match was well-received by Lucy's family. Her father waxed generous and to show that his daughter was a fine prize, bestowed an ample dowry. Lucy would see her father studying Jonathan's tall commanding form and would imagine he was thinking he had been wrong about her after all if such a man still wanted her.

Aunt Madeliene wept for an hour. "You will be so far away, Lucy."

"Nonsense. I will be the wife of a sea captain. I will

be able to come home whenever I wish. I have only to accompany him."

She knew she would never wish it. She knew she would try to forget this world as if it had never existed. And she would try to forget France as well. Most of all, she would try to forget a certain sun-bleached grave—

Guilt weighed upon her as her aunt brightened and, putting on spectacles, began to rummage among pictures of wedding gowns. Her heart ached at the thought of parting forever with Caroline, who had gone abroad with Charles without even hearing the news.

"I must be gone before they return," she thought, and broached the matter to Jonathan.

"Can we not be married soon? I am eager to see our island."

He laughed, delighted with her enthusiasm. "Nothing would please me more, but I have no house for you. We must wait until summer when it will be built."

"I cannot wait, Jonathan."

"What a very immodest thing for a young lady to say," he teased.

Lucy flushed. "There is a reason—"

He nodded. "It is that Charles Ashton is still in love with you. We have a mutual interest in the success of his marriage, since he is my very dear friend and the bride is your cousin. I will go and arrange a place for you. I will send for you."

She went to London to see him off with a boatload of tars and settlers and a number of indentured servants, who could not pay their way. She watched until the sails were no larger than the cresting of a wave and felt angry that these people should all see her island before her.

Then she remained in London with much to do, since Jonathan had left instructions about china and crystal and silver. He had made lists of furniture that should be ordered, and he, not Aunt Madeleine, had even decreed the design of her wedding gown, an elaborate creation of satin and Brussels lace.

Lucy was amused at his interest, dismayed by the opulence of his taste. "Jonathan, can we afford all this?" she had asked.

"Enjoy it, Lucy, and don't worry your head. It's an investment. We've a position to maintain, and you will see it will be well worth it to show we are substantial. The Queen has made me master of Hazard Island, and I cannot live like a fisherman. I must show I am not to be trifled with."

She had not thought of it in such terms before. She had thought only of a pretty home, a successful fleet, but she supposed he was right. Everyone on Hazard Island would be there at the sufferance of Jonathan Rathrock. It was his island. The tars; the settlers; those poor semi-slaves, the indentured servants—her husband would be master of them all. She knew what Galen would have thought of it. She knew what *La Flamme* would have written, and it gave her an unsettled feeling in her stomach.

She did as he directed and spent his money with a flourish that set her father's friends agog. She was not above enjoying the gossip that she was marrying great wealth. Wooden crates were stacked all about the house where she was staying when she received the letter from Jonathan.

> *Dearest,*
> *I have just completed the purchase of a fine clipper, and you shall make her first voyage to Canada. I have an invitation for you to stay at the home of his excellency, the governor of Nova Scotia. That province borders ours of New Brunswick, and he and I have become good friends. He will have someone to meet you at Halifax, the capital and the nearest large Atlantic port to our island.*
>
> *You may call me judge when we next meet, for I have been appointed a magistrate of the court of common pleas. It will help me to keep order on the island. I may even marry people. Would that I could marry you to me this very instant, happy thought!*
>
> *The ship will sail on the twenty-fourth, which should be about a week after you receive this letter. But if that does not give you enough time, she will wait for you. She is at your disposal. You will have no trouble finding her, I'm sure. Her name will be* The Lucy Maid.

She was to leave England at last, a ship had been named for her; yet Lucy threw down the letter in a pique. How could he offer her the governor's invitation as though it were such a treat? She did not want to visit the governor. She did not want to go to Halifax. She wanted to see this new life she had been promised, his island that was to absorb her like a patch of sea fog in the forests on its cliffs.

Still the excitement of leaving gripped her. She could not help going to the docks the very next day to see the ship that bore her name. Her ill humor dissolved at the sight of its tall, raking masts and over-hanging bow. She stood for a long time, imagining how it would be under sail and studying her name in fresh black paint.

Gradually she became aware that someone was standing beside her. She glanced around at a girl in a tired-looking alpaca dress. She could not have been more than sixteen, and her face was pinched under her bonnet. "Please, miss, are you Miss Hamlin who is going to marry Captain Rathrock?" she whispered, when she saw she had Lucy's attention.

"I am."

"Please, miss. I must go to Hazard Island, too. There's nothing for me, if I don't—except the workhouse or worse. There's no one would marry me. It was one of his tars, you see—a year ago next Michaelmas. If I was to get to him, I'd make him see he ought to do right by me."

"You haven't your passage, of course?"

"Six pounds ten, nothing more." The red-rimmed eyes begged Lucy to say it was enough.

"You could indenture yourself."

"No, no. It's too long. I've a child, you see. He is with me mother—eight months old he is. I must come back." The girl burst into tears, and Lucy, drawn to her by bonds the pathetic ragamuffin could not guess, slipped an arm around her shoulders.

"There now, what's your name?"

"Annie Watts, miss."

"Meet me here two days from now at six in the morning. You shall go, Annie. You shall be my personal maid."

It was an extravagance Jonathan had not authorized, but he would see that she needed a maid. He would approve. She would say it was to keep up their position.

Annie was there, pale and determined, her belongings in a faded brocade reticule. Lucy was struck again, not only by the similarity of Annie's situation to hers aboard the *Kumrah*, but by a similarity in character between her and this urchin.

"It is so much the same, and yet not the same at all.

It is the love that's the same, for the child, anyway. I wonder if she can love the man as I did Galen. I wonder if her luck will be better."

Lucy stood at the railing and watched the figure of her Aunt Madeliene recede with the English coast. The square white sails fluttered out, and below the Union Jack a flag was run up which Lucy had not seen before—the Rathrock crest.

Lucy had never sailed like this. The boat responded to the winds with a coltish glee, and Lucy could not tear herself from the deck. A joy surged in her that this wonderful vessel bore her name, and followed everywhere by the worshipful Annie, she wandered about, savoring her proprietorship, asking the sailors questions. "What makes her go so fast?" she asked.

"It's a mystery, my lady. Some say she's a hog in her keel—a twist, that is. She fell onto her side when she was launched."

"How many miles can she make in a day?"

"She logged four hundred once. But that was when Captain Rathrock was at her helm to try her out. He sails her like a madman when he wishes, beg pardon, my lady."

"Then I shall be there soon," thought the impatient Lucy. She spent her time training Annie, and though the girl had to be shown everything from how to pack a crinoline to arranging the cap of her new uniform, she was an apt pupil.

"You shall curtsey to the captain, so, when he sees you," she said, demonstrating. But it was not an easy feat to master on the rolling ship. Annie pitched forward on her face time after time, until both mistress and maid were weak from laughter. It was the first time Lucy had seen the girl laugh.

She was glad for Annie's company, since aside from that of the sailors it was all she had on the ship. A member of the Nova Scotia legislature and his wife traveled with them, but the wife, viewing the journey as an ordeal, remained seasick in her cabin, tended by her husband, who, when he crossed the deck from time to time on some errand, was the butt of sailors' jokes.

"There he goes, lads, escaped again. She'll have him back before we've gone another mile!" they would call to each other among the rigging.

"You'd think him a bridegroom to judge by his hurry,

but just look at his face! It's obvious he's not had the pleasure even once, or perhaps it's no pleasure!"

If they found Lucy within earshot after having made some such tasteless observation, they would call out, "Beg pardon, my lady," and grin down at her, for they had formed quite a different opinion of her than of the legislator's wife. To a man they approved of the captain's bride-to-be. And if Lucy felt a possessiveness toward the ship that bore her name, the sailors felt the same loyalty and possessiveness toward her.

She was a rare one, they said among themselves, this slender, dark-haired girl who had discovered a love of the sea they had supposed a woman could never experience. Once on a calm day, she inveigled a few moments at the helm, and at night, after a dinner of salted fish, she would have a chair brought out and she would sit listening to the sounds of the concertinas. In the morning as they went about their work, they would listen for the sound of her lovely voice singing the chanties she had liked best.

She learned the names of all the sails, the skysails, the stay sails, the port studding sails. She spoke of ties and yokes and boom irons, of mizzens, buntlines and top gallant sheets.

She wondered why they called her "lady." She was not titled. Even Caroline did not truly have a title yet.

They raised the evergreen coast of Nova Scotia, and Lucy frowned as the spires and rooftops of Halifax grew closer. The frown grew deeper as she saw the legislator's wife handed into a dory. Then it was her turn to go and the old devil, which should have been stilled, rose in her.

"How much further to Hazard Island?"

"A day with good wind, my lady."

"Send a message to the governor then. Thank him for his offer of hospitality, but I have decided to stay aboard." The sailors cheered when they heard the news.

A great excitement grew in her as the ship sailed on. She paced the decks, asking every hour or so, "What is it we are passing now?"

"Port Medway, my lady," came the answers, "Western Head, Mouton Island."

And finally, as the coast dropped from sight, "We are in the Bay of Fundy."

She borrowed a glass and studied the small, foggy islands of spruce and balsam that rose from the ocean like pieces of lost forest. Each time she knew she was not seeing *her* island.

Then she saw the great, rocky cliffs, the waves beating them like invaders at the walls of a fortress. She saw the magnificent greenness, the gannets flying into the mists, a beach sparkling under a spot of sun. She gave a cry, even before the watch in the crow's nest had sung out. The crew caught her excitement, and as the island grew, they pointed out the sights.

"There is Shipwreck Head, and that is Wailing Widow Cliff. See how it is shaped. You can see the nose and the chin, and they say the hawkweed that grows on top is her long hair blowing. When there is a storm, the wind howls about her, and she moans like a woman. It is horrible to hear. They say it is the ghost of someone who lost her man in a wreck at its foot."

"Was there such a wreck?"

"Aye, many. The tide is swift and treacherous. It can take a ship and dash it against the cliffs as though it were no more than a log.

"Over there on that neck of land is the Hazard Light. No one will live there now, so we've only bells and buoys to give us warning in the fog."

"Why will no one live there?"

"It's a desolate little cliff. The tide comes up thirty feet, and for twelve hours a day you cannot get to it from the main part of the island. Nothing is there except trees and rocks, and the gannet and guilemots that nest on it have taken it as their own. If you want to see it, though, you can walk across at low tide, with only a trickle in the strait."

Lucy's attention was drawn from the lighthouse by a cry, "The borers!"

Every sailor had left her side. Dead ahead were a line of column-like rocks, rising from the sea like the ruins of an ancient city. They seemed like great ocean monsters with kelp streaming down their grizzled faces. They appeared to leap from the sea, then sink beneath it again, as huge waves tossed around them. Lucy guessed that this impression gave them their name. Horrified, she saw that the ship must pass among them.

They were so close to the rocks she could see the separate strands of the brown kelp. She could see the little shells of the sea animals that lived there. She shut her eyes, knowing that she had come all this way, only to be smashed into pieces at the island's very gates.

Then, disbelievingly, she felt the boat turn into the wind and heard the command to drop anchor. Somewhere on shore a cannon fired a salute. Lucy Hamlin was home.

PART II
The Island

Chapter 1

The harbor was full of fishing boats, aground at low tide, crouched like nesting ducks on long, gray stretches of basaltic sand. A small schooner rode high in the water. On the piers were mountains of slatted, curve-roofed lobster pots, and everywhere great snaking coils of black fish net dotted with red floats lay like seaweed washed ashore.

She caught sight of houses, their shingles shining silver in the sun. They were low and cozy with chimneys of old, red brick and flat-roofed dormers. Vines clung around porch posts, and smoke drifted along the beach from the weathered smokehouses, smelling sweetly of fish and slow-burning saltwater wood.

The crew of *The Lucy Maid* snapped to attention and forming a double line, saluted as the island's new mistress passed through. From the dory Lucy waved her handkerchief to them. Then, eagerly searching the shore, she saw someone else to whom she wanted to wave. A fierce pride rose in her at the sight of Jonathan Rathrock on his island, standing like a beacon, the early April wind whipping his bright hair, the gold buttons on his coat glinting in the cold sunshine.

"Jonathan!" she cried. He did not return her wave, but she did not mind, for somehow the motion might have spoiled the symbolic look of him against the backdrop of his island. The thought flitted through her mind that perhaps the proprietor of an island of forty thousand acres would not wave like an ordinary mortal. Then, as the boat reached the pier she saw that it was a high quality of rage that made him unlike an ordinary mortal.

She shrank back into the boat with a terrible dismay, for his rage frightened her more than the wrath of her father or Lord Ashton. Here was her lord for the rest of her life, his features hard and drawn, the coppery tones of his mustache and his scowling eyebrows like fire among the rocks of Hell, sparked by his smoldering eyes. Annie cowered behind her mistress. The sailors themselves seemed to cringe.

She had come all the way across the ocean and now, as she was handed ashore, she wanted more than anything to scramble back to the water, like a netted fish escaping. Instead she forced herself to meet his blinding gaze.

"I am sorry, Jonathan." she said. She knew he was angry because she had not remained at Halifax.

"I hope you have a good reason, Lucy." His voice was as cold as his visage was fiery.

Her mind floundered; she could not think. With a curt command he gave instructions for Lucy's baggage and for Annie, who did not seem sorry to be left behind like a piece of equippage. He guided Lucy to a carriage, and they set off briskly on a winding dirt road. On one hand lay the ocean with a beautiful pebble beach. On the other, fields led up into forests, and the road rose as they entered the chill of the woods. Fog swirled through the spruce on cold, aerial pathways. She heard the clicking of a red crossbill as it flew and saw violets blooming in great coverlets among the fern of the forest floor.

She glanced at Jonathan, hoping he could not be as angry amid this beauty, but the shadows of the woods made his face darker still.

"I did have a reason, Jonathan," she ventured. "It was because—because I felt so—left out."

He looked at her uncomprehendingly. "Left out? When you are to be my bride?"

"But you were doing everything, and I was not even allowed to see the island!" Her voice gained a little strength. She found the courage to feel wronged.

"You have made a laughingstock of me, Lucy!" he burst out. "What shall I do with you, coming here without a chaperone, and our wedding day not even set? What of the governor? Did you not think of the opportunity you ruined for me? Do you not realize that his friendship is important to us? Did you not think what a hindrance you might be to me here, I who must arrange a safe place to leave you, while I tend to the thousand things I must do? You must not think first of your selfish whims, Lucy Hamlin, if you are to be mistress of Hazard Island."

"You are right, Jonathan. I will think of Hazard Island first." She was so mortified she did not notice that his expression softened. She did not notice that she had pledged her allegiance not to him, her husband-to-be, but to the island, or that he, glancing at her with interest, approved.

"Well, I must think of something to do with you," he said in a gentler tone.

The road had made a loop and come out onto a rocky plateau, fringed in leafless alder. She could see the village again below and *The Lucy Maid* at anchor. One house stood some distance from the others. It was grander than the rest, with twin chimneys, and in a style Lucy had not seen before on the island, had columned corners and a pedimented doorway. Behind the house stretched an orchard, and around all grew a natural curtain of hemlock, shielding it and setting it aside.

"What is this place, Jonathan?" she said, as he turned into the drive.

"It is the home of Fitch Treadway, who has more intelligence and ambition than any other man on Hazard Island. He owns three fishing boats, and someday he will have more."

As he jumped from the carriage, a man came out of the house. Lucy watched curiously as the two met and shook hands.

They were of the same height, the islander brawnier, the captain looking more lithe. The captain's features were cut cleanly. The little ledges of his brow and upper lip were like tiers of a rock garden supporting the rampant growth of his eyebrows and mustache. The islander's features were more imprecise, as though he had happened by chance, weathered by storms like the island cliffs.

What interested Lucy most was that the islander showed no sign of deference to the captain, but stood in his rough shirt and nankin trousers, eye to eye with the proprietor of Hazard Island. The captain folded his arms across his chest; the islander lighted a clay pipe. They are rivals, she thought in amazement, wondering that this islander should have the effrontery to consider himself the equal of the captain who had fought on most every ocean of the world.

The men shook hands again, and Jonathan returned to hand her from the carriage. He gave her into the hands of Fitch Treadway and his wife, Polly, and without saying when he would return, he drove away.

Lucy had never seen a house like the Treadways. The

low ceilings lay on rough beams of tamarack, and the polished pine floors were covered with hand-hooked rugs. Much of the furniture was rough hewn and simple, but here and there was a piece of breathtaking fineness—a Sheraton sideboard, a Windsor chair, a set of Rockingham china ornamented in gold. When Lucy exclaimed on these things, Polly Treadway told her that they had been brought from Boston by her forefathers and Fitch's.

"You are Americans?" Lucy asked in surprise.

"No, never. Our families were all Englishmen. When they could not be Englishmen in Boston, they fled. It was in the winter of 1775."

"And they came from Boston to Hazard Island?"

"Yes, but not by choice. T'was St. John they were after. But a storm caught the ship and dashed it against Wailing Widow Cliff. Eight men and six women scaled that pinnacle in the night, a thing that has never been done since. It was only death biting at their heels that gave them the power. In the morning the great tide had receded, and the ship was aground. They went down by another way and brought ashore what goods they could save and buried what bodies had not been swept away. Two of those men were Fitch's grandfather and mine, and the town that you see is the one they founded. The name of it is Shipwreck, and the main road they built across is named for them, too, Tory Road."

Polly Treadway was a plump young woman, only a year older than Lucy. She had a gay disposition and a head of chestnut curls, worn in bunches of ringlets. When she laughed she laughed too loudly and tilted her chair back on its legs, so that Lucy thought she would go crashing to the floor. She was fond of her gardens, fond of making and eating American johnnycakes. She was fond of Fitch, and fondest of all of the *pièce de résistance* of her life, a little towheaded baby in a cradle near the fire.

The baby's name was Josh, and when Fitch Treadway looked at his son, Lucy saw all the blaze of ambition of which Jonathan had spoken.

"May I hold him?" Lucy could not help asking, and Polly handed him into the arms of a mother who had been so long starved for the touch of a child. The memories stirred by the soft, heavy warmth almost made Lucy cry, and she hid her agitated face against the baby's silky hair. "I shall have one myself as soon as I can," she whispered. It was a promise she made to herself, though she spoke the words aloud. "I hope I shall have a dozen!"

"I hope I shall, too," said Polly. They had met on rich grounds and a friendship had begun.

Lucy's room had a pine four poster bed, covered by a wedding ring quilt. A portrait of Queen Victoria, one of several in the house, testified to the Treadways' loyalty to the Crown; and there was a window with a view to the harbor. Day after day she would sit for hours watching in the early morning as the boats slipped silently out to sea.

Jonathan had not returned. It was almost as though he had chosen to forget that she was on the island. She would fume at being so ignored, planning how she would remonstrate with him when he appeared. "I shall be very cool," she would think. "Perhaps I shall even say I am indisposed." Then suddenly she would be terrified that he had changed his mind about marrying her, and she would dart to the door to search Tory Road for the dust of a horse that might be his.

Annie, who had helped unpack the trunks and hung the magnificent wedding dress in the darkest closet to prevent yellowing, slept on a pallet in the kitchen. She went freely about Shipwreck, asking questions at the docks. The man she wanted was at sea.

"On the Captain's whaler, he is," she told Lucy. "He won't be back for months."

"He will be surprised to see you," Lucy ventured.

"That he will, miss!"

"And what will you do if he doesn't marry you then?"

"He'll marry me; I'll see that he does," returned Annie, with a thrust of her little jaw. And Lucy, in the face of such confidence, worried no more about Annie.

For fear of angering the Captain further, Lucy went out only with Polly. She walked about being introduced everywhere, watching the women slitting and cleaning herring or laying cod on the wooden flakes to dry. Wherever she went she remembered the names of everyone she met and the names of all the children, cataloguing them like treasure. And they were treasure—all this wild lovely island and everything that existed upon it. They were to be her life.

Polly Treadway did not dirty her hands on fish. The daughters and sisters of other fishermen were hired to care for the fish from Fitch's boats, and Polly had servants to do her heavy work as well. She cooked and made elaborate clothes for the baby, and finding Lucy had been in Paris, made her talk and talk about it.

Lucy would tell about the cafés and the shops with their wares of silver gilt, ivories and polychrome statues. She would recall the House of Worth dresses, the winter walks on the quays, plays at the Italiens in which she had seen the great actresses of the day.

"Oh, how could you ever leave it!" Polly would cry, and Lucy, jerked from her reverie, would realize that she did not miss Paris at all. Thinking of it only filled her with a sadness, a longing for Galen. But with every day the sadness grew sweeter, more mellow. Galen and Paris were becoming a lost, though beautiful, dream. The quality of unreality she had predicted about all she had left behind was taking hold like a powerful sedative.

She wandered in the fields behind the Treadways' house, and finding narrow sheep trails, followed them. Lilacs and columbine were beginning to bloom. She found a waterfall and a beach to scramble down to at low tide. There were flat rocks to lean against, and once she counted fifty harbor seals, dry and yellow from the sun, sleeping on the ledges of the exposed shoals. She would climb back up to the cliffs and look out to sea, studying the brush weirs in which the islanders trapped the herring. The weirs were all named, like boats, for some characteristic or for the wife of the fisherman who had built it. But Lucy had not learned the names, and one looked exactly like the other.

Two weeks had passed, and still Jonathan had not come. How long should she simply remain here waiting? Should she seek him out and learn the worst? She had no idea how to go about it, and she was afraid.

Then one day while Lucy was playing with little Josh, Polly rushed in from the garden. "The captain's carriage is coming!" she cried.

Lucy had just time to push at her hair and skirts before he jumped down; and lifting her in his arms, spun her around, setting her all awry again. He was in a marvelous mood; his anger had completely vanished.

"Would you like to go for a drive?" he asked, and without waiting for an answer, he swung her up to the carriage seat. "Ah, Lucy, it is good to have you here. I am a curmudgeon sometimes. Do you forgive me?"

She could not do otherwise when his eyes twinkled at her as they did now. "You were a long time coming,

Jonathan," she said with a smile, "if you were so glad to have me."

"Oh, but I have not been on the island at all this past week. Let me tell you what I have done. I have bought another ship, a mast ship to haul tall pine and spruce to England. Better yet, I have convinced three ship builders to come to the island to take advantage of the fine timber. We shall build our own ships, Lucy, and when we have enough, we will build for others. We shall be known throughout the British Empire for our fine ships!"

She was delighted with the plan, and when he admitted he had on his person drawings of the square riggers he intended to build, she dug boldly into his pocket to find them. "And your company, Jonathan," she asked. "Does that go well?"

"Oh, exceedingly! I persuaded Charles Ashton to invest in it, and where his money goes, that of others always follows."

She smiled with satisfaction and thought to herself she must never let him know who had really persuaded Charles. She was good for him, she congratulated herself. She helped him in ways he did not even know.

"Where are we going, Jonathan?" she asked.

"Why, to see the town of Hazard. It is only half built, but it will be a fine place someday."

Hazard looked much like the village of Shipwreck, except that it was new and raw, and the smell was of sawdust instead of fish. The sound of hammering echoed emptily from the cliffs behind it.

"What do you think of it, Lucy?"

She frowned and looked out to sea, where no more than half a dozen boats were moored. "It has not a good harbor, Jonathan."

"No. There is only one good harbor on Hazard Island, and that is at Shipwreck. There one must run the borers, but it is deep and without a reef, and that is the harbor we will use."

"Then why didn't you build the houses there?"

"My tars and sea captains and shipbuilders among the fisherfolk? It would never work."

"Why not? They are all people of the sea."

"Ah, Lucy, I must have my own town."

She saw what he meant. He was not content to build onto something begun by others. He pointed to a frame building on a knoll and asked how she liked it.

"Is it something special, Jonathan? It has about it a certain serenity, an exaltedness in that spot with the sea to its back, and the slope to its front."

He laughed wih delight. "It is to be the church, Lucy. I am having it built for our wedding. The stained-glass windows came with you all the way from London in the hold of *The Lucy Maid*, and the very first time it opens its doors will be in honor of our marriage."

A queer feeling gripped her as she looked at the church. She seemed to pass into the future, seeing all her daughters—all save one—who would be married there, and her sons and their children for generations to come.

He led her to another spot not far from the unfinished church, where the wind blew softly though a curtain of larch. Below, the land dropped away and terns dived at the white foam of the waves.

"And what of this spot, Lucy?"

"It would be a fine place for a picnic. The sea wind has a special quality here. It has a kind of comfort."

"This shall be our grave, Lucy. I have picked it especially."

She stared at him. "You plan too much, sir! I am not ready to have my grave chosen!"

He laughed at her shocked face. "One has only to look at you to see that! But a grave can be beautiful, too. Ours shall not be memorials of sorrow, but monuments to our accomplishments."

"Jonathan—I am interested in our lives, not our deaths. Show me where we shall live. Show me our house!"

"That I shall not!"

"Why? Isn't it built?"

"Almost. But it is to be a surprise. You shall not see it until your wedding night."

She teased him to tell her something about it. "You shall see it soon enough," he said. "Ask me to show you anything but that."

So she settled for everything else, and all that spring, whenever he had a moment to spare, Jonathan Rathrock courted Lucy Hamlin. They went walking through fields of orange and yellow hawkweed, purple clover and blue-eyed grass; explored sphagnum bogs; watched tree swallows feeding at dusk. He discovered her interest in sailing; and taking her out in a dinghy, taught her to tack about the harbor.

Once he took her aboard a small schooner to St. John

on the New Brunswick mainland, where he introduced her to society at a ball.

He took her to see the thriving shipyards and wharves, telling her that more than half of the great ships operating out of Liverpool had been built here. "And the gold rush to California—that has helped business, too. Shipload after shipload of passengers want to sail around Cape Horn. There will be plenty of work for our builders."

"Look, Jonathan. There is even a steamship," Lucy said. "Shall we build steamships, too, on Hazard Island?"

His face darkened. She was appalled at how her casual remark had affected him. "Steamships!" he spat. "They are the invention of idiots who understand nothing about the sea. I would sooner go to the bottom in a leaky catboat than command one of those iron monsters!"

"But aren't they very fast?"

"*The Lucy Maid* is faster, with a good wind. Every fine clipper is. We shall build only clippers and square riggers on Hazard Island. We will have none of these spiritless iron things!"

"Yes, Jonathan," she said, frightened at how she had offended him. She promised herself never to subject herself to his anger by mentioning steamships again.

He showed her King's Square, where the gardens had been laid out in the form of the British flag by loyalists who had fled America. She saw the terrifying black rapids of the reversing falls, where the force of the tide pushed water upstream, making its flow change direction every twelve hours. On the streets of St. John, Lucy was bumped by a staggering woman about whom hung an aroma that reminded Lucy sharply of another time and place.

"Why it's hashish, Jonathan!"

"Yes. It is the way some poor, weak women compensate for their loneliness while their husbands are at sea. Sailors bring it here from China."

"Have we hashish on Hazard Island?"

"I have never heard of any, and I hope I never will."

Chapter 2

By July the church was finished, a graceful structure with a roofline of broken peaks and windows and doorways that arched with the belltower to the sky. The chancel carpet, altar vestments, stoles and chalice veils brightened the chapel with colors of green, white, scarlet and purple; and pine pews still smelled of the forest and sparkled with new varnish. But it was the stained-glass windows that were the outstanding feature. Lucy had never seen any like them, and she would look long at them, wondering whether she liked them.

She was certain she liked the window behind the chancel. There a gull rose in flight, and in the morning, when the east light shone through, the bird seemed to be winging away into the sunrise.

The other windows gave Lucy a different feeling. Most of them dealt with distress at sea—a drowning sailor holding to a mast and raising his eyes—to meet his God? A woman clasping her hands in prayer at the ocean's edge. These windows reminded her of the times God had failed her, and she decided that every Sunday for all the years of her life, she would focus her attention only on the flying gull.

They were married on the thirteenth of July, 1850.

Stepping from the brougham he had sent for her, Lucy walked up the hill to the church, through a field of daisies, and bluebells and creeping juniper. In the warm sun her cheeks were the color of the rugosa roses picked for her bouquet from Polly Treadway's garden. Halfway up she paused, her veil blowing in the sea wind, and looked at the church that was as white and bride-like as she—and more virginal.

For an instant the image of Galen Le Blanc shimmered in her mind before she thrust it away forever. The wind whipped her heavy satin skirts, sweeping away the past, urging her on to the vaulted door of the church.

As she started down the aisle she was taken aback that

the faces turned to look at her were not those of the fishing people of Hazard Island or even those of the captain's tars and settlers. Strange faces, these—ladies in gold brocades and crape bonnets, gentlemen with shirt frills that stood out at right angles and dress coats with tails to the knees. She should have guessed! The gentry of New Brunswick, who meant so much to her bridegroom! How far some of them must have traveled for this event!

Suddenly she was aware of the show the captain wanted her to make, and she trembled, half with rage at being shown off so, like a prize pig, and half with fear that she should prove inadequate. But as she reached the chancel, her resentment melted at the obvious pride in Jonathan's eyes. How very handsome he was in his velvet-collared dresscoat and his two waistcoats, one of sky-blue and one of white embroidered satin!

She liked the strong way he said his vows, as though for all the world to hear, and the certainty with which he pushed the gold wedding band onto her finger. Soul and body, she gave herself into his hands, as he lifted her veil for his kiss; and as they stepped triumphantly into the sweet summer air, the church bell began to ring.

Because there was no proper hall as yet on the island, the wedding celebration was held outside. Tables laden with fresh-caught lobster, fiddlehead greens, Jamaican rum and spruce beer, island strawberries and cakes were set under the trees where one day the churchyard would be. The merriment lasted all day. Lucy murmured to all the ladies; she danced with all the men, including the governor whose hospitality she had snubbed. Her dress grew heavier and heavier; her knees ached with the weight of her satin and petticoats. The captain was pleased with her, and displaying a side of him she had never seen, played a concertina and sang in a fine baritone.

"My husband and but half known to me," she thought, wondering what other surprises were in store. He took her away in a shower of rice, and leaning against him, she fell half asleep in the carriage as they rode through the dusky evening, the cool air resonant with the song of crickets.

"We are here, Lucy."

She stirred and lifted her head from his shoulder. "Oh, Jonathan!"

In the moonlight stood a milky, dormered house. Six double columns supported a long, low porch; and a great curve of bannistered steps swept down to the ground. It was an exact replica of the drawing she had made him on Gibraltar, so long ago, and it told her more than anything ever had how deeply she affected him, how much he longed to please her, to have her approval.

The house of his dreams had been built to her vision, and it filled her with a wonder and gratitude she had no words to express. Nor had Jonathan words for the moment, since he was a man who could not easily speak what was in his heart. Perhaps in all his life he would never make another statement of love as strong as that he made with the house.

"Come, I'll show you the inside," he said. He set her down from the carriage and led her up the steps. Pausing at the door with its shining cut-glass fanlight, he lifted her with all her heavy petticoats and carried her over the threshold.

Painted china lamps glowed in the large rooms that opened on either side of the entry. The many-paned windows were curtained in damask and Indian muslin, and on the Adam mantels models of the ships of the captain's naval career were already displayed. The drawing room had a Brussels carpet; squat, tufted chairs and inlaid tables. In the dining room a long table, overhung by three fringed lamps on pulleys, told her her husband wanted to do much entertaining. Everywhere pedestal jardinieres were filled for her arrival with the dark-veined blossoms of swamp laurel.

"Oh, Jonathan, it's perfect!"

He grinned like a schoolboy. "Not perfect yet, Lucy, but to be made perfect by you. The paintings have not been chosen, and you must add touches like needlework footstools done by your own hand. Otherwise it will not be home."

"I don't sew well, Jonathan." A sudden apprehension swept her. She could at least have told him that.

He laughed and, lifting her face in his hands, kissed her lips softly. "You, Lucy Rathrock, will do whatever is necessary. That is the way you are."

She thrilled, hearing her new name for the first time, and ceased to worry, trusting herself because *he* trusted her. He took her hand. "You have not seen the upstairs."

He led the way, telling her that the bannisters had been

carved by a craftsman in Halifax, pointing out to her maps of his various campaigns that hung in frames on the papered walls. The upstairs hall was dotted with islands of Persian rugs, but along it, many of the rooms stood empty.

"For you to finish, Lucy," Jonathan said. He did not say "with children," but that was the way Lucy saw it, and the dim rooms seemed filled with the quiescent spirits of babies yet unborn.

"This is your room, Lucy. See, this door opens into a dressing room, which in turn opens to mine."

She took in white lace curtains framing a dormer window, a vanity of gray sycamore, a half tester bed and a fireplace with a dainty gilded cornice. The great bed with its baroque carving and elaborate hangings seemed to overwhelm the otherwise cozy room, but perhaps it was only in her mind that it loomed so large.

"It's delightful, Jonathan," she said. "You have done it to suit me, and I did not even make you a drawing of this."

But Jonathan's mood had changed. He was no longer interested in the house. "Turn around, Lucy, and I will unfasten you," he said with a grin. "You will have to make do tonight with no maid to help you. I have arranged for us to be alone. Your Annie will not arrive until tomorrow."

She turned willingly, with a trembling wave of anticipation. How long it had been since she had known the pleasure of a man! Memories of the glories of sexual contact swept over her, and she prayed he would mistake her blush of excitement for one of maidenly shame.

He sent her away to the dressing room, where she found her trunk neatly unpacked, her night things set out. She stood naked before the mirror, assessing herself, her body in a fever. Dropping the cool gown over her hot skin, she loosened her hair so that it covered the outlines of her breasts. She supposed she looked very well. She remembered that he had seen her in a gown before and that the sight would not be new to him.

This gown, though, was not like the other. It was made of the thinnest chambray, and the neckline, set with blue ribbons, came low on her round, white shoulders. The curves of her hips and thighs shone through easily. There was even a shadow at the joining of her legs, a darkness like a swift island current between soft limestone banks.

She opened the door cautiously and spied on him. His wedding suit lay folded over a balloon-backed chair, and her heart raced at the sight of the empty black trousers. He was standing with his back to her, wearing a long, white nightshirt and smoking a pipe.

The air was permeated with the masculine odor of tobacco. He was so much larger a man than Galen; he seemed so much more powerful. Suddenly the reality of the moment overwhelmed her. She felt near fainting and swayed against the dressing room door, pushing it open.

He turned at the sound, catching her in his arms as he rushed across the room. "Lucy, dearest, I am so sorry. How thoughtless of me."

For what was he sorry, she wondered as she felt herself lifted. How very light she had become in nothing but her nightdress. It was as though the lightness in her head had affected her body. His hand gripped close to her breast. She gasped and seemed to be floating.

She floated down, down onto the bed, her dark hair spreading onto the goosedown pillow. Jonathan flung out a window, and a fresh breeze played over her nearly-naked body, rippling her thin gown and blowing it above her ankles.

He turned away, tapped his pipe into the fireplace, and scattered the ashes. So that was it! He thought the smoke had made her dizzy.

"Please forgive me. I've no experience as a bridegroom, of course."

Of course not. Nor experience with innocent girls. But experience. Had he smoked that pipe in some brothel in Tangier?

Had he had experience with innocent girls, he might have realized that it was a category that Lucy did not exactly fit, that her swoon had been caused by more than a mixture of vague apprehensions and tobacco smoke. He sat on the bed beside her, and gently pulling her gown below her breasts, took them in his hands. Stroking them, he lowered his lips to the quivering buds of her nipples.

She gave a strangled cry of passion. "Love, don't be afraid," he murmured. "I shall try not to hurt you. I promise it will not be as bad as it is made out to be."

She was not frightened, but a kind of anger rose in her. "If I *were* frightened, if I were a poor, terrified virgin," she thought, "he would not stop, for all his pretty words, until he had had his way."

The demon of his sex—where did she remember that phrase from? Caroline had spoken it, describing poor Charles on the night of Lucy's ball. Poor Charles, whose demon could be nothing beside the appetite that thundered in the captain, for, even as he comforted her, his hand slid into the intimate channel of her body, and he lifted her gown above her waist, kneading her buttocks in his strong grip.

Her own sexuality raced to meet him. She tugged at his nightshirt. "Jonathan, take this off."

He glanced at her in surprise. Weren't young girls stupefied by the sight of male anatomy? He had intended to be delicate and keep it on, but it was an encumbrance, and with a huge sigh, he flung it from him and stood in all his arrow-straight manliness—the broad muscled shoulders, the slender hips focusing on the meaningful part of him below, which seemed to fit its owner with its aura of command.

He threw himself on her now, his reserve gone with his clothing. She felt him enter, and her body thrust up, struggling to receive him into the deepest reaches of her being.

"Lucy!" Spread-eagled beneath him, the weight of him engulfing her, she looked up into a face as angry as it had been when she debarked *The Lucy Maid*. "Lucy, do not behave like a harlot!"

She looked at him blankly.

"Do not writhe and twist about. It is not what a lady does."

"How do you know? Have you made love to so many ladies?"

"It is none of your affair what I have done. I am your husband. Do not question my word. Did you learn this disgraceful behavior from your Frenchman?"

"I learned only not to deny what is in me, and I have done nothing shameful. I have only tried to love you!"

She was furious, and tried to shove him off her. But his desire rose again, and he pinned her harder against the bed, wrapping his arms tightly about her, hurting her breasts, crushing away her breath. She lay as passionless as he could wish, gripping the bedsheets with bloodless fingers while he beat against the walls of her body. Then he was spent, and rolling away from her, stumbled off to his own bed chamber.

Lucy wept like any disillusioned bride, and in the

morning her body ached as though she had indeed been a virgin the night before.

She supposed that when he had accused her about her Frenchman, he had accused her of loss of chastity, but Jonathan never mentioned the matter again, whether from some shyness or from a desire to torment her with doubt.

Servants had arrived and Annie herself came to help Lucy dress. Lucy was so glad to see her maid that she almost threw herself into the girl's arms. At breakfast Jonathan was as gracious to her as though nothing had happened.

He took himself from the island on business that had come up suddenly and was gone for several days. Returning without warning late one night, he came to Lucy's bed. She was stiff and proper with Victorian fear, and when it was over, he stroked her hair, brushed away her tears and told her that he loved her.

He was willing to forget her transgression of the wedding night along with all it might mean. Indeed he never wanted to speak of it. That she did so perfectly as he wanted her to now, he took as a sign of her devotion, and it made him feel a special tenderness toward her.

She was a woman who did what was necessary without fuss. He had said so himself. He was content and felt that he had chosen well.

Chapter 3

Lucy busied herself with the arrangement of the household; and never, she thought, had a bride had such a task. Every routine must be established where nothing had been before. Goods had to be acquired and placed in a house that had not yet all its pantrys, and instead of a wise old housekeeper to help her, she had only Annie and a handful of young indentured girls who had come with their husbands or in search of husbands and who were usually to be found in corners, weeping for the loss of English home and family.

Lucy often felt like crying herself. She did not know a porringer from a pudding cup or a paring knife from a butcher knife. She had no way of knowing whether her cupboards were well-stocked; and it seemed that every day cook came howling to her for some commodity that did not exist on Hazard Island, but which could not be lived without.

Finally Lucy took the carriage and, driving across the island, threw herself on the mercy of Polly Treadway. The household improved after that and was full of companionship and laughter as the well-versed Polly taught Lucy the complexities of coping with island life.

Lucy began to be pleased with her management of the house and, longing for some recognition from Jonathan, wanted to cry out to him, "Am I not doing well?" He, however, pushing away his plate of shad or chowder, seemed to take the smoothly-running house as a matter of course.

So, she was especially delighted one afternoon when he came in with his twinkling, mischievous expression and catching her around the waist as she stood on tiptoe on a stool, demanded, "Do you think me an old skinflint, Lucy? I have never given you a wedding present."

She forgot the high shelves of the linen closet she had

been inspecting and cried excitedly, "Oh, but I never thought of a present! You have given me the house!"

"That is exactly the point. You are inside too much. You are losing that bit of tan which you should not have, but which becomes you so. Let the house go its way now, until winter, which will be time enough for pallor." He led her to the stables and bursting with pride, showed her the fine white gelding he had bought her.

"I have not forgotten that once I had to shoot your mare," he told her. "I have not forgotten how you love to ride."

She hugged him in her excitement and kissed him on the mouth. It was the first time *she* had ever kissed him, she reflected later. Taken by surprise, he had responded to the soft pressure of her lips. Each had been kissing the other, and it had been very pleasant. Jonathan had not objected.

The animal was an Arabian, so she gave him an Arabian name, Kumrah, after the ship on which she had begun her African adventures. In speed he was far removed from the sluggish vessel, but like the *Kumrah*, he opened up a new world.

She rode every day. In the morning, wearing her olive riding habit with its polka skirt, she would go tearing along the pebble beaches, urging her mount into the water, wetting them both with lacy foam, and stirring up clouds of sandpipers and fat dowitchers. In the afternoon she might take Tory road to Hazard to inspect the new buildings or go the longer way to Shipwreck to visit Polly or to ride about near the piers and smokehouses. When she wished to see no one at all, she would wend her way to some sunny cliff or tether her horse at the edge of a quivering bog to search for little orchids called grass pink.

Early in September the weather turned chill. The Labrador current made the water numbing, and all around the island fishing boats could be seen removing netting from the weirs to mend and store away from the destructive winter storms.

On Sundays when Lucy drove to church in Hazard, a great number of fishing boats rocked in the bitter winds of the shallow Hazard harbor. Their anchorage did not seem safe, especially in winter, Lucy thought, considering how little she knew yet of island ways.

The pews were occupied every Sunday now by the captain's tars and settlers, but not by the fishermen, who had long had their own chapel in Shipwreck. The tars came to a man, looking awkward and rough, out of place. They did not dare stay away, Lucy thought, for fear of the captain.

On Sunday morning the fog would be so thick that the carriages would be lighted, wending up the slope on the new road, like a chain of sparks from a bivouac fire. In the gloom of the sanctuary, when the organ was hushed, she could hear the empty thud of waves against the cliffs, and the wind screeched about the new walls as though outraged at finding impediment where before it had swept free. Lucy knew of no other place like it on Hazard Island, save for Wailing Widow Cliff. She thought that the captain gloried in it, that he had chosen the site for that very quality, so that the power and vengeance of God might seem to be visited on the worshippers in their very pews.

Jonathan had chosen well, Lucy thought, for if there were a God on Hazard Island, God was the wind that filled the sails, left them limp, or ripping them from their cleats, sent sailors smashing to their deaths.

Jonathan preached every Sunday, leaving Lucy sitting alone in the front pew, her eyes fixed on him or on the shadowy gulls behind him. It was his duty, he said. One could not expect a circuit preacher from the mainland more than one or twice a summer and not at all during the winter. And no one else on the island was half as qualified as he. He would be remiss if he allowed the devil to take the souls of his islanders for want of a church.

Lucy knew this was only an excuse. He enjoyed himself in the pulpit. How well his booming voice fit with the roar of the wind and the thunder of the sea! He cried forth sermons of hellfire and damnation as though they were a part of the symphony of the place, and he was right in doing so. The idea of God as love would have seemed as foreign here in winter as field flowers in the raw November air.

What Johnathan did, he did well. The most irreverent tars sat rigid as bowsprits and the brims of ladies' bonnets trembled as if stirred by the force of his breath. Behind the congregation the empty pews were eerily attentive, seeming already inhabited by the souls of the sinners who would one day sit there when the island's population had grown.

Frequently Jonathan's sermons touched on sins of the flesh. She knew these diatribes were directed mainly at his womanless sailors, but at such times she could never keep from her mind the picture of him naked at her bedside, his eyes burning, not with righteousness, but with lust; and she was glad to be in the front pew, where only he could see her blushes.

She was sure that he noticed them, and she thought that perhaps it even pleased him to see her decorously distressed by the subject. He would never have another preacher in his church, Lucy was certain. Jonathan Rathrock wanted to be king on Hazard Island. And he would be, in every way, for there was nothing to stop him.

Sunday was Jonathan's favorite day. During his walk to the church door during the final hymn, the brimstone would evaporate. Fresh air would sweep into the sanctuary, releasing everyone, including Jonathan, from the oppression of religion. He would slap backs, call greetings, and finding several of his ship captains, would invite them for Sunday dinner of jugged hare and ragout of breast of veal.

Rarely was a woman among the company, since most of the wives still remained in England, but Lucy was allowed to remain after the meal, as a kindness, so that she should not be lonely. Grateful for the favor, she would sit quietly with her sewing, saying almost nothing, but listening and storing away talk that few of her sex ever had the opportunity to hear.

The gray afternoon would wear on. The gentlemen would drink port, massala and West Indian rum. The talk would grow louder, the stories more colorful, the plans for the future, grander. It could reach a kind of crescendo, and then the guests would begin to depart in the dusk. They would have a light supper of cold rabbit and Cheshire cheese, and then Lucy would excuse herself and go upstairs.

She would dress herself as carefully for bed as though she were going to a ball, for she would know he was coming. Her stomach would quiver with a queer mixture of carnality and dread. As his footstep sounded in the hall, she would tense, and the tips of her breasts would grow hard with excitement and fear. He would knock politely, and she would tell him to come in. Never once did she make any excuse to send him away to his own room.

When he entered she would blow out the light, and at that signal, he would strip himself naked and then her as well. "It is all right for me to be naked, so long as it is he, not I, who makes me so," she intuited. She delighted in his appreciation of her body, and wondered if that were all right, too. She had a feeling it was not, but she could not help herself. She could not help it, either, that the sight of him still inflamed her. The tension would grow as he caressed her. Her legs would tremble as he pushed them apart to make room for himself. She would throw her head to one side on the pillow and hope that this time she would not feel passion, all the while longing to do so. She would force her thoughts far away to what should be ordered from London on the next ship or to some dress she was having made.

Sometimes she would be almost successful. Other times nothing she could do would help, and almost painful waves of passion would flood her. She would feel she was choking, that she would die unless he would receive the love she so needed to give him.

She would be seized with panic, and only the fear of displeasing him in bed, which seemed greater than the fear of death, kept her from the actions that nature so strongly urged her to. Once without the slightest effort on her own part, she reached that ecstasy she so often had with Galen. With a strangled moan, she buried her face in the pillow, and Jonathan, mistaking the cry, apologized for his roughness.

When he was finished, he no longer went to his own room, as he had on their wedding night, but slept beside her, cradling her naked body next to his. Her agitation would slowly seep away, and she would take comfort in the closeness.

"Why am I not pregnant?" she would wonder sometimes, as she lay there. "I have been married over four months. It did not take so long with Galen. Indeed it had been only ten months after their first coupling that Alyce had been born. Had she been conceived that very day that Galen had taken her up beside him on the steps of the palace, and they had seen the throne of Louis Philippe carted away to be burned? Is God punishing me for Alyce, she wondered? For if Lucy had little faith in a

175

god who helped her, her belief in one that hindered had not been eradicated.

"Oh perhaps it is in my nature," she would think. "Perhaps if I did not hold back, it would happen, as it did then—" But there was no hope of discussing the idea with Jonathan, and every day as she left her bedroom, the empty rooms along the hallway seemed to accuse her.

Caroline expected a child momentarily. Her letters to Lucy, a month or so out of date by the time they reached Hazard Island, were a chronicle of her adjustment to matrimony. Charles was a considerate husband; she loved him more than ever. The baby would be a boy, of course, to inherit the title. Old Lord Ashton had already announced a list of properties that would come to his grandson at birth.

The marriage act had shocked her. "My dear, I did not leave my room all the next day!" she had written. But the torment had been brief. "It was but three months until I knew I was with child, and he has not come to my room since. But I had found a way to cope with it. I imagined that my body had been left behind as I flew up to the sky. I would close my eyes and think of perching on one cloud and then another. I would think of soft, lovely colors, more beautiful than any earthly thing. Then it would be over, and I could come down—"

This bit of ingenuity amazed Lucy. "She loves him so much that she smiles sweetly through it, though it disgusts her in every fiber"—or did it, for the softness and the lovely colors were not so far removed from Lucy's experiences with Galen. "Can it be she likes it, but she cannot admit it, for it would make her that kind of woman that I am always in danger of becoming?"

Lucy experimented with her cousin's method, but it did not work for her. Lucy did not seem to have a mind that could leave her body behind. When her soul reached out for the sky, her body surged up, too. She had to marshal every strength in her being to hold it back, while the pretty clouds floated on past. It had been a close call, and she never tried Caroline's method again.

Polly Treadway was Lucy's dearest friend on the island. Jonathan did not approve, but that did not put an end to it. "Must you go there so much, Lucy?" he would grumble.

"I must. Do you forbid it?"

He laughed, and displayed a greater knowledge of his bride than she had suspected he had. "Forbid you, Lucy? I would never forbid you. I had as well order the tide not to rise. There I would stand, looking very foolish as I was submerged like Lighthouse Head." He played with a coil of her hair, smiling in an oddly suggestive way, and she wondered if, in his nightly explorations of her, her body unfolded her secrets to him in some manner she knew nothing of.

"Polly Treadway is the wife of a fisherman," he said.

"She is the wife of the most intelligent and ambitious man on Hazard Island except you," she countered. "You said so yourself."

"I have not changed my mind, but Fitch Treadway is my tenant. He pays rent to me and must stay in his place. And no matter what his intellect, he smells of fish. Make your friends among the wives of the sea captains when they come next spring. Better still, among the ladies of St. John. I will buy a cutter and put her at your disposal to take you there whenever you wish. There! Isn't that more exciting than Polly Treadway? You shall have a ship when most brides consider themselves lucky to have their own carriage."

"Save your money, Jonathan. It would be a foolish expense. I have no wish to go to St. John."

"Very well. I will use the money otherwise, and you shall not go to St. John, so long as you do not go to Shipwreck so much."

"Jonathan—"

"Yes, dearest?"

"Why is it that everyone calls me 'lady,' when I do not possess any title?" It was a question she had wanted to ask ever since the journey on *The Lucy Maid*.

"It is because you are the wife of the owner of Hazard Island. We are the closest thing to royalty here. Don't you like being queen of Hazard Island?"

"Not nearly so much as you like being king. Can you not give a royal order that I am to be addressed as Mrs. Rathrock?"

He did not rise to her gibe about his kingliness. In fact he did not seem to recognize that a gibe had been made. He frowned. The heavy, flame-like eyebrows knit in a way she did not like. "I will give no such order, Lucy. It is done from respect for you, and respect is what we must have to keep Hazard Island running."

Whatever the captain's formula, it was working well. Shipwreck Harbor was full of ships. Lucy could scarcely keep track of what vessel was in port with a load of rum and sugar from the West Indies and which had departed for England with lumber or with beaver skins for which the sugar was traded in St. John. Shingles and cordwood, hundred-foot spruce for masts, the omnipresent herring; all shipped away load after load. Such was the rich-running life's blood of the island.

Stiff white curtains hung in the windows of the new houses at Hazard, and it seemed that a sideboard and a crate of Wedgwood jasperware, preceding its lady, arrived on every boat from London. A new tavern had been built and stocked with barrel-shaped pewter tankards.

Captain Rathrock was much pleased with himself and whistled about through the grayness of South Cottage. No such levity relieved the gloom of winter at the Treadways, Lucy noticed. When Fitch was there, his countenance was darker than the December sky. Polly would play with the baby, coaxing him to toddle across the pine floor or to lisp the words he was learning. Strangely, the sight of the baby seemed to make Fitch's mood worse, and he would leave the house to stalk away in the direction of Shipwreck.

What could be wrong? He had been an amiable man and had doted on Polly and the baby, Josh. At last Lucy could stand it no longer and burst out with the question to Polly.

Polly did not want to answer. "It is better that we not speak of this, Lucy."

"How can that be when we are friends, and there is something that hurts you?"

"It is *because* we are friends, and I want us to remain so."

"Polly, there can be nothing that would change our friendship."

"Very well, then," said Polly, her eyes suddenly glistening with tears. "If you must know, it's that husband of yours! He has forbidden the fishing boats the use of the harbor at Shipwreck. They must all moor inside the shoals at Hazard, where there is no protection. You cannot imagine the force with which sou'westers strike there! Sooner or later there will be a disaster; we will all be ruined. It is one thing for the Queen to grant our island to a stranger, but quite another for us to be denied the harbor we have had for eighty years!"

"Can't Fitch tell this to Jonathan?" cried Lucy.

"He has tried. The captain thinks he knows more than all of us. He cannot be swayed."

"I shall have a word with him myself," said Lucy.

"Oh, Lucy!" Polly gasped. "He will not listen to *you*, a woman! You will only make trouble for yourself!"

"We shall see," said Lucy.

Lucy spoke to Jonathan that very night. He scowled, and she sensed the anger rising in the depths of him, surging up like heat into his face.

"There is no help for it, Lucy. I must have room for my ships in the deep water harbor. The fishing boats are not as important."

"But they will be destroyed, Jonathan!"

"And who informed you of this?"

"Polly Treadway."

He gave a snorting laugh. "So! That vacuous little woman is the source of your worry! *She* knows better than I! I have inspected the harbor, and if I must point it out to you, Lucy, I am a man of some naval experience. There will be little damage to the boats. It is only natural that the fisherman resent giving up the Shipwreck harbor, but they will adjust. What is good for my ships benefits us all. And as for you, Lucy, you will leave Hazard Island to me and take care of your part, which is the management of South Cottage and the raising of children."

"I am sorry, Jonathan. Perhaps it is only because I do not yet have any children to raise."

Her apology did not cool his anger. He stared at her, as though to see whether she had meant an accusation. So he had been thinking of it, too! A shudder of dread passed through her just before he lifted her, crinoline and all, and draping her over his shoulder, carried her upstairs.

Though it was only dusk, he stripped her and threw her on the bed with as little ceremony as though she had been an overcoat.

He used her roughly, the blazing heat of his wrath seeming to pass to other parts of him. She felt it spill inside her, burning the core of her body, and she screamed with a terror that he had never before inspired in her.

"We shall see that you have children to raise, madam!"

he said. The great weight of him lifted from her, and he went away, as though satisfied that he had dealt well with a challenge to his domination of Hazard Island.

She lay still, holding the seed inside her, as if afraid that if she moved it would sear her again. She felt the fluid in her like a powerful medicine. "It is doing its work now," she thought. "Even now I am becoming a mother again. I will be put in my natural place and bother him no more. I shall have a fine row of sons to testify to my worth." Lulled by the notion, she fell asleep, and the half-seen faces of the young men who would be her sons floated through her dreams.

Somewhere deep in the night one face became clearer than the rest. She woke with a start to find that Jonathan had come to her again.

He was a man of determination, and he had put his mind to it that there should be a child. Lucy knew no more peaceful nights. The anticipation she had once had drained away, and each inevitable encounter became an ordeal. The row of empty rooms that had held such promise on their wedding night now seemed a burden heavy with the weight of a life's work to be done.

Chapter 4

The time had come when Lucy should have heard news about Caroline's baby, and every morning she would wrap herself in her pelerine and climb to the open widow's walk of the cupola to stand in the wind and peer through a glass at the ships far away in the harbor. On days when she saw a new one she thought had come from England, she would not go out at all, but would pace nervously about the house, waiting for word. Finally she would send the stable boy to see if there were a letter. There never was.

One day the captain's whaler, home from Galapagos, rocked at anchor. Glimpsing it through her glass, Lucy drew in her breath. Annie's sailor was home.

The girl's face was impassive that morning as she went doggedly about her duties—cleaning a pair of shoes, polishing Lucy's silver hand mirror, mending the flounce on a dress that Lucy had carelessly torn on a bannister when she had run down to meet the captain. When Annie had done everything, she dropped Lucy a curtsy, which she had now learned perfectly.

"Do you mind, my lady, if I have the afternoon off?"

"Take it. Take all the time you need. Good luck, Annie!"

The girl said nothing. During her months on Hazard Island, she had become completely the servant, and she seemed to have forgotten that she had once given Lucy her confidences.

It was almost dark when Annie returned. She looked haggard and exhausted, and the strings of her bonnet had tangled into a knot beneath her chin.

"Shall I heat the water in the bath stove, my lady? I'm late with it, I know."

"No, no. It is you who need a hot bath—and a strong cup of tea."

"I have my work, my lady." The idea seemed to sustain her, and Lucy, not daring to tamper with such pride, let her go about filling the tub. The girl worked silently until Lucy could stand it no longer.

"Annie, did you see him?"

"Yes, my lady."

"Well? Will he marry you?"

"He says the baby is not his. He says I have no proof."

"What will you do now, Annie?"

"I will find a way to make him do right. He will marry me yet and take me home to my baby."

"But if he feels as he says, he may leave you. He may make your life wretched. Can we not think of another solution?"

Annie shot her mistress a rare look of contempt. "All very well for you to say, a lady with a fine home and husband! You could never guess what it is like to leave your little one who has never yet called you 'mama.' There is no other way, for who would have me with a child? And I will not desert my baby!"

She left Lucy to sink into the hot bath, her heart aching with thoughts of Alyce. "Where are you now, my angel?" she wondered. "Dead? Ill-used and miserable? Or safe against some warm bosom with no need of me at all?"

The last thought was almost as painful as the first two, and it suffused her heart with jealous longing. She was so subdued at supper that Jonathan asked if she were quite well. She thought he seemed almost disappointed when she said that she was.

Nothing yet, Jonathan! Nothing yet!

The storm Polly Treadway had predicted came that very night. Rain, hurled by the wind, clattered against the windows like buckets of pebbles, and thunder shook the ground like the footsteps of a sea monster come up from the depths to walk the beaches. The wind whined a dirge of a hundred voices, so human, so steeped in the horrors of hell that Lucy leaped from her bed and ran like a child through the dressing room to Jonathan's room, to the comfort of his masterful male presence.

A dazzling bolt of lightning illuminated him, struggling with his braces in the center of the room.

"Jonathan! You are not going out!"

"Of course. I must see what's to be done."

"You are not going to leave me alone!" she cried without a thought.

He looked at her amusedly, thrusting his boots over his foot straps. "Would you rather go with me? In those petticoats of yours, the wind would take you like a piece of thistledown! Go and read, if you cannot sleep. A new book came for you today on the *Obiah,* a thing by Dickens, I think. It's in the library."

"You did not tell me!"

"If I had, I should not have had your company all evening," he said, and was away down the stairs, leaving her in a confusion over whether to be angry because he had withheld the book or flattered at his testimony to enjoyment of her presence.

She had never been in a storm like this; she was used only to the gentle showers of England, and thinking of the captain's high good humor, as he had left, she had a new idea about her husband. "He has chosen this place precisely because it is so wild and can never really be tamed. Wildness has been his life. He would go mad without it.

She took his advice and tried to read. The suggestion had been wise. Lucy had had few enough books to read since coming to Hazard Island, and the storm could not compare in interest to *David Copperfield.*

Half an hour later, she was deeply absorbed when a drumfire of thunder shook the house. The room flashed white. A great, splitting crash followed the volley of sound, and the room went completely black. Lucy found herself on the floor, unsure whether she had been thrown there or had dropped down from fear. Dark spots, ringed in red, swam before her eyes as she struggled to see.

"It was only lightning," she told herself, every part of her shaking with shock. She knew at once she was wrong. A cold freshness swept through the house where only stuffiness had been before, and on the breeze wafted the smell of smoke.

"We've been struck! South Cottage is on fire!"

She did not think of fleeing. Jerking on a tasseled bell cord to summon the servants, she ran upstairs toward the top of the house, where the wind swooped through like an evil ghost escaped from the attic.

South Cottage must not burn down! She had not known until this moment how much she loved this house that she had sketched on Gibraltar, this home that Jonathan had built as a tribute to her, and which embodied his dreams and hers of empire and dynasty. She had not realized that she had developed a loyalty that belonged not to Jonathan or to Hazard Island, but to South Cottage itself. It must not be a cinder before they had even begun!

Her mind assessed the situation with a strange coolness. There were Annie, two parlor maids, a stableboy and herself. Cook had taken to her bed with gout and would only budge if need be to save her own life.

Shrieks reached her ears from the servants' quarters. *They* had thought of escape! She called out in a voice of command which, though she did not realize it, was worthy of the captain. Their frightened voices fell silent as they obeyed and mounted the stairs after her. In the upstairs hall the smoke was suffocating. Lucy tripped over a brass candlestick that had blown to the floor, and a circular walnut table on a tripod base went rolling past like a wheel from a Roman chariot.

In the captain's bedroom a hole loomed in the roof. From one part of the hole a skelton arm of a tree stretched groping fingers inside. She saw at once that the huge beech tree in the front yard had toppled onto the house. A parrafin lamp had blown over onto the bed, and now the goosefeather mattress was a bonfire, the side hangings blazing as well.

Lucy organized a brigade of buckets to the cistern in the kitchen. She worked feverishly, thinking nothing of it that her servants rushed again and again into the heat to bring her water which she trusted no one but herself to dispose of over the flames. The fire was *her* enemy; it was her own personal battle, as much as if it had been a sword duel.

Vaguely she was aware of a scream from Annie. She felt the girl tear away her dressing gown, and, scarcely comprehending, saw the line of fire like a trimming of bright feathers along its edge.

Then there was only the smell of char, a darkness and the howl of wind rushing through the hole in the roof. The sound offended her more than she could say. In her nightgown she climbed from a chair onto the polished rosewood bureau and stuffed the aperture with comforters. Knowing this temporary measure could not long stay the violation of the house, she sent the stableboy out to find spare lumber left from the building of the cupola.

After she had thanked everyone and sent them away,

she closed herself into her own room, and, changing her wet gown for a dry one, slid into her bed. The rain had turned to a solid patter, and just before she fell asleep to the sound of the stableboy's hammering, she was aware of a great welling of exultation and self-satisfaction. Drowsily she understood that she and the captain were alike. She, weaned from her girlhood by the cannonades of Paris, would always be as much in need of excitement and challenge as he.

She woke again while it was still dark. The rain was softer, muffled, and Jonathan stood over her, his face white, staring at her as though he thought her a corpse.

"Lucy—"

She reached up and put a finger over his lips. "I have taken care of my part, which is South Cottage, but you will have to sleep here with me tonight. We have had a certain inconvenience with your bed."

He did not seem to mind the inconvenience. He looked weary, but when he climbed into bed he clasped his arms around her. She pillowed her head on his shoulder. It was a luxury she had never had, except after sex. But then came an even greater luxury.

She felt him become aroused. His hands caressed her, reaching under her gown to the softness of her hips. He rolled her onto her back and entered her so gently, so feelingly that she was aware of it only as an enormous sense of well-being. Something seemed to melt in both of them, and their bodies rocked together.

He could not have accused her of wanton behavior, since there were no longer two beings, only one that moved and breathed with a passion independent of either of them. What he did came from a depth in him he had not known; she knew a release perhaps greater than any she could remember. When it was finished, he drew back and looked at her. She saw a newness, a wonder in his eyes, as though he had awakened from a kind of virginity. She saw that he had known love as he had never known it before.

"Lucy, you are magnificent!" he whispered, stroking her hair.

She remembered another who had liked to call her that, and the two voices seemed to blend into one.

Chapter 5

The destruction of the storm was tremendous. Lobster and horned sculpin lay in dead heaps on the beaches and among the grasses of the cliffs where the great storm tides had tossed them. Laminaria, torn from its submarine forests on the ocean floor, lay with its great ruffled leaves and rubbery stems across the steps of the Hazard Church. The town had not fared badly. Here and there shutters were missing; someone's hen house had blown over.

In the harbor the tale was different. The waves rocked with the flotsam of demolished boats. Only here and there was a hull left whole, floating eerily upsidedown. Debris had washed up everywhere.

Jonathan and Lucy stood together in their new closeness, surveying the ruin. "What will you do?" Lucy asked.

"I will have to build breakwaters. I think it can be done, and next time the water will not come with such force."

"Next time! What about this time, Jonathan? The fleet is destroyed. The islanders have lost their livelihood."

"Don't be so dramatic, Lucy. It is a natural disaster of a kind our islanders have dealt with for generations. They will rebuild."

His assessment of the situation proved as wrong as his judgment that the damage would not occur in the first place. A bleakness settled over the island as impenetrable and pervasive as the winter fog. Unable to bear the grimness, Lucy no longer went to Shipwreck at all. One or two families made plans to leave the island. The others stayed. They had inhabited Hazard Island too long; they had no knowledge of any other place. Elsewhere they would not have survived, any more than an island star flower taken from the forest shade.

They blamed the captain utterly. They spoke to Lucy

kindly, almost with a pity that she should be married to him and endure him in intimate ways, but she saw in their eyes that she, too, was tainted with the Rathrock name.

Even Polly Treadway could not quite separate her from Jonathan. "Don't you see, Lucy? You are to bear the sons that will rule my sons, just as your husband rules my husband," she replied when Lucy remonstrated with her. "That is what none of us can quite help seeing when we look at you—that you shall be the means of continuing the Rathrock domination forever."

Lucy saw. Indeed it was the role she intended for herself. But she had not seen it exactly in that light. She stood that night, looking long into the mirror, her hands over her stomach, wondering if a tiny oppressor grew inside her. No, her sons would be wise and gentle. She would make them so, no matter what Jonathan wanted.

She told Jonathan for the first time that night that she felt unwell, and he, thinking he understood the cause, gave her a tender smile and turned aside.

The islanders could not rebuild, Polly explained to Lucy. Oh, many times before they had done so. One boat or even half a dozen might have been sunk or damaged in bad weather. But a man could work from another's boat until he could raise money to replace what he had lost. The destruction had always been limited, and the relatives and friends of those hit could band together to help. They were all down at once, now.

"We have hardly a boat left. We cannot buy them and we cannot build them. We have not the tools or the skills."

"The captain has shipbuilders," Lucy said.

"But they are busy with his ships. The captain will always put that first. And even if they would build our little boats, we would not have the money to pay."

Lucy could not get the shipbuilders off her mind. Then at last a letter came from Caroline, or rather from Charles. The baby had died at birth, and Caroline had been ill for a month.

> *"The doctor says it is grief that will not let her recover,"* Charles wrote. *"It is a great deal to ask, Lucy, but could you come? It might help her if you were here."*

She threw down the letter and ran to beg the captain for passage. Halfway down the stairs she slowed thoughtfully. Something about that letter, something unspoken that Charles had not intended to say or even known he had said.

"What if I go there and Charles remembers his old love for me? What if that is not yet dead? Caroline may see, and it will be as bad for her as the loss of the baby."

She did not go, though it took almost more strength than she could muster to hold herself back.

Lucy had almost forgotten about Annie, though the girl was beside her daily. She was so quiet and had such stolidity about her that she was as much a fixture as the baize dust cover on the dining room table.

A time came, though, when Annie could not be ignored. For suddenly Annie brightened the winter-dead island with the leaping flame of scandal.

It began on Sunday morning, while the cold fog pressed its dusky fingers to the church windows. Lucy, her head bowed drowsily, was half-listening to the captain's sonorous prayer, her feet toasting on the hot cloth-wrapped brick she had brought from South Cottage.

Into the moment of stillness following the captain's "amen," into the breath of time before the shifting of bodies and clearing of throats, shrilled a feminine voice, transcending its vulgar accent with righteousness and purpose. Before the altar stood Lucy's little maid, her finger pointing at her lover. As he cowered in the pew, she accused him with astounding eloquence.

"Edward Moore, look on me, before this congregation! You who took me in my ignorance when I was a child of fifteen! You who left your child fatherless, and its mother with no hope except that someday God would make it right. Look on the heartbreak and the misery that is your doing! Think of your babe a thousand miles away, crying for his mother! Do you dare sit here in the house of God and deny it? Your soul will be damned if you do!"

She paused, and the wind whistled down through the bell tower, fluttering the pages of hymnals. There was not a worshipper who did not quail, feeling that God had breathed a warning. Annie felt it, too. The Almighty had given her a sign. Her voice rose triumphantly.

"Edward Moore, come here to his altar and fall on your

knees to beg forgiveness! Pledge your troth to me before these witnesses!"

Edward Moore was deathly pale, still as stone. Then suddenly he leaped up as if breaking from shackles. Lucy caught her breath. Annie, her hands clasped prayerfully, gave a sob of thanksgiving.

But the sailor did not walk toward the altar, and as if fleeing the vengeance of God, he rushed from the church.

In confusion and mortification Annie whirled on Jonathan, who, dazed with astonishment, still stood at the pulpit, out of control, for once, of the conduct of the church. "Captain Rathrock, you shall decide, since you are judge on Hazard Island. If God will not make him wed me, you shall. You shall sit in judgment on him and make a decision!"

Jonathan was aghast. His brow darkened, and his features arranged themselves into the most thunderous of expressions. He pounded the pulpit resoundingly with his rock-like fist and in a tone that brooked no question, called for the final hymn.

He strode down the aisle to the door, and, not stopping there, vanished into the heavy fog. With him went the discipline of the congregation. The hymn ended midway in a clamor of voices. The organist stopped playing. Lucy ran to the altar and, lifting Annie from where she had fallen in a spent heap, made away with her to the carriage, half carrying her slight form. She looked about for the captain and not seeing him, ordered the carriage home. Annie must be got away at once, and, judging by Jonathan's face, it would be all the better if he and Annie were not together on the ride.

When the church was left behind and the only sounds were those of carriage wheels and the cob, Annie lifted her face to Lucy. "There now, my lady, did I not tell you I would find a way?" Her eyes were triumphant, but childish, asking for praise from her mistress. Lucy could only return a frightened stare.

"The captain will make 'im marry me, won't he, my lady? The captain will do what is right?"

"The Captain will try to do what is right, Annie," Lucy said, and Annie, not noticing the slight difference in words, sank back, comforted.

Having canceled Sunday dinner of Westphalia ham with champagne sauce and truffled roast chicken, Lucy put the girl to bed and sat in the library waiting.

It was almost night when he slammed into the house, and as he stormed into the library, she saw with a tremble of surprise that his anger was not for Annie, but for her. He paced about, hands clasped behind his Saxony frock coat. Lucy shrank into her chair.

"You knew of this, Lucy! You brought that girl here, well knowing! Do not deny it. I could see by your face that you were privy to her tale. Show me the references by which you hired her, if you wish me to believe it is not so."

"I do not wish you to believe it is not so."

He sprawled onto a couch with a great groan of frustration. "Oh, I shall never understand you, Lucy! It is obvious that you have a brain, a good one for a woman, and yet there are times when you seem to fly in the face of everything it must tell you. There are times when you act with less sense than the commonest toy of a female."

"Jonathan, do not waste your energy in ranting at me," she said. "It is not really I you are angry with, but yourself. You are upset about the thing you must do. You are not happy to have to decide Annie's fate."

He looked at her quizzically. "Hers and Edward Moore's and some child's I have never seen. Well, you are right that I am not happy about it. But you are the one who brought it on me. You brought that girl here without the slightest thought of the scandal that might touch us. Now I must sit in judgment on the lover of my wife's maid. Could anything be more ridiculous?"

"I cannot think of anything, Jonathan, but it is you who created the situation. You wanted to be magistrate on Hazard Island and had yourself so named. If you had not, this would be the business of the court of common pleas at St. John."

"Humph! *They* would make short shrift with Annie! They would send her packing!"

She heard in his tone that he would do differently, and a wave of hope lifted her. "I will ring for black tea and cold mutton, Jonathan," she said. "You must be famished."

"Yes, yes, please do," he returned, still agitated, but growing calmer. "You see how it is, Lucy. It is only her word against his. There is no proof on either side."

"There is the baby. That is real enough."

"Ah, Lucy, you are biased. You must disqualify yourself. And I must set a date for a tribunal to hear both sides of the argument."

"You have heard them already, Jonathan. She says he fathered her child, and he will say he did not touch her. And if there are witnesses who might put the lie to one or the other, they are across the sea in England."

"Yes. But I must deal with the formality. And it is my responsibility to decide. I do not like it, Lucy!"

The captain's first court case was slated three days thence, to be held in the drawing room of South Cottage. Invitations were sent to the leading citizens both of Shipwreck and Hazard. The island hummed with speculation. The captain was short-tempered and distracted.

Annie gazed on him first with adoring trust and then with growing doubt. He had been the husband of the mistress she so loved, and hearing his tempestuous sermons in church, she had deemed him something beyond a mere mortal. Her young mind now grasped the fact that he was only a man and unsure of himself.

One night, brushing Lucy's hair, she was overcome by tears, and on her knees, wept into her mistress's lap. "Oh, I am lost, my lady! He is a man and will decide for his own kind. It is the way of them! It will make him beastly unpopular with his tars if he decides in my favor. He thinks of that!"

"Indeed he does not, Annie! He is a man, but a better man than that! He will deal justice as he see it. Otherwise his men would not respect him so."

She went away a little consoled.

On the morning of the hearing the servants rose early, and grates that were usually cleaned by six were done by five. The clatter waked Lucy from an uneasy sleep. She lay tensely, her eyes closed, trying to put the day away from her by sinking into slumber. At last she gave a great sigh and sat up. Jonathan had already gone from bed, and she was alone. Automatically she started to ring for Annie, then drew her hand away from the bell. If the poor child still slept, let her be. Lucy would make do by herself, this one day, although it was an inconvenient time for it.

She hoisted herself up and opened her wardrobe. It would be important to the captain that she look especially nice today, she thought, chosing a plaid taffeta with a round waist and a sash that tied in front with floating ends. The bright colors would make her look less pale, she decided, braiding her hair in circles, which she decorated with ribbons.

She was really unwell. It was the strain of the last days, she supposed. How odd that when the future of three human beings was to be decided, she had had to think more about polishing silver, dusting porcelain and preparing baked duck and lobster with pineapple cream.

"It is almost as though we are giving a ball, but we are not having any of the fun of it," she thought. "I have not danced in such a long time, not since the day I was married and that in a dress that was like ballast. Perhaps I shall speak to Jonathan about it when this is all happily past. She twirled a little dance step across the floor, and suddenly she was so dizzy she careened back on the bed.

"I shall be better when Jonathan has ordered that scoundrel to marry Annie," she thought, but it was a kind of sickness she had known once before, in Paris, and she recognized that what was wrong would not go away. She lay there with a mixture of joy and fear coursing through her as the knowledge bore in.

She ought to tell Jonathan at once, but going downstairs, she saw that Jonathan had closed himself behind the paned-glass door of the morning room, away from the bustle of the house. She started to go in, but then, seeing a stoniness in his face that she dared not approach, she went on past. Had he made a decision? It was impossible to tell.

Outside a crowd was beginning to gather on the lawn. A gang of tars played concertinas and guffawed over their hapless comrade who must stand before the captain. Wagons and carriages brought the curious as well as the invited. Lucy sent out great pots of tea, platters of Genoa cakes, and pigeon pies. The long case clock struck eight.

The captain left the morning room and marched out to the drawing room. The wan-faced Annie was brought in. A hush fell over the assembly. There was no Edward Moore.

The spectators fidgeted. The captain frowned in annoyance. "Where is the man? Does he dare to flaunt my authority? Get up a party to search for him. He cannot have left the island, for it would be the ruin of anyone who gave him passage."

But Captain Rathrock was wrong. Edward Moore had left the cold island for perhaps an even more inhospitable clime. Just before noon they brought his body back from the bottom of Wailing Widow Cliff.

The sailor's grave was the first in the churchyard where the wedding guests had danced. Lucy's illness grew worse, as she blamed herself for ever having brought Annie to Hazard Island. Jonathan had been right about that, and she was struck with a horrible remorse.

Had the humiliation driven him to suicide? Or had a distracted misstep sent him to his death as he stood searching the horizon for an incoming ship whose captain might sign him aboard unawares?

It scarcely mattered. Edward Moore and the hope his existence had held for Annie was gone. The girl's grief was almost more than Lucy could bear, even knowing that her own sorrow over Alyce would soon be eased by the birth of the child she carried.

"What shall I do, my lady?" Annie begged.

"It is a problem for which there is no perfect solution, Annie. I know how you feel."

"You cannot!"

"Yes, I can!"

Something in Lucy's voice made the girl pause in her weeping and look at her mistress' face.

"I had a little girl, Annie. Her father was murdered and she was stolen away."

"You, my lady!"

"I have never told anyone since, and you will not tell anyone either. If my little one had not been stolen, I should have arranged for her support after I had married, and that is what we shall do for your child."

"But no one will marry *me*, my lady. Especially not now."

"I am married, Annie. I shall do for your little son what I would have done for my daughter. You shall have a huge raise in pay and send the money to your mother to keep him in good style. When he is grown we shall see that he has a profession."

"But the captain—"

"He will not know. He does not bother with the household accounts, and he has no idea, anyway, what a lady's maid receives in wages."

Annie wept in gratitude. For as long as she lived she would worship Lucy Rathrock, and the secrets of one of them would be safe with the other.

Chapter 6

The experience with Annie had unnerved Lucy. She wanted Jonathan to love her. She wanted an experience like the one they had had after the great storm, a joining that would restore everything to a happy perspective, obliterating the coldness that was more in her heart than her body. She could not ask for his favors, of course, so she shifted herself in bed so that her breast seemed to fall against his hand. She felt him shiver with longing.

"Is it all right, Lucy? You are not well."

"Is it all right, Jonathan," she answered in a voice of wifely patience.

He loved her, but with restraint. The freedom and closeness of the night of the fire were gone. "What's wrong, Jonathan?" she dared ask.

"I suppose I am still dwelling on the death of that sailor."

"Don't. He was worthless."

"Yes, he was scum, but I feel responsible for his death. When I am responsible for someone's death, I like it to be a worthy opponent. I did not mind it when I killed men in battle."

Edward Moore's death diminished him in some way. She knew he still thought of her part in it and she did not mind a day or so later when she told him she was pregnant, and the physical part of their relationship vanished from the scene.

Winter passed on into spring. Long before the lupine bloomed its pink, white, and violet, the captain, like an animal wakened from hibernation, put out to sea.

She missed him violently at first; then a kind of defiance set in. She swore to be as independent as he, to mold herself a life in which he would be only the accessory she seemed to be in his. "It will be easier when there are children," she thought, for the bargain she made with herself was a hard one. Whenever she thought Jonathan due, she could not stay away from the wind-stunted forests at the edges of the cliffs. Heavy with child as she was, she would follow the bits of wool that marked the sheep trails and find her way to a spot where she could catch sight of the sails of *The Lucy Maid,* looking like a flock of low-flying gulls on the horizon.

She was happiest reading away long hours, supervising the planting of lilac bushes and Canterbury bells along the porch, or exploring some little nook of shade to find the green-centered white blossoms of bunchberry growing there. She worked at knitting the little garments she was supposed to make, invariably ending in a tangle and tears of frustration. When the mess proved beyond her powers of rectification, she would be almost glad. Then she would go to her desk and write a little note for a housemaid to take to Polly Treadway.

Polly would almost always come to her aid. They would set little Josh to play on the carpet, and while Polly put Lucy's needlework to rights, Lucy would send for the cakes and pastries that so pleased all three of them.

"Oh, if only I could pay someone to do this!" Lucy would rant. "Why must the mother always sew things herself?"

"It is natural—like a bird feathering its nest," said Polly.

"It is not natural for me! It's Miss Alpin's school all over again. I expect any moment to have my fingers rapped!"

Polly did not really understand, but she said sympathetically, "I would do it for you, except that Fitch would be furious to see me stitching clothing for the heir to Hazard Island."

"But that is what you are helping to do at this very moment! Doesn't that bother you?"

"It is just a baby to me, the baby of a friend and sweet, like all babies."

Those afternoons, her loneliness assuaged, Lucy would be almost glad that Jonathan was at sea. She and Polly were relaxed and free together, not dreading his footstep, his disapproval, no less than Fitch Treadway's at seeing them together.

Polly did not provide the caliber of company Pauline once had, but her simple good-heartedness was a balm. Intuiting Lucy's terror of the approaching birth, a fear that grew, like her girth, with each day, Polly tried to reassure her. "There is nothing at all to it," she would insist complacently. "The tales you hear are simply made up by women who want to feel important and get the sympathy of men. When Josh started to come, I thought it was only indigestion. Lucky that Fitch went for the midwife when he did, for she had not been in the house half an hour when out popped my little one like a pie from the stove."

Lucy, uncomforted, could only stare at her friend in disbelief, unable to share with her or with anyone the incredible pain of her confinement in the convent. The memory of that rending of body and soul, of her willingness to surrender to death was with her daily. At night it took on larger proportions, and the blowing tree shadows prowled the bedroom walls, stalking her like the hyenas at bay beyond the African campfires.

She knew she must make peace with the phobia. "I am a married woman," she told herself, "and I must deal with these demons every year or so until I am forty." When Jonathan was beside her in bed, she slept better, and yet, she knew even he, for all his masterfulness, could not intercede for her. The moment was coming; nothing could prevent it.

Her fear made her pregnancy far different from the one preceding the birth of Alyce. She was tense and thin of face, and she knew moments of panic when she longed somehow to rip the child from her. Just as quickly they would pass, and ashamed of herself, she would cradle her bulging stomach and rock herself gently, as if to soothe the small being who depended on her.

Summer drew to a close, and Lucy had scarcely noticed that it had been there at all. She had not ridden Kumrah or given a party. She had even been too ungainly to pick up pretty colored pebbles from the beaches. Autumn scattered showers of gold leaves across the lawns of South Cottage, and Lucy, seeing them float past a window, would mistake them for clouds of butterflies, so lost on her was the demise of summer.

The last week in September Jonathan went to sea one final time. She had not expected it, and she was stupefied. "You cannot go. The baby will come in two weeks. You will not be here."

"Lucy, I must go. I have business in Jamaica. Most likely I shall be back, but if I am not, it is no matter. What could I do? It's a woman's job, and I would not even be allowed in the room. I would only sit downstairs and drink a season's worth of our best madiera without noticing the taste."

He chucked her under her chin, but she glared at him, thinking that he was deliberately escaping even his minor role in the unnerving event. He saw his tactics were wrong and added seriously, "I have alerted the doctor in St. John, and a cutter in Shipwreck Harbor stands ready night and day awaiting your word to go for him."

"A doctor! But I had thought to have the midwife. Polly says she is very kind."

"Kindness is not what will be important. You will have the best."

"But, Jonathan—"

"Lucy, when will you stop listening to that fishwife? I forbid you to have anyone but the doctor, and that is that."

That night, when he had gone, the specter of the unknown doctor joined the shadows on her walls. She had a special fear of the doctor she could in no way have told Jonathan. The midwife would merely stand by to help pull the baby out, but the doctor would be more learned, more thorough. If he examined her, he might realize that she was not a mother for the first time. It would be mortifying enough for him to know, but suppose he felt it his duty to tell Jonathan? What would happen then?

Her dread of the birth became overshadowed by her fear of the doctor. Daily she felt more certain that she would be discovered by him. She wept to think that the loss of Galen and Alyce might not have been payment enough for her transgressions against society's rules.

Then one night the shadows were shadows no longer. Howling down from the walls, they crowded in hungrily, gripping her with envenomed fingers, rendering her body stiff as death with pain. She fought them with her willpower, which was all she had, searching the onslaught for openings in which to catch a ragged breath of air. She bit her lip to keep from screaming until a trickle of blood ran onto the linen pillowcase.

The bell cord hung tantalizingly, and yet she did not pull it. No one she could summon could frighten away these beasts. The doctor grew in her mind to a stature greater than any of them. The demons were hot and real, and she might be capable of routing them. The demons were familiar, since she had encountered them once before, and she had had months to study them since they had returned to haunt her. She had dealt with them at Alyce's birth, and now she realized that she had acquired a certain skill and confidence. But the doctor was cold, alien, and it would not be possible to fight what he saw as his duty.

The demons gained ground, and the pain seemed to shake her body, tossing it in involuntary convulsions, like a dog toying with a bone. It was a stage she remembered and not fighting it, she waited for the rending sensation that was to follow.

The bedcovers grew wet and cold with perspiration, but still it did not come. She longed for it, for the moment when the apparition of the nun would float into the room with her welcome command, "Let go! Let go!"

The dawn began to glow in rosy halos through the bed hangings. She struggled to push back the curtains, as if to admit some powerful friend come to her. But the morning was her enemy, too, unconcernedly spilling its light like gold sovereigns in dappled circles on the carpet.

Instead of the nun's message she heard the distant scraping of a grate. The light had awakened the servants, and Lucy knew she had lost her battle to deal with the birth alone. Any minute someone would come to light her fire, and she would be found. She was so weak and spent that she could not lift her head, and realizing that if she were found unconscious, she would lose all initiative, she groped frantically for the bell pull.

A young housemaid appeared, her cap set hastily on hair that had not been brushed. Lucy saw the extremity of her state reflected in the girl's big, frightened eyes.

"Go—for the midwife!" Her voice, disobeying her husband, seemed totally strange.

"But the captain said—"

"Don't dally! We haven't time to send to St. John," she said truthfully. And then, to repay herself for her night of silent suffering, she unleased one scream of agony summing up all she had borne and sending the maid fleeing as though Lucy's demons were at her heels.

She must have fainted. The next thing she knew a cold cloth was bathing her forehead. Her eyelids fluttered, and she gazed up into a compassionate face.

The midwife's hair was white and soft as her immaculate fanchon-style cap and the white apron she wore over her skirts. Her features were soft, too, as though time, instead of making them craggy, had worn them silky and comfortable as old bed linen. She reminded Lucy of her Aunt Madeliene, but she had not that lady's ascerbity. It was almost as though the mother Lucy had never known had come to her in this form. She gave a sob and reached out weakly, longing to be taken into those arms.

"Don't worry, little mother; we'll have your baby in no time." She pushed Lucy back, and went about her business.

"Why doesn't it come? I know it is time!" She wished she could choke the words back into her throat. If it were her first baby, how should she know if it were time?

The midwife did not appear to notice. Her mind seemed elsewhere; her brow had knit. Lucy had almost decided the old woman was deaf and had not heard when she answered, "It is because the poor child is in all wrong. Feet first, it is. Grab to the bedposts, dearie, and I will give a yank."

Lucy clutched the smooth curves of the turned walnut headboard. The passage of the baby was nothing like the moment of Alyce's birth. The pain, which should have receded, became her very soul. Unimaginable parts of her tore and ripped. Then suddenly it was over. She stopped screaming, and more horribly than anything, there was silence.

The midwife held a blue, lifeless baby. Lucy did not weep; instead a strength swept through her. She flung herself up from the bed, and snatching the child in one hand, sloshed water skimmed with ice into the marble wash basin.

She plunged the child into the frigid bath. The blue and gold Caughley pitcher fell and shattered, and the child burst into screams.

Lucy had just time to see that the baby was a girl before she fainted.

Chapter 7

Something was wrong with the new Rathrock daughter. It was not only that she wasn't very appealing with her straight, dark hair and splotchy complexion. Something was not right about one of her legs, and when the doctor from St. John looked at it, he thought that it had been done by the midwife at birth.

"She will be a healthy child, but she will always walk with a limp," he predicted. He prescribed long weeks of bed rest for Lucy. "You are lucky, Mrs. Rathrock," he told her. "You will heal in time and bear other children."

Lucky! Lucy hardly knew whether to think so. She did not think she could bear to face childbirth a third time. And yet, she must. Jonathan could never be satisfied with progeny of one lame girl. He had wanted a dynasty. There must be a son She must give Jonathan one or both their lives would be meaningless. And she would do it or die trying.

The little girl, named Madeliene for Lucy's aunt, lay in a cradle near her mother's bed and screamed as though the terror of her birth would not be stilled. Lucy, looking down at her child, wondered if she must blame herself for the baby's infirmity.

"It was I who saved her life," she would think. Then again, "No, it was I who did not send for the doctor. And everyday that I look on her, I must know that in a way the illicitness of my love for Galen Le Blanc has been visited on her."

She would lie back, sighing, thinking long on the complexities of life that had caused this to happen. "Was it wrong to love Galen as I did? Oh, I knew that it was against the law of society—but wrong? I could not help it; it was the core of my being to love Galen. If only *he* had married me, I would have been an honest widow. Alyce would have been with me now, and this would not have happened. He is to blame." The ideals of Paris were past, and in the days she lay abed, there rose in her an awful resentment against her dead lover.

But she had little time for dwelling on Galen. She had the captain to consider. Each day the dread of his return increased in her until it was as great as her earlier fear of the birth itself. She would hear a creak in the hallway at night and shoot up in bed, heart thudding. Each time her sudden fright would seem to communicate itself to the baby, who would waken and begin her hideous howling. Lucy would have to quiet her herself, for the nurse was to come from England and had not arrived.

She would rock her and sing lullabies, which went unheard in the wailing. She would give the child her breast, and Maddie, seizing it with disconcerting force, would manage to nurse and cry at the same time. Lucy was bewildered. Why did the baby cry so, when she was neither hungry nor wet? Lucy could only divine that something inside drove her as though she sensed she was out of kilter with the world or it with her.

It was hard to love Maddie. It was not only that she was not the boy she should have been or that she was unprepossessing and had a deformity. It was that Maddie seemed to refuse to be loved.

"She needs love," Lucy would say, and she would dose out her affections to the baby as though they were castor oil, planting resolute kisses on the squirming, screaming infant.

Would she ever be able to deal with this child? In spite of herself Lucy would find herself comparing this dark little scrap of humanity to the beautiful Alyce, who had once nestled so companionably against her bosom.

She was sleeping late one morning, exhausted from the sleepless night, when a round of cannonfire brought her from slumber. *The Lucy Maid* was in port, for the Spanish guns the captain had captured in battle saluted the arrival of no other ship but the one he commanded.

An hour later his boots pounded up the stairs. He did not look at Lucy at all, but went straight to the baby and with nothing of the fearfulness of new fathers, lifted her from the cradle.

Lucy was astonished to see a pleased, almost foolish expression come over his face. Maddie gave a little sigh, and as though she had been waiting for him, ceased to cry and snuggled against his shoulder.

Jonathan said nothing about the baby's not having been a boy. He did not seem to blame Lucy for that, but she thought he blamed her for everything else. When he had put the baby down, he paced the room, as if the wind of his walking cooled an anger that would otherwise ignite him like dry twigs. His unruly red hair whipped like flame. His eyebrows and mustache melded together in the glow of his fury like lines of burning brush, and it was not difficult for Lucy to think of him as a walking bonfire, like the one she had extinguished in his bedchamber. If only a bucket brigade could extinguish Jonathan!

"Lucy, you disobeyed me. If you were one of my tars I should have you flogged!"

She could not help a smile. "No doubt the punishment will be worse, since I am your wife." How pallid a flogging sounded after her night of labor, her nights of dread. He might deny her new clothes or an outing to St. John and presume her devastated, but the real punishment he would deal he would not think of as punishment at all. She supposed he would try to make her pregnant again as soon as possible.

"There was not time to send for the doctor," she said. "It was the midwife or nothing."

He looked at her curiously, as though scenting the lie. "Did you feel nothing, Lucy? Ah, if I had been here—"

"I did ask you to be here!"

"Yes, and I shall be everytime hereafter when a child of ours is born. I was wrong to think it was not my responsibility," he said surprisingly. "The blame is mine."

"No one is to blame, Jonathan," she said. She knew her words were useless. She saw his mind shift about like a hand of playing cards. He was a man of action and could not wallow in his guilt. He would do something to cleanse himself. She had only a moment to wonder what.

"That midwife, Lucy! Has it occurred to you that she may have done this on purpose?"

"On purpose! Oh no, Jonathan!" Lucy had never been so taken aback. "One has only to look at her to know she is kind! On purpose! Why?"

"Because it was a Rathrock baby. When she jerked on it, she could not even see, most likely, if it were male or female. A deformed heir to the island! The fisherfolk would appreciate that!"

"Oh, Jonathan, it can't be!" she said aghast. "I could not bear to live where there was such cruelty!" She sank in the bed as though she would pull the covers over her head. "Have we made such enemies then?"

"They have never forgiven me for the storm that wrecked their boats—as if I myself raised that wind. Perhaps they view Maddie's deformity as just retribution. But whether they do or not, the midwife is incompetent. She shall not be allowed to practice any longer on Hazard Island. Babies shall not be maltreated here, be they those of yeoman or gentry."

"You will only make a fool of yourself if you forbid the midwife to practice. People will call her anyway. She is beloved. I loved her myself."

"What sentimentalists women are! You can say that even while you look on our own daughter. Only think, Lucy—it was you who rose from your bed to save her life, while the midwife did nothing. Perhaps she meant to let Maddie die. No, I shall expell that woman from the island, and we shall import someone of competence." His pacing was no longer angry; now it seemed to churn energy for the generation of his ideas.

"Hazard Island must have more than just a midwife, Lucy. It must have a doctor to take care of all our emergencies. I shall institute a tax to pay him a good wage."

"That will be very well for Hazard, Jonathan, where everyone is getting rich from shipping. But in Shipwreck—"

"Shipwreck will do as Hazard does, Lucy. Do not tell me how to run my island!"

He confided in her no more. When he was home, he played incessantly with the baby, the pair of them seeming to forsake their woes in a strange kinship. When Jonathan arrived, Lucy would dismiss the weary nurse for a few hours' rest, and more than likely she herself would fall asleep in the absence of the baby's screams.

She knew only that a tension grew about South Cottage, and that two tars with muskets were always on guard in the entrance hall, resting their weapons against the tall chairs with the Rathrock crest, playing cards on the table that held the silver bowl for calling cards.

Once she heard shouts in the night and running to the bedroom window, saw Jonathan gallop away toward Shipwreck. A queer orange glow lighted the sky, but Lucy was not yet allowed to climb to the cupola, where she might have got a better view.

She did as she usually did when she wanted information. She invited Polly Treadway to tea. Polly was not eager to talk about the incident, but at last in answer to Lucy's queries, she answered, "The captain's cutter caught on fire; didn't he tell you?"

"The new one? The one with the coe horns and swivel guns? Jonathan will be sour as bonnyclabber! How could such a thing happen?

Polly looked dark, the expression sitting oddly on her features. "It was the boat that was to take the midwife from Hazard Island."

Puzzled, Lucy leaned forward as she poured tea. "I don't understand, Polly. What has that to do with it?"

"Maybe it wasn't an accident. Maybe it was a warning!" Polly's brows arched knowingly.

"Polly! Do you mean it was arson?"

"I mean nothing. I wouldn't tell you, even if I knew. But that monster you are married to had best watch his step!"

"Jonathan is not a monster! He will get a doctor for the island, and it will be better."

"He has a nerve deciding what is best for women who are not even his kind! A doctor! A man, of course! I will not have a man coming about me that way, and neither will most women in Shipwreck. It's another woman we want for birthing. My Fitch will not sit by and let your Jonathan decide who is to attend my confinement. And as for his wretched tax—"

Lucy was not interested in the tax. She had fixed on the implications of Polly's previous statement. "Polly! Are you expecting a child?"

Her friend blushed and burst into tears. "Polly! What's wrong? You wanted more children!"

"Yes, but not like this. Who knows what the captain may do to anyone he finds conspiring against him—" She stopped, realizing she had given too much away.

"It was Fitch who organized the burning of the boat," cried Lucy. "Yes, I see that. He is the natural leader of the islanders. And Jonathan knows it, too. Fitch is another who had best watch his step!"

She lay in wait for Jonathan that evening, huddled on a brocade drawing room sofa, beneath a new set of

Audubon bird prints and a lithograph of Baudin's "Cockatoo." "Well, Jonathan, what are you to do? Will you have more boats burned or will the midwife stay?"

He stared at the unexpected sight of her. "How well you look this evening, Lucy! I did not think you would be downstairs until dinner."

"You did not answer the question, Jonathan," she insisted.

He came and sat down beside her. "You think I am a fool, Lucy?"

She said nothing. Her chin tilted upward. She had told him her views before. He gave a long, weary sigh. "Well, you are right. I will let the midwife stay."

She drew a deep breath. "And what of those who burned the cutter?"

"Fitch Treadway!" He spat out the name with a scowl. "Perhaps I should put him into the new stocks I've built outside the jail."

"Jonathan! You have not constructed such an odious device on Hazard Island!"

"Why not? It will make wrongdoers think twice," he grinned. "My rents will be paid, for there is no price too high to pay to avoid being a public laughingstock."

"And Fitch Treadway?"

"I shall not have him put in stocks, as much satisfaction as it would give me. Fitch Treadway is too valuable a man to waste in animosity. I shall have him on my side."

Lucy clapped her hands in a gesture of approval. "Oh, excellent. Do you have a plan?"

"Indeed. This winter my shipbuilders shall build a fleet of fishing boats, finer and larger than any of those destroyed by the storm. I shall hire the islanders to run them, and they will make more money working for me than they eved did before."

Lucy approved the idea, remembering that she herself had thought of the shipbuilders as a solution. Most of the islanders applauded the maneuver also. How buoyant she felt when she heard her husband cheered by the dozen or more heads of Shipwreck families he invited to the library for the unveiling of the new scheme. How proud she was then of her husband, how proud of the Rathrock name!

Hazard Island will be whole, she thought, and he has made it so. He has overcome his pride with wisdom!

But there was more pride to be overcome than Jonathan's, and Fitch Treadway's was of a height no one could scale. Fitch Treadway not only refused to sign onto the captain's fleet, but he went about from house to house and made fiery speeches at the ancient Shipwreck pub, urging others not to sign.

Jonathan was furious, since it was Fitch he had wanted most. "That fool!" he would rave. "He tells them not to give up their independence. He tells them that Shipwreck must maintain an identity separate from the Rathrock empire."

"And what do they answer, Jonathan?"

"They shake their heads and say nothing. They will be fed and clothed and do honest work. Their families will have plenty. What more could a man ask?"

"You yourself asked a great deal more of life," she reminded him.

"Ah!" he said scornfully. It was obvious that when he defined himself as a man and when he called the islanders such, he meant two quite different things.

"One cannot eat independence," he would cry. "Only look at Fitch Treadway. There he stands with nothing but a few sheep and what fish he gets with a handline. No food in the cupboard, a child on the way, and yet he will not work for me! I have never seen such a fool!"

And yet it began to seem that Jonathan almost gloried in Fitch Treadway's stubborness. He called Fitch to the library and offered to build a huge trawler and make him her captain.

Fitch stood there calmly, arms folded. "Nay, Captain. It's generous, but I'll go my own way."

"And what way will *that* be? Do you mean to starve with your wife and children?"

"Nay, Captain. I will catch enough fish for us to eat if nothing else. I will find a way."

After Jonathan had had some such conversation with Fitch Treadway, he would pace about the house charged with a peculiar excitement. "He has such faith in himself, Lucy! He cannot survive, yet he believes he will. He should be scrambling for any bit of flotsam like a drowning man, but he has not the slightest aura of haste about him."

Fitch Treadway, standing alone, fascinated Jonathan more than he ever had before, and it was easy to see that the captain had moved Fitch from the category of men which included the fisherman and had placed him in that other category with himself.

Chapter 8

That winter Hazard Island glowed with good will. Lucy regained her health, and wearing a fur-lined highland cloak with a capuchin hood, she would gallop about the island on fair days, glorying in her newly-found freedom. Her face looked so girlish, so happy, as she sped past that everyone who saw her had to smile; and without trying at all, she promoted friendship for her husband.

"The beautiful Mrs. Rathrock," the fisherman would say. "To think she is a mother, that slip of a thing!" And their load seemed lightened as she went skimming past, her cloak rippling out behind, her hands in gauntlet gloves gripping the reins, white clouds of steam from Kumrah's nostrils blending with the everpresent island mists.

She went often to see Polly, but just as often now she rode to Hazard to pay her duty calls to ladies who had arrived on the island in the summer and who had visited her or left their cards. On these visits she went more formally by carriage and usually returned bored and depressed by her hostess' longing for the civilized world.

Hazard Island did not bore Lucy. Even in winter there were a hundred different vistas of sea to be seen and forests to be explored which in summer were too tangled. The frigid air excited her. She loved to follow the trails of small animals in the snow. And when Jonathan was in a very good mood, she would tease him to take her ice skating on a small bay which remained frozen all winter.

There would be fires along its edge, and a moon would come up over the expanse, making it shine as though with a magical internal light. Jonathan was a skillful skater. He would pull her after him, twirl her, spin her, until she felt she floated in the crystalline night. She would surrender to his power, letting her feet fly where he sent her while her gleeful laugh sang into the air.

"If only I could be so pliant in bed," she would think. Jonathan had begun to love her again, but the ecstasy they had known that one time had not returned. Her body would be tense with a need for expression; a matching tenseness in him told her she dared not release herself. The moment had gone; the inhibitions, the taboos held sway once more.

But here on the ice, her spirit unlocked to him. They seemed to move in a kind of accord, and she felt the depth of his love, his admiration.

"What are you thinking, Lucy?" he asked her one such night.

"Oh, I was thinking of the very first time we danced, Jonathan. Do you remember that?"

"I do. It was a waltz. And you asked me if I could not be satisfied with England as an island. What do you think now?"

"That I could never be satisfied with England either."

"You wore camellias in those fussy ringlets, and I was bereft that I was not the lord who would carry you away."

"Bereft, Jonathan? Really? I am glad. You were quite beyond my experience of men, and I had no idea how to deal with you."

"Ah, what a coquette you were, Lucy! I declare, I believe you are becoming one again. Let us have a ball at South Cottage and put an end to all this discontent you tell me of among the ladies. You shall flirt the whole evening with me as you did for the space of that waltz."

She embraced the idea gladly. How long it had been since she had worn a new evening gown. She ordered a pale yellow moire with sleeves *enboufant* above the elbow and a skirt with flounces looped up with bows of silk ribbon. It was not the House of Worth, but the dressmaker in St. John would do the best she could, guided by pictures of the latest fashions from *The Englishwoman's Domestic Magazine* and *The Illustrated London News*.

Lucy was so caught up in the project that her mind worked on it constantly. She was thinking of table decoration and entertainment so deeply as she rode one morning that she almost did not heed the call of an old man from Shipwreck who was out hunting rabbits.

"Mrs. Rathrock! Don't ye be going to Lighthouse Head!"

"Why not?"

"There's someone there. Some stranger."

"Do you mean *no one* knows who he is?"

"No one. Camping, he is. In the old light tower. There's a glow at night—of a fire inside or of some ghostly thing, some say. A poor soul fallen from heaven to that awful spot. Stay clear, Mrs. Rathrock!"

Lucy had never been to Lighthouse Head. Just as South Cottage occupied the gentlest part of the island, so the Head was the wildest, the windiest. She had thought of going there, but always she had turned back. She was afraid of the tide that raced blackly between the two parts of the island, growling like a hungry sea monster, the white teeth of its froth gnawing at the rocks above its smooth obsidian swirls. At low tide the descent was treacherous, the violence of the waves etched like a memory into the jagged cliff.

But the matter intrigued her. "Jonathan," she said that night when they were in bed, "have you heard that someone is living on Lighthouse Head?"

"Yes, I have heard it," he returned, tucking the down-filled comforter around him.

"Then will you go there in the morning and see who it is?"

"Certainly not. I do not like the Head any more than anyone else, and I do not care who it is, so long as he does not give trouble. I have other things to attend to."

"But perhaps it is a criminal."

"If so, he is not wanted on Hazard Island, Lucy. It is none of my concern. Why does this interest you so? Go to sleep."

Lucy herself could not have said why. She tried to think it was because she worried about a possible threat to the island. Or perhaps it irritated her that she had allowed the Head to keep its secrets from her so long, when it was part of the island that was her own. Or it could have been simply the challenge, the call to adventure which had not come her way for a time?

Something immutable about herself, something she could never successfully do battle with, drove her to her horse the next morning, across the island to the edge of the cut, where she stood looking at the desolate rocks and the wind-stripped trees on the far side.

A form *was* moving there, but a very small form,

blending with the rock. An animal? Some goat that had strayed at low tide?

But the fisherman had said a light. Lucy kept watching. The form straightened and stood upright. A person! But a very small person—a dwarf—or a child! A child lost on Lighthouse Head? But what a peculiar child! It seemed to be dressed like a boy, but when the wind caught its hair, it blew out like a long, gold banner. "If only I had Jonathan's glass!" she thought.

She would have to do something about the child. She would have to go across. Her neck prickled as she made her way down a splintered ladder. Ice, made of spray thrown up from the waves and from long tails of the receding tide, glittered and dripped in the sun. The enormity of her undertaking rushed in on her as she clambered over icy boulders.

"Suppose I slip and break an ankle or a leg. No one would find me, and the water would come—"

No one would find her, except, of course, the child, for as Lucy completed her scramble across the gorge, she glimpsed movement again on the Head. Her gloves tore as she fought her way toward the plateau. The slope was gentler there and only a few weatherbeaten boards marked a kind of long-neglected catwalk.

"Hello! Hello there!" she called. The Head was silent, except for a screech of disturbed gannets, sounding as though it had been learned from the low-voiced shriek of the wind.

"Hello! I know you're there. Come out. I'm a friend!"

A little head poked up. Cunning blue eyes gleamed at Lucy with something almost like a sense of fun. This child whoever it was, was not frightened.

"Aren't you cold without a hat? Where are your parents? Well, do make me some answer. Are you a boy or a girl?"

The child made no reply. What beauty its face had, the features, as if spun of nailsea glass, the chin, heart-shaped, the cheekbones high even in the baby softness. But the eyes—how could such a tiny child, no more than four, she guessed, have such uncanny eyes? As Lucy watched the expression in the magical orbs shifted. The next second the child vanished.

It was used to hiding and eluding and without thinking what that might mean, the frustrated Lucy plunged in pursuit, in and among the grotesque spruces, across crevices streaming with wiry, frozen kelp. Now and then a flash of gold led her higher, toward the barren cliffs where the gannets and guilemots nested. Like a cloak thrown over the sea, velvet-black birds surged out, flashing orange-red legs. The terrain became sub-arctic; the growth was hummocky, like tundra, and the spruce became sparser, giving way to shrubby cinquefoil.

The child, having begun in fun, ran in earnest now. Lucy sensed growing panic in the number of stones knocked loose, and in the direction of flight, a seeming homing toward the great forboding tower of the gray lighthouse. Running *to* someone, Lucy realized. She should turn back, she thought, before she was led into this undefined danger. And yet she pressed on, driven by a concern for troubled children deep-rooted by the Belgium convent.

"Lucy!"

The voice rang in triumph from a cliff above. It was a voice she would have known in Heaven or in Hell, and suddenly she was as frozen as the kelp, as rime-frosted as the ground. It was some trick of the soughing wind. Even so, she trembled and prayed she might hear it again.

"Lucy!" The voice was louder and more insistent. It was not the wind. "Truly I did fall crossing the cut," Lucy thought. "I struck my head, and now the water has taken me and I am dead." How beautiful was death that she should hear this voice in it! Her head lifted without her willing it, as though to offer praise and thanksgiving at last to the Almighty, who was kind after all.

She saw at once that Galen Le Blanc, on the ledge above her, was no celestial vision. Every nuance of his body was remembered as he came scrambling down to her. The beloved face was against hers, tougher than it had been; and the arms that held her were harder. And yet everything was the same. The mouth kissing her brought the same flash of love and passion, and she gave herself to the frenzy of it while tears froze on her cheeks.

Unfastening her cloak and his, he pulled her to a sheltered spot on the mossy hummocks and wrapped their two bodies together as one. From the distance of her rapture, she wondered what had happened to the child. *Alyce,* she thought, choking with disbelieving sobs.

The child with the beautiful face and strange eyes was her lost daughter.

"We'll go to the lighthouse," he said. "There's a fire."

At first it seemed even colder inside the lighthouse. A flight of stone steps led up from the bottom floor, and there on the next level, the fire burned cozily and the aroma of woodsmoke hung thick. Beyond the kitchen were two small bedrooms, limp mattresses strung across cannonball bedsteads. On one bed lay a small cloth doll.

Alyce had been sent away, for his hands moved familiarly inside her bodice. A button broke from her skirt as he shoved down inside it. It might have been yesterday that she had last felt his touch, so right did it seem, and her body strained helplessly toward him.

"I shall never love anyone but him," she thought, just as she had when the monarchy of Louis Philippe had fallen, and he had taken her for the first time.

Everything that had been so long hopeless within her, all that had been repressed, seemed to explode inside her. And then suddenly she pushed him away, no easy task, for he clung to her as though he had become a part of her.

"Galen! Galen, I am married!"

"I know you are married. It could not be helped. You thought I was dead."

"I saw your grave!"

"I paid some Turks to dig it. How else was I to be free? How else was I to remain alive? I was under sentence of death because of the boat I tried to commandeer to sail back to you. Oh, the agonies I have suffered, Lucy, since I have known you found not me, but my grave! But I have found you, as I would have done, had it taken a thousand years."

"And I should have waited for you, but I thought I could not. There was Alyce, so I went to Africa. *You* stole her from the convent!"

"Yes. I knew you would never be able to care for her, so I disguised myself and sneaked back to France. Pauline told me where to find the baby. My disguise must not have been very good, because we were quickly on the run again. But together. We have each been all the other had. You have not been easy to find. I risked my neck in England, but your cousin would tell me nothing. We traveled from continent to continent, Alyce and I. I suppose it was fated that we should cross paths with a sailor from *The Lucy Maid*. 'Lucy's a beautiful name,' I told him. 'But not so beautiful as the lady she's named for,' he replied. And when he sang your praises, I knew he could mean no other than my Lucy."

He lifted her expertly and carried her to a bed. "Now I shall know completeness again."

"Galen!" she cried, nearly hysterical. "I am married!"

"A mere inconvenience, Lucy. I don't blame you. You shall leave him of course, and come with me to the United States. There is one place I have not a price on my head."

"Leave him! I have a child, Galen. And I have given my word! You were right; marriage *is* a prison. You failed to imprison me and now another has."

"You have a child by me, too, and you have given me your love. You married, of course. You were forced to do so. You struck a bargain with Jonathan Rathrock for your survival, just as I did with the Turks. It is the foulness of society that is to blame—the society we fought. No covenant is more sacred than the one you made with me. You are mine, Lucy."

Somehow her skirt and petticoats were on the floor. Her bodice had gone as though of its own accord. Her ripe breasts shivered inside her thin chemise, as he loosened its strings, lifting them into his hands to warm them with its touch.

She stared down at herself as though she had never before seen the delicate tracing of blue veins that the nursing had brought, the swollen plum-colored nipples. With a cry of anguish she leaped up, and snatching her heavy cloak about her, fled from the lighthouse without stopping for her clothes.

She ran headlong, starting rockslides where her feet hit uncertainly, falling and jumping up again before her body had even settled. If he followed her, if he caught her, she would be lost.

But Galen did not follow. She gained the main part of the island, and mounting Kumrah, galloped home, mindless of the dangers of such speed on the icy road.

Straight up the polished stairs of South Cottage she

ran, into her room, where she threw off the cloak before the bright hearth and climbed shivering into bed.

Two days passed before Lucy rose again, as if the torment of her soul left no strength for the mundane functions of her life. She thought back on her marriage to Jonathan. Was it true that she had made a bargain with him for survival?

Yes, of course, it was true in a way. She had been the cast-off of Charles Ashton, a woman of questionable reputation and no prospects. Her father had meant to send her off to a life as a governess, if anyone could be found to have her. How *should* she have survived if not for Jonathan? "Even as a mere governess in England, I should not have lasted," she thought, "while here I am queen of all I see."

And yet it could not be said that the bargain had been made cold-bloodedly. She remembered how he had stood by her on Gibraltar and how she had missed him afterward. She thought of the kiss he had given her when he had come to Callow Hill to ask her hand. How charged he had been with adventure, with the triumph of his success in acquiring his island! Even then she had loved Jonathan Rathrock in a fashion. And now?

What was between them had grown stronger. It was a love that had almost never been defined in bed, and yet at least once, it had been. There was a comradeship, a mutual dependence, a jointness of purpose. He did not treat her as Galen had, as an equal, but he admitted that she had a good mind for a woman. He terrified her with his temper, but never struck out at her. He demanded obedience, but when she could not give it, she could circumvent him. He scorned her advice—and then took it, more than he would ever admit.

If Galen had married her, how would it have been? But Galen had had his mind on higher things. And she had not asked for marriage. She had taken up his challenge to fight the forces that made women as dependent on men as she had been on Jonathan.

Jonathan Rathrock had chosen well in Lucy. "You are a woman who can make commitments to which no persuasion, no hardship, can ever make you false," he had said, and he had been right. For beyond her longing for Galen, her commitment held her, just as it had that moment on the bed in the light tower.

They would bring Maddie to her, and she would weep both with devotion for the little cripple and with yearning for the wily Alyce scampering on the cliffs.

Jonathan, all concerned, hovered at her bedside. "What are all these scratches on your hands?" he asked her once.

"Nothing. I fell from Kumrah and landed in a blackberry bush."

"You fell! Perhaps you are injured in a way you do not know. I'll send for the doctor from St. John."

"No. I only rode too far and caught a chill. I shall be all right, Jonathan."

He knew the tone of determination and was content. "You will have to wear black evening mittens to the ball on Friday," he reflected, studying the scratches.

The ball! She had forgotten it! It was the first major entertainment that had been given at South Cottage. It must not be a fiasco! The next morning she left her bed for the duty of attending to it.

Every floor was polished, every window washed, the chandeliers dusted. The silver and crystal were brought out and the facet-cut centerpieces with hanging baskets for sweetmeats. From the steaming kitchen came a succession of delicacies: stuffed partridges in aspic, roasted truffles, lobster au gratin, liqueur-flavored jellies, meringue baskets, charlotte russe.

The winter island afforded no flowers, but there were pine boughs and juniper berries in startling contrast to asparagus fern and fan palms brought in from the conservatory.

Lucy worked with a frenzy. The maids drooped with exhaustion, and if they thought that their work was done, Lucy was sure to require a brighter shine on the woodwork or decide that the prisms of every light must be removed to wash away the oil soot. But the wall Lucy threw up against thoughts of Galen was not enough. What would he do? Had he really gone from the island to where she would never hear of him and Alyce again?

Each morning when she rose and every afternoon when worked lagged, she would think of Kumrah idle in the stables. She would want to ride off across the island to catch him before he vanished, this time forever.

Jonathan was pleased with the house. He was pleased with Lucy in her pale yellow dress and a Runic necklace, her hair done in a new way, rolled over hair pads that only recently had arrived on her order from England. She liked the satisfied way he looked at her, with a mingling of gratitude and pride. He danced the first dance with her over the honey-colored floors of the drawing room and morning room, between which the double folding door had been pushed open to make space.

Three violinists from St. John sat before a flower stand of ivy geraniums, gilt buttons flashing on their crimson waistcoats as waltzes wavered into the air.

"We have done well, Lucy," Jonathan said.

"Yes. Everyone has come. Even the governor and his wife."

"But I meant more. Our dream is coming true. We are becoming important. Our ships rule these waters as the fleets of Britain the Atlantic. Our blood will run deep on Hazard Island."

"You have not a son, Jonathan." It was an apology, the first time she had dared to hint at the disappointment she knew was in his heart.

"I would not change Maddie," he said gaily. "Next time we shall have a son. Hazard Island can wait one more year for its heir."

She shuddered at the thought of a new pregnancy, but she was a woman and childbirth was a duty. The dance ended and she turned away, looking for a glass of wine to banish the dismal thought. When a hand touched her elbow familiarly, she thought it was still Jonathan.

"Yes, dear?" she said absently.

"That is a start at least," said a voice too soft for Jonathan's.

She whirled. "Galen!" Where had he got those clothes while he had been on the run, she wondered, for she had never seen him so resplendent as in this flowered damson waistcoat, mosaic watch guard and pair of primrose-colored gloves.

"I have come to take you away, Lucy," he said into her stupefied silence. "Dance with me or we shall be noticed."

She danced with him, tripping over the bottom flounce of her gown, her face flushing with the wonderful closeness of him. "Galen," she gasped at last, "you're mad! You were not even invited!"

"Of course not," he said. "One does not invite a thief, and that is why I come tonight, to steal away the most priceless Rathrock treasure."

He had a look about him, an exultation that reminded

her of the time she had helped him elude the police on the Dover ferry. How he had stirred her, even then, with his determination to right the world single-handed! Suddenly she felt the old emotions of revolt rise in her. A current of freedom swept her. She was again *La Flamme*, for whom no restriction of society held terror. She would go with him anywhere!

He sensed that his ploy had worked, and he danced her toward the stairs. "Pack a reticule. Meet me at the stables."

She resisted, and they swayed away like a boat missing dockage. "I have given my word to Jonathan!" she whispered. His hand tightened at her waist. "Your heart knows it is not married to Jonathan Rathrock! Come with me or every day of your life will be a lie!"

He swung again toward the stairs, and this time she ran up, like a kite blown in a gust of wind, while he still held the string of her heart to guide her.

Suddenly screams bore in on her, intruding on the beautiful sense of unreality that had come over her. The baby was crying in a soul-consuming way, and instinctively she turned in at the nursery. The night nanny was standing helplessly in the center of the room holding the child, whose perspiration-dampened gown showed that the siege must have gone on for many minutes.

"Why didn't you call me?" cried Lucy sternly, taking the baby. Maddie's arms and legs flailed as she screamed even louder.

The nanny looked astonished. "But it's nothing unusual, my lady, as you well know. And you were dancing."

It was not the crying that was unusual, but the nanny could not be expected to understand why Lucy was aroused to such protectiveness.

"Go and get the captain!" she ordered.

"The captain! Bother the master over a crying baby!"

"He is the only one who can calm her."

She held Maddie until Jonathan came, feeling eerily that the baby cried so because she had been born without innocence as another might without a toe or finger, and that she sensed already the misery of life. She thought that Maddie seemed glad to prevent her mother's flight. "How dare you forget your duty to me?" her resentful wails seemed to say. "I who will always be a cripple because of your affair! Do you think I will let you have him now?"

As she left her lover to cool his ardor in the night air of the stables, an equal, weary resentment grew in her. Her husband came and comforted their daughter until she fell asleep, and watching them, Lucy wished she could be so comforted herself.

Chapter 9

After the ball she climbed to the widow's walk each day to look with a spy glass toward the part of the island that was Galen's hideaway. Or was it his hideaway any longer? Had he gone? She had seen no sign since she had left him to wait for her that night. She had never known a spot could look as vacant and desolate as the Head, its emptiness echoing the emptiness in her heart. A gull would lift off lazily, and she would think for an instant the movement was human; or the grasses would blow and she would think she glimpsed Alyce's hair.

They had gone.

She was beginning to accept the idea, and then one night at dusk she saw the light in the tower wink on. It was still there after dinner and even in the small hours when she crept from her bed up the black steps of the cupola. It came the next night and the next, haunting her with its presence. At last she could stand it no longer, and mounting Kumrah, rode off to the spit.

Galen came down to the cut to meet her as she clambered over the rocks. He did not reach out to kiss her, and she did not know whether she was more wounded or relieved. "Ah, Mrs. Rathrock," he said scornfully.

"Galen, you are lighting that tower on purpose to torment me!" she accused.

He smiled wryly. "A beacon to love, Lucy? It is you who make it so. I have merely taken a job."

"A job!"

"Your husband was kind enough to offer it to me. Hazard Island has long needed a lighthouse keeper, and since I am living here the idea seemed sensible. I am tired of running. I will be of some use here, doing, as usual, a task for which others have no stomach, and trying to bring light where there has been none."

"You have met my husband!"

"He came to see me a day or so after the ball."

"What did you tell him?"

"The truth," he said, smiling at her flabbergasted look. "I said I was an agitator with a price on my head."

"You know there will be bloodshed if he finds out what you have been to me!" she cried.

Galen shrugged. "So he is a violent man at times. You forget that I disposed of a share of gunpowder in Paris myself. Perhaps I will spill his blood instead of he mine. Either way it would be ended. But I shall not be the cause of it. It is not with him but you that I have something to settle. I shall not make another move toward you, but I will never leave Hazard Island until you come, too."

"And Alyce?"

"I shall keep her from you until you are ready to be her mother."

For days longer Lucy frequented the cupola, staring hollow-eyed at the pinpoint of light that marked as well as shoals, the location of her heart. Then one morning she declared that the steps were too steep to be safe. Maddie would be walking soon and must never wander there with her twisted leg. And she ordered a workman to nail boards across the door.

For Lucy Rathrock time and meaning had dissolved into that small glow of light which burned in her heart, though she no longer saw it with her eyes. It guided her husband's ships and the new fishing fleet past treacherous channels and among the dreaded boring stones. Hazard Island had a new aura of civilization and security. Every wife slept better at night, blessing the captain for the light—all except Lucy, who knew that it burned no more to save ships from wreckage than to lure her life onto reefs.

Each night it made its statement of constancy; it glimmered its promise across the dark rocks and the waves. It spoke of a faith in her love that was almost insolent.

Head bowed in church Lucy would hear the captain end his prayers, "God bless this island and the light that leads us home to her. God protect the Hazard Light."

She would pray that she would never answer its summons. He had said he would stay until she came, and she believed him. He had a will as strong as the New Brunswick ironwood tree, which could hardly be felled. Could she outlast him? In every fiber he believed in what he was doing while she was divided. He had that advantage over her. But she at least was set into a life. Could a man like Galen, whose great talent was the moving of others, exist indefinitely as a hermit on the barrenness of Lighthouse Head?

In the spring he built a weir and acquired a small boat. After that he would be on the docks in Shipwreck several times a week, taking his catch to the smokehouse. The fishermen were wary of him; he was a crimnal, they'd heard. But the shy little daughter drew them. Lucy would ride to Shipwreck in hopes of hearing word of the pair.

The little tyke helped her father with the nets, Lucy was told. Indecent that was, for a girl. As for Galen Le Blanc, he was peculiar, given to odd pronouncements. One day he had remarked that Queen Victoria had less claim to heaven than any fishwife, having contributed to the world not even a crate of dried herring. Such sentiments did not ingratiate him to the islanders, who perceived, not a compliment to themselves, but only an insult to the Queen.

"He'd not speak so of a French king," they mistakenly declared.

"Ah, he'd be rotting in Newgate Prison if the Queen caught him. He fled England, they say."

Lucy would be amused at how little Galen was understood. There were no revolutionaries on Hazard Island, and Galen did so need an audience. Only one man did not laugh at Galen Le Blanc. Fitch Treadway would suck on his pipe, and his eyes would darken like small sphagnum bogs, collecting all manner of thought from the wind-reddened tributaries of his face.

"Le Blanc has more education and more vision than anyone who has yet lived on Hazard Island," he said once, while Lucy sat at tea with Polly. She noticed that he did not exclude himself or Jonathan. She did not quite like it for some reason, and the comment did not leave her mind for days.

In midsummer, just as the water arum bloomed its finest in the island ponds and the air was heavy with the scent of balsam and meadowsweet, Polly Treadway's baby was born and, having given one wail to mark its existence, died.

Lucy was sent for at once. There was something of relief in the arduous task of comforting her friend, who had gone innocent and unfearing to childbed, for here was a matter that banished the Hazard Light from every corner of her mind.

Polly clutched Lucy's arm and put a pair of inlaid mother of pearl scissors into her hand. "Go and cut a lock of his hair for a mourning ring," she begged. "It must be no one but you."

She went into the room where the baby already lay in its tiny coffin, and snipping the fine-spun curls, her hand grazed the cold cheek that should have been soft and warm. Suddenly her heart broke, not only for this infant, named Jeremy, but for Alyce, the child whom she had lost in another way.

She followed the baby to its grave in the Shipwreck churchyard, and Jonathan, to her surprise, went with her. She knew that he went out of kindness, but Fitch Treadway glared at him over the mound of his son's grave, and Lucy shuddered at the look in his eyes.

"Why did he look at you so bitterly, Jonathan?" she asked as they drove home.

"I suppose he thinks I came to gloat. I did not, of course."

"Of course not! Why would he think you had?"

"Because if he had not made the trouble over sending the midwife away, if he had not organized everyone against the tax, we would have had a doctor on the island, and most likely this would not have happened."

"But it was Polly who insisted on the midwife. She would not have the doctor. He did it for her. It wasn't Fitch's fault."

He looked at her ruefully as they pulled into the lane of South Cottage, and Maddie ran down to meet them with her queer, listing gait. "Polly Treadway is a foolish woman, but it is not always easy to keep from blaming oneself. I should know."

She sighed, as he swung the little girl into his arms, and wondered if he thought her a foolish woman, too.

How quickly Maddie grew! It seemed to Lucy that the first word she lisped was "captain." And so she always addressed her father, always captain, never Papa. Jonathan thought it was delightful. Never a voyage ended that he did not arrive with presents—a babyhouse peopled with silver figures and furniture of ivory and rosewood— japanned tinware for her tea parties, a kitchen doll whose skirts opened like a cupboard on shelves and hooks for tiny copper pots.

When he was leaving to go to sea Maddie would inevitably hear him, and rushing from her room in the pinkening dawn, she would beg to be taken to the docks to see him off. "No, Maddie, no," he would say, but there would be no conviction in his voice. A sleepy nanny would dress her while he waited, and they would all leave together.

"She is spoiled," Lucy would think, lying tense and wakeful, hearing laughter in the drive. "And she is wilful, like me, only more so. I was a pretty girl at least, and Maddie will not be. Handsome perhaps, if it were not for that limp. She has a kind of strength about her that would be attractive if she were a man. And if she had been a male, she could have run Hazard Island without a bobble, limp and all."

In the grayness a love would well in Lucy's heart which later in the day would be hard to transmit to her daughter. Beginning with the morning porridge, the trouble would start. "The captain said I might have cake!" Maddie would declare and push the bowl away.

"Maddie! Your nose will grow long with such lies!"

" I shall get my cake from cook herself," Maddie would declare; and then Lucy would have to bar the door with her body, for cook was more terrified of a tantrum from Maddie than of a scolding from Lucy.

After a few token spoonfuls of the cereal had been shoved down, Lucy would face the agony of dressing her. There was so much to get on—the drawers and leglets, the petticoats and dress, and lastly the hair to be brushed while the protesting Maddie squirmed under the bed, smearing dust on her freshly-starched pinafore. Lucy and the nanny would struggle together, and Lucy would read the nanny's mind wondering how soon she could make her beau suggest marriage. The young nannies never stayed long. They married sailors with a rapidity which made Lucy think that Maddie drove them to unusual coquetry.

"If only we had another child perhaps that would help," Lucy would say, but only to herself or Polly. Jonathan did not see any problem with Maddie; since when he was in the house, the tension went out of the air.

Had something happened at Maddie's birth to prevent another pregnancy? She was driven at last to see the doctor in St. John. She blushed crimson explaining her problem and was even more embarrassed when nothing was wrong. Though Jonathan said nothing, Lucy's sense of worth began to seep from her. She paid less attention to fashion journals and took less pleasure in the island. What would become of it without a Rathrock son?

"It is not my fault," she told herself angrily. But she believed it was. She believed that it was the longing of her body for the kind of love she had known in Paris that prevented her conceiving. That was an affliction no doctor could cure. She herself must provide the cure, and she fought more than ever to put Galen from her mind. But what she banished in the day came back at night, repression making it the stronger in her dreams. One night she woke from a particularly vivid imagining to see Jonathan sitting up in bed looking down on her speculatively.

Instinctively she pulled the covers tighter about her as if the unfulfilled fever of her body might be visible through her skin. She wondered what she might have moaned in her sleep.

"Lucy, do you remember the first winter we were married—the night my bed caught fire in the storm?"

"Yes, of course. And you have never slept there since. Are you afraid it will happen again?"

He smiled at her teasing. "I had a different reason. I wanted to keep something I found here that night. But it slipped away almost at once. Do you know what I mean? Did you feel it, too?"

"Yes, Jonathan." She touched his cheek. He knew less about love than she did, she saw suddenly. He seemed as hesitant and confused as a boy.

"I have been lonely for that ever since, Lucy. Could you not love me again that way?"

"I dare not, Jonathan. It would make me baggage."

"No, no. I have lain with whores and never known the pleasure I knew that night. It was more than pleasure; in that moment I thought I conquered all my oceans. I suppose it made the difference that I love you."

She leaned across him and reached for the china cottage on the bedside table, glowing with the night light of her mortar candle. "Very well, then. Let us burn the bed again. It will make a cheery blaze in but a minute."

He caught her, both of them laughing as he pulled away her gown. He waited then for her to strip him of his nightshirt, a thing he had never done before, and they tumbled together naked and unabashed. Her fingers caught in the bright mane of his hair; she pulled his face to hers, and their bodies moved in beautiful unison. When it was finshed, she would not be parted from him, and her tears of release ran down onto his cheeks.

Jonathan had acquired a wisdom, but within the month the joy that attended the big half-tester bed had ceased. Lucy was pregnant.

"Jonathan, do not stop loving me!" she begged. "It will hurt nothing."

"I am not such a fool as to take such a chance with my heir, Lucy. God knows we have waited for it long enough." And he gave her a censorous look, as if the activities of the past weeks were all at once lewd and unsuitable, since she was a mother-to-be.

She felt betrayed, and the betrayal spoiled her happiness at having conceived. "No sooner does he start the baby than he is finished with love, and I am left with the discomfort to come. Oh, *he* was not that way. How different it was when I carried the child of Galen Le Blanc! Galen did not treat me as a brood mare!" Her husband had had her for a moment, but now a reserve grew between them again. They were partners in the production of an heir, and in little except that were they united.

Through the months of her pregnancy Jonathan withdrew from the coldness of her bed to his own chamber. He spent long evenings smoking and talking with his ships' masters, and when they had gone, he would criticize her for reading instead of doing needlework.

"It is no wonder you cannot sew," he would rage. "You never try. You have not made one gown for the baby."

"Maddie's will be good enough," she would reply, and she buried herself even more deeply in the books. The challenge of Jonathan's dream had paled. She longed for the life she had had in Paris. She longed to be *La Flamme* and move the world. When she could stand it no longer, she would go to her davenport desk and pen articles, which she would throw into the fire before Jonathan came home. And she had the door to the cupola unboarded, so that she could climb up to gaze on the shimmer of the still-constant Hazard Light.

Even so, the months of her pregnancy were happier than those of the previous one that had produced Maddie. Spring came, and Jonathan did not leave the island. He would be gone all morning to the docks, never missing the arrival of a ship, and in the afternoons he would climb restlessly to the cupola to scan the sea with his glass.

"Jonathan, it is better than three months yet," she would tell him. "You have time for one voyage at least to Jamaica or the Bahamas."

"I will stay here, Lucy," he would answer.

So there were picnics and long walks on the beaches. They built huge sand castles with Maddie on the gray sands and watched the bottle-nosed dolphins at play beyond the surf. They searched the woods for puffballs and beaver dams to delight the little girl, and they sailed about the harbor in a sloop-rigged dinghy.

The fishermen were less happy than Lucy to have Jonathan on the island. He poked in everywhere, reorganizing, banishing sloth and inefficiency wherever he found it. He boarded one boat after another, complaining of dirt, of faulty rigging, of waste in fish scales not swept up for the making of buttons and paint. And if the miscreants did not immediately step to, Jonathan had them thrown in stocks. Scarcely a day passed that the town of Hazard did not have the entertainment of watching one of them with the island's black flies and mosquitoes buzzing about his nose while he was helpless to fend them off.

"Jonathan, you must find some other way," Lucy would say. "They are fishermen after all; it is not the Navy."

"Ah! In the Navy a man would be flogged. This is gentle punishment, Lucy. It is a fishing fleet; but it is my fishing fleet. It shall be run to the utmost of its potential, and if there are those who cannot measure up, then we will weed them out."

A number of fishermen did leave the fleet. Once they would have had no place to go, but now a long, ramshackled structure on Shipwreck's waterfront provided an alternative. Fitch Treadway had started a cannery.

It had astounded everyone, including Jonathan Rathrock. Captain Rathrock had marched about South Cottage, clapping his hand to his forehead. "How did he get the Bank of New Brunswick to sponsor him! He has nothing!"

"He has a sound idea, Jonathan, and he has himself. He can hardly fail. The Bay of Fundy is so rife with lobster that they are used to fertilize the corn. All that is needed is a way to get them to market, and we have ships for that."

Jonathan had been quick to see that the cannery would benefit him as well as Fitch Treadway. He gave his permission for the construction, and since he reserved a percentage of profits in rental of the land, he did not mind when Fitch succeeded so well in lobster that he branched into salmon.

The cannery provided a substantial source of cargo for the Rathrock ships, which suited Jonathan exactly. "Hazard Island is a family," he was fond of saying. "We are all interdependent."

But Fitch Treadway, although he was growing rich, did not seem satisfied. Unlike Jonathan, he was not the "family's" patriarch. He took to wearing velvet waistcoats and built a new house which he called North Pines.

"North Pines—South Cottage," Jonathan fumed. "He is trying to be as important as I am!"

"Fitch will spend all his life trying to best Jonathan," Lucy would think, "and God help us if he ever finds a way!"

Jonathan would tip his hat and snarl a "Good day" to Fitch when they met. He knew that he needed Fitch Treadway. The threat, the opposition, provided his life with a meat that was as essential as the garnished round of veal on the dinner table.

Jonathan imported the doctor that summer, at last, instituting the tax to pay him and building him a turreted house outside Hazard where he could be summoned quickly to South Cottage. There was much grumbling in Shipwreck about the location of the house, about the tax and about the timing of the doctor's arrival, just before the birth of the captain's child.

The awful dread grew again in Lucy, as it had before Maddie's birth. "It is simply something that I do not do well," she told herself. And she would try to banish the terror by yanking the bedcurtains around the brass tester or more simply by pulling the quilts over her head.

The first harbingers of birth came to her softly. She seemed to be drifting over strange, green waves. Eider ducks coasted by and sea gulls fluttered on the crests. She wakened in disbelief. It could not be so gentle. And yet, what else? She called for Jonathan.

After he had sent for the doctor, he held her hand through hours of steady pain. The sundering came quickly, catching her by surprise, and in panic she gripped her husband by both arms. That was all. It was over that easily. Jonathan left her side even as the baby cried. She heard cannon begin to fire and knew that he had signaled the salute from the cupola.

She did not have to be told that the baby was a boy.

She had got the knack of it at last. Thinking back over the hours of her confinement, they seemed almost pleasant. The heir of Hazard Island about to make his appearance—Jonathan beside her, more totally caught up with her than she had ever seen him with any of his ships, his face awed at her grit in a sort of contest which, though new to him, impressed him as much as though it had been done with guns or swords. How lovely it had been to bask in his admiration! She had almost been grateful to the pain that made her seem so important to him.

What triumph, what utter justification of her existence she had felt that moment she had seen the red, twisting baby in the air; and amid its screams, the cannon had begun to fire! It was the sort of exultation that Jonathan must know when an enemy stronghold had surrendered to his siege or when he had guided one of his clippers unscathed through a hurricane. The same kind of need that kept Jonathan at sea now ran in Lucy's blood, too. She wanted to birth child after child.

Jonathan treated her with a new reverence. She accepted it without question, not knowing whether it came because she was now the mother of his son or because of the struggle he had witnessed. Whichever, she took it as her due; and when she went downstairs again, she carried herself with more dignity. She had accomplished the utmost life required of her. She had fulfilled her pledge to Jonathan, who had once sworn that no one but she would be the mother of his dynasty.

A dynasty? This one tiny boy who could be held cupped in the palms of two hands? Bryan Rathrock, quickly nicknamed Brye, lay quietly in his cradle as though studying the weight of his destiny. He would be handsome, Lucy saw. Already his fawn-colored curls glimmered with titian Rathrock highlights, while his features, beneath his father's full brows, had a beauty that almost reminded her of his half-sister, Alyce.

She had been almost afraid to pick up the little jewel-like baby, on whom, more than any number of diamonds and rubies, the Rathrock fortune depended. But at length he had given a cry, and she had lifted him, expecting a tirade like one of Maddie's. Instead he had sighed and snuggled against her bosom as though recognizing home. She was touched as she held him there, the sun setting, glowing through the window, diffusing into the lacy fineness of his hair. She knew he would be her child, just as Maddie was Jonathan's, and that the love between them would have a simplicity, a purity she had yet to experience.

Chapter 10

She had not seen Galen Le Blanc since he had begun to keep the lighthouse, swearing he would not leave the island without her. But that winter in the company of her infant son, her life was content. She was no longer afraid of her French lover, believing her life could not now be destroyed by her love for him. His face came to her mind only infrequently, thoughts of Paris, almost never. She thought herself mature and sensible, newly poised and self-assured. The flights of youth were past with all their wonder and their troublesome consequences. Why did Galen stay? He had said forever, and she supposed he might waste his life senselessly on Lighthouse Head, keeping his vow simply to spite her.

When she looked to the light now, it was only with thoughts of Alyce, she told herself. Galen's life was his own to spoil, but not Alyce's. What would become of her, growing up in isolation there?

The more Brye with his sweet baby ways reminded her of that long-ago time with Alyce in the convent, the more determined Lucy became to do something about her. One bright spring day she had Kumrah saddled and set off for the Head. It was the soft kind of day the island rarely knew. Only a few wisps of fog lingered in the woods, like birds lost from the flock. The tall lupines melded their pastel colors against the sky, and a purple finch sang a long, twisting song from the top of a dead spruce. Once in a while the road would come out of the forest into a field smelling like new hay from the delicate, pale green hay fern that grew there. The day lulled Lucy. A few baby lobsters were playing in the trickle of water in the cut, as Lucy climbed down the rickety ladder and hiked up the riflecloth skirt of her new riding habit to wade across. As before Alyce waited on the other side, as if an uncanny sense had told her of Lucy's approach.

She had grown tall and lithe, and the softness had gone

from the expressive framework of her face. Though she was still dressed like a boy in an oversized cambric shirt and a pair of cut-off trousers, she was as beautiful as though she, like the lupines, had been born of the spring morning. Lucy caught her breath, fearful she would run away as she had the other time.

"Alyce!" she called.

The little girl showed no sign of flight, almost as if an earlier training to run had been replaced by admonitions to stand her ground. She shifted a straw basket on her arm and studied her mother.

"Mrs. Rathrock?"

"Yes. How do you know who I am?"

"My father told me. You came here once before."

"And you have remembered all this time!"

"Of course. You are the only woman who has ever come here. My father said it was because you have more heart for adventure than other women. I am going to feed fish heads to the seals. Do you want to come with me?"

So they clambered up and down the cliffs of Lighthouse Head, Alyce showing Lucy all her favorite places, speaking in a soft French accent like Galen's. Galen was out with his fishing boat and that gave mother and daughter the entire afternoon together. Lucy was the first friend Alyce had ever had, and she saw worship begin to dawn in the child's eyes.

"Don't you wish you lived with other children, Alyce?" Lucy asked.

"I don't know. I have a flock of sheep—well, there are four of them—to play with. And some eiders. We feed them every day and twice a year we sell their down."

"Why does your father stay here in this lonely spot?"

"We are waiting for my mother."

"Your mother! And where is your mother?"

"I don't know. There was a war in France, and my mother and father became separated. My mother was beautiful and wrote for my father's paper, and she even fought in the streets. I am going to be like her when I grow up. My father says she will find us someday if we are patient and wait for her."

"Wouldn't you sooner go away from here, Alyce?"

"No. I pray every night that she will come." Alyce looked out across the bay, and her blue eyes filled with longing. Lucy gripped the rocks to prevent herself from throwing her arms around her daughter to acknowledge her.

The child gave a sigh, and broke the mood in a grown-up way, saying, "Would you like some tea and sponge cake? I have some at the light tower."

Lucy accepted the offer and found the kitchen she had visited long ago made gay with bits of shellwork and childish watercolors. They were still sitting at the table when Galen came in. The mixture of passion and triumph that suddenly suffused his face told her what interpretation he put on her presence here.

"Go outside, Alyce," he said in a low voice.

"But, Papa—"

"Go!"

Alyce fled, and Lucy, her heart lurching, leaped from her chair, feeling as vulnerable as though she were naked. She thought he would seize her in his arms. Already she felt faint with anticipation.

Instead he looked at her warily. "So! Have you decided to leave that husband of yours?"

"No, Galen."

"Then what are you doing here? I told you you could not see Alyce until you would be a proper mother!"

"Do not order me about so. You will begin to remind me of Jonathan. And do not tell me what right I have. For if I have not been a proper mother, neither have you been a proper father."

"I?" He seemed genuinely astonished.

"Only look at her. Has she a dress to her name? Or a bonnet?"

"She wears what is practical for living here."

"Ah! That is exactly the point. Alyce should not be living here. She will grow up thinking she is a mountain goat or worse. Where is she to learn culture, manners, all that she needs?"

"I have not neglected Alyce's education, Lucy. She is well-schooled. She has even begun to read Greek plays."

He was standing very close to her, too close, she realized suddenly. The current of his attraction pulled her like a swift undertow. His face rippled with memories, not faded over the years, but set more deeply with the passing of time. His love for her had been his whole life; the love she had given him, she could not reclaim. All the while she had thought herself in control he had nourished her love with his singleminded devotion, presenting it to her now stronger, more compelling than ever before.

He took her chin in his hand and tilted it up. "We will take her away, then, Lucy. Come, you have done your duty by Jonathan Rathrock. You have given him his son. Now come away with me. Climb to the top of Wailing Widow Cliff and throw off your hat and your shoes. Everyone would think you were dead. It would be that simple."

"No!" She choked out the word. It would mean leaving Brye! Her Brye motherless! Or worse, in the clutches of a stepmother. She could more easily have shared a lover with another woman than Brye.

His hands took her shoulders, hurting her with his grasp. "Once we overthrew a king, Lucy, and now you share a bed with one. I will not say you are married to one, for I do not recognize that marriage. Well, so it be. Hail, Queen Lucy!"

"Galen, go away from here. Take Alyce, whose future matters to both of us. I can never come to you."

"You will come, Lucy. Someday you will be through denying what you are."

"Let me go, Galen!"

He released her, though she felt a reluctance in the lessening of his grip. "Do not worry about Alyce," he said in a softer tone. "Even though she stays on Lighthouse Head, I will make something fine of her. She will be more than something to be auctioned away to a husband when she is eighteen. She has your love of books and your talent with words. I may make a novelist of her. A lady may at least pen romances. Go quickly if you must. Think of the tide. It will be coming in."

He turned his back on her, and she wished that he still held her in his hurtful grasp, protecting her against the deeper pain she felt as she ran out of the tower and across the head to the cut. An angry froth was rushing over the rocks. Lucy was soaked to the waist when she reached the other side, so rapidly was the water rising. Wide-eyed and breathless, she looked back, realizing how foolhardy she had been to risk the crossing. But the fate she would have succumbed to on the other side had been certain. It was a much-shaken Lucy who returned to South Cottage and took her baby son into her arms.

The housemaids remarked on it among themselves. "How Mrs. Rathrock does dote on the little one," they said.

"Yes, she but goes for an afternoon's ride, and she acts as though she thought she would never see the tyke again!"

And they chuckled at the devotedness of mothers.

Night after night the Hazard Light winked on, and Lucy, watching it in the soft spring air, gradually formed a plan. She could not have Galen, but she would have Alyce. The captain might not approve Lucy's idea, but Lucy had learned a simple way to get around him. She had only to wait until he departed on one of his longer voyages, and then she could do as she wished. She would live in dread of his return, of course, though at times he did not even notice the changes she had made. On other occasions he ranted, but the matter would have been accomplished and he seldom bothered to put it to rights.

Lucy intended to start a school for a few of the daughters of Hazard's sea captains. Some one of the island's governesses could be recruited to deal with the troublesome needlework, while Lucy herself would teach academics. A school would benefit Maddie wonderfully. She would have companionship every day and learn to handle herself among other children. Jonathan would be pleased with that. If Maddie liked the school, he would probably allow it to continue.

But her other daughter was the real reason for the school. Would Galen send her? She wrote a note to him and sent a messenger with it to Lighthouse Head. He made no reply, but on the first day of classes, there was Alyce in a fresh blue dimity dress and a white apron, her golden hair loose, curling about her shoulders.

Teacher could not rush to embrace pupil, so Lucy, fighting to contain her joy, made do with a smile for Alyce, whose eyes lighted with relief at the sight of her friend.

Alyce was a stranger; Maddie, a cripple. The half sisters for whom the school had been planned became the misfits of the class. Alyce's beauty did not seem to make up for her peculiar, reclusive father, nor Maddie's exalted social position for her handicap. Lucy saw the situation with a heavy heart. The two girls were learning, but what they were learning was not pleasant. Lucy wished she might talk to Galen as any mother might to her children's father, but she knew she dared not cross to the Head ever again. The hermit of the Hazard Light had surrendered a battle in sending Alyce to the main island, but now that he had, Lucy was not certain she was glad she had won the point. What bliss to see her child before her every day, but at what cost to Alyce?

The two little girls did what was natural. They became friends. It was an odd alliance—the tall, graceful Alyce and the dark, listing Maddie. They were different in every way: One was shy; the other, bold. One was poor; the other, rich. And yet it was clear that they loved each other dearly.

"May I stay, Mrs. Rathrock?" Alyce would beg when the lessons were over. "I can help Maddie with the spelling."

It was only an excuse. One trait the girls did share was a quickness at books. Maddie would have her lesson in hand. And Alyce, schooled by Galen, was such a challenge that Lucy was sometimes driven back to books herself.

The three of them would have tea together in the nursery, sometimes joined by Brye, toddling adoringly after Alyce. He had found his way quickly through Alyce's shyness, and a mysterious accord had grown between them. If Brye cried, Alyce sensed the reason even before Lucy, and when Alyce became downcast over her schoolmates, Brye could make her smile.

Those afternoons, surrounded by all her children, Lucy would be unbearably happy, wanting to lock the flying hours away forever. Maddie would do imitations of some other little girl in the class, smoothing her skirts with such uncharacteristically prim gestures that they would all break out laughing.

"Oh Maddie, that was unkind," Alyce would declare and look at Lucy, who would be required to second that it was. She would do so half-heartedly, sighing and wishing that she had had a friend like Maddie during her own girlhood at Miss Alpin's school.

"Am I becoming a Miss Alpin?" she would wonder uneasily. "I am only doing what is necessary, teaching my daughters to be ladies."

If Lucy lived a lie as Jonathan's wife, as Galen had said she did, she lived another in the classroom, watching Maddie struggle with waxwork and her first cross-stitch sampler and with penwipers for the Captain's birthday present. Beside Maddie, Alyce would sew neatly, her underside as precise as the top. The two girls reminded her of herself and Caroline, especially since Maddie sometimes seemed the older, ordering servants about, snatching tarts from the kitchen while Alyce stood silently agog.

South Cottage was a happy place that fall—and then Jonathan Rathrock came home. He had brought a tea set of Bristol blue glass for Maddie and a large box of sugar comfits. The little girl was delighted. "Oh, Captain, thank you!" she cried. Then she stowed the presents carefully away.

Jonathan frowned in surprise. "But aren't we to have a tea party? Your dolls have not had such elegant dishes before, and I'm sure they're hungry for comfits. I will ring for a pot of real tea—"

"No, Captain."

"Why not?"

"I will wait for Alyce to open my comfits."

"Who is Alyce?" asked Jonathan, and so he learned at once of Lucy's school. All South Cottage trembled at his wrath. It seemed that his anger shook down the last golden leaves from the birches along the drive, and all at once winter bleakness settled over the house.

"My wife, a schoolmistress!"

"Why not, Jonathan? I am better qualified than any woman on Hazard Island. You have always said yourself that I have a good mind for a woman."

He brought the palm of his hand down on a sideboard, setting a display of japanned iron picture trays to rattling. "Of course you have a good mind, Lucy. The point is that you are not required to use it in such a coarse manner. You are a lady, and your cleverness should be confined to witty conversation at the dinner table."

"Jonathan, don't be such a hypocrite. You know I have never confined myself to dinner table chatter."

"You are right, Lucy. I do know it. I knew it in Algeria. I suppose I knew it even before that. I suppose I thought you would be different when you were my wife."

"And so are you sorry you married me?" she cried, but he stomped out, slamming the door at that moment so that she could not be sure he had even heard her question.

Once he had told her that South Cottage and the raising of children were her domain. He had come every night to her room to make her pregnant and put her in her proper place. And now that there were children he insisted on running the nursery, too.

Jonathan moved the school out of South Cottage and

built it in Hazard. He hired a young woman in London to take Lucy's place, and so Alyce was taken away from her mother again, except for those afternoons when lessons were finished early enough for her to come home to South Cottage with Maddie. Lucy would watch from the upstairs windows for the carriage to turn into the drive, waiting to see if one little girl would alight or two.

Perhaps because Lucy resented what Jonathan had done about the school, she did not become pregnant again. It was as if he had made a sham of her role in life, and subconsciously she was making one of his role in the bedroom. They did not find the satisfaction in which Brye had been conceived, and sometimes both of them seemed to tire of the effort of lovemaking, and of the pretense of a fulfillment which was complete. "I shall never know it again," Lucy would think and a chill would come over her when they had finished.

Stories began to come to her, brought from the servants quarters by her faithful Annie. The captain was looking for satisfaction among the girls of Shipwreck. It was a new turning in their relationship, and she knew the tales must be true. She would hear him go out in the night, and thinking of him in the arms of some fisherman's daughter, she would be unable to sleep with the humiliation of it.

She would slip into Bryan's room, where she would rearrange the covers he had kicked away. Almost always the little boy would stir and reach out his arms, "Mama, stay!"

"If I don't, he will cry," she would think, and she would slide gladly down beside him, letting his arms go around her neck, finding a peace which in a very few years must surely be gone.

Chapter 11

Looking out the window one autumn afternoon, she saw Maddie running across the lawn, her body rolling with the terrible effort of her twisted leg, her dark curls loosened from their pinnings, swirling about her head like a cloud of unruly blackbirds. "Mama, it's Alyce!" Maddie cried, as Lucy dashed down to meet her.

"Alyce! Is she hurt!"

Maddie gasped and tried to get her breath. "Someone said something dreadful to her in school. I don't know what it was. Alyce is going home to her father! But she cannot, Mama! The tide will be coming in!"

"Alyce knows about the tide, Maddie," Lucy said, but the thudding of her heart denied the calmness of her words.

"She will try to cross ahead of it!" Maddie insisted. Somehow Lucy knew that Maddie was right. An injured Alyce would flee to the light tower as surely as a gannet to the shelter of its nest.

"Go and have Kumrah saddled," she commanded, and running into the house, she closeted herself in the drawing room while she unfastened the metal hinges of her cage and let it drop away. She did not have time to change to a riding habit, not even time to find a maid to take the cage upstairs. As she ran out to the horse, she wondered what whoever found it would make of it.

"Stay here, Maddie," she called, urging Kumrah into a gallop. She was more grateful than she had ever been in her life for her fine horsemanship, since the road to the Head was little-used and dotted with washed-out holes and big spruce limbs from the last storm. At first she thought to intercept her daughter easily, but the road was empty, and as every new curve swept out silently, Lucy's fear grew. The roar of the tide sang in her ears as she neared the cut.

"Alyce!" she screamed and thought she heard an answer.

The cry came again, only the screech of an auk, followed by the strident call of guillemots. Peering over the edge of the cliff, she glimpsed something reddish on the stairs. "Alyce's dress!" She thought. "Alyce is still within reach!" But quickly she saw that it was only the russet of blackberry leaves, turning in the brisk autumn air. Far below something white fluttered close to the hissing plumes of the rushing tide. Alyce's apron, flapping out over the swooping rolls of green water, as she bent to remove her shoes.

"Alyce!" Lucy called, but the girl, intent on her business, did not look up. Perhaps the wind had blown Lucy's voice away, but she did not dare to wait to call again. She started down the steps after Alyce, as the girl, clutching her shoes, waded into the edge of the water and began to climb from boulder to boulder over rocks that were not yet submerged. She moved with long-accustomed sureness, yet if she slipped, the water would already be over her head. Lucy was on the lowest step above the water when Alyce, seeming to be blown over in the fierce wind, tumbled into the froth.

Lucy dropped her hold on the ladder and without hesitation plunged in after her. The water came only to her shoulder, but it dragged at her heavy skirts. She tore them off, letting them sail away, a strange flotilla, as she struggled toward her daughter, who had gained a hold by tangling her hands in the thick kelp of the rocks.

"Mrs. Rathrock! I can't swim against the currents, and the rocks will be covered in a minute!"

"Let go and hold to me, Alyce! The water is not over *my* head!"

Trustingly the girl put her arms around Lucy's neck. The sudden weight pulled Lucy backward, and her feet lost their hold on the floor of the cut. She floundered, regained her footing and fought for the far bank. A sudden wave struck her hard between her shoulders. Water surged up into her face, and she went under, choking. She thought she would drown; then she was lighter and floated up. Alyce was gone!

"The water did not jerk her away!" Lucy thought wildly. "She let go on purpose to save me!" Catching sight of Alyce's white-aproned form swirling inertly, she reached out, grasping a seaweed swirl of her daughter's hair. It tugged her after it into the deadly current, but Lucy fought back, forced to swim in the ever-deepening water.

She managed to turn the girl's face out of the water. Was she dead already? Her eyes were closed, and she floated pale and inert. Had her head been hit against rock? Lucy hated Hazard Island in that moment—the ever-present wind, the sound of the sea which she had not been without for so many years until its rhythms seemed like those of her own breathing. She felt the ocean draw her and Alyce into it, merciless as the carnivorous sundew which spread its fatal talons for insects on the ground of the island's bogs.

In the moment that she felt she could breathe no longer, she knew an overwhelming rage and lashed out at the water, as though to injure it with the last of her energy. Her foot struck something solid, and hope charged her dying strength. She realized she had been flung against the wall of the cut and finding a hold, struggled out with Alyce, shouting for Galen, mindless of the fact that she wore nothing but her bodice and pantaloons.

Alyce lay with her head pillowed on the hummocks of cinquefoil, its tiny yellow flowers like gold stars thrown from her flaxen hair. Lucy's body heaved and shook; the spit itself seemed to shift and sigh with remorse. The rocks Alyce had clung to had vanished beneath smooth curls of water. The howl of the tide had an angry sound, as though having lost its prey it would at least drown Lucy's cry for help.

"Galen!" she screamed, her voice more primal than the screech of the terns wheeling above the tide in search of gray-green cod. Even as she screamed, he was there, bending over their child. She had not seen him come. He seemed to know what to do, and as he pushed water from the child's lungs, Alyce stirred in his grasp.

"Lucy, how did this happen?"

She heard her voice at a great distance now. "I don't know—something that happened in school."

"You and your school! This is my reward for listening to you!" He wrapped his coat around Alyce and carried her toward the tower. Blaming herself as much as he did, Lucy followed, her wet, half-naked body shaking uncontrollably in the raw wind. Galen did not appear to notice her condition; she did not expect him to. Neither of them thought of anything but Alyce.

She built up the fire and found a blanket to put around

herself, while Galen arranged the child in bed. Suddenly Alyce's voice rang out frighteningly. "Papa! Mrs. Rathrock has drowned!"

"No, Alyce, she is safe."

"I am here, Alyce," said Lucy, hurrying to the bed. Alyce slipped her cold hand into Lucy's.

"You saved my life, Mrs. Rathrock."

"And you mine, when you let go of me. Why did you take such a chance, Alyce, crossing the tide? What did the children say?"

Alyce hesitated and turned her head away. "Oh, they said my father was a madman."

"You are used to such things," cried Galen. "What else?"

"I don't want to speak of it, Papa."

"What else?" he demanded roughly.

"Go away and I will tell Mrs. Rathrock," she said. Galen gave an impatient sigh, and with a glance at Lucy, went out of the room.

"What Alyce?" Lucy probed gently when the girl still did not speak.

"It was about my mother, Mrs. Rathrock. They said Papa was crazy to wait for her. They said she was probably a serving wench he knew only for a night."

"She will come, Alyce," Lucy heard herself say. How was it that she made this promise which could not be kept?

The child sighed and turned her head on the pillow. "Why does she take so long?"

"It must be because she cannot come. It must pain her almost more than she can bear to be away from you."

"I wish you were my mother, Mrs. Rathrock," said Alyce. She smiled, comforted and closed her eyes to sleep.

Staggering up, Lucy went back into the kitchen to stand before the fire, her chest ready to burst with the agony of repressed sobs. "She is asleep," she said.

"Are you satisfied now, Lucy, since you have exposed her to the spite of your arrogant Hazard brats?" he answered in a voice so hard she scarcely recognized it as his.

She whirled on him. "You are the one to blame! She cannot live a recluse. If you had taken her to Boston or New York—if you had not come here—"

"I would not have come if you had not married Jonathan Rathrock!"

"And perhaps I would not have married him, if you had

married me first! I might have gone to your family as your widow—"

She stopped, seeing his face gray as she had never seen it, even when he had been wounded in Paris. "Galen!" Alarm was in her voice.

"You are right, Lucy. It is my fault. If I had it to do over, I would not relish revolution. I would not care a straw for anything that might harm the ones I loved. Your Jonathan has always been that way. How shallow I used to think him when I first came to Hazard Island! Perhaps you were right to marry him; perhaps you are right not to leave him."

"Oh, Galen! It was because you were the way you were that I loved you so."

"You must get out of these clothes," he said, pulling the blanket from her shoulders.

"Galen—Oh, Galen, it *is* my fault, too," she murmured.

"It will be all right, Lucy. I'll take care of you. Remember I have seen you naked before." His hands moved gently on the strings of her chemise, and when she gestured to stop him, he stayed her with a kiss on her fingertips.

Suddenly her sobs came easily, flooding her with relief, almost as though he untied her heart strings along with those of her camisole. When he had taken off everything, he loosened her hair from its tortoise shell combs and wrung it, letting droplets of sea water hiss into the fire. That was all of her he allowed himself to touch, except with his eyes, but she trembled as though the caress had been physical. She knew with terrifying certainty that her body must betray her before the fall of the tide released her.

He wrapped her in a dry quilt and led her into the other bedroom, watching as she sank gratefully into the sagging bed. "Oh, Lucy, I am so tired," he said. He spoke not of the weariness of a day, but of years.

"And I, too, Galen," she answered, overwhelmingly aware of the burden she had carried. She felt the bed sink as he moved his weight onto it. Without hesitation she turned to be folded into his arms. They lay that way for a long time, while the water wailing about the quiet cliffs made escape from the truth impossible.

Slowly, inevitably, their love seeped between them, binding them in the ultimate way. Their bodies moved and turned together tentatively at first, each seeking the long-remembered wonders of the other. Then with a quickening, the weight of the years fell away. They wept together and lay until dawn in the luxury of each other's warmth.

It was as true as the very first time that she loved him.

Chapter 12

All Hazard Island knew that Lucy Rathrock had spent a night on Lighthouse Head. All Hazard Island talked. It was the choicest gossip in anyone's memory. There had been the cage left discarded in the drawing room. The skirt and petticoats that fishermen had rescued half a mile to sea. Anyone could imagine how that had left Mrs. Rathrock clad. And that man at whose mercy she had been for twelve terrible hours had not been known to have enjoyed the company of a woman in all the years he had been on the Head. Scarcely a soul believed that Lucy had not been ravished, that she did not bear the shame of it. Even Polly Treadway looked at her in a strange, embarrassed way.

But the worst thing of all was that Jonathan was not angry. She had made a laughingstock of him in a way she never had. At least half the islanders thought that the Frenchman would have worked such charm on Lucy that she would not have resisted, and the island buzzed with jokes about the cuckold captain. He would declare that the tide might never again recede from Lighthouse Head, they said. He would put a special tax on the French. Or think of that Frenchman in the stocks!

Jonathan, only mildly surprised at the venture, did nothing. And when Lucy, wracked with guilt, burst out an apology, he kissed her forehead lightly, replying, "Ah, Lucy, did I not tell you even before we were married that I knew you would always cause talk?"

She had done what was necessary without fuss, where another woman might have hesitated from modesty or fear. He admired her in that special way he had, and somehow it was all quite different from when she had disgraced him by holding school at South Cottage.

Jonathan and Lucy grew closer in those days. The lewd stories about the captain and his Shipwreck girls faded away, as if a loyalty kept him home. He, prideful, dared anyone to smirch Lucy's name; and she desperately granted him every consideration, every affection in her power to make up for the completeness of love he deserved from her, which had finally become impossible for her ever to give him.

If she could not give him that, could she not at least give him more sons? Had a key turned somewhere inside her, decreeing that if her sons were not Galen's, she would not have more sons at all? Was this the consequence of the lie she lived?

Such a scarcity of sons among the two leading families of the island! Polly Treadway had given birth to a dark-haired girl named Susan, who was beautiful from the moment of her first cry. Caroline, in England, had suffered the birth of a daughter, too. Her letter was blistered with tears as she wrote of her love for her daughter and of the rage of Lord Ashton that the child had not been a boy.

The doctor says there will be no more children, and so the title will pass from our line. Charles seems sad sometimes, but he says he is only glad that little Sarah and I are safe. He loves us both, and I am more in love with him than on our wedding day. But if ever a man deserved a son it is he!

Caroline wanted Lucy to visit England in the spring, and Lucy found the notion appealing. She would take Maddie and Brye to meet Caroline, and she herself would see the baby, Sarah. Surely she need not worry now that Charles Ashton still loved her. Surely it had been long enough! It would be nice to leave Hazard Island for a while. It would help to get her mind off Galen Le Blanc.

"Jonathan, I am thinking of going to England in the spring," she said one evening as she sat across from him in the drawing room, helping him sort out a packet of mail, a tea set of white cream ware between them on the carved ebony table. He shifted some papers he was reading, gave a grunt of annoyance and did not look up.

"It will be too dangerous."

"Dangerous! I have never been afraid of the sea!"

"It is not the elements that will be dangerous. There will be war. You see, here it is right on the first page of this newspaper. Mississippi, Florida, Alabama, Georgia and Louisiana have already joined South Carolina in seceding from the Union."

"Oh, that business! That will be over in no time. The abolitionists will have their way as they should. It will have nothing to do with us."

"I hope not."

He did not mean to be comforting, for he knew she would never leave it at that. She was the kind of woman who should be prepared for what was coming. She should not be sheltered from the truth.

"What do you mean, you hope not?"

"I mean that we are standing too close to the stove for comfort. There have always been those in the United States with the idea that Canadian lands should be under native rule. There is always the idea of expansion and annexation."

"Then we shall sit very still, shall we not, Jonathan, so that no one will notice we are more than a piece of rockweed adrift in the bay."

He smiled at the hint of command in her voice. He felt rather pleased at how well she understood him. "You think I cannot bear not to be in the fray. You think someday the wind will blow the smell of gunsmoke over from the mainland, and I will find a way to become involved."

"I would not be surprised, Jonathan."

"No, no. My fighting days are over. Hazard Island is what is important and what we must make of it for Brye. We shall be as still as a little petrel in its hole, just as you wish. We will be careful with Hazard Island."

She was reassured, but not entirely. She felt a threat, an insecurity that was completely new to her. She saw suddenly how deeply she was rooted here, as much as South Cottage itself, which was no longer raw and fresh, and seemed to flow naturally skyward from the comfortable plantings of rugosa rose and Rhodora. The little birches that had once framed the drive like graceful children had grown taller than the mother house. And Lucy herself had become almost part of the soil. Bleakness, loneliness, the torment of the Hazard Light—these, too, she had known here, and they helped her belong on the island as she had never belonged anywhere, even in Paris. When she drove home with Jonathan after some evening's excursion, every lighted window of South

Cottage was inexpressibly dear to her, filled with the warmth and the meaning of her life.

"The war will not come to Hazard Island," she told herself, as she followed the familiar sheep trails with Maddie and Brye. In April Fort Sumter was fired upon and Abraham Lincoln called for a militia of seventy-five thousand men. Lucy shuddered and wished she might tuck her island with its freshly-blooming violets and blue flag into her dresser drawer along with her pearl vinaigrette and her rose-cut diamond pin.

Suddenly Lucy's nightmares of an end to Rathrock control of the island began to shape into reality, but it was not the Union that coveted their domain. The threat came from within.

Jonathan stormed into the house and shut himself into the library without any dinner. They tiptoed about all evening. Then the children and servants went to bed. Lucy sat in the drawing room, waiting. The Westminster chimes of the long case clock struck one. Lucy put down the Alexandre Dumas she had been reading. "It has been fifteen minutes since I turned a page," she thought. She studied the library door dubiously, wondering what choler she would unleash on herself if she opened it. Curiosity got the better of her at last and she cracked the door to peek in.

He was sitting arms crossed, legs out-stretched toward the fire. "Come in, Lucy," he said quietly, not turning to see who was there.

With the merest crackle of petticoats, she crossed the floor, slipped into a needlepoint chair and waited. He reached for her hand, covering it in his great, rough grasp. It was not what she had expected.

"Lucy, you have been a good wife, building me a home in this uncivilized spot."

She flushed in the firelight and thought of Galen. "I might have done better."

"I have been thinking how I should despise myself if I had nothing to offer you but ruin."

"Ruin! What a strange idea when you have been nothing but successful—when our ships dock in ports all over the world and our builders cannot keep up with orders!"

"It is Fitch Treadway," said Jonathan flatly.

"Fitch Treadway!" She felt herself go pale. She knew the kind of man Fitch Treadway was, and if Fitch had found his way, she was more frightened of him than of all President Lincoln's men.

"Fitch Treadway has filed a lawsuit against the Crown for possession of half of Hazard Island."

She let go of his hand and gripped the arms of the chair, her fingers closing tightly over the smooth rosewood claws. "But how dare he! Against the Crown! It is the most audacious thing I have ever heard!"

"Yes, isn't it! But I have had word of it just today from my solicitor in St. John. Some ancient document has been unearthed—a deed of some kind nearly a hundred years old, belonging to some Treadway ancestor."

"Jonathan, that can be nothing. He cannot possibly succeed. The Queen herself granted you Hazard Island and that will take precedence over this claim. If worse comes to worst, we are still richer than Fitch Treadway to fight him in the courts. And it will not come to that, Jonathan. What I do not understand is why Fitch Treadway has limited this grandiose scheme. Why does he not sue for all of Hazard Island? It would be as feasible."

Jonathan sighed. "It is because Fitch Treadway is an honest man, Lucy. And intelligent. If it were anyone but he, I would not give it a second thought. Fitch has no need to sue for the entire island, for we cannot exist without the north. If Fitch Treadway were to control the Shipwreck Harbor, it would be the end. What *I* do not understand is why he has waited so long—nearly a decade —to make his move. Well, let us go to bed, Lucy. We are in a strong position, as you say, and the fight if it comes, will not be tomorrow."

Jonathan Rathrock felt better since he had talked to Lucy. He had accommodated the situation. His outrage had faded into a not-unwelcome anticipation of the sort of struggle on which he thrived. He made vigorous, grateful love to his wife and slept soundly, one arm flung across her breasts. He expected to best Fitch Treadway, and it would do him good.

Lucy lay wakeful, her unease just beginning. She had an idea why Fitch Treadway had waited so long to do this. Fitch was intelligent, but not educated. Fitch had not thought of the maneuver by himself. Her stomach tightened with the memory of Fitch's admiration for Galen Le Blanc. Galen, who had studied in Paris, was well-versed in law. He was the only one on Hazard Island who could have envisioned this. How had it come about? Had Fitch sought Galen, or had it been the other way around? Had Galen decided, in either case, to try to destroy Jonathan, since she would not leave him? Every man who loved her seemed to suffer because of it. Was it Jonathan's turn now?

Galen would have dug this deed from the record books, and a lawsuit inspired by Galen would amount to more than she cared to admit. Louis Philippe had underestimated Galen Le Blanc; it had been the sort of misjudgment that had toppled him from his throne. She must never be guilty of the same mistake. "We overthrew a king, Lucy, and now you are married to one," he had said. There could be no doubt that Galen was hatching another, though smaller, revolution.

What could she do? She could not tell Jonathan. She fell asleep and dreamed of the sacking of Tuileries. She heard the jeering of the throng, saw the rabble in wigs and laces, but strangely the palace had changed. The rooms had become those of South Cottage. She woke with a start to an uncanny silence, broken only by the cadence of the sea and one far-away cry of a puffin lost from its fellows in the night. She slipped out of bed and, pulling a shawl-sleeved mantle over her muslin nightgown, went up to stare out at the Hazard Light, burning with the Morning Star in the blackness.

The lovers of Paris had become enemies at last. She knew nothing she could say would turn Galen back. He would pit himself at destroying Jonathan as much to serve justice as because Lucy stood beside him. "I must not allow Galen to win," she thought. "It would be as if I destroyed Jonathan myself." And she vowed that she would defend to her last breath her husband's dream and her son's heritage.

Soon everyone on the island knew about the lawsuit. That summer as she rode about there was a touch of malice in the smiles of the fisherfolk as they greeted her, a hopeful bit of insolence in the way they took off their hats to her. Fights broke out between the Shipwreck fishermen and the Hazard tars. It seemed that every week Jonathan had to hold court to dispense with the misdemeanors that piled up. He tried to deal with each impartially, though he himself had been the object of the dispute in almost every case. He would come out rubbing an aching head and calling for a glass of brandy. Each decision was vastly unpopular with one side or the other.

Then one August afternoon a frigate of Her Majesty's Navy stood in the Shipwreck Harbor. Since the captain of the vessel was an old friend of Jonathan's a fine dinner was ordered up from the kitchen. The children were scrubbed and dressed in their best. Lucy wore her hooped earrings and her cabochon brooch with a new moire gown trimmed with blond lace. She did what a wife was supposed to do; filling flower horns and silver epergnes with summer flowers, supervising the table setting, the preparation of the brown, Madiera-flavored soup, the baked fish in claret sauce, the filets of hazel grouse, the breaded mutton cutlets, the almond cheesecakes. She smiled and looked beautiful, all the while frozen at the thought of what it might mean. She had seen the dispatch that lay on Jonathan's desk. It bore the seal of the Crown.

It came from Queen Victoria herself.

The food had no taste; the hours of banishment while the gentlemen smoked and drank were intolerable. She heard Jonathan's laughter and wondered if it could be genuine. The dispatch must concern Fitch Treadway's lawsuit; what else could it be? It was the first such message that had ever come to them, and a Naval ship had come especially to bring it.

She dismissed the nanny and put the children to bed herself, reading them stories to divert her mind, and feeling almost annoyed when they fell asleep, leaving her alone with her anxiety. She went to bed herself with a book. When it was nearly daylight, Jonathan came in whistling.

"Jonathan, you are very drunk!" she said, starting up from the pillows.

"Ah, that I am Lucy," he agreed. "I was enjoying the company of old friends." He clapped her across her backside.

"It is almost morning!"

"Yes, it will be a beautiful day."

"Jonathan, did you have such a fine time that you forgot to open the Queen's dispatch?" she demanded.

"I didn't forget. But I did have a fine time. I feel very good."

She clutched him about the neck, his jollity affecting

her. "It's all right then, isn't it, about Fitch Treadway's lawsuit?"

"Fitch Treadway's lawsuit! Whatever are you talking about? The letter had nothing to do with that!"

"Well, what, then?"

"The Queen has made a request of me. I am to run the Union blockade with my ships to bring cotton out of the South for England's textile mills."

"Jonathan! You promised we would not get involved!"

"So I did, Lucy. But I did not foresee this. You are not a child. You know sometimes a promise must be broken."

He groaned impatiently as she burst into tears. "You cannot leave Hazard Island now!" she cried.

"I must. The Queen asks it."

"It can only be a request. She cannot order you to do such a thing. You are no longer an officer of the Navy."

"Nevertheless it is my duty. Have you forgotten that it is because I performed my duty that we have Hazard Island at all?"

"You are glad to go, Jonathan," she accused.

"Well, I don't mind admitting that I am. I am sick of the atmosphere here. I am tired of all this bickering, and I shall be glad to be at sea, doing something with a little adventure. I am tired of being a merchant seaman."

"I though so! You care more for glory than for your son's future. Oh, what a fool I was to listen to you, Jonathan Rathrock! You with your dream of land and family! How could I have believed you when I knew that gunpowder was in your blood! It has come out finally!"

"There, Lucy," he said mildly. "Don't worry so. Remember I am well-seasoned at such things. Most likely not a shot will be fired."

"I suppose you would not think of sending some of your captains instead."

"What! And stay home myself? How little you understand of a man's world! I would lose their respect. And that would be all I need on top of this Treadway trouble."

"Doesn't it bother you at all that you will be aiding the cause of slavery?"

"I have no love of slavery, Lucy. You know that. But I am on the Queen's business. I am in her debt."

"In her debt! I thought Hazard Island was granted us because *she* was in *your* debt! What shall you say when you stand before your maker, accused of helping to oppress those poor black wretches?"

He sighed and gave her a whimsical look as if to say that she might have a thing or two to account for herself. "I shall say I served England, Lucy, which, right or wrong, is the highest duty I acknowledge."

She glared at him, filled with rage and disgust. A sudden repugnance overcame her for all the nights he had spent inside her body. "Go, then, Jonathan. But when you come back, do not expect to come to my bed."

He sobered and stared at her. "You cannot mean that, Lucy!"

"I do mean it, Jonathan." She was trembling at the enormity of what she had said.

He knew her well enough not to question her further. He rose and went, without a word, to his own room.

She threw herself down on her bed and stared at the blankness of the dusky ceiling. She knew what he would do: he would go again to the girls of Shipwreck. For the moment she didn't care. She wondered what *she* would do, how she would face the rest of her life.

Chapter 13

Jonathan Rathrock did what he had to do. The cost to him was enormous. He gave up the intimacy of the woman he loved. He surrendered the possibility of more sons to continue his line.

Everything rested now on Brye, and in the days before he sailed, the captain gave more attention to the boy than he had before. Brye was only seven, but already he had his own little dinghy to sail on the island's bays. He knew his way about the docks and was familiar with each of the captain's clippers and New Brunswick square riggers.

The sea had laid claim already to Bryan Rathrock, yet he was unlike his father. Like Jonathan he loved sailing ships and loathed steamboats, but it seemed he loved the clippers more for their beauty than for the challenge and that it was the ungainliness of the steam vessels that offended him. He knew things about Hazard Island Lucy had never discovered—the nesting places of Savannah sparrows in the tall grasses beyond the beach, the exact day of August when the last of the shearwaters would head south to nest. He told his mother that the storm clouds at sea were big velvet pillows and he sang her songs that he heard in the wind.

He would make a good sailor, but he did not seem to care about power. And he would stare off across the water while his father explained to him the responsibility that would one day be his.

He was only seven. Was it any wonder that he had no interest in generations of Rathrocks to come? He himself had scarcely left the cradle. But Maddie, at nine, could tell you how much sugar filled a ship's hold and how many loads of Treadway lobster were hauled in a given month.

On the morning Jonathan was to sail, Lucy knew a

moment of panic. "Jonathan," she cried, "whatever shall I do?"

"Do?" He patted her cheek. "Why you shall keep South Cottage shining and polished and order yourself one of those new riding hats we saw in *The Ladies' Treasury* last week. It will be handsome on you."

"Jonathan, there will be more trouble when you have left the island."

"I don't think so. I have put good men in charge everywhere. And I am not going forever. I will be back before you know it."

She climbed up to the widow's walk and watched the sails of *The Lucy Maid* fade over the horizon. When she went downstairs, the house had a strangely hollow feel, and going to the library, she walked about, fingering his ink stand and pipes as though to reassure herself of his existence.

His rancorless acceptance of her ultimatum had shown her a dimension of him she had not suspected. She knew for the first time the depth of the integrity that had made him go. And to her great surprise he had acknowledged her right to her integrity as well. There had been no threats, no recriminations over her decision not to share his bed; and these circumstances had so raised him in her eyes that she felt a shiver of passion whenever he came near her. And when he spoke to her in the courtly way, with longing half-veiled in his eyes, it was all she could do to prevent herself from crying out a retraction.

A fine mess she had made for herself, insuring that her bed would be empty for the rest of her days! She envied the girls he would sleep with, though she thought they would never satisfy him. He would never want anyone but Lucy, that elusive fulfillment that had finally slipped completely away.

Lucy had no idea of repeating her infidelity with Galen. She owed Jonathan that much. Jonathan's motives in the quarrel had been pure; she wished she were sure that she had been as honest. Had it been that she hated slavery so much, or had it been partly that she had been looking for an excuse to quit her marital duties? Had it been that she had not been able at last, as Galen had predicted, to live that nightly lie?

Lie? It had not all been a lie, not all these years, not even after she had shared her body with Galen in the light tower.

Jonathan returned as he had promised, grinning and triumphant, acknowledging a salute of gunfire from his island. He had about him that aura of unknown places that he always had when he returned from the sea, and this time there was something additional—a sense of peril overcome.

"Was there trouble, Jonathan?" she said conversationally at dinner.

He paused in wolfing his favorite welcoming dinner of braised goose and glazed root vegetables. "No trouble. Ah, we were fired upon once. It would have done you good to see how *The Lucy Maid* outran the Union Navy! They didn't know what to make of us, those Yankees! Their frigates might as well have been wash tubs beside *The Lucy Maid*. We took only one shell, through the mizzen."

She shuddered and reach for her goblet of wine in the candlelight. "I am glad it went so well, Jonathan."

"Oh, marvelously well. Do plan some entertainment for us—a dinner party, even a ball. I shall want some gaiety on Hazard Island when I come home again."

"Again!"

"Yes, of course. I must go and go until the cotton that is available is brought out. It will be most of the winter. That is another reason we must have parties. It will be especially lonely for you during the bleaker months."

"You are very thoughtful, Jonathan." Once she had railed at him and had lost. Now she could do nothing but play her part, and she was determined to play it well.

"I suppose your hat has not arrived yet," he said. "Well, no matter, we shall ride about tomorrow and see how things are faring. We shall take Brye and Maddie, too. They would like that."

She knew he had more reason for taking her along than simple desire for her company. He was calming her fears, showing her his faith in the firmness of his control of Hazard Island. And it seemed that he was justified.

The shipbuilders worked away amid their hawsers and copper spikes. The docks were busy with timber, salt, a load of eiderdown, and fish scales to be sent to a button factory in Boston. And the sweet haze of smoke from the wooden smokehouses told that the captain's trawlers had brought in their catch.

He went each night to his own bed, while Lucy, in the next room, listened to the sounds of his retiring, hoping that he would come through the dressing room door and tell her he had had enough of her female silliness. But would she love him so much without the pride that kept him away?

Her body ached for him, as it never had in all the years of their marriage. But she could not go to him either, without being overwhelmed by a sense of his mastery over her, so she lay alone, thinking how strange it was that she could love him only if they were apart.

All that autumn he came and went. Cotton bales were stacked high on the docks and were carried away by slower, more prosaic ships to England. When the captain was home he was always in a good humor, and there were parties at South Cottage.

Fitch Treadway's lawsuit was almost forgotten. Nothing had happened. Nothing was going to happen. The island seemed to settle back, content with the diversion of watching the captain's cutter unload his wealthy, fashionable guests.

Polly Treadway came to visit South Cottage, for the first time since her husband had filed the lawsuit. "What worries you, Polly? Is it the lawsuit?" Lucy probed, seeing how melancholy her friend looked.

"Please, Lucy, let's not speak of *that*!"

"We are friends, Polly. We can speak of anything. We have done so before."

"Well, then, truth to tell, I am not eager to be mistress of half of Hazard Island. And Fitch is wrong to go against the Crown, but he is my husband and dearer to me than the Queen."

"Ah, that's it! The suit has become a quarrel between you!"

Polly's eyes blinked in astonishment. "Heavens, Lucy, I would not presume to tell Fitch what I think! Not about matters such as that! But he is wrong. Even if he wins, we will never be gentry like you and the captain. It is in the blood. We are rich now, and how I suffer! Oh, the servants Fitch hires—the chambermaid who wakes me every morning with her rattling, the governess who keeps the children to their lessons and will not let me play with them, and the cook who will not cease putting Bordeaux into the fish chowder."

Lucy laughed and passed her guest a dish of chocolates. "It cannot be that you are unable to run North Pines,

Polly. Only think how you helped *me* when I first came here as a bride."

"That was different. I told *you* what to do and *you* told the servants. It is in the blood, Lucy! Even if we were to become landed, it would make no difference. I would never be the great lady of Hazard Island!"

"But you would try?"

"Fitch would like it, so I would try."

Lucy sighed. "You are luckier than you know, Polly, to care so for a man that you would try anything."

When Polly visited South Cottage, her children Josh and Susan came with her, a circumstance for which Lucy was not totally glad. Though Brye adored Josh, four years his senior, they were already rivals like their fathers. When Josh threw down the challenge, Brye was always ready to pick it up. Lucy would clutch the porch railing, her knuckles as white as its paint, as she watched them race away on their ponies.

"Brye, you are smaller. You cannot do everything that Josh does," she would say sternly.

"I am a Rathrock, Mother," he would reply and jerk away from her grasp. There seemed no way she could keep him from Josh Treadway.

The relationship between the two little girls, Maddie and Susan, was simpler. They did not like each other. Susan Treadway was cool and beautiful, poised beyond her years, and her voice had an ever-present smugness. Her thick auburn hair lay in soft coils about her neck, resting like sleeping kittens, and Susan had a habit of reaching up to stroke them as if indeed they were her dear pets. Susan would not find it foreign to *her* to be the grand lady of Hazard Island, if ever she should have the opportunity.

Maddie never missed a chance to make Susan lose her composure, whether by interrupting or contradicting her, by dumping a cup of milk into her silken lap or, most directly, by laying a blow to her shin. Maddie, slumped into a Berlin wool chair in the drawing room, would study her prey, her dark eyes sharp and glimmering. Susan, as much as Josh, threw out a challenge. To expect Maddie not to torment Susan was like asking a dog not to chase a squirrel.

Lucy would scold and punish uselessly. "If my heart were in it, perhaps it would make a difference," she thought. But unfortunately, Lucy enjoyed seeing Susan discomfitted almost as much as Maddie enjoyed the discomfitting. Then one afternoon Maddie outdid herself by thrusting a pin into Susan's new inflatable crinoline, the latest thing from London.

Susan jumped about, uttering little screams, clapping her hands over her skirts, turning and twisting like a cat after its tail, as she tried to cover the puncture, which hissed impolitely as her petticoats went limp.

Lucy jerked a hysterically mirthful Maddie out of the room and up the stairs. "Young lady, your father shall hear of this," she threatened as she shut them away in Maddie's bedroom.

"The captain will think it is funny, Mama," said Maddie, gasping for breath.

"It is not—" said Lucy, but this was one lie that she could not manage. She choked, tears of merriment rolling down her cheeks. She knew she had taken Maddie away, not so much to punish her, as to cover her own overpowering merriment. Surrendering to hilarity beyond her control, she sobbed and shrieked with glee.

When they were finished laughing, holding their sides and wiping their eyes, there was a new glow between them. "You may spank me, now, Mama," said Maddie. "I deserve it."

"No, Maddie, I am done with spanking you." She was done suddenly with a number of things. She was no longer in danger of being Miss Alpine, who had so tormented her in her school days. She reached up unexpectedly and unfastened Maddie's curls, combing them out and forming plaits around her ears. "There now, that is more becoming. From now on, you shall be what you are, which is something quite wonderful; and you shall not try to be what Susan is. When you are grown, the best of men will see that you are not silly, like Susan!" (Or weak, like Susan's mother, she added in her heart. For though she loved Polly, she had always admitted some justification to Jonathan's assessment of her.)

"The captain likes my curls," Maddie said, doubtfully.

"He shall see that this is better," Lucy promised.

The girl studied herself in the mirror. "I will never be beautiful like you, Mama."

Words of contradiction formed on Lucy's lips. But the new Lucy did not utter them. Instead she took her daughter by the shoulders and said firmly, "No, but you will have such intelligence and spirit that you do not need to be." And she went away, leaving Maddie bewildered at her flaunting of this paramount measure of feminine worth.

Lucy set about replacing Maddie's flounced dresses with princess robes and redingotes. "I will teach her to be elegant," she thought.

Maddie remained dubious. "The captain admires that dress," she said, as Lucy disposed of an organdy with puffy gabrielle sleeves.

"Exactly so," agreed her mother. "He admires the dress when it is the woman he must admire." And both of them waited to know what he would say.

The days dragged on. The captain was overdue. For a fortnight, Lucy disciplined herself not to worry. Each morning she went hopefully to the cupola to search the winter horizon.

Brye came to her one night as she sat sewing. "Mama, the captain is lost, isn't he? Am I the master of Hazard Island, now?"

"Your father is only overdue, Brye," she told him. He sighed with relief, and she saw responsibility slide from his small shoulders.

Another week went by. The island stirred like a bear, untimely awakened from its hibernation. The rents fell due and nobody paid them. The captain's solicitor came to see Lucy.

A trustee must be appointed for Brye, he told her, on the unhappy possibility that the captain did not return.

"I cannot allow that, sir," she told him. "My husband is in charge of this island." She felt a quiver of a terrible dread.

"But, my dear Mrs. Rathrock, there are things that must be attended. The matter of Fitch Treadway, for the first. His case will come up for a hearing soon. It will be a strong one, I warn you. I have seen the papers. Hazard Island must not be leaderless now. We will bring someone competent from England—"

"No one in England is competent to run Hazard Island!" said Lucy. "We will not discuss the matter further until there is proof that the captain is dead."

All too soon that proof came. A listing square rigger, one of the southern convoys came dragging into the harbor, riding peculiarly in the water, its sails torn and gray.

She ordered the carriage and rode down to meet it, Brye slipping in almost unnoticed at her side.

"Where is her captain?" she demanded of a sailor.

"Still aboard, my lady."

"Then I shall go out at once," she said, and had herself handed into the first dory.

"Mama! I am coming, too!" cried Brye.

"Stay here! This is not for children!"

He put a determined foot on the ladder. "I must hear what has happened to my father!"

She looked at him standing there, his chin set, his face pale with fear, his hair blowing. He was right, she thought. He would face the moment at its rawest and later he would have the memory of it. Not for Bryan Rathrock soft-spoken words in the nursery to tell him his father was dead. Though she did not realize it, her relationship to her son had shifted. She had taken over Jonathan's role, honing the boy to his future.

She had second thoughts even before they reached the vessel, for she could see part of the rigging in shreds and patched holes in the hull. Half the ordinary complement of sailors snapped to attention as Lucy lifted her silk skirt over the debris of the deck. As if it were a uniform, all of them wore bandages; and everywhere lay patches of rust-colored gore.

Lucy whirled on the high-ranking officer. "Where is your captain? Why is he not on deck to greet me?"

"Begging your pardon, my lady, the captain will see you in his quarters. He cannot walk."

The captain's quarters had an awful stench. Behind a splintered desk sat a cadaverous officer, the lower half of his body tucked under the kneehole in an attempt to hide from her delicate sight, the remains of a leg that had been shot away.

"Mrs. Rathrock, you should not have come! I would have sent word!"

Lucy clutched Brye's hand, whether to give courage or to receive it, she could not have told. She felt faint, but her chin tilted up. "I must hear it from you yourself." The words came out softly, as though mats of Georgia cotton blocked her throat. "What has happened to *The Lucy Maid*?"

"Sunk. Off Charleston."

She bent forward and put her gloved hand into the grime on the desk top. "Did you see it, sir?"

"I did, Mrs. Rathrock. On fire it was. There was a fog that night over Charleston harbor. The Federals were bombarding from the barrier island and the echoes of the cannonade from Fort Sumter and Fort Moultrie and a half a dozen other Rebel strongholds shook the decks on the ships. We had run past the patrol boats in the blockading squadron, and Captain Rathrock led us on under the barrage, since more danger was behind than in front.

"But at the harbor entrance was an ironclad, hiding low in the water. Its hundred-pound shot disabled one of our three ships, and the crew had to abandon it with no more than one or two life boats put down. *The Lucy Maid* signaled for us to run, but she herself remained, flashing in from the fog to pick up the wrecked crew, while the ironclad sent its rounds after it. What a thing it was to see! What a hero Captain Rathrock was! What skill he had!

"Skill could not be enough against the ironclad, but Captain Rathrock seemed determined that it would be. You could see how he hated that monstrous, propeller-driven craft in the reckless swoopings of *The Lucy Maid*. The turret of the ironclad glowed with a fury, and then it hit home. *The Lucy Maid* blazed all at once from her mizzen to her skysail. And we escaped into the mist as the patrol ships chased us."

The captain's head drooped. Lucy was terrified that he was unconscious or dead. "Captain! Were there survivors? Did the Federals take prisoners?"

His eyes flickered open. "From that fire? It is not likely. I know of none."

"You know nothing more of my husband?"

"No, Mrs. Rathrock." The other members of the battered crew could tell her no more. Night and smoke and fog had obscured vision. The harbor had been filled with the cries of the drowning, and a man had tended to notice in detail only what was happening to himself. It seemed certain that Jonathan Rathrock had gone down with the beautiful clipper he had named for his bride.

"Father was a hero, Mama," Brye said as they went home. His face was still pale, and he hung very close to his mother. "But, Mama—"

"Yes, Brye?"

He looked up at her, his eyes troubled. "I would not have been a hero. I would have sailed away and saved my ship and my crew. More people would have been happy that way. *You* would have been happier, wouldn't you?"

She gave her son a long glance, studying his earnest face. "Yes, Brye," she said at last, "but I am only a woman. I cannot explain to you about heroism."

"Who *will* explain it, Mama?" he asked.

"I don't know, Brye. I don't know," she said, and she damned Jonathan's irrational hatred of modern ships and she prayed that Brye would not be like other men, always finding reasons to die.

Chapter 14

The idea that Jonathan might be alive in some Federal prison haunted her. She decided to write a letter to President Lincoln, and going into the library where her husband's presence lingered heavily, denying he could be dead, she penned half a page. Then suddenly, knowing it could not be sent, she tore it up.

"How stupid I am!" she berated herself. "I would only be alerting the Union that Hazard Island is an enemy!" And she knew with despairing resignation that there was no way of knowing whether Jonathan was alive or dead for as long as the war lasted.

Every day the bell of the Hazard Church, which had first rung on her wedding day, tolled in memorial for sailors whose women accepted their loss. "You must have a memorial service for the captain, too," said Polly Treadway gently. "It is indecent that you do not."

"I will be indecent then, and it will not be the first time. I do not believe that Jonathan is dead."

As the days passed, Lucy shook herself out of shock. The period of mourning would pass. The island would begin to move again. She remembered the solicitor and his threat of a trustee for Brye. "No trustee can run this island as it should be run," she would think, pacing about, the military heels of her balmorals tapping on the pine floor beyond the floral baroque rug of the library. "And yet Brye is too young, of course."

There seemed no solution unless—and an idea began to grow in her mind, an idea so daring that she scarcely allowed herself to entertain it. Still, it would not go away. One morning she came downstairs very early, and lighting a fire for herself so she should not be disturbed by the maid, she took up her pen and wrote to Charles Ashton.

She was a long time composing the letter to the first man who had ever loved her. How often she had hoped that that love was dead! And now suddenly she prayed that some spark of youthful passion still glowed, just enough to make Charles do what must be done.

> *Dear Charles,*
> *You will have heard by now of the fate of* The Lucy Maid *off Charleston. Do not worry about me or the children, for we are well and confident that Jonathan will return to us at the end of this dreadful war. But I am writing to you about a problem only you, as the most influential shareholder of the Hazard Company, can solve.*
>
> *Believe me, Charles, no trustee from England can comprehend the working of what has been built on Hazard Island. It was an ever-present challenge to Jonathan himself.*
>
> *Dear Charles, I have never asked for a favor before, but now I beg you to make me the trustee. Grant me this and we shall prosper—*

The sight of the words on paper awed her. She hesitated, drew a great shuddering breath, signed her name and reached for the seal.

"Lucy," said a voice behind her.

She spun in her chair and looked up into the face of Galen Le Blanc. "What were you writing? Was that letter for me? You had that marvelous look of purpose you used to have when you penned articles for *Le Revue Démocratie*. How I used to sit and look at you in our pretty little house. You were more beautiful than any woman I had ever seen, caught up in something greater than yourself, beyond your own beauty."

"Galen! How did you get in here?"

"Why I said that I had come on a matter about the Hazard Light. And I have. Have you not watched it burning all these years?"

She leaped away from the desk as he approached her. "You were not announced!" she cried wildly.

"No, there was only one silly little maid about. I flattered her into admitting me. This is not the first place I have ever got into in an unapproved manner. Lucy, why have you not come to me? Have you some foolish idea about mourning? We must not waste any more time, dearest. The rest of our lives will not be long enough to make up for what we have missed."

She steadied herself and with one quick flick of her

hand, she yanked the draperies shut. "Do not touch me, Galen. I shall scream if I have to. I am not coming with you."

She was frightened that he would not heed her, and she braced herself against the brass grille of the silk-backed bookcase as if to find there the will to resist his touch. But he did not take those few steps that might have shattered her life. For all his sensuality, Galen Le Blanc was an intellectual, a believer in minds. Lucy's mind had rejected him, and he did not attempt to make her body obliterate that rejection. Perhaps he did not realize it was possible.

He crumpled, from his feet to his face, as if he had been destroyed with a charge of dynamite. He sank into a chair, almost unrecognizable, the strength, the defiance blown away. The suddenness of the change left Lucy breathless. She had won too easily and with a cry of distress she stepped forward to comfort him. Quickly she stopped herself, her fingers clutching the bookcase. She remembered that Galen was not beyond resurrection.

He looked at her with awful, betrayed eyes. "Why, Lucy?"

"I—am not certain that Jonathan is dead."

"No, it is more than that. Let me see the letter. What was it that made you look the way you did? You have not yet sealed it."

She handed it over silently, and he read it, a rueful smile coming to his lips. "So! You ascend the throne. Was it this lust for power that made you such a fine revolutionary in Paris? I did not realize it."

"Galen! Do not be absurd. It is not power that I care about!"

"What, then?"

"It is—" She spoke slowly, putting something into words for the first time. "It is that when I married Jonathan, I committed myself to something more than him. I did not know it at the time. I was young, and I thought a woman wed no more than a man. But I married all his dreams, the destiny of his line. I married Hazard Island."

"You mean Brye. Do you think he needs this? That he can be happy nowhere else? We will take him with us, Lucy. We will take all the children. We need not sacrifice!"

"No, Galen." She shook her head sadly. "I must stay here." And feeling stronger having said all she had, she dared to put out a hand and touch his hair. "Galen. This lawsuit of Fitch Treadway's. You will see that it is dropped, will you not? It is me you are fighting now and not my husband."

His head came up and some of the old fire returned to his eyes. "Certainly, I will not, Lucy. I shall work even harder in the cause of Fitch Treadway. This island belongs to Fitch Treadway by a justice higher than that of the Queen. *He* is meant for Hazard Island, and *you* are meant for Boston with me, though I must wrest the entire Rathrock empire from you in order to have you! Here is your letter to mail, or shall I take it down to Hazard myself as I go?"

A month later Lucy Rathrock was made trustee of her son's interests on Hazard Island. The appointment was the subject of much astonishment over the island, and many jokes were made in the cozys of the pubs both of Hazard and Shipwreck. They took to calling her Captain Lucy, and wondering lewdly how it would be if she took over as ship's master in a crinoline.

Lucy, unflapped, dug into Jonathan's papers, interviewed sugar buyers, contracted for the shipping of shingles and lumber, and sent off a convoy of mast ships. Finally she called a senior captain to the library and ordered him to arrange another expedition to Charleston.

"Charleston, ma'am? For cotton?"

"Of course. It still stands in warehouses there."

"But—" The captain seemed bewildered.

"Are you afraid to go? I shall find someone else."

"I am not afraid, only I thought you were opposed to blockade running."

"I am. But Captain Rathrock gave his word. We shall go south until we have done all that is to be done. Oh, and Captain, I have purchased two of the new propeller-driven blockade runners to do the job."

"You have, Ma'am! Ah, Captain Rathrock would never approve of that. The captain would never have anything but sails!"

"I said that Captain Rathrock's word would be honored, sir, I did not say that we would do everything as he would do it. I am in charge now!"

She knew sleepless hours after she had seen the blockade runners leave Hazard Island. She was sending men perhaps into battle, perhaps to their deaths, and she could not even go with them as Jonathan had to risk his life along with theirs. "Am I equal to this?" she would wonder, wishing that she might have stayed in that pleasant world of kitchen and nursery. God had made wind, men steam engines, Jonathan had used to say, and Lucy rather typically had chosen to depend on men. What if the engines failed? What if there were a slaughter, like that last time with *The Lucy Maid?*

She would drift to sleep and waken suddenly, hearing some creaking in the house that reminded her of Jonathan's footsteps when he had used to come in at dawn from some voyage. She would shoot up in bed, thinking he had come back to deal with her, whether alive or as a ghost. And the thought of him alive was only a little less frightening than the idea of the specter.

By day Lucy did what her lights told her. She did not ignore Fitch Treadway in the gentlemanly way her husband had. She called him to South Cottage and announced there would be a huge increase in the rate for carrying cargo from the cannery.

"Mrs. Rathrock, you know we cannot pay it!"

"Perhaps if I had less expense of lawyers I would not have to charge it!"

"That is blackmail, Mrs. Rathrock! How can you do that, and you such a friend of Polly's!"

"It must be done, that's all. We can exist quite nicely together, if only you will drop this suit of yours."

Fitch Treadway set his jaw. "I believe in the deed, Mrs. Rathrock. I cannot drop the suit. We will just have to get along without each other. It will be hard on the Rathrock enterprises, too."

He was right, of course. The cannery had always produced a great deal of business for the Rathrock ships. But it would not make a critical difference—would it? They would have less income for a while, but in the end Fitch must capitulate, for he would have to take his fish to the mainland somehow and unload and load it again. The Hazard Harbor was too treacherous to attract ships other than Jonathan's to load the catch. That was the way it had been when they had come here, and Fitch Treadway, living hand to mouth, like the others, had been only a little better off than the rest.

She was jolted from sleep one gray predawn by the distant reverberation of the captain's Spanish cannon. Grabbing on a mantle and a pair of slippers she dashed up to the cupola. Through the spy glass she saw the two new blockade runners coming into the harbor, two triumphant dark spots on a horizon of swirling snow.

Gleeful as a young girl at the sight of her suitor, she spun down the stairs and jerked the bell to waken Annie. "Go and get a groom and send him to Shipwreck with the carriage for the captains of the two ships that are mooring. Then come back and help me dress."

Frustrated with the complexities of the feminine toilette, Lucy struggled with her pantaloons and camisole, her openwork silk stockings, the ever-present petticoats, the linen engageantes which must be fastened under the bell sleeves of her dress. She was in a hurry, and yet she wanted to look especially well. She dusted on a bit of pearl powder and frowned with impatience while Annie draped her hair round her ears and turned it into a plaited bun at the back of her head. She was especially glad for Annie's company these days, perhaps because she was cut off from the companionship of her own sex, since becoming Bryan's trustee.

The feminine exchanging of visits had stopped. Lucy, always rather bored by it, had no time for it, now. And yet she missed those leisurely afternoon chats, the communion, however imperfect, of her sister women. Even Polly Treadway did not come to South Cottage, since Lucy had raised the cargo rates. A rivalry which had been only the thing of men, had become personal.

The path she blazed was lonely. In all the world she had only Brye, who adored her, for company, and in a sense, Maddie, who seemed to admire her. Sometimes it seemed she had not even energy for these two. The new relationship between her and Maddie had sunk to a memory, like the coals of an untended fire. Left to a governess, Maddie wore her hair in ringlets again. As for Brye, he did not make his sweet confidences to her anymore. He seemed almost frightened of her, since she had taken over his father's work of readying him for his manhood. It made sense, Lucy thought, regretfully. He had always been afraid of the captain. But he would thank her when he was grown, when he was proud of the person he was because of her.

She was only doing what was necessary, she told herself, but that was not exactly the truth. Lucy was enjoying herself. No one would ever guess to look at her that she had denied herself her lover, that her husband was lost at sea. Lucy glowed with fulfillment. Her cheeks often were so high with color that the island women whispered that she painted them. Lucy enjoyed Annie's companionship that morning, but when she heard the sound of carriage wheels in the drive and twisted away from the last ministrations of the hair brush, she needed no one.

Lucy Rathrock was in her element as she tripped downstairs and slipped behind the great oaken library desk to receive the captains of the blockade runners. She had told Galen that she did not care for power and that, she was beginning to realize, was not exactly true. Though she had not lusted for it or sought it for itself, she enjoyed this ordering about of men and ships, the grappling with problems, the glory of achieving solutions.

And now in this cold, snowy dawn, she knew the first of the kind of victories she had envied Jonathan. The library was frigid; she had neglected to have the fire lighted, but Lucy herself did not really need it. She pointed to the grate, blamed the oversight imperiously on a maid and ordered a breakfast to be brought for her and the visitors. "Black tea, as soon as possible, biscuits, eggs, shad and a loin of mutton."

The captains came in noisily, laughing and boasting, regaling her with the kind of tales she had used to catch fragments of from her exile of needlework. They had run in to Charleston under a heavy barrage, slipping past the harbor guard without a murmur. Then as they had been ready to leave, the cotton loaded; the moon had come out from the clouds, pale and bright as only a southern moon could be. They sketched eagerly for her the climes she had never visited. The March wind that had been as warm as May, the silhouettes of great spreading trees and rows of balconied houses on the shore. A Navy frigate had spotted them then and had sounded the warning with a shot across the bow. The Rathrock ships had run for it. Two Union vessels had given chase. One had been left far behind. The other, in a fever of pursuit, had carelessly cut across channels and had run aground on one of the harbor's lurking sandbars. The new blockade runners were the fastest things on the water, the captains said. They were ready to go again and again.

"Do you mean they are faster than *The Lucy Maid?*" she demanded.

"No, my lady, nothing driven with shafts will ever be faster than *The Lucy Maid.*" They spoke of the clipper with as much reverence as of a dead queen. "But *The Lucy Maid* was harder to maneuver, and if the wind failed—"

She nodded. "Very well. Every member of the crew shall have a bonus for his bravery. Can you make ready to sail again in a week?"

The captains left, and Lucy paced about the house to work off her excitement. It was not enough. She must do something to top it off before she could rest. She remembered the old quarrel between her and Jonathan over the matter of steamboats in the first year she had come to the island. She had dared then to dispute his word. But now!

"You were wrong, Jonathan," she thought. "Sails are not always best. It has just been proven. And now I shall prove how very much *I* am the one who controls Hazard Island. I will buy a steamship, and everyone will know I am my own person and not just the echo of my husband."

She was surprised to find that this had become important to her, that Hazard Island should not only prosper, but that she should have the credit for it. She shrugged the thought away. Hazard Island must have steamships sooner or later. Lucy would purchase them now and anticipate the times. Delighted with her own boldness, she worked happily, sending off inquiries on the matter.

Sometime before noon her endeavor was interrupted by the announcement that Fitch Treadway was waiting to see her. "Why, send him in at once," she said. It could mean only one thing. Fitch was capitulating.

He stood before her stormy-faced. "Mrs. Rathrock, I have come on a matter concerning all of Hazard Island. It is greater than the rift between us."

"A rift I hope will soon be healed."

Fitch Treadway looked at her incredulously. "It will never be healed any more than the cut between the island and Lighthouse Head will close. It is, like that, a natural thing. But there are still matters on which we must work together or none of us will survive."

"And just what matter have you come about?"

"Blockade running, Mrs. Rathrock. It must cease at once!"

"Cease! Mr. Treadway, do you know what we have just accomplished? We have run a Union gunboat aground—"

"I do not find that a cause for rejoicing, Mrs. Rathrock,

especially I do not favor the cause of the South. I did not think you did, either."

"I don't," said Lucy, feeling a little confused, "but the Queen—"

"The Queen! The Queen! Do you know that two Union ship are patrolling the island? Does that man you have in the light tower tell you nothing? They have been there for days, and no one the wiser, except that that girl, young Alyce, has let the matter slip. If they missed seeing the blockade runners that came in this morning, it is a miracle. Do you know what will happen if the Union discovers your little game? They will send a force to occupy Hazard Island and annex it. *That* will put a stop to this blockade running!"

She was frozen, helpless with terror. "What shall I do? The blockade runners are in the harbor—"

"Scuttle them, Mrs. Rathrock! With their cargo!"

"Scuttle them! But I have just paid—"

"Their purpose cannot be mistaken like that of a clipper, Mrs. Rathrock. You should have thought of that. Do it quickly before they cost us all of Hazard Island!"

She ordered the ships scuttled and went to bed ill and shaken. So soon had the glory of morning turned to defeat. "Oh, Jonathan, I am only a woman, after all!" she thought, and wished she could remain indefinitely, trembling under the quilt with a case of vapors.

Her respite lasted only until the next morning when her maid came in with the news that a United States Naval cutter was in the Shipwreck Harbor.

"In the harbor?" she cried fearfully, clutching the covers.

The maid looked at her peculiarly. "Yes, my lady. Her officers have sent word that they are coming ashore. They wish to see the proprietor of the island."

"Very well, then. Go and start cook to preparing a luncheon. Beef sirloin with glazed onions, turkey and oysters—oh dear, I have not time for all these domestic details. Tell her to prepare the best of whatever we have. And to serve the best wine. Send Annie here at once."

She dressed very carefully, chosing one gown, then discarding it in favor of another, expounding the credits of a third to a patient Annie. Oh, if Jonathan could be here! Then she would be sent away to do nothing more than see after the china and crystal!

"Well, I am a woman and that cannot be helped," she

decided. "I cannot deal with the Union officers as a man would, but perhaps I may find being a woman an asset after all. I must be steady without being abrasive; I must be charming without being a coquette. And there is one other thing I must do. I must send for Fitch Treadway, who is at present the best *man* on Hazard Island."

And she went downstairs and had the Union officers ushered into the drawing room, where the atmosphere was more feminine and conducive to politeness.

How easy it was, after all! They had come to see the captain. Certainly they expected nothing of his wife. She thought quickly and said that her husband was on an extended trip to England. The officers cleared their throats and balanced dainty teacups. They had come on a matter of some delicacy, they said.

"Please," she cried, "do not be shy of mentioning it to me! We are neighbors, you know. I am sure that if we can help the Union in any way—"

"It is a matter of two blockade runners that were sighted in the Bay of Fundy, Mrs. Rathrock," they began, almost apologetically.

"Blockade runners! Do you think they might try to come into the harbor? Oh, I should be afraid of such a lawless lot. No better than pirates! Do stand in the harbor to protect us!"

They smiled, amused, and traded their tea cups for mugs of rum and birch beer. They relaxed and sampled lobster au gratin and stuffed oysters. Not many of their expeditions turned out so pleasantly. Not often did the alleged enemy turn out to be so lovely. Not often was a luncheon given in their honor and attended by the highest society available, including numbers of attractive ladies.

Lucy had planned well, but one guest appeared whom she had not expected. Polly Treadway, answering the summons that had been sent for Fitch, who had not been found. Polly was no help at all, for she fainted away at the sight of the Union blues in the dining room. Carried off to the morning room, she recovered after a few whips of a camphor and rue vinaigrette, which one of the guests wore in a heart-shaped locket hung from loops of silver snakes.

"Lucy! It has happened! We are annexed!"

"No, of course not. We would never go so easily, without even a fight. Anyway, you and Fitch have little to fear. *You* have not been running the blockade. *You* do not have a grant from the Crown that will be invalid in the case of annexation. Don't worry so. The Yankees are not barbarians. If they come, it will not be burning and looting and violating women."

"There is the lawsuit, Lucy. That would be invalid, too, and that is what Fitch lives for," said Polly, and she did not go in to luncheon, but rode away limply in her fine landau.

After the Union officers departed, Lucy sent for Galen Le Blanc. He stood before her on the flowered library carpet, water from a misting rain dripping from his wide-brimmed shooting hat.

She could not help frowning at the hat, until finally with a mocking gesture, he whipped if off and made her a bow. "You wished to see me, my lady?"

She ignored his sarcasm. "You did not tell me about the Union ships, Galen. And you knew the danger."

"Yes. You are right, Lucy."

"Why, Galen?"

"I should think you would know why. Did I not tell you I would have you if I had to wrest the entire Rathrock empire from you to do it?"

She went gray with something beyond anger. A sob rose in her throat, and her hand closed over a cameo paperweight on the desk. Her arm rose as though to strike him with it, and she saw him flinch instinctively. Something in that movement made her regain her reason.

"When you first came to Hazard Island, my husband generously allowed you to stay and perform a useful task. Now you are no longer fulfilling that duty satisfactorily. I can do nothing but expel you from the light tower!"

He gave a short laugh. "Expel me! You need me, Lucy. There is no one who would replace me."

"I can do it!" she cried shrilly. "I am mistress of Hazard Island."

"You used to be *my* mistress," he said wistfully. "I would have to tell that."

"You dare to threaten me! I can threaten you with worse! I have only to give your name to the magistrate at St. John, and you will be off to England to stand trial for your part in the Darby Mill riot and whatever else you did! I could have you wasting in prison. Perhaps you would even be executed!"

He smiled ruefully and put his hat back on his head.

"Ah, Lucy, it does not matter. I love you, and you know I have always been willing to die for a cause." He kissed her forehead lightly and went away.

Lucy dropped her head onto the desk and wept.

Chapter 15

Galen Le Blanc did not leave Hazard Island. The light burned steadily through the spring fogs. And Lucy did not make good her threat against him. Time drifted on. Pressure became greater on Lucy to hold a memorial service for Jonathan and to erect a monument in the churchyard.

She went sometimes to that spot overlooking the ocean, where he had said that their graves would be. She would sit with her skirts spread out around her, watching the darting clouds of sand swallows that nested in the sandy banks below. She would ingest the smell of the ocean, listen to the cries of herring gulls and black-bellied plovers over the boom of the waves. How full the churchyard was of empty graves, of monuments to those presumed perished on the Charleston expedition! How unfair it seemed that Jonathan's plot should remain only in field daisies and primroses, when he would want the most imposing monument of all, to show that he was the captain, even in death.

But Lucy had had enough of empty graves one nightmarish day long ago in a Turkish cemetery. She had accepted death when she should not have, and because of it, Galen had been taken from her forever. Now she would cling to hope as long as any could be left. She had a phobia of empty graves that made her will stronger than that of most other Hazard wives.

She was aware, too, as she looked about the churchyard, that she was not the only one holding onto hope. The captain's plot was not alone in its vacantness. She knew that these other women would lose hope, too, if she "buried" Jonathan. She would wonder, after all, if she were doing them a favor. Better, perhaps that they should give up and return to their families in England as others already had. Better that they take new husbands from among the tars than to struggle on, raising gardens and sheep, working in the smokehouses to supplement the death duty she had paid.

Scarcely ever did she pass Wailing Widow Cliff, which commanded the best view of the sea, without seeing one of them standing there, staring irrationally after some ship, which, without doubt, rested on the bottom of Charleston Harbor. One young bride had thrown herself off. Of all the Charleston casualties, hers was the only occupied grave.

Fitch Treadway lost his case in court and gamely filed an appeal. He would have a better chance in a higher court, where points of law might outweigh awe for a grant of the Queen's. Business was not so profitable as when Jonathan had been in charge. Fitch was still refusing to pay Lucy's shipping charges; and although the new steamship had been a success, Lucy did not have capital to order more, after the loss of the two blockade runners.

"Tom Cory is waiting to see you, my lady," she was told one afternoon as she returned from an inspection of the docks.

"Tom Cory!" she cried, and rushed into the library without even removing her cloak. Tom Cory had been on *The Lucy Maid*.

She felt she was seeing an apparition standing there, he was so thin and bloodless, his face so sallow that it had no more color than the surrounding air. His clothes were ragged, and his eyes had an unchangeable gaze of startled horror.

Seeing him she stopped, almost wishing he *were* nothing more than a ghost, a ghost that would fade away without answering the question she had to ask.

"Tom, sit down."

He turned about dazedly as if he had not been aware that the room had chairs. She took his shoulders and pushed him down. He had no more resistance to him than if he had been a package she was setting there.

"Tom? Tom?" He blinked at her uncomprehendingly; then meaning rose to his eyes as he remembered what he had come to say.

"All gone, my lady," he whispered dully.

"All? All? Think, Tom. Was no one but you picked up from the water?"

"There were three more. Joseph Banning, Edward Dreppard, Ted Hopkins. All dead now of a fever in prison. We dug a tunnel together, but only I was left to escape."

"And those were the only Hazard sailors? What of the captain?"

"No one else, my lady. No one else."

She ordered herself mourning dresses of black bombazine trimmed with crape. She erected the monument and wept as though the grief were fresh.

And then the Union Navy began to harass Hazard Island, commandeering a load of sugar for its own use, circling the harbor and taking target practice at the features of Wailing Widow Cliff.

When the "nose" of the widow was blown away, Lucy's fury knew no bounds. "Haul out the cannon," she ordered. "Position it so that we shall have a good target if they do it again."

Fitch Treadway urged against retaliation. "It may be taken as an act of war, Mrs. Rathrock."

"We must show them that Hazard Island is not to be trod upon. They must see we are not defenseless."

"Please, Mrs. Rathrock! You are not yourself just now!"

She supposed it was true. She had not been the same since the news from Tom Cory. Sometimes she felt she was almost becoming Jonathan, thinking with his mind. It must be that, since she knew that her position was no longer temporary, since no one would relieve her until Brye reached majority; she needed more to rely on her husband's judgment than on herself.

"It will be only one shot across the bow, Mr. Treadway. We will only be protecting ourselves, as is our right."

The whole island heard the reverberation of that shot and seemed to shrink back, as if it might make a moat of air between itself and the ocean. The gunboat went away without reprisal. This very circumstance made everyone sure that this would not be the end of it. No one knew exactly what kind of resistance Hazard Island could make, but from Shipwreck to Hazard watches were kept and guns were oiled and polished.

Evening came. A queer sort of light made the island look like a browned photograph. A heaviness foretold a storm. Horse after horse came pounding up the drive of South Cottage where the tall birches and the ancient beeches already whistled and swayed, protesting the rude gusts. The message of each horseman was the same. A battleship was bearing in on Hazard Island. Each informant looked to Lucy for instruction. Hazard Island realized suddenly how much it had come to depend on Mrs. Rathrock.

"Shall we send out ships to fight?" someone asked.

"No, of course not. We have only the cutter with swivel guns and one other, lightly armed. It would be a massacre."

"We must do something, Mrs. Rathrock, or tomorrow we shall not be Englishmen!"

She fought down panic, her mind spinning. She was more frightened than she had been even when she had fled Paris with Georges dying in her lap.

She looked at Brye, white-faced beside her, and made her decision. "We shall have to stand off the landing party," she decided. "We shall organize every gun on the island. Fitch Treadway shall be in charge."

That was the thing to do—turn the matter over to a man. Let Fitch Treadway save the island for the Rathrocks. How ironic that he could not protect his interests without protecting hers, too! She wondered what Jonathan would think of it.

When everyone had gone, she sent the children to bed and sat in the drawing room alone with only one lamp lighted. She did not know how much time passed as she sat hypnotized by the shrieking of the wind.

"Mama!" The soft voice melded with the tumult of the storm, and Lucy looked up, jolted, thinking almost that some banshee gust had taken soul. Maddie came out of the dimness and, encouraged at not being told to go back to bed, sat down at her mother's feet.

"Mama, is there no way we can turn out the light?"

"Turn out the light? Then we should be in the dark."

"Not this light, Mama. The Hazard Light. The battleship will wreck without the light to guide it. We don't need guns to save Hazard Island. Hazard Island can save itself."

Lucy stared at her daughter with sudden respect. Maddie, who was a native of her island, had a better understanding of it than she. Hazard Island was a power unto itself. It had no need of protection.

"But the tide is up, Maddie. No one can get across to the Head."

"Can't you give a signal?"

"I can't think how." She sent Maddie back to bed then,

frustrated with the child's unabated pushing of an idea that would not work.

She paced the floor, for the idea had become imbedded in her mind like a painful splinter. The Hazard Light must be put out. But it did not seem that the problem was in getting the message to Galen. He must already know of the battleship. He would have seen it. And yet the light glowed, a beckoning finger of destruction. Galen would not help her. He was pledged to wrestling her empire away.

Finally she went upstairs and changed into the chamois riding trousers which she had ordered in an uninhibited moment and had never worn. This was not a time for modesty; she must not be encumbered by a skirt. She fastened on her hooded highland cloak, and going to the library, took down a rifle, which hung over the mantle. The rain beat on the folds of her cloak as she went out to the stables and saddled Kumrah herself.

The horse balked and reared as Lucy tried to lead him into the storm. Lightning popped exposing the scene as though for a camera. The photograph would not have been blurred, for the trees seemed to suspend their thrashing, shocked at the thunderclap. The lightning seemed to come from every side as she rode. She had the fantasy that a savage force of soldiers was in the woods. They were shooting at her from everywhere, and the heavens were merely joining in the lust for her annihilation.

She must get through! She rode with her head pressed against Kumrah's neck, she and the animal wincing and dodging as one as limbs came smashing down and derelict lobster pots rolled past. She reached the edge of the cut and looked toward the black sea, where the battleship must lie. She shuddered as she thought of the men on board, the rampant sea sucking at their very feet. *They* would be thinking of wives and sweethearts they might never see again, women like her, for whom they made their sailors' valentines of scrimshaw work on bone, knitting sticks and apple corers.

"How can I do this, I who am a seaman's widow?" she wondered. She looked at the great pale moon of the Hazard Light and raising the rifle to her shoulder, took aim. She shivered, and the shot went awry. "I must not be a silly female, not now," she told herself, her resolve firming. A warmth seemed to prickle at the back of her neck. She imagined Jonathan behind her, strengthening her with his ghostly presence. She fired again. Still the light shone. She fired again and again. A sob escaped her, lost in the anguished howls of the breakers in the cut.

"Oh, it is so much harder than I thought! If only I had got Jonathan to let me practice. He might even have taken me out riding for rabbits, if I had not disliked guns so after those days in Paris." She spent the last of her ammunition and sank down on the wet earth, weak and without hope.

When she raised her face again, there was a queer darkness, as though the clouds pressed closer than before. At first she did not realize what had made the change, then, looking across the cut she saw that nothing of Lighthouse Head was visible. No silhouette of land, no tower. The Hazard Light, after all its faithful years, was out.

Had the Head been torn from the island, washed away like a piece of rockweed? She could imagine nothing else. The rain beat down urgently, the droplets stinging her cheeks. The courage that had sent her into the storm had vanished with the need. She could face the elements no longer; and remembering a small cave nearby, she led the horse carefully inside and sat shivering, wrapping and rewrapping her cloak around her and wishing she had flint for a fire.

"Well, it is done, however it happened," she thought. "The light is out. Will that be enough?" Then out of the blackness on some distant promontory, another light winked into view. It quavered at first as though someone held it. Then it was still, steady, beckoning. She held her breath, fascinated, locating the new light in all its relationships.

"Why, it is a trap! Whoever follows that light will go onto the borers! No one could run the borers in the darkness, not even Jonathan himself!"

Who had thought of this? It was a ploy that was almost certain to work. The light was high, and the urge of the seamen to head for its warmth, its promise of safety, would be all but undeniable. She watched it for half an hour, as it beamed its monstrous lie across the water.

Then a scream, the first of many. The dreadful smashing of wood and rock. She left the cave and rode home through the storm, trying to outrun the wind that carried the shrieks of the drowning to her ears. Great gusts worked lecherous fingers beneath her heavy cloak, lifting it, spinning it out from her body, exposing her to the violation of wind-rushed currents of rain.

"Go, Kumrah, go!" she urged, and the beast seemed to respond to the awful need in her voice. When she stopped to take shelter again, she caught sight of the light. Now it was moving, not going anywhere, wandering up and down in the night.

South Cottage stood out from the rain, every light blazing. Fitch Treadway ran from the doorway to seize the bridle and lift her down. She stared at him dazedly.

"Why are you here? Why are you not organizing the rescue?" she demanded.

"We can do nothing, Mrs. Rathrock."

"You must!" Beside herself, she drummed her little gloved fist on his chest.

"We would only be sending Hazard men to their deaths along with the Americans. You'll not find a soul to venture out tonight."

She drew a long breath and regained herself. "Yes, of course. Have the cliffs patrolled all night to see if there is anyone to whom we can drop a lifeline."

Fitch Treadway smiled ruefully. "That is being done. And do not speak to me as if I were your lackey. I am Treadway of North Pines. Do not become confused, Mrs. Rathrock!"

With such suddenness did they resume their role of enemies. She missed the solidness of his support. She knew that she needed Fitch Treadway. Unable to sleep that night, she went up to the cupola and stood for a long time. Many lights moved on the shoreline. She found herself studying them, trying to pick out one that was different from the rest, one that had helped to send a shipload of sailors to their deaths. She thought something must mark that light, that somehow it must burn more feverishly than the others, like a soul searching its way to lost heaven. She could not pick it out, and yet she was certain it was there.

The dawn was a dreadful thing, for terrible as the night had been, the morning was worse. The storm abated, and Lucy rode on the beach, where every line of waves washed up more wreckage. A figurehead lay face up in the sand, gazing with blank wooden eyes at the calamine blue sky. Around it other faces as still as hers lay carved into grotesques by the hand of the sea, their eyes as empty as the wooden ones.

It went on for days, until it seemed that Hazard Island would be plagued forever with this washing up of bodies and debris with every tide. Men worked the stretches of sand constantly and put out in boats all around the island to reclaim bodies hung up on rocks below the cliffs.

And there was salvage of tobacco boxes or metal match boxes shaped like dogs' heads. Somehow these domestic trinkets, snapped up at once by their finders, spoke more of the loss of humanity than did the remains of their dead owners. Lucy had accomplished her purpose, but at what cost! Hazard Island would be safe for a long while. The Union would not soon risk another battleship on her shores.

Lucy thought often of the person who had carried the light to mislead the ship. She had supposed that someone would come forward to claim the credit and perhaps to demand a reward for his service. No one did. Many had seen the light, and as no one owned to having carried it, the stories told about it began to take on a quality of the supernatural. The phantom light, they called it.

As for the Hazard Light, no one mentioned that. No one was very surprised that that Frenchman had done his duty and shut it off. Lucy could not fathom it. With every day that passed, it seemed more and more that she could not let it go. He could have destroyed her, and he had not done it. The shock of Tom Cory's arrival and the sinking of the battleship began to wear slowly away.

"Why, I have no husband anymore. That need not keep me from Galen, any longer."

There were other considerations, of course—the scandal that would be caused by a liaison between the mistress of Hazard Island and the hermit of the Hazard Light. "Dare I marry him when the period of mourning has passed?" she wondered. "It would be enough to keep tongues wagging for the rest of our lives! Would we be acceptable in St. John society, I and my lighthouse keeper? Would people notice how charming and well-educated he is? And what mischief would he get into, my Galen? It might affect Maddie's opportunities for marriage and as for Brye, whatever would *he* think?"

She mused this way for a week, rather enjoying her flirtation with the idea, imagining Galen at South Cottage. And yet, the more she dreamed about it, the less feasible it seemed. She could not picture Galen in Jonathan's black oak dining chair—Galen, smoking pipes after dinner with the ships' masters they would be required to entertain. Galen in her bedroom was a more likely fantasy, for she had replaced the great half-tester she had shared with Jonathan with a canopied cast brass bed, which was airier and more suited to her tastes.

But marriage, if it came, could not be for another ten months. And Lucy tired of day dreams. The first of the lilacs bloomed by the porch railing, the morning she set off for Lighthouse Head.

A few eiders waded in the cut, searching minnows, as Lucy went down the steps. The air had a clearness, a sense of newness. She felt herself become younger, lighter, as she waded barefoot in the numbing stream. On the other side, she began to run, not stopping to put on her new, fringed Adelaide boots. Her cheeks had flushed, her hair had half-fallen from its pinnings when she burst into the light tower and ran up the stairs.

He was sitting at the little handhewn table, reading a book over a cup of tea. He looked up mildly, surprised but not expectant. "Well, Lucy, have you come in person to pay my month's wages?" He had about him a calmness that almost alarmed her.

"Why did you turn off the light, Galen?"

"You were shooting at it. Who else could it have been with such excellent nerve and such horrible aim."

"And?"

He brushed crumbs from his nankin trousers. "I was a coward, Lucy. I could not bear to have you fail. I could not have your spirit crushed. I would have you whole, with your precious island or I would not have you at all."

"Then have me!" she said joyfully, and jerking at the fastenings on her mourning dress, she shoved it away to the floor.

Chapter 16

The next years on Hazard Island were the happiest of Lucy's life. The island prospered; Fitch Treadway, deprived of Galen's help, lost his lawsuit; and several times a week, Lucy slipped away to Lighthouse Head. She would leave early and make the trip on foot, so that her mount would not be missing from the stables. She would keep to the sheep trails and the woods to avoid making a habit of being on the road.

On these occasions, the faithful Annie would announce that Mrs. Rathrock was indisposed or that she was taking supper in her room to rest. "Your mother works hard," she would say to the children's protests. "She deserves some time for herself. And you, Master Brye, and you, Miss Maddie, are old enough to amuse yourselves with concerns of your own. Master Brye, work on your arithmetic. Miss Maddie, your needlepoint wants finishing."

They would groan and sneak off to play cards together. They dared no stronger disobedience, for years of consuming devotion to the Rathrock household had honed in Annie a terrible righteousness. She was no longer the slip of a girl Lucy had brought from England, and when her jaw clamped and her bosom heaved, she was no more to be ignored than God in the burning bush. Only Annie of all the Rathrock servants had ever been able to bully Brye and Maddie.

Annie guarded her mistress' secret with a fierceness equal to that of the great racing tides that wrapped the lovers safe from discovery on every long, sweet night. No one on Hazard Island guessed, except Alyce, from whom the secret was not long kept. She had returned from gathering dulse for the cooking pot that first evening and had found them sitting together, arms about each other in companionable embrace. Galen had taken her by the hand and introduced her to her mother.

"Now she is here, Alyce. You see, I always told you she would come."

The delighted girl had reacted with a maturity that Lucy thought was beyond her sixteen years.

"Oh, Mrs. Rathrock, ever since I was a little girl, I have dreamed that my mother would be like you!" she cried. "Mrs. Rathrock! But I cannot call you that! Shall I call you 'Mama'?"

"I would like it," Lucy said, choking back tears as her arms closed around the daughter she had last held as an infant.

"You two will need privacy," Alyce had said briskly, when the hugs and kisses were finished and the fire had burned low during the tale of her parents' separation. And she had gone to move her things to a higher floor of the tower.

"Really, Galen, how does she know so much? She acts as if she understands what love is all about."

"She does," replied her father complacently.

"She does! But that is scandalous! I knew nothing when I was her age! Who is the scoundrel who told her? You should box his ears at the very least."

Galen gave her a sidelong smile. "It would be difficult to do, Lucy. I am the scoundrel."

"You! You of all people should preserve her innocence, Galen! You will make a loose woman of her."

He sighed and placing both hands on his knees, gazed out at the gannet-flecked sky. "I have been both a mother and a father, and I have done what I thought right. Knowledge will not make her licentious; it will make her wise. *She* will not lie on her marriage bed a human sacrifice in the name of modesty. *She* will know what it is young men are after when they come about, and she will think twice before she favors them with her smiles."

"So. You have taught two women about love, Galen."

"Have I? Was the other you?"

"I had no idea what it was all about until you took me into your arms. I hope you are right about Alyce."

In truth Alyce was no coquette. But somehow her very lack of posturing made her all the more beautiful. If she were to mince her walk instead of striding about with that long, easy gait, she would seem less sensual. If she wore a cage instead of relying on petticoats, she appeared less supple, and the wind, blowing against her as it always did, would not reveal the round curve of her hips. And the frank gaze she turned on men was somehow more exciting than the veiled promises of the flirt.

When Alyce walked about Shipwreck on some marketing errand, every male eye followed her. And when she went out to help her father collect the herring from his weir, other boats found excuses to maneuver closer to watch her lissome form and see the play of the sunshine on the glowing, golden banner of her hair, which she still wore loose like a schoolgirl.

Lucy grew more and more apprehensive about Alyce. She came and went with never a by-your-leave. She might even catch a ride across to St. John on some boat from the island, and they would never know she had gone until she returned in the evening and sat with her face buried in some book or newspaper she had bought there.

"Alyce, would you like to go away from here?" Lucy asked. "Perhaps to some school in England or France? There would be no problem with expenses—the Rathrock money would equip you. When I was at Mme. Fichaud's, we would go to plays and to museums and cafés. We would walk along the quays among the vendors and the booksellers and think that all that mattered in life was teeming there. The people, the great buildings, the music, the paintings! Don't you want to see it all, Alyce?"

"No. I would not fit in in Paris—or any other such place. And what is in Paris does not matter to me. I am content to read about it in books."

Alyce's attitude frustrated Lucy. Alyce was beautiful, and she was brilliant. How she would shine on the Continent! She would be eccentric, but room had been made there before for eccentrics.

"Do you intend to write books, Alyce?"

"I like to put stories down on paper sometimes. Why do you ask that?"

"Your father told me once he wanted to make a writer out of you."

Alyce smiled a secret little smile, and Lucy was suddenly aware that Alyce had a mind of her own, even where Galen was concerned. "Oh yes. He thinks to make me independent, so that I shall not be the slave of some man. It is all in his mind as orderly as a law book. But my father does not understand how a woman feels. I will not allow myself to be his contribution to the cause of justice. My life shall be warm and full of babies and kisses and laughter."

Lucy sighed, feeling suddenly very old. Why had *she* not said these things to Galen so long ago in Paris. *She* had not been following her own heart when she had lived with Galen as his mistress, but striving blindly after his ideals. Could it be that this daughter of hers was wiser than she?

and I will send it to Charles Ashton, the captain's dear

"Well, Alyce, should you write a novel, give it to me, friend. He can get the ear of any publisher in England."

Alyce did not write a novel. She went humming about Lighthouse Head all summer, looking especially lovely, her unabashedly-tanned skin striking against the honey of her hair and the pale, sprigged muslin of her dresses. Galen never knew quite where she was, for she seemed as ephemeral and as difficult to put in place as the shifting sea breeze. She dug in the garden, her long, slender fingers bare of gloves; or she went handlining in the boat. He might glimpse her as she scrambled over the rocks to collect the sheep. But more and more of the time, Alyce was not to be found at all; and when she returned to the light tower, she always sang, and her face glowed.

Then one morning she told her father why.

The commotion in the front hall of South Cottage was terrible to hear. A commanding voice bellowed demands to see Mrs. Rathrock; and but for the French accent, Lucy, closeted in the library with her work, would have thought it Jonathan. The silver dish for visitors cards hurled through the air as Lucy came into the hall.

"I said now! I will not wait!" declared Galen Le Blanc.

She stood there astonished, ink dripping onto her dress from a pen she had forgotten to put down.

"I must see you at once!" he said, and seizing her arm in a way that made the servants gasp, he pulled her back into the library and shut the door.

"Lucy, you must do something! Alyce is your daughter. Surely you must have known!"

"Known what, Galen?

"If you do not know, it is almost too awful to tell. Pour me a brandy."

"I shall pour myself one, too, if it is so bad. Now—tell me. I have to know."

"She is in love with a sailor, and she is determined to marry him."

"And the sailor?"

"He came to the Head to ask for her hand. Young Tom Cory. He is only a deck hand and will never be much more."

"Tom Cory is a good man, Galen. If he had not been, Jonathan would not have taken him to Charleston on *The Lucy Maid*."

Galen made a face of disgust. "He cannot even read and write. And what is worse, he does not care. He has no ambition and no talents except that he is rather good both at playing the fiddle and dancing. I suppose that deciding whether he will do one or the other or both at the same time is the largest matter ever in his mind. Lucy, tell me that I do not have to accept this along with everything else I have suffered!"

"I will talk to Alyce," she said.

He sent Alyce to South Cottage that same afternoon. She came in trying to look serious and not succeeding and smelling of fresh air and balsam, which must have crushed its perfume into her dress as she lay in some meadow, undoubtedly not alone.

"So, you have had a proposal, Alyce."

She flushed. "Yes, Mama."

"That is very nice, but you are too young. And this man—what has he to offer? You cannot possibly be happy with an illiterate. We will send you to a boarding school for a year or two and you will see how you feel when you return—"

"I will not be sent off, Mama!" Alyce's voice was soft like her father's, but she had drawn herself up, and the little heart-shaped chin that reminded Lucy of Galen, was set. "You ask what he has to offer—he has love and constancy. His life will revolve about me like the earth around the sun. He is handsome and gay, and he will allow me to lead the life I always have. He adores me so that whatever I do is perfect. If I take off my shoes on the beach, if I will not wear a crinoline even in church, that is perfect because I do it. Only think, Mama, what better solution could I ever find for my life? I am what I am, Mama, the daughter of the hermit of Hazard Light. It cannot be changed, and I do not want it changed. I will make my own decisions, as my father taught me, and I have decided to marry Tom Cory and live forever on this island, which contains everything and everyone I love."

"And Tom Cory—is he one of those you love?"

"Oh, yes!" she cried, and the joy bubbled in her laugh and shone in her eyes.

It was not a case of a young girl swept away by the thrill of her first suitor. Alyce had a wisdom, a perspicacity far beyond her years, a result perhaps, of her early wandering and years of isolation with her intellectual father.

Galen was forced to accept the marriage. The effort seemed to drain Galen more profoundly than the failure of the revolution or Lucy's refusal to leave the island with him. He fell in with the wedding plans laconically, allowing Lucy to order him a short frock coat of blue diagonal, a double-breasted, white drill waistcoat and gray angola trousers for the occasion.

Alyce was married in September in the Hazard Church. The first chill gusts of autumn tugged at the veil behind her wedding bonnet and rippled the lace insets of her skirt. And around her neck hung the emerald locket that Galen had given Lucy in Paris.

Since the wedding was sponsored by South Cottage, it was well attended. How good Mrs. Rathrock was to that poor girl, people whispered. What an interest she had always taken in the motherless child of the lighthouse hermit!

Lucy could not have told why tears flowed down her cheeks. Was it because Maddie, the maid of honor, tried so hard to cover her limp that her face was a grimace of anguish? Or because Brye seemed bereft that he was too young to wed the girl unknown to him as his sister? Or was it because Galen looked so splendid and proud and at the same time so worn and old? Or that this beautiful bride, whose mother had been loved by a nobleman, was marrying a man who could not even read or write?

Bride and groom had no such mixed emotions, and when Lucy saw the way Tom Cory looked at Alyce, her doubts were almost quelled.

The wedding celebration was held at South Cottage,

a kindness to a bride who had no proper home, and a gesture to the sole survivor of *The Lucy Maid*. After the hours of dancing, the feast of jugged hare and lobsters, roast truffles, fruits and cake, the pair was sent off on their wedding trip to the West Indies, a gift from Lucy.

Nobody thought it strange that night that Galen remained long at South Cottage. Indeed, he had no place to go, since the tide had long since covered his access to his light tower. That night, for the first time since the approach of the Union battleship, the Hazard Light did not shine. Nobody but Lucy thought it was symbolic, of a courage that had finally failed, a purpose given up at last.

They sat companionably together before the fire like any mother and father of the bride, Galen reclining comfortably on Jonathan's long-seated lounge with its bobbin-turned barley-sugar woodwork; Lucy, more primly, on a chintz-cushioned basket chair. And when they knew that everyone else had gone, they held hands, talking over the events of the day, how beautiful Alyce had looked and how young and confident.

"If only she might stay that way, Galen!"

"Yes, yes!" agreed Alyce's father with a sigh.

Lucy closed her eyes, remembering that day when the steps to the Hazard Church had not yet been finished, and she had walked in that same sea breeze up a hill of daisies to Jonathan. How full of hope and energy she had been! How ready to begin her life, to propagate ships and sons for Hazard Island!

Oh, if she could recapture the way she had felt then! If she could stand as a bride before that altar!

She opened her eyes and studied the profile of her lover, who was staring into the fire. Suddenly her heart was beating furiously, and when she spoke, she had to discipline herself to make the words come out casually.

"Well, Galen, shall we be next, now that Alyce is wed? What a shame if you do not wear that suit again, when you look so handsome in it!"

What heaven to sit here with him like this every night! She did not care what would be said; she did not care about the consequences. But Galen's expression did not change. At first she thought that he had not heard her.

Then he said very quietly, "No, Lucy. It's too late. Neither of us wants to leave Hazard Island now, and I have not the strength to live at South Cottage in the shadow of Jonathan Rathrock. I am the hermit of the light, now, not the Galen Le Blanc you loved in Paris. I am the keeper of the light. It is all I shall ever be."

Chapter 17

Before the leaves flew again, Alyce had made Lucy a grandmother, bringing forth little Adam Cory with the ease that Lucy had once hoped she herself would produce heirs for Jonathan.

In the United States the war had ended, and with the lifting of the blockade, the Hazard shipping interests flourished. Lucy was thinking of buying another steamship with the new capital.

One night in October she lay propped in bed, studying plans that had been sent to her. Outside the wind whistled teasingly, a mischievous fury, rattling the gold-coin birch leaves in the rain gutters like change in a pocket, singing ghoulishly of winter. At first when she heard the sound, she thought the peculiar cadence was her imagination. It was the wind. It was not the first time she had imagined such a thing, but it was the first time since Tom Cory had come back to the island with his tale of *The Lucy Maid*.

Tap, tap. She willed the sound away. She pulled up the covers and thrust her head beneath them like a child. Even muffled, the sound became louder. She pushed the covers away and sat upright, her eyes large, her face white.

Jonathan Rathrock's footsteps! It could be nothing else!

How often she had heard them just so in the night, during the years of their marriage! And yet they were not quite the same. They did not come as quickly. They dragged in a disembodied way.

Closer! With a practicality born of desperation, Lucy thrust the steamship plans under the mattress. Feeling faint, she reached onto the bedside table for a mint vinaigrette she had unpinned from her dress. The flowered porcelain knob of her door turned slowly, and she dropped the vinaigrette, thrusting her fist against her mouth to stifle a scream.

"Lucy! I am not a ghost." He stood there, thinner than she remembered him, his red hair flecked with gray, and where there had been only a mustache, now there was an imposing beard.

"You look different, Jonathan, but not like a ghost," she managed to say. She did not mean the beard; she meant a certain seasoning, like the wood of a ship that has survived every punishment of the tides, a certain exciting strangeness that the years had marked on his face.

He stroked the growth on his chin. "Ah, yes. I grew it to cover a scar across my chin that resulted from a tangle with a Yankee saber. Can you get used to it, Lucy?"

"Oh, yes, Jonathan!" And action coming at last to her numbed body, she flung herself at him, knocking away the mahogany cane that he carried.

He swayed and staggered and the two of them fell backward onto the bed. He did not ask her if the ban on loving her was lifted after all these years. He simply raised her night dress above her hips and used her with a potence and meaning that his long ordeal had created in him.

She responded in a rapture, her head light, her breath coming in long surrendering moans. Her hands clasped his hard hips, and she held him as though to imprison him inside her as surely as he must have been in some Union dungeon. He was her husband, the substance of her existence, the man who could master her, make her cared for and mindless with his love.

He shuddered and lay still, not stirring from her arms, as he looked lingeringly around the familiar room. "Lucy," he said finally, "I do not like this bed. It is ridiculous."

"We will change it, Jonathan," she sighed. A great lassitude crept over her, a kind that she had not felt since the hours following childbirth. She had done her job. The master was home, and she was a mere wife again.

During the years of his internment in a Union prison, Jonathan Rathrock had assumed that his empire lay in ruins. Those years had been especially miserable because Jonathan had refused to identify himself or the port from which he had sailed.

Jonathan Rathrock had come up fighting from the fiery waters of Charleston Harbor, drawing a cutlass and upsetting the very boat whose crew had pulled him in, his clothes and hair singed with the flames of his beloved ship.

They would not allow him to drown after that, as he would have preferred, but kept after him until he was hauled aboard a man-of-war and subdued with a clout of a musket across his skull. And he had awakened to sunrise at sea, a melancholy mixing of the empty, gray sky with endless empty water, which made even such an old sea dog as he feel lost and soulless. They had brought him a tin pot full of "water bewitched," tea sweetened with molasses, and sea biscuit and cold salt beef. And he had eaten manacled to a chain cable.

They had refused to tell him if any of his tars had been saved—perhaps they did not know—and they urged him to identify himself so that his poor wife, wherever she might be, could be informed of his safety. They had realized he must be the captain of the expedition, a feather in their caps, and he had been treated with respect for the gallantry with which he had fought. But Jonathan had given them no satisfaction. He had gone his way to prison, saying nothing, never knowing if Hazard Island had been annexed, never knowing how Lucy or his heir, Brye, or his adored daughter, Maddie had fared.

His laugh boomed everywhere on the morning after his return to Hazard Island. He could not keep himself from squeezing Lucy's waist, even in public, as he viewed the busy shipyards, the well-stocked warehouses, the vessels of his fleet riding proudly at moorage in Shipwreck Harbor.

"Ah, Lucy, what a jewel you are! You, the trustee! How well I chose when I chose you! There is not another woman who could have done it! How did you persuade the company to appoint you—ah, let me guess—you asked it of Charles Ashton, shameless thing that you are, and he arranged it. The rascal has never ceased to love you!"

She let a merry flush admit what she had done. "Jonathan, you never told me before that Charles still loved me," she said, turning serious. "You must have guessed it in all the visits you made to Grandemas on your travels."

"Yes, but it would not have pleased you to hear it, Lucy. You wanted him to love Caroline."

"Doesn't he love her at all, Jonathan?"

"Yes, in a way. I believe she is happy. And now about the lawsuit, Lucy. Do not tell me that you worked your wiles on Fitch Treadway! I would not believe that!"

"No wiles, only good lawyers, Jonathan." She did not tell him about her attempt to bring Fitch to heel with higher cargo rates. He would learn soon enough how much money she had lost with that maneuver. And if Galen had not left Fitch on his own— She shuddered at what a homecoming Jonathan would have had then!

"So. You do not take credit for winning in court, Lucy. But I'll wager that Fitch Treadway would have had Hazard Island one way or another if he had had you behind him instead of Polly."

"Poor Polly. Do not joke about her, Jonathan. I am afraid she is very ill. She has not been herself for a year."

"Ill!" said Jonathan with a snort. "I saw her this morning, and she is nothing of the kind. She has become an opium addict with those glazed eyes of hers. She will be staggering before long."

An opium addict—Polly! Lucy realized at once that he was right. She had seen women like that often enough in St. John—the stuff was easy to get. She had seen some of the widows of the Charleston expedition turn to it. But Polly? Polly had a husband who adored her, and she had never seemed to want anything more.

She had not the leisure to think about it, for Jonathan suddenly demanded to see his grave. "Oh, the monument!" she cried aghast. "I must have it removed at once!"

Jonathan, standing back, viewed it from this angle and that. He admired its silhouette against the light from the sea, and he sighed with satisfaction, as though his soul were truly resting there. "Do not have it taken down, Lucy," he said finally. "You will only have to put it back someday." And he kissed her there in the caressing sea wind, just as he had once before, when he had first showed her the place.

Jonathan Rathrock liked his monument. He took to walking about in the churchyard after services to have a look at it. "I need a bit of air," he would say. "I must clear the sticky odor of all that lavender water the ladies wear from my senses."

Lucy would always refuse his suggestion to come along, so he would commandeer Brye instead. It gave him a fine sense of permanency to stand there with his son.

"Captain, when shall I go to sea?" Brye would ask.

"Soon, Brye. You shall be my cabin boy. We will ask your mother."

"She will not want me to go."

"She knows you must."

"Captain—when I am dead, will my monument be as high as yours?"

Jonathan would give the boy a wry smile. "Higher, Brye, and that is an order. But you shall not be so lucky as I to have one before you are gone."

Lucy felt that her own days were numbered. She had not dared to tell Jonathan about the steamship she had bought. Nothing else she could have done could have angered him as much. The steamship was just now gone on a long journey to the Sandwich Islands, but any day it would be returning. On the morning after Jonathan had come home, she had burned the plans for the second steamship in her bedroom fireplace.

Lucy would steal out of bed each dawn, and throwing on a cloak, go out into the cold, bracing air of the cupola to search the horizon with a spy glass. At last she saw it, no more than a small dot, black against the pinkness of the sea, but unmistakable with its heavy, awkward build. She fled downstairs and putting on her riding habit, mounted Kumrah and struck out across the island.

She had it in mind to be gone the whole morning, but it was too cold for such a venture. Her hands, even inside her kid gloves, seemed to freeze to the rein, and her stomach, heedless of the peril awaiting her at home, rumbled inelegantly for the breakfast she had not eaten. She paused on a rise and reined in, looking back at South Cottage where curls of gray smoke rose from both chimneys. "I must face it sooner or later," she thought, turning and looking with a shudder to the harbor, where the steamship was just making port.

Jonathan was seated at the dining room table before a spread of pigeon, herring, eggs, and muffins. His chair was turned sideways, and he was looking through the bay window with a spy glass.

She stopped, paralyzed with fear, and wondering why he had not already struck her dead with the force of his anger.

He turned to her gaily, "Lucy, take a look at that outlandish craft that is putting in to Shipwreck. See all the soot and smoke coming out of it. It looks like a factory that has put to sea. How do they manage to navigate in that fog! I wonder what it is doing here. Perhaps they have been forced to make port for a whiff of fresh air." He laughed at his own witticism.

"It is coming home, Jonathan," she said, flatly, darkly, into the laugh. "It is a Rathrock ship."

Johnathan did not say anything. He seemed unable to speak. He stared at his wife. She stared back, braced and afraid. Then, finding herself unscathed, she could stand the wait no longer and plunged to the offensive.

"It is the way of the future, Jonathan, and Hazard Island must look to the future to survive. The steamship has produced a good income, and the great clipper ships will be gone one day—"

Her blasphemy roused him from his confoundment. His face went red, then purple. His formidable chest heaved like stormy sea swells, and his eyes tore her like swords.

"By god, Lucy! Sails are the soul of the sea, and as my name is Jonathan Rathrock, they will never be gone from Hazard Island!"

What did leave Hazard Island was the steamship. Jonathan had said that sails were the soul of the sea, but prised that he did not simply scuttle it, such was his fury. She half-expected to be shipped off herself with the boat. Jonathan sent it to St. John to be sold. Lucy was surwhat he had meant was that they were *his* soul. All his manhood, his self-esteem, all that was noble in his character was built upon the sail. She had emasculated him with the steamboat, and she wished, for his sake, more than her own, that she had never purchased the thing. Strange to remember what a sense of power it had given *her* at the time, a reaction exactly the opposite of Jonathan's.

Jonathan did not speak to Lucy for two weeks. He went about with a wounded expression and did not come near her bedroom. That part of their marriage was off once more, and this time it was his doing. She wondered if he would ever desire her again.

Before long, however, Jonathan was forced to speak to Lucy. The island had too many complex problems about which she now knew more than he. "Lucy, what is this Confederation everyone is talking of?"

"It is the joining of all the provinces of Canada under one government, Jonathan." Confederation was something she had wanted to keep from him as long as possible. She knew it would upset him.

"That will not be good for us! We should not have as much influence over the laws that affect us. It is a certain thing?"

"There will be a vote, and the climate is ripe for its success. Many in New Brunswick have been frightened by the Fenian thing."

"The Fenian thing?" He looked at her blankly.

"The American Irish, many of them veterans of the Civil War, would like to invade Canada and hold part of it hostage for the return of Ireland."

"That is absurd!"

"Perhaps. That is what they said about Paris in 1848—in 1847."

He sighed. "Well, if it is not the United States or Fitch Treadway who is trying to take Hazard Island from us, then it must be the Fenians or the Confederation. I hear that Galen Le Blanc has been campaigning up and down the island in favor of this joining of the provinces. He will be for the Fenians, too, if I am any judge of character. No matter, he will not be listened to. I must do some campaigning myself, among the legislators in the New Brunswick Assembly. I shall be gone for a while, and you may look after the island, so long as you buy no steamships!"

So this was the Galen who was so broken, who would never be more than a hermit! But the hint of social change, and he had regained his spirit. The idea made her long to see him again, glowing with that purpose he had had when she had first known him.

A day or so passed, and Annie announced at dinner that Mrs. Rathrock had one of her headaches. Lucy would have every slice of the cake, it seemed. She would be wife, part-time manager of the Rathrock empire, and Galen's mistress. And a mother again, it soon became apparent. She thought the child was Jonathan's, conceived in the great power of their first coupling after his return, but she had no way of knowing but that the quieter poetry of Galen's love might have produced it.

Power and poetry. She admitted to herself she must have them both, and climbing to the cupola to gaze out at the misty beacon of the Hazard Light, she knew she would go there again and again as long as she lived.

PART III

Sarah — 1875

Chapter 1

Sarah Ashton, only child of Caroline and Charles Ashton, expected at any moment to die. The gale had been blowing since before dawn, seas washing over the bow of the three-masted New Brunswick square rigger. Through the wail of the wind came the racketing screech of the flock of petrels, storm birds of the Atlantic, that followed the ship like harbingers of death. The storm jib was up, the sky sails taken in, and only an hour before a young tar who had gone aloft to repair a line had been blown loose and had fallen into the taut belly of the mizzen. There he had floundered for an eternal moment, flailing and screaming before he spilled to his doom, an insignificant dot in the pudding thickness of the fog. The ship's captain had not turned back. Indeed he could not have, for the wind was shoving them ahead with a mastery that defied the interference of Man.

She blamed the captain anyway. It was an indication of the savagery she expected to find on Hazard Island, whither she was bound, very much against her will.

It had all happened so suddenly—the railway accident that had ended a holiday excursion. Her dear mother and her gentle father dead. Sarah had thought she would die of the pain; then, when she had thought she could stand no more, there had come these other shocks. Her magnificent home Grandemas, taken from her for the residence of the new lord, a cousin for whom she had no liking.

She had had no place to go, and then suddenly it appeared that she had a place worse than no place. Among her father's papers a document surfaced, making Jonathan Rathrock her guardian. And that was the end of it. *He* might have quartered her in some appropriate boarding school, but he had refused outright, and had insisted that she come to Hazard Island. How very high-handed of him to take her away from everything she had ever known! Of course she had always been told how forceful he was. Caroline Ashton's eyes would light with amusement every time she repeated the story of how the captain had swept her cousin Lucy away to be his bride. But then, Lucy had wanted to go.

Sarah most certainly did not, and she had already decided she did not like Captain Rathrock. It was not a spur of the moment judgment. He had come to Grandemas from time to time over the years. He had always frightened her with his huge frame and his voice that boomed as no one else's ever did in the quiet, serene mansion. Sarah had been wont to hide in the pie chest during his visits.

"Go below, Miss Ashton!" said the captain of the square rigger at her elbow.

"I shall stay here," she said, pulling her soaking cloak more tightly about her. "I shall be seasick if I go below!"

"If you remain on deck, you'll be swept overboard," he declared.

"I'll take my chances."

"You're a plucky woman, Miss Ashton, but it's my chances you'll be taking as well. I'm to deliver you to Captain Rathrock; and should I fail, I would lose everything—my command, my reputation, even my family's home on Hazard Island."

"Is Jonathan Rathrock really so powerful?"

"More than you can imagine. Now go below, Miss Ashton. We shall put into Shipwreck soon, and it is not the easiest port in the world to make, as its name might tell you."

She went, reflecting how far he had mistaken her motives for remaining in the storm.

Not pluck, but craven fear had kept her there. If she must face death, it must not be helplessly in a tiny cabin. She must be able to see the toppling masts, to reach out her arms to grapple with the boiling green waves as they swallowed her.

A scrape of metal made her start with new alarm. He was locking her in!

"There, you'll be safe and snug, Miss Ashton!"

She threw herself against the door, beating on it with her fists, kicking it. "Captain! Captain!" But he was gone and her screams were as lost as the cries of the petrels. She fell onto the bunk and indulged in tears.

Safe! She knew what he meant. By such a definition, she might be safe drowned at the bottom of the ocean, for it was her virtue he was speaking of. Her chaperones, a new lieutenant governor and his wife, had gone ashore when the ship had dropped anchor at Halifax. No one was left to "defend" her, as if any of the sailors, who had eyed her so furtively since Liverpool, would have a moment to come and ravish her before the boat sank. She was as tucked away as part of the cargo, and she felt as owned.

Anger began to intrude on the fear. She welcomed it. She nurtured it. "We shall see about this!" She would complain to her new guardian, who had such power. She rose and pushed open the lid of her trunk. There were all her gowns, her best dinner dress with its front of blue satin and its train of red velvet, her polonaise dresses with their flounced underskirts, her Guernsey costume of fine knitted silk that she had worn for so many pleasant games of tennis on the lawns of Grandemas. Small use they would be to her now! She was in mourning and must go to her fate, be it Hazard Island or the ocean bottom, dressed like a little black crow.

Oh, if she had used those dresses when she had had the chance! If she had not spurned her mother's advice to select one of the young men who had vied for her hand when she had been the success of last year's London season! Then she would not have been shipped away, dispossessed and miserable, an exile.

But life had been lovely, made all the merrier because her grandfather, Lord Ashton, had died several years before, removing his gloomy presence from her life. He had never loved her; he had made her mother miserable over her failure to produce the boy that Sarah should have been. And her father, who had always tried to make it up to both of them, had been the lord. Sarah had been having fun, and she might marry at any time. She had laughed at her mother's urgency. She had not comprehended the thing that could happen. Her father had not been able to save the title for her, of course, and his money had been almost gone from bad investments.

All the young men had gone now. Not one had stepped forward to save her from her ruin. What chance would she have on Hazard Island? Oh, doubtless they would arrange a suitable marriage for her, probably to some oafish colonial. The sooner she was off Captain Rathrock's hands, the better, no doubt. She could not expect much from a man who had dragged her halfway across the world against her will.

She stripped off her wet dress and let it drop, as the lurching of the vessel sent her tumbling across the floor in camisole and petticoats. Staggering to her feet, she braced herself against the bunk and delved into the trunk, grateful at least that it was here, instead of afloat in the wash of the forecastle, like the trunks of the crew. The mourning clothes, with their crape borders, were all on top.

She shook out the best of the black dresses, the one she had been saving for arrival and changed her petticoats for her nicest one, threaded with yellow ribbons and trimmed in Honitron lace. In case one might be undressing at South Cottage in the presence of a maid, she told herself, while in the back of her mind lurked the thought that if she were to wash ashore drowned it would not be amiss to be well dressed either.

"You will be the loveliest woman ever to land on Hazard Island," her grandmother, old Madeliene Hamlin, had asserted, but that had been loyalty speaking, Sarah thought.

Sarah had inherited her mother's beauty, but the months of grief and shock, the omnipresent black that never let her forget, had drained away the color from her skin and her hair, which had been a sunny gold like Caroline's, was dull sulphur.

She would not be the most beautiful woman ever to arrive on the island, she thought. That distinction would still remain Lucy Rathrock's. Sarah looked once more at the miniature she had studied so many times during the voyage. This young girl, pictured with the merry smile and the plump clusters of ringlets, did not look formidable. *She* must be Sarah's ally on the island, for certainly it could not be the captain.

And yet the two of them were such different women. Sarah would have never sailed away willingly from her happy home, not even had a church been built especially for her wedding as it had for Lucy's.

Or was it only that Sarah had never really been in love—with a man or an island or with any kind of life that was unexpected?

"Ah, Lucy was a fine girl, but always discontent with a life of drawing rooms and tea cozys," Grandmother Madeliene had said. "Hazard Island caught her imagination, and I think perhaps she was as much in love with the idea of it as with Jonathan Rathrock himself. But there is one way the two of you must be the same."

"What is that, Grandmother?"

"She wed for love. Oh, I thought she was a fool when she threw away Charles Ashton's devotion the way that she did. But it turned out well, and Charles would never have been happy with Lucy the way he was with your mother."

"Mama made Papa very content, I think," Sarah said. "But when Captain Rathrock came to Grandemas, it was never a happy time. Mama would ask after Lucy, and the captain would talk on and on about her. Papa's eyes would have a look I never saw on any other occasion. Mama would keep smiling, but her face would seem like stone. And after I was old enough to understand, I thought that Papa had never stopped loving Lucy."

"Perhaps he never did, but Caroline was wise enough not ever to let Charles see that she knew, not even when he made Lucy the trustee for little Brye."

"And Lucy did her part, too, didn't she? She never returned to England though she loved you and mother so. How strange to think I have never seen her and after all those birthdays and Christmases she never forgot. I remember a silver toilette set and a pedlar doll with its basket full of wares—"

"Promise, Sarah," her grandmother said, cutting her short.

"Promise what?"

"That you will marry for love, like Caroline, like Lucy."

"But—"

"Promise. An old woman who will never see you again can go to her grave easy that way."

It would not be an easy promise to keep. Whom should she find on Hazard Island to inspire a passion in her like that her father had inspired in her mother or Captain Rathrock in Lucy? She who had had the pick of the London crop and had chosen no one!

Was that the very reason that she had not married? Because she had set her sights too high—on a rare kind of marriage like that of her father and mother? On Hazard Island her chances would be much worse, especially with her dowry only a fraction of what it had been before.

She had thought of becoming practical, of marrying anyone suitable, even an amiable widower whose wife had worn away from a dozen childbirths. Anything to avoid spinsterhood, to avoid being a burden forever on the Rathrocks. She would not be the first woman ever to make up with a brood of children what she had missed in a man.

But there was Grandmother Madeliene, looking at her fiercely from beneath the ribbon-encircled caul of her breakfast cap, and with a sinking heart, she had promised.

Beyond the porthole, the heavy rain stretched on forever, consuming the universe. Then from the decks came a shout. "The borers! The borers!" The terror in the cry made her press her face close to the glass to see.

Like great black giants the stones sprang from the water, the foaming ocean streaming from their faces. Then, eerily, they were gone, covered by another onslaught of waves. Suddenly, on the upsurge, the ship was among them. She heard the distant shrieks of the sailors, and unable to look death in the face after all, she closed her eyes.

"There she is! The Hazard Light, God bless her!"

The voice was swept away on the wind. Instinctively, her eyes blinked open. Through the mist came a small, slender shaft of golden light, far away, disembodied, as it came from Heaven itself.

She heard a cheer go up. "We're through! We're through!" Finally the key turned in the lock of her door. "We've dropped anchor, Miss Ashton. Home port!"

With shaking hands she fastened her mother's brooch at the throat of her dress, and pricking her finger, drew a drop of crimson blood.

She was ready to go ashore.

Chapter 2

Though the sea was still heavy, she debarked several hours later on the first boat to leave *The Racing Cloud*. This also was interpreted as bravery by captain and crew alike.

"Wait until morning, Miss Ashton. The sun will shine for you then."

"My relatives will have come to meet me. I mustn't keep them waiting." It was true that she did not want to begin by having Captain Rathrock think her a weak, burdensome female. She imagined his temper rising like the island's enormous Bay of Fundy tides as he drove home without her. But more than that she had a compulsion to leave the ship.

The idea of one more night in its airless quarters was intolerable while she could glimpse the soft, round outlines of hills in the distance. How could anyone be in love with the sea, as she had always heard that sailors were? How could anyone want to spend his life going back and forth across it?

I shall never marry a sea-going man, she found herself thinking. I would never understand him. And then, horrified at how such a qualification would dim her already not-bright hopes, she reneged, deciding instead only that she would never set foot on an ocean-going vessel. "Unless it takes me home to England," she whispered, as she stepped into the dory.

In the April air everyone's breath frosted. Icy waves sloshed over the side of the craft, and Sarah was soon soaked once more and chilled despite the dry three-decker cloak she had put on. The evening was dusky, the tide rising when the boat reached a rough pier laden with head-high piles of fish net and red floats.

Her skirt caught a rusty nail on the ladder, and she tore a three-cornered rent in it, but Sarah's elation at being ashore was such that she hardly noticed. She poked the tear shut and forgetting she was a sodden girl in unbecoming mourning clothes, forgetting that she did not want to be on Hazard Island at all, she twirled about toward the shoreline and greeted the island with a laugh.

"You're a merry one, Miss Ashton. We can always use a bit of gaiety on Hazard Island." She gave a start and saw a huge man standing behind a mountain of black nets. His hair and beard were streaked with gray, matching exactly the weathered boards of the dock. Everything about him was outsized, from his black boots to his bulky coat to his large-bowled pipe. Such an aura of strength emanated from his person that if she had not known Jonathan Rathrock by sight, she would have been certain it was he.

"Who are you, sir?" she said stiffly, trying to regain her dignity. "And where is my guardian? Captain Rathrock was supposed to meet me here."

"I'm Fitch Treadway, at your service. Captain Rathrock's at sea. It's Brye you'll be wanting."

"Brye? Do you mean Bryan? Captain Rathrock's son?"

"Yes, of course."

"Then why isn't *he* here to meet me? Where will I find him?"

"Most likely he's had trouble with the carriage. He has a fancy four-in-hand. Wonderful for racing on fine days, but not such good in the mud." Fitch Treadway seized the handle of her trunk and bending down, lifted her belongings easily onto his back. "I'll drive you to South Cottage myself."

"Drive me! Oh, but I couldn't allow it!" She looked around wildly. The sailors who had come ashore were already vanishing up the pier into the night. Her glance sought the lights of *The Racing Cloud*. How she wished her captain had come with her instead of staying aboard to supervise repairs to the rigging!

"I cannot possibly go driving off in the dark with a man I do not know!"

"And I cannot possibly leave you here alone in the rain, Miss Ashton." He looked perplexed. "I own the fish cannery and I am well-known on the island. It will be all right. Come along, Miss Ashton."

"Is there no place nearby I can wait for my cousin?"

He looked thoughtful. "Well, perhaps the public house. Ladies do have luncheon there now and again, though there'll be none there tonight, of course."

"I'm sure it will do very well," she said, relieved, scarcely wondering at his look, half dubious, half amused.

In a few minutes she was before a warm fire, still shivering, a cup of hot tea pressed to her lips. The place was almost empty. In one corner several men in whipcord trousers and woolen shirts sat over pewter tankards of ale. They looked her over in astonishment, then looked away. These fishermen would talk about her when she had gone, she thought. If she were so lucky as to ever go, she added as time passed.

In a room below a card game seemed to be in progress. From time to time laughter drifted up, accompanied once in a while by howls of dismay. She began to wonder what she would do if the establishment closed before Bryan Rathrock came. Fitch Treadway had left to go and check his sheds, and he had not said he would be coming back.

"Is South Cottage far from here?" she asked the proprietor at last.

"Far enough. At the other end of the island. If you are waiting for the captain, you had better forget it. He's at sea."

"I am waiting for Bryan Rathrock," she said.

"Well, make yourself comfortable then." He smiled at her, and she wondered why she did not like the smile. "Is that black you're wearing for your husband, dearie?"

"Why he is becoming impertinent!" she thought. "How dare he?" This was what she had come to already. She felt ill and knew suddenly that she must be out of sight of his leering eyes.

"Do you have a room I may rent for the night?" she asked.

He grinned at her. "I have a room that will serve the purpose nicely. Come over from St. John to visit, have you?"

She could not make herself answer him. He was too uncouth and she was too exhausted. She gathered her things and followed him up the stairs.

The tiny room was under the eaves. Its ceiling was barely high enough for her to stand up straight on the uneven, creaking floor. Frigid wind seeped in at the little window, lying like a blanket of cold on the handhewn bed beside it. She had only the light of a single candle, but all the same, she was glad to be left alone here and with a sigh, she locked herself in.

"Why didn't I tell that horrible little man that I am

Captain Rathrock's ward? He would have behaved better then. Perhaps it is that I have not even become used to *not* telling people that I am Lord Ashton's daughter. I have been concentrating on accepting the idea that I am no one."

She noticed that the fire was unlighted, and rather than call him back, she tried to light it herself, holding the flame of the candle against the logs. The candle sputtered and went out, plunging her into darkness. She gave a cry of despair and then undressed in the lightlessness and crawled into the cold bed.

As she lay there shivering, her eyes grew accustomed to the night and focused on a comforting glow from the window. Now and then she heard a laugh outside, a crunching of footsteps. And at last, exhausted, she dropped off to sleep.

A sound awakened her. She knew she was no longer alone in the room. For a moment of terror she was too frozen to move, and in that moment the bed sank with a heavy weight, warm breath fluttered at her ear, and a hand slipped familiarly around her breast.

Her head swam, a torrent of indescribable emotion rushed through her. She knew somehow, even before the man spoke that he could not be the horrible little proprietor.

"What a clever game to put out the light!" he said. "Are you Adele? Georgiana? You cannot be Susan! I know. Suppose I make love to you first, and then I shall guess. I shall guess soon enough that way. But quickly—give me a kiss. I haven't much time. I'm expected at home. I was to meet a silly cousin of mine—"

Fury put motion to her shocked limbs. "Indeed you were, Bryan Rathrock!" she cried, shoving him off and rising up, clutching the covers around her.

He stumbled backward with a gasp of surprise. A chair crashed to the floor. She heard the striking of a flint. "Oh, please do not light the candle!" she cried.

Then in the low of the light, his face wavered into view, handsome but unseasoned, blue eyes disbelieving, trying to regain composure.

"So you are Cousin Sarah! What an addition *you'll* make to South Cottage if you go playing many tricks like this!"

"Tricks! I have not been playing tricks! It is you—"

"What was I to think when I was told a lady had taken a room and was waiting for me there?"

"You might have thought of your duty to your cousin. I might have spent the night on the pier and died of pneumonia there while you—"

"By Heaven, Cousin Sarah! You sound like one of my old nannies!" said Bryan. Strands of Rathrock red sparked as he ran his hand through his sand-colored hair. A smile trembled at his mouth, and he gazed at her appealingly, looking in truth like a child trying to charm his nurse out of a switching.

And in spite of herself she was almost charmed. He had a talent for that, this cousin. And how he must use it! On Adele, Georgiana, Susan! She wondered if he could use it on his mother as well.

"The damage is done, Brye," she sighed. "Go downstairs, and I will get dressed and we will go to South Cottage now."

He thrust his hands into the pockets of his small-collared Oxonian jacket and looked disconcerted and embarrassed all over again. "Oh, Cousin Sarah, it would have made matters so much simpler if you had gone there with Fitch Treadway as I thought you did."

"Well, we will forget all that, Brye."

"I am afraid we cannot forget it. It's really your fault, Cousin Sarah. If only you had stayed on the boat as we expected you to, then we would not have started the card game—"

"So, it was you I heard downstairs. You were here all the time!" She could scarcely believe she had nearly forgiven him a moment before. "And when you learned I was coming ashore, you could not interrupt your precious game long enough to drive me home!"

"I wanted to, Cousin Sarah, but it was impossible."

"Impossible!"

"Because I had lost the transportation. Now I have won back the horses, but not the coach. So you see, we are stranded, unless you can ride bareback on a rather spirited mare."

She stared at him, almost as dumbfounded as when she had first felt his intimate touch. This could not have happened to her in England. She would not have imagined that it could have happened anywhere. She drew a deep, shuddering breath and said, "Well where is this person to whom you have lost the carriage?"

"In the cozy drinking killibogus—that's spruce beer and rum, an island favorite. The Indians used to make it."

She shuddered again. "Indians! I suppose they are lurking somewhere to scalp us!"

"Why, there are no Indians at all on this island, Cousin Sarah, and only a few friendly ones who come to sell mayflowers in St. John."

She sighed. "Well, there is that to be thankful for. Go outside and wait for me. I shall have a word with your friend."

After she had hurriedly fastened on the blue-ribboned petticoat and struggled with the bone buttons of her mourning dress, they went down together, Sarah blushing at the idea of seeing the proprietor again, Brye whistling under his breath, maddeningly unabashed.

In the cozy a fair-haired young man sat with black Wellington boots propped on a table. "Hello, Brye," he said. "Who's this? She's rather prettier than last week's."

"May I present my cousin, Miss Sarah Ashton," Brye said. "Cousin Sarah, this is Josh Treadway."

Josh brought his feet down with a bang. Sarah heard Brye stifle a laugh. She might almost have laughed herself if she hadn't been so angry.

"Josh Treadway! Then Fitch Treadway must be your father!"

"My mother says so," said Josh, collapsing into laughter now himself, his face flushed with drink.

"If your father knew what really happened to the horses and carriage—" "Oh, but he does!"

She was astonished. "Then he lied to me. He said Brye was probably stuck in the mud." She felt a particular insult because she had taken Fitch Treadway to be a man of honor. She must remember that she could not trust her own young judgment. She studied Josh's face and saw the family resemblance, a resemblance that was more than physical. There was the same solid certainty of self-worth in his easy posture, the same ambitious tilt to his chin.

"I'm sure my father never lied to you," said Josh. "He told you there'd been trouble with the carriage. It was what we decided he should say."

Thinking it over, she remembered that Fitch Treadway had said only that the carriage was fine for racing and not much good in the mud. They were all allies, three men against a woman, and though it still surprised her that Fitch Treadway had taken their part, she was beginning to be calmer.

Josh saw laughter tremble at Sarah's mouth and said with a grin, "We have treated Miss Ashton badly, Brye. I'll lend you the carriage for now. You'll have trouble enough at South Cottage, especially if the captain finds out it was me."

They were friends. That was evident in the easy way they went out together, each with an arm draped roughly about the other's shoulder, but there was something else—Josh had seemed almost pleased at the trouble Brye would be in because of him.

They brought the carriage around. Josh handed her up to Bryan with an elaborate courtesy and stood waving drunkenly as they drove off. The rain had almost stopped, and the night was very quiet, the silence broken only by the horses' hooves, the squeaking of the wheels and the distant hum of ocean waves. "Did you have a good trip, Cousin Sarah?" said Bryan, as though he were meeting her only now.

"Perfectly dreadful. I hate boats. They are prisons without so much as a tree or blade of grass outside one's cell."

"How peculiar," said her cousin. "I cannot get enough of sailing, and it's the very freedom of it I love."

"The captain would not lock you into your cabin during storms, no doubt."

"He did that?" Brye said in surprise. "I shall certainly speak to him."

"I should like to see him flogged!"

"It would take my father to tend to that," Brye said off-handedly.

"Do you mean Captain Rathrock really has people flogged!"

"On occasion. Why not? The island is his, and everything on it exists at his whim. I do, and so do you, now that you're here. And *The Racing Cloud* is my father's ship. But if you did not like the *Cloud*, just be thankful you were not on *The Lucy Maid*. She had a twist in her keel that made her the fastest thing in the provinces, and my father sailed her like a madman."

"Wasn't that the clipper that was lost off Charleston?"

He gave her a quick smile. "So you have heard of that. If only I had had a chance to sail her! My father always said that I might when I was ready. And I would have made three hundred miles a day all the way to Melbourne. I say, Cousin Sarah, I do apologize for tonight. You won't tell Mother what happened, will you?"

"I can think of no reason I should cover up for you," she said.

"Nor I either," he agreed. "But at least do not tell her that it was Josh I was playing cards with." And leaving her to wonder about the oddity of this request, he urged the horses faster. He made the carriage fly over the dark, rutted road, as though he were rushing to his doom while distracting himself with the race.

Sarah hardly knew what she had expected of South Cottage, but whatever she had, the name was misleading. It was not a cottage at all, but a stately white mansion with a row of black-trimmed dormers, like a line of winging gulls. It had twin chimneys, painted white. The doorway had a large fanlight above it, and the sidelights were set with rows of square panes in hues of rose and gold. Light shone softly through onto the lacy silhouettes of the birch trees that lined the curving drive.

The house was topped with an enormous widow's walk, and had, of course, a view to the sea. Its classic elegance and simplicity made it one of the loveliest places she had even seen. Stepping down from the carriage, she gave an involuntary sigh. It seemed like a home in a way that Grandemas never had and a hope flashed in her that somehow it would truly be her home, and return to her on this distant island something of what she had lost.

"We'll have to let ourselves in," said Brye. "Everyone will have gone to bed."

Treading lightly in his heavy boots, Brye led her into a dark hallway. Pausing, he lighted a paraffin lamp and in its glow hardwood floors gleamed, smelling strongly of lemon. The bannisters of the staircase, sweeping down, were likewise polished to a sheen.

"What am I to do now, Cousin Sarah?" he whispered. "I must wake someone, I suppose. I cannot show you to your room myself. It wouldn't do, I daresay. Well, I shall ring for Annie. She is fond of me, and perhaps she won't tell mother the hour."

"Brye? Is that you? You're very late. Did you find Sarah?"

On the stairs stood a woman, her dark hair loosened, streaming down her back, the lacy edges of her nightdress showing beneath her robe. She was not the girl of the miniature, and yet Sarah would have known Lucy Rathrock anywhere. The nubile youth had been replaced by self-assurance, and despite the lines at the corners of her eyes, she was still a great beauty. She would be so at eighty, Sarah thought. There was something more than physical about it.

"Cousin Lucy!" Sarah exclaimed, hurrying eagerly into her embrace, as though she could not believe her good fortune at finding another female on the island. Lucy hugged Sarah to her, her body still slender and firm, not gone soft and plump as Sarah's mother's had before her death.

After the long trip, Sarah needed to be drawn to such a sanctuary. She missed the softness, and too quickly Lucy drew back, holding her at arm's length. Her sharp eye examined Sarah as though she had been a bolt of silk. Nothing about Sarah's bedraggled person escaped her.

At last she said thoughtfully, "How familiar you are, Sarah. You've your father's eyes, and your mother's voice. It's as if I have known you always, and at the same time have never known you at all. I remember that brooch. How strange to see it after so long! Whatever kept you so late? Was there a problem on the *Cloud?* Her captain is very competent."

"Oh, no, I came ashore early—" Beside her Brye tensed, drawing in his breath. "I waited at the public house for Brye. He had—some trouble with the carriage."

Lucy's eyebrow went up, and she turned on her son the same look of inspection she had given Sarah. "Trouble, had you, Brye! Well I have always told you that silly carriage was impractical."

"You're right. But don't worry, Mother. Someday I will lose it in a card game and be well rid of it."

"No doubt." Lucy's mouth had the expression of the miniature, as though she were suppressing merriment. "Brye, go and see what has become of Sarah's luggage. She has had a hard welcome to Hazard Island, and we must let her get to bed. I'll ring for Annie to show her the way."

She pulled a cord, and in a moment, Sarah was being led up the shining stairs by a billowy, taciturn servant who did not appear to approve of her at all. "Here's your room, miss," she said.

It was beneath one of the dormers and the walls sloped cozily, adorned with flowered paper. Potted plants sat on a window ledge, and a light-colored four poster and dresser and a papier-mache chair completed the furnishings.

"Is this American?" Sarah asked about the bed and dresser.

"Not a bit," sniffed Annie, offended. "It's all New Brunswick maple, commissioned by the captain himself." Next Sarah thought, she would admonish her not to scratch it, but at that moment Brye came in, helping a stable boy with her trunk.

He lingered behind in the hallway after the others had gone, and giving Sarah a little squeeze around the waist, he whispered in her ear, "You're a peach. You got me out of a scrape. I can't think why."

And later as she lay, still agitated, unable to sleep as the last of the rain drummed quietly down, she couldn't think why either. But she knew she would never forget this night, or the intimate touch of her exciting cousin, who lived so freely and loved so recklessly.

Chapter 3

As lightly as a kitten, something landed on Sarah's bed. She opened her eyes to sunlight streaming into the pretty room. A little girl was watching her, her chin cupped in her hand.

"How late you've slept, Cousin Sarah."

"Have I? And who are you?"

"I'm Lily. Lily Rathrock. Haven't you heard of me?" Lily was breathtakingly lovely, with a delicate bone structure, translucent skin and eyes of wisteria blue. Her dark hair, in sausage curls, was pulled into two bunches. She was a small Lucy, except for those eyes, except that she seemed more fragile and promised to be an even greater beauty.

"I've heard of you. You're the baby of the family, born after the captain returned from prison."

"I'm not a baby," she scowled. "I'm eight. You've missed breakfast. I've brought you crescent rolls, and there's an apple, too." She unfolded a linen napkin carefully. Sarah was ravenous, having eaten little on the *Cloud* the day before.

"And do hurry, Cousin Sarah," Lily said. "We mustn't be late for church. The Rathrocks never are."

"Church!" Sarah cried. "I can't possibly go to church. I haven't had a bath! And my hair!"

Sarah clapped her hand to her head as Lily said chidingly, "God does not care about your hair, Cousin Sarah." It was a comment too old for her years, and Sarah supposed it was something that had often been said to *her*.

"My clothes! I shall look a fright. What will everyone think?"

"They will not think you a slugabed or a heathen, which is what Mama says people think when one stays away. Mama says you must go. And you must not look like a bit of flotsam as you did last night. Annie and I are to see to it."

"Oh!" Sarah said, stung by the thoughts that had been behind Lucy's kind welcome. "Your mother is very high-handed, Lily!"

"Of course. We all are. It runs in the family, people say. Hurry. There's a fire in the kitchen and Annie is steaming you a dress."

Annie took her over, tugging and patting, frizzing the front of her hair in a fringe as was the latest fashion, turning the sides back to join the chignon. Annie worked with a frown and an expert hand, and more than once Sarah yelped at a tug on her hair. "Please be careful. It will hardly matter how neat it is if it is not still attached to my head!"

Annie, never pausing, only noted that Sarah was too pale and bid her bite her lips to make them rosy. At last with a black-bordered white handkerchief added to her costume, she took her place beside Lucy in a landau more sedate than Brye's four-in-hand. She looked as though she had been truly washed and starched instead of merely patched together.

She saw the island that morning from Tory Road, which ran the length of it, like a ribbon strewn carelessly by a child, going around each molded hill. Sometimes when the land rose, she could look back and see circle after circle of road where they had been. The island seemed tame then, but at other times she woud catch a glimpse of jagged cliffs leading down to the sea and of long wind-stunted slopes of evergreen forest. Weirs dotted the blue water, speckled gulls topping every one, and velvety black guilemots dived for sand eels. Everywhere lupine was beginning to bloom.

The town of Hazard was a scattered collection of shingled houses, shimmering silver in the sun, some built almost upon the road, others away from it, close to the sea, as though each builder had been obsessed with the need for one or the other. A few houses were white, trimmed in black, in imitation of South Cottage. They reminded Sarah of so many stiff maidens at a lawn party, an impression reinforced by neat gardens and Priscilla curtains at the windows.

The church was high on a knoll, overlooking the sea. Three arrow panels of stained glass lifted skyward to the steep roof and from the chapel door uncut grasses spilled down, sprinkled with pink and yellow wild flowers and violets. Sarah cast a side-long glance at Lucy. This was the church where she had been married, the one that had been built for her wedding. Sarah tried to imagine how Lucy would have looked, standing at its door with her captain on a summer morning, her veil and skirt blowing like the grasses in the sea wind.

Lucy, impressive in her leghorn hat with follow-me-lads streamers, gave no sign that her thoughts were kin to Sarah's. She was frowning, looking up at the roof. "Brye, the wind has blown loose a piece of the cornice. Please remember to send a workman tomorrow."

"Yes, Mother," said Bryan, and jumped out to hand them down from the carriage. A flush rose to Sarah's cheeks as they took their places in the Rathrock pew. She was on display to all the Hazard faithful. The church was full, and she guessed that some of the worshippers had come as much to see the Rathrock cousin as to praise their maker. Certainly every head turned in their direction.

"Courage, Cousin Sarah," Brye whispered. "It's not only you. They are always interested in Mother and Lily."

Hoping for a neutral spot on which to fix her gaze, Sarah turned her eyes to the stained glass along the sides of the church and met the terrible glance of a drowning sailor. She turned away with a shudder, her dislike of the island strengthened. She caught sight of Fitch Treadway beside a pretty, plump woman with an odd, vacant stare. A chill ran through her, as she felt herself faced with something she did not understand, but with which threatened her.

"Mrs. Treadway is a sweet woman—one can see that— and he cares for her—his attitude is so gentle. And yet something has been terribly wrong in her life," Sarah thought. "Could it happen to me?" She had to know the nature of this new menace, and turning to Brye, she whispered, "What is the matter with Mrs. Treadway?"

"She's an opium addict," he replied. "She's been at it for years now, in spite of everything Fitch Treadway can do. Don't bother your head, Sarah. No one can help weak women like her."

"But what caused her to become an addict, Brye?"

"Who knows? She is wealthy and loved and has everything a woman could want. They do not even go to church with the fisher people any more."

Not satisfied, Sarah mused on the matter until the final hymn.

> *Almighty Father, quick to save,*
> *Whose hand doth rule the ocean wave.*

It would always be the same hymn, she was to learn, but this Sunday morning as the slow, sonorous sound drifted over the pews, a terrible loneliness swept over her as it occurred to her that she like Lucy must stand as a bride before this strange altar, if bride she were ever to be. And there, at that font, she was seeing for the first time, her children would be baptized if children she ever had.

Her longing for home became unbearable; and to her horror, a sob rose in her throat, and tears began to trickle down her cheeks. Brye looked at her sharply. Then, leaning forward, he propped his elbows lazily on the back of the pew ahead, blocking her from everyone's view except that of Lily, who was seated beside her. When the benediction had been pronounced, he took her hand and led her quickly through a side door.

"I'll show you the family plot, Cousin Sarah. I'm sure you'll find it interesting." Blinded by tears, she saw nothing until they were inside a large iron-fenced enclosure, the two of them hidden by a group of larch trees. "Hackmatack," Brye called them.

"There now, nothing like a friendly hackmatack. You would have had to meet everyone, and you are not up to it. We will say you felt faint, which will be understandable after your long trip. Mother will not care for it, but it will be acceptable. Lily will have told her the truth, anyway. Lily is in the enemy camp, I warn you."

"This is very kind of you, Brye," she said. He did not ask what was wrong, and she liked him for that. He was returning the favor she had done him by not mentioning the card game, she thought. Had she told about his escapade, she suspected that she, too, would have been "in the enemy camp."

"Oh, it's not kind at all," Brye was saying. "You are only making it conscionable for me to run from that pack for once. I am set upon each Sunday. It's a scheduled event, like afternoons at the Roman Forum. I counted four marriageable daughters in the congregation."

"Goodness! Do not tell me girls don't interest you,

Brye," she said and immediately flushed crimson, overcome with memories of confusing sensations which she dared not admit were pleasurable.

Brye did not seem to notice she was flustered. He thrust his hands into his pockets and stared out over the sea. "I am not interested in marriageable daughters," he said.

"But you must be the most eligible bachelor on the island," she said, thinking of it for the first time. "You will own it someday."

"Yes," said Brye, uncaringly.

"Well, aren't you *glad* you will own all this?" she cried.

"That's the joke of it, Cousin Sarah. Nobody can own Hazard Island. Hazard Island owns itself. Even my father doesn't understand that, but then the captain only came here. I was born here, and every breath I have taken has been of Hazard. Hazard Island is as much master of us as we of it. Someday the captain will learn it. Come, we'll talk of something else. I haven't shown you the graves."

"Who is buried here?" Sarah asked, uncomfortable with the conversation, which was unlike any she had ever had with a man.

"Why nobody is buried here," returned her cousin. "Nobody at all. We've been here only a quarter of a century, and there haven't been any casualties. Yet, of course."

"But, Brye, you are most disrespectfully *sitting* on a grave!" It was a full-length slab of marble. Above it stood a monument with its back to the sea.

"This? This is only the captain's grave."

"Your father's? But I—oh, dear!"

"Do relax, cousin. Remember I said nobody was buried here. It's Father's grave, but he's not in it. The slab is canted. Do come and look for yourself."

"Really, Brye—" But he grabbed her arm and pulled her down to a crevice beneath the stone. Instantly two awful eyes peered out at her. She screamed and broke free.

Brye burst out laughing. "Jemima, come out," he coaxed, and a calico cat emerged. "It's Jemima's favorite place. She's the graveyard cat and not very friendly. I wouldn't pat her if I were you."

"I have no inclination to," she assured him, still quaking. "Why does your father have a grave, Brye, if he is not dead?"

"Oh, it's the monument Mother put up when he was

lost on *The Lucy Maid.* Father is rather proud of it. When he sees the monument he sees the future—all the generations of Rathrocks that will inhabit Hazard Island. Power—for eternity—that is what the captain is all about."

Brye paused and dug into his pocket. "Jemima," he called, unwrapping a packet of fish scraps.

"Why, Bryan Rathrock, you're a fraud," she cried. "You intended to come here all along. It wasn't because of me!"

Brye looked surprised. "I never said it was, Cousin Sarah. I said you made it conscionable. I've done you a good turn, sheltering you in my hidey place. Next Sunday you will be on your own, and this spot will be taken. Look, there's Mother, getting into the carriage." He hurried her out of the enclosure, across the lawn.

Lucy was not angry, though Lily's smug, curious face informed Sarah she had told all. "We have made your apologies," Lucy said coolly. "Next week you will feel better, and you will be eager to meet the congregation."

"I'm sure I shall, Cousin Lucy," Sarah replied, and trembled at the off-handed way that Lucy Rathrock gave orders.

Chapter 4

The next Sunday, relishing her position center stage no more than before, she tackled the job gamely. Brye did not escape either. Perhaps he had been given a scolding by Lucy, or maybe he only wanted to see the show.

Several young bachelors were presented to Sarah. One, an officer on leave from naval duty at Halifax, asked if he might call at South Cottage. Lucy answered that they would be delighted and whispered aside to Sarah that although this Desmond Crandell was not really wealthy, people said he would one day be an admiral.

The Treadways came to speak to them, Josh giving high signs to Brye when Lucy and Lily were not looking. It didn't matter if Sarah saw. She was trustworthy, an uneasy participant in their collusion. The Treadway's daughter, Susan, tall and elegant, her olive skin heightened by rose tones, stood by in annoyance. When she looked at Brye from under dark lashes, it was not the shy glance of other girls, but the knowing challenge of a coquette.

Brye, slouched against a tree, acknowledged the look with a grin. It crossed Sarah's mind that he had allowed himself to be a part of the after-service socializing because of Susan. *She* had not been among the marriageable girls of the previous Sunday.

A similar idea must have occurred to Lily, for on the ride home, she suggested that Susan had not stayed away from church, as she had said, to avoid spreading her cold, but to keep Brye from seeing her red nose.

"Do not become a catty female," he admonished.

"God does not care about red noses," Lily replied, in variation on a favorite theme, "any more than Susan cares about other people's germs." Brye, not disagreeing, let the matter rest.

Whatever Brye's feelings toward Susan, he was out of the house often until very late, perhaps finding girls at Shipwreck who were not quite marriageable or playing

327

cards with Josh. She wondered if he were imitating his father, for the servant girl who cleaned Sarah's grate had hinted of the wild life the captain led these days when ashore.

You cannot be Susan, he had said that night at Shipwreck, as he had slipped his arm around her in bed. Because Susan Treadway was of too good a family to dare to make an impromptu rendezvous at an inn. But Brye had hoped, Sarah thought. With what reason?

She envied Brye his free life. It was a new experience for her to hear someone come up the stairs in the small hours, whistling and humming in a mysterious, self-satisfied way. Often it was all she could do not to fling open her door and rush out to beg him to tell her all that had happened. She had had a taste, that one night, of a sort of life she had scarcely guessed at before, and she longed to be a part of his conspiracies again. It would not do, of course. Even if she had dared, she would not have known how to approach him. She remained a proper and frequently bored young lady. She told herself that she missed the social life of London, the shopping excursions, the friends of her own age and sex.

With Captain Rathrock at sea, Lucy was too busy to drive out visiting often. She spent a large part of her time in the study, working over island business at a huge desk with many pigeonholes. She issued licences, oversaw rents, settled minor disputes, ran the captain's fleet.

To Sarah she spoke about new draperies for the drawing room or of the quality of vegetables in the salad, exactly as a man might speak, conversing with his aunt or sister. In her peculiar hybrid role, Lucy seemed to have lost the ability to deal with women as women, and Sarah wondered if she were the same with Maddie, who was away at a young ladies' school at St. John.

"She refused to go to England," Lily said, rolling her eyes. "Maddie's horrid; you'll hate her." And every two weeks a letter arrived, addressed in a scrawling, undisciplined hand.

Lucy would say, "They have not improved her penmanship yet," and she would carry it away. Sarah was never privy to any of its contents.

With summer the island bloomed, and Sarah's mourning, which had kept character with the landscape in the lingering April bleakness, was as out of place as an unleafed tree. The wind itself seemed to try to blow her away like a winter cloud when she went out walking.

She welcomed the push of the scent-laden breeze. If it could not blow the mourning black from her body, at least it fluttered the dark veils over her heart. She began to find her favorite spots, just as Lucy had found hers so many years ago. But Sarah did not like the cobbled beaches or nooks in the sea cliffs as much as Lucy had. The spots she liked best were the sphagnum bogs where the rough ocean seemed a thousand miles away. She loved wandering over the lacy, pale green covering of the springy bog, among the pink flowers of swamp laurel and fragrant white ones of Labrador tea.

Sarah fancied herself quite alone in the bog. The silence was unbroken even by the hum of black flies and mosquitoes, since the pitcher plants and sundew set their traps for these and kept the bog free of insects. But one day as she paused beside a clump of tall swamp cotton, a scrap of laughter drifted to her from beyond a thicket of heath and huckleberry. The girlish laughter brought Sarah a curious step closer. She was thinking perhaps to make a friend, to join in the merriment, but as she peered through the branches she glimpsed a man and a girl. Brye! And Susan Treadway? No, some other, for with her back to Sarah, her hair was long and golden. Brye had his hands on her shoulders as he kissed her on the forehead. Nothing about the kiss seemed the way she would have expected Brye to kiss a girl. It was—worshipful.

Brye walked off suddenly, passing so close to her in the thicket she did not know how he missed seeing her. Startled, she took a misstep backward, and her feet were sucked under in a spot where the sphagnum had not taken hold. She grabbed instinctively at a Rhodora bush, shaking its foliage. The huckleberry crackled, and there was the golden-haired girl, holding out her hand.

"Hold on, I'll pull you in," she said. Her grip was uncommonly strong as she hauled Sarah to solid earth. "What a pity! Your boots are all ruined. You're Sarah Ashton, aren't you? And your father was a lord."

"Yes."

"Well! I have been wanting to meet you, but this is a strange way to do it. I used to come to South Cottage a great deal, but I don't so much anymore."

"Is it because of Brye? I saw you together. It's only honest that I tell you that."

"I didn't think you came to spy. But yes, it's because of Brye. Nobody must know he's in love with me."

"I won't tell—but why? Doesn't Captain Rathrock approve of you?"

She laughed, looking even more beautiful than before. "He would not, but I am married already. I am Alyce Cory, and I am not in love with Brye."

"Then why—"

"Why do I meet him? Because he needs someone. Because he has always loved me. He almost wept on my wedding day, when I was hardly more than a child, and he was even younger. Because I do love him deeply and understand him in a certain way."

"Like a little brother?"

"Ah! Exactly so. But he does not want to leave it at that."

"Oh," said Sarah perplexed, "I don't understand why he needs someone when every eligible girl on Hazard Island has set her cap—"

"That is the very reason," said Alyce. "He says he will love me forever, but when he has found the woman who does not covet him because he is Jonathan Rathrock's heir, he will forget this silly love for me."

"And what if he does not find such a woman?"

"He must," said Alyce. "How lucky that Brye says you are to be trusted, Sarah." She swept her long hair over her shoulder and picking up a bucket of blackberries, said, "I must get home. I live on Lighthouse Head, and the tide will rise soon."

"Lighthouse Head? But I thought that only a hermit—"

Alyce's laugh pealed again. "People are slow to change, Sarah. They will still call my father, Galen Le Blanc, the hermit of Lighthouse Head, even though he is a member of the Parliament and spends most of his time in Ottawa. He was elected from the island right after Confederation with the backing of Fitch Treadway.

"Captain Rathrock was quite piqued, since my father ran against the captain's own hand-picked man. My father has got new railroads laid, and people all over Canada say he will be prime minister someday. While he's away, my husband Tom and I run the light. Oh, and my son Adam, whom all of us adore beyond anything in the world. I teach the Hazard school. That was Mrs. Rathrock's idea, so that I should not waste the good education my father gave me. *He* always wanted me to be a novelist, but somehow it was not right—a girl from the wildness of the Head writing for ladies in their cozy drawing rooms."

"Perhaps the ladies would have liked the excitement of your books."

"I doubt it. Those on Hazard Island have little use for me. They think it's their husbands I excite. I don't mind. I am very happy being with the children. Walk down to the school with Lily, someday, Sarah, if you're in want of a chat." And lifting her skirts, she disappeared behind a group of young larch trees, calling back when she was out of sight, "Be careful of the bog, Sarah. It's dangerous to come here alone."

So now Sarah had her wish. She was involved in Brye's intrigues again, keeping a secret more serious than the loss of the carriage in a card game. Somehow Sarah was not glad.

No wonder Brye slipped off to the captain's grave to stare out at the ocean and dream of Alyce! And while he tried to relieve his feelings with his shenanigans, he had about him an intensity that hinted that his love was not the passing fancy of a boy.

The more Sarah saw of Alyce, the more she admired her. The frankness of her mind Sarah would never be able to emulate even if she dared. And her uncorseted body and uncoiffed tresses had a beauty that hair pads and skirts flattened with ties could never produce.

Sarah walked often to the school, daydreaming in the summer air, and for want of a better subject, Lt. Crandell often figured in her thoughts. When would he come to call, she wondered. Had he forgotten? Or found someone of greater interest?

She strolled on the beaches, where bits of polished, pearl white glittered everywhere among the gray rocks. Bones of fish and whales and of shipwrecked humans, too, it was said. One beach had rocks of speckled green and gold, sienna and pale orange. Behind it, high sand hills formed a pocket beach, where she could watch small fish trapped by the tide in its wine-red water.

She had discovered that the door of the staircase that led to the widow's walk at South Cottage was not locked, only jammed. Working carefully, she had loosened it and climbed to the top of the house, where, it appeared, no one had been for years. The stairway was musty, unwaxed, filled with cottony spider webs, and reaching the top, she was always doubly glad to be out in the fresh wind.

She loved the commanding view—of everything moving on Tory Road, of tiny forested islands, like small boats afloat in the Bay of Fundy, and especially of what could not be seen from any other point, the lighthouse spit, which intrigued her more than any spot on the island.

The lighthouse itself was half-hidden behind a slope, but she could see its rock tower and an aura of danger and desolation hovered about it, as real as the gannets circling in to their nests of its rocky heights. Perhaps it was the sense of the unknown and the unknowable that drew her to watch Alyce's home so closely.

She would stare out at it, never seeing any sign of life, never thinking of going there herself. Then one afternoon, she saw a flash of color. A woman climbed skillfully over the rocks and disappeared down toward the lighthouse. The dress had been a blue or lavender polonaise, not of a style that Alyce would wear, and Sarah remembered that Lucy, when she had last seen her, had been wearing that hue.

In an instant, before she had even wondered what Lucy might be doing on the Head, she had decided to follow her. Her long tedious days after the night with Brye had made her brash and reckless. Without knowing it, she longed for adventure, any semblance of it she could find. She did not realize that something was stirring in her, coming to life with the island summer like a long-dormant seed put down in fertile soil.

Soon she was striding down a narrow part of the island, following an almost overgrown footpath, below which were tidal cliffs on either side, covered with haystack mounds of kelp. Without warning, the path ended. Now the cliffs were below on three sides, and a gut separated the spit from the rest of the island. For a moment she stood indecisive, overwhelmed by the perilous-looking descent. But Alyce must make this climb as regularly as Sarah climbed the stairs to her bedroom. Lucy had made it, too, so it was not really that dangerous, even for a woman.

As for the water below, it looked shallow enough to wade easily, so she gathered her skirts and started down, thinking of the captain of the *Cloud,* who had run the borers because he was from Hazard and must not be afraid of it.

Reaching the bottom without mishap, Sarah pulled off her laced slippers and clockwork stockings and waded into the swirling, ankle-deep water. On the other side, the climb was not so difficult. Suddenly an explosion echoed over the rock. Gunfire! What could anyone be hunting? There could be no deer on these rocks. They would make a poor home even for a rabbit.

Another shot rang out, knocking away a bit of stone above Sarah's head. Stricken motionless, she cowered. "Look out, you idiot!" she managed to shout. "Someone's here!"

"I know, mademoiselle!" The voice so soft and musical, the French she had always associated with grace and romance, contrasted nightmarishly with the wild-haired man who stood arms akimbo at the top of the lighthouse spit. "Go back!" he shouted. "You'll be trapped by the tide!" The gun rested in his hand, and he seemed all too ready to fire it again.

Sarah obeyed at once. She could not believe how much deeper the water had become in those few minutes. As she stepped into it, the current caught her heavy skirts, tugging them like an angry dog until she plunged headlong into the water. Struggling to her feet, she gained the far side and scrambled up the cliff to safety. She looked back at the man she knew must be Galen Le Blanc, the former hermit of Hazard Island, who might one day be prime minister.

From a distance, he was less appalling. The hair that had seemed lunatic was merely whipping in the breeze; the gun was held loosely at his side. What was happening beneath Sarah was more fearful. Water churned into the gut with awful force. Each moment it rose perceptibly higher, covering the kelp, the ladder, the cliffs. White water raced where she had waded a short time before and frothy geysers spewed where it slapped the great boulders. When she looked back at last to the craigs of the lighthouse spit, Galen Le Blanc had disappeared. The channel was impassable. Only then did she remember Lucy, trapped beyond it.

Her first impulse was to go crying to the nearest person for help, though what help anyone could give, she could not imagine. But the nearest person was a long way off, and her progress was slow, since she had dropped her shoes and was at the mercy of every stone in the road. By the time she drew near habitation, she had decided it would be more prudent not to tell her story to just anyone. She would go straight to South Cottage.

It was Lily she met, all agog at her appearance and full of questions. "I tripped and fell in the water," Sarah tried to tell her.

"Where are your shoes? Why does your sleeve have a tear?" the child persisted.

"Where is Brye?"

"Off somewhere. Wait until supper; he'll be home. Cook is having his favorite, mutton cutlets and apricot fritters. What do you want with Brye?"

Sarah didn't answer, but went to make herself presentable and to watch from her bedroom in hopes of seeing Brye on his return. When the bell rang for dinner, she hurried down on the chance she might find him in a hallway.

He was already at the table with Lily, and he startled her by broaching the subject so on her mind. "Where is Mother?" he asked.

Before Sarah could speak, Annie, coming in with a soup tureen, answered, "Mrs. Rathrock has a headache; she sends her apologies."

And then Sarah understood.

Chapter 5

It was almost more than Sarah could grasp. Lucy Rathrock, grand dame of Hazard Island, wife of the flamboyant sea captain, was having an affair with a member of Parliament who might become prime minister. Slowly awe superseded shock, for she saw how great a love it must be. The consequences to either, were they found out, would be disastrous!

What a scandal it would make! Galen Le Blanc would be ruined, of course. And as for Lucy! She shuddered to imagine what the captain might do—to Galen—to Lucy! And how close Sarah had come to exposing them!

Sarah grew more and more amazed at Lucy. She was everything her mother had told her—and more! Caroline had told her daughter about a Frenchman who had claimed Lucy's love and who had died in Africa. She had told her how the captain had swept her away to New Brunswick, and Sarah knew of her own father's great devotion. Three great loves, and here, it seemed, was a fourth. Why was it men felt such passion for Lucy? And what was it like to return that love?

She must never breathe a suggestion of what she had seen, but it was not easy to put it from her mind. That night she dreamed of it and thought she blurted it to Lily, to Brye, to a sea captain with a flushed, furious face who shouted, "Out with it, my girl!" She awoke, trembling, sure that she had cried the story aloud. And she lay thinking about the tides, wrapped protectively about the lovers, howling until dawn, concealing their forbidden love.

Lucy was at breakfast, looking calm and fresh, and, a knowing eye might think, radiant. She drank black tea while she dealt with business of the day, telling Brye to see why a certain load of smoked herring had not yet been shipped.

Sarah could not look at Lucy, and heat kept rising into her cheeks. She was thankful Lucy did not know about her guilty discovery.

But later in the day when she sought the cupola, the door to the stairs would not open. At first she thought it merely jammed again and pushed against it with her shoulder. Then she saw that it had been nailed shut. Lucy had not said a word, but she had guessed.

Galen Le Blanc would have told Lucy of his encounter with Sarah, but Sarah's face at breakfast must have told Lucy that Sarah's appearance on the spit had not been mere coincidence. Lucy hd remembered the cupola and had checked the door. Perhaps she had even seen footprints in the dust of the stairs.

What were they to do now, Sarah and Lucy? They must live here together and pretend—for how long? Until Sarah married, whenever that might be.

How Sarah longed for a great love, like one of Lucy's, especially one that would take her from Hazard Island. She took to studying Lucy to see more what sort of woman attracted such passion. She noticed a great vitality, a scooping up of everything life had to offer. Lucy had a firmness of manner, a gaiety, a simple certainty of her own beauty that was not kin to vanity. Sarah could not emulate her any more than she could Alyce. Sarah was too quiet, too easily content. Though she had thought herself an accomplished belle a year ago, she had found on this distant island a woman who had her bested in ways she had not even known one could be bested.

Yet this same woman was an adulteress, and Sarah could not quite meet her eyes. She wondered if Lucy were capable of meeting hers, but there was no way of knowing. They would pretend. "Half of life is pretending," Sarah's mother had used to say when she had protested the hypocrisy of some social chore. "Life would be intolerable without it."

Fortunately they were provided with a distraction. With almost no warning, Maddie arrived at South Cottage.

Nobody told Sarah anything. It was a family matter, and Sarah was not really family. Maddie, it seemed, was coming home in disgrace. The servants were busy cleaning her bedroom, washing curtains, setting her bedding to air. By mid-afternoon, when Brye was dispatched to meet here on the weekly ferry from St. John, an atmosphere of tension was building about the house. The place was dreadfully quiet. Servants no longer sang at their work. Lily had retreated to her room, and the far-off clatter of supper being readied in the kitchen reminded Sarah of the rattle of an approaching storm.

The carriage arrived with the darkening of night. Maddie stepped down, throwing her shoulders forward as she walked in a way that exaggerated her limp. It was a display for her mother's benefit, Sarah thought, seeing Lucy frown. Maddie was a handsome girl, but the flounces on her dress bounced with her limp, and her black hair was done in a mass of curls that looked silly above her strong eyebrows.

"Well, Mother," said Maddie, "this is still the same dreary place, I see."

And to Sarah's surprise, it was a dreary place, though yesterday it had seemed pleasant.

"It is still South Cottage," said Lucy with a sigh. "Come and meet Sarah."

Maddie did not give Sarah the perfunctory little embrace she expected, but instead stood looking her up and down as her mother had. "Well, Cousin Sarah," she said, "you are quite pretty. It will be a perplexing matter for the gentlemen whether to try for your beauty or my fortune. You and I shall have the sport of it until you are married off."

It was an astonishing speech, but Sarah would learn that Maddie usually said what she thought. And what she thought was often not the conventional thing. The most predictable thing about her would be her stormy unpredictability, as if her major strategy in life were to keep everyone as off-balance as she herself, listing about on her lame foot.

"How do you do, Cousin Maddie?" said Sarah. Maddie's brows knitted and a flicker of irritation crossed her face. She was annoyed at not having got more response.

But if Sarah disappointed her, surely, Lucy did not. That night Lily and Sarah hung over the stair railing, listening to the argument raging behind the closed doors of the library. It must have begun discreetly, but Maddie had a love of shouting. Her voice boomed out with defiant joy. Obviously she did not care who heard, so Sarah did not feel guilty in her position on the stairs.

"Nonsense!" Maddie would shout to whatever her

mother said. It appeared to be her special word. Soon Lucy took to using it, too.

"Madeliene, you cannot go about endangering your good name!"

"Nonsense. I am Madeliene Rathrock, and I may do as I like."

"Nonsense. Nobody can do as they like. You've come home from school too soon, and no matter what excuse we give, peple are going to talk. A young lady cannot afford talk."

"Nonsense!" said Maddie. "I am an heiress and can afford anything at all, including talk. Talk will not change the fact that I am rich and well-provided for. Let us say that I was dismissed because it was impossible to teach me embroidery. Everyone will believe that. It's well known that I am helpless at such things."

"So am I, but I have always tried—"

"Oh, nonsense," said Maddie. "I wish I were a man. Then I should have Hazard Island as my inheritance. I wish the captain would leave it to me anyway. Brye doesn't want it."

"Nonsense! Nonsense, yourself! What a thing to say! Hazard Island is Brye's birthright. How could he not want it? As for you—what's to be done? You cannot just sit here like a lump from now on. Your father should be home in a few days. I will leave the decision up to him."

Maddie became more subdued. "It is to be so soon?" she said.

"Yes. Captain Harkness told me last week when he made port that he had berthed near the captain's ship in Shanghai and that your father was loading to leave within a fortnight."

"Well, then we must begin to polish all the silver, and the whole house must shine like the forechains on the captain's clipper. What a bore! I don't understand what's so shameful about tarnish; it's simply a process of nature." On that note Maddie exited from the library with Lucy behind her, looking grim.

It had been an altogether interesting discussion, especially considering Lucy's recent indiscretion on lighthouse spit. Sarah thought Maddie must believe herself at least as free as her mother, and Lucy was demanding of her daughter standards of behavior she did not adhere to herself. Or was she? Was it only not causing talk that was important?

Maddie was recalcitrant, but she did not disregard her father. No punishment Lucy could have dealt could have been worse than that the captain must pass sentence. In the days that followed, while floors were polished and dust from the rugs was beaten into the summer air, Maddie sat morosely watching. And at night when the wind rose, Sarah could hear her leave her bed, since her room was next door. At first Sarah did not understand the reason for this pacing about in the night. Then she realized that the wind disturbed Maddie because she imagined it filling the sails of the captain's ship, bringing her father and her punishment ever closer.

Something of Maddie's dread began to grow in Sarah, too. It was difficult to think of Maddie's being afraid of anyone. Since Maddie was frightened the captain must be very worthy of fear, and though Sarah had not transgressed, she would lie sleepless, too.

Maddie had left school without permission, Sarah had learned. A search party had found her wandering in the dark, and the rumor, via Lily, was that a man had been involved. It was hard to believe that the ungainly Maddie, like her beautiful mother, had a lover.

Finally, one night, hearing her begin to walk about, Sarah slipped out of bed and knocked on her door. "As long as neither of us can sleep, we might be less lonely together," she suggested. Maddie was too astonished not to let Sarah in, and after she had, too distraught not to talk to such a willing listener.

"It was an awful school, Sarah—you cannot imagine—no, it might have suited *you*."

"I can guess. Any place must be dreadful where you are made to be something you are not."

Maddie looked at Sarah as if trying to decide if she were making fun. "And those horrid gowns," she said. "The captain has them made for me in London. By a dressmaker who has never seen me, naturally. The captain simply orders what is latest and most expensive."

"Why don't you stand up to him, Maddie, as you do to your mother?"

Her face went ashen. "Oh, I couldn't possibly. He might do what he has always threatened—send me to England to be educated. That is what I'm so afraid of. I would die in England. I *will* die before I'll leave Hazard Island. My dust will remain forever at least."

Stupefied, Sarah saw that she meant it. Before she would leave Hazard Island she would kill herself and become the first to occupy the Rathrock plot. And even in death she would anger the captain, Sarah thought. He would have wanted that honor for himself.

No doubt life in England would be miserable for Maddie. No doubt she loved Hazard Island. But was that all? Was it a man, more than an island, she could not leave?

The two became friends, in a way, after that night, although Maddie, unused to sharing confidences, was uneasy that she had done so. "I can think of no reason I should like you, Sarah," she would say. "With you as an example of London-bred girls, I haven't a chance. You are my doom."

She said it so much that Sarah began to feel guilty, imagining herself already standing before a sepulcher, to blame for Maddie's demise. "You are only being dramatic," she would reply. "I was not responsible for your escapade. You should have thought."

"I did think. I knew it was a gamble, but I did not intend to get caught."

"Suppose I were your salvation, instead of your doom?" Sarah said one day.

"I certainly don't see how!"

"By being such a shining example to you. We shall seem to be inseparable, and you shall imitate me until the crisis is over. It will be like children playing follow-the-leader. And it will be only a game, because you are Madeliene and always will be. We will never be alike."

Maddie was entranced. To fool the captain was exactly to her liking. By merely acting a part that did not fit her, she would not lose face with herself. She set out at once to see how well she could do it.

Sarah began by arranging Maddie's hair in a simpler style and spent hours in her room subtly altering her dresses. "So he will see an improvement at once without ever knowing what caused it," she explained.

"But won't he notice the difference?"

"Men never notice such things. They only know whether a woman is attractive or not."

"Do they? Well, Mother will not care. She is too busy to bother."

Maddie's voice was wistful when she spoke of her mother. She had Lucy's interest in island affairs and would have loved to take part. But Lucy confined her conversation on such matters to Brye, who would answer with preoccupied grunts, thinking, no doubt, about some young blade's adventure he was about to undertake in Shipwreck or across the bay in St. John.

So instead Sarah and Maddie wandered about the island, Maddie showing Sarah the nest of an eider duck, a point where seals and walruses came to swim, a lake of seawater where edible seaweed grew.

One gusty, overcast day, when the sky was full of gray, rolling clouds, Maddie challenged her to climb the Wailing Widow Cliff, springing up lithely, proud of her native's ability.

"Lie in the grass and look over," she advised when they reached the top. "It's supposed to resemble a woman. You can see the profile of her face. There's the brow and the nose, and the long grass here is supposed to be her hair. And see what a view she has. She is turned toward the sea, ever looking for her lover."

"Something seems to be wrong with the nose," Sarah observed.

"Yes. During the Civil War an American gunboat used the Widow for cannon practice. Mother had the captain's own cannon brought around and fired back. There was no end of trouble over it. A mysterious light led the ship onto the reefs; a ghost light, people say. Scarcely a stormy night passes that someone doesn't glimpse it on the cliffs."

A strong blast of wind buffeted the cliff, and suddenly the air was filled with moans. They very earth seemed to emit terrible, wrenching sighs, which rose into screams, then gradually faded into soft shivery whines and died away. As Sarah lay thunderstruck, Maddie shook with uncontrolled mirth.

"Sarah, you should see your expression!"

"Dear god! What was that?"

"Some people say its the spirit of a woman who came here year after year to look for her man and finally threw herself over. A woman did jump from here after her husband was lost in Charleston Harbor. And a man who was to marry Annie was found dead at its foot. But it's only the wind. The way the rocks are formed makes it howl like that. You should hear it in a gale! They say that it sobs with a grief beyond human endurance. A man from Shipwreck heard it, and his hair turned white, so they say."

"I must make certain not to hear it then. I should look silly with white hair at my age. You brought me here on purpose to scare me, Maddie."

She laughed again. "So I did. You wanted to learn about Hazard Island, didn't you? Well, you are learning."

Sarah *was* learning. About the island. About Maddie. Then one night she awakened to the knowledge that something was very different about the house. She lay hardly breathing, not knowing what had disturbed her. It had not been the wind, since outside it was dead calm. And there was no sound from Maddie's room.

Suddenly a tapping began, coming closer and closer with a hollow, disembodied echo. She thought of ghosts at once. They were still in her mind from the day on Wailing Widow Cliff. Nobody had said that South Cottage had a ghost. She wanted to pull the covers over her head, but knowing she must not be overcome by the mysteries of Hazard Island, she rose, and pulling on a dressing robe, slipped out into the dim hall.

The sound was coming toward her. She pushed herself flat against the wall of an adjoining corridor, out of the moonlight that spilled onto the floor. The apparition she saw frightened her as much as any she could have imagined.

The man was handsome, but she had never seen a man handsome in such a fearsome way. The whites of his eyes flashed like bleached whalebone in the moonlight; his jaw jutted, the whiskers extending like field artillery. The nose was classic. The eyebrows, like Maddie's, were fierce, outlines of mountains thrust up into the high expanse of his forehead, and his hair like wings of flame from its center parting. The tapping came from a walking stick he carried from habit to support an injured leg on which he limped hardly at all.

Sarah pushed closer to the wall, praying he would not discover her. Then another door opened.

Lucy in a thin nightdress came into the corridor. Jonathan Rathrock stood gazing at his wife's bare shoulders in the moonlight. With only a sigh, he gathered her into his arms. The formidable old sea dog laid his cheek against Lucy's as though resting at last on a welcome pillow.

Sarah could not doubt the devotion of either party in that intimate embrace.

Chapter 6

Captain Rathrock was home. South Cottage became a gay place, for the captain loved a good time, and he was happy to be back on his island after a long voyage. There were guests for dinner, guests for tea, guests who played whist far into the night, who smoked fine cigars, drank the best whiskey and reminisced of their naval exploits until the small hours of the morning. The captain hunted duck and small game, and when he was in an especially fine mood, he would play the concertina.

From the first he liked Sarah, who was much surprised to have such a champion. She could think of no reason he should be more than tolerant of his wife's relation, but he seemed interested in everything about her and pleased to have her on the island. Apparently he had had good notice of her from the master of the *Cloud*, whom she had wanted to have flogged. Her unwonted reputation for spunk was going to stick.

"This little lady refused to go below passing the borers in a gale," Captain Rathrock would say proudly, introducing her to someone,

"Whether one is on deck or in a cabin makes little difference," Sarah would demure. "One is still at the bottom of the sea, if the ship goes down."

He would be amused. "You don't like ships, do you, Cousin Sarah?"

"I loathe them, Captain," she would answer, having decided to navigate a course of candor.

"We shall have to change all that! You will learn to love them," he would insist. He would throw back his head and laugh, but all the same she would cringe inwardly, wondering what he had in mind, positive it was something disagreeably specific.

She hoped he noticed the change in Maddie as they had planned. Sitting amid the scrolled shells of the uncomfortable Chippendale garden chairs, the two girls would work needlepoint for hours. The captain, passing that way would glance at his daughter quizzically, as if trying to decipher a puzzle.

"Sarah is showing me a new stitch," Maddie would say. "Sarah is so clever."

The captain was clearly baffled. He could not understand why Maddie should take to someone who so constantly outshone her, but he was pleased. Sarah saw that her friendship with Maddie could only improve her stock with him, though she had not planned it that way.

At first he declared himself too busy to deal with Maddie. "Really, Lucy, it's most annoying," Sarah heard him say. "I must attend to Brye's problems. Why can't the girls be your province?"

"I'm sorry, Jonathan, but I've given my word it will be your decision."

"Oh, very well," he muttered, stalking away.

Finally he sent for her. Sarah, at Maddie's behest, was stationed in a room above the library, where, Maddie said, one could hear, even if there were no shouting. "I expect there will be plenty. You will not have to strain your ears," she said with a wan attempt at a smile.

But he was gentler than either of them had supposed, and his voice had a certain tenderness when he spoke to his daughter. "You've been in another scrape, Maddie."

"I have, Captain."

"You could not help it, I suppose. You are going to tell me how well-intentioned you were."

"I am not. I meant only to make myself happy, and I thought it more important than the feelings of my parents." Maddie's voice, though shaking, rang with the defiance she could never stifle.

"You must tell me who the man was."

"I would sooner die!"

"You are always making dying an alternative, Maddie. It is not a fair threat. I will not ask you if he left you pure. No doubt you would sooner die than tell that, too. You are aware that should an infant appear, I will be required to shoot *someone*. Well, I will think about this further."

The captain did think about it further. The next Sunday he took the pulpit and preached a fiery sermon on the virtues of womanhood. Perhaps there was not a woman in the congregation who did not quake as he thundered of the obedience owed to husbands and fathers by the weak-minded sex that was prey to notions of vanity and romantic love.

It was all falderol, Maddie declared later. "He doesn't really like his women that way. He married Mother precisely because she was not obedient. Obedient women bore him. It's an idea he pays service to when things are going badly for him. It means he really doesn't know what to do about me. And he enjoys being the tyrant."

"Maybe he will count on his sermon to have chastened you sufficiently," Sarah suggested. They both cherished a faint hope he would.

In the end he gave her a choice. Though the alternatives were both abhorrent to her, the decision was easy. "You are a grown woman, Maddie," he told her, "and it is high time you came out. You have shown much more polish of late, and I am confident you have the maturity to handle your debut. If, however, you do not agree, you shall be sent straight away to England, where one last effort will be made to endow you with the proper graces. Which will it be, Maddie?"

"I will come out, Captain," she answer in a small voice.

He grunted, unsurprised. "I expected as much. You must put your heart into it, and your mother and I must hear not one word of discontent. You will make a good show of it, if you use your willpower. It is much the same quality as mine."

Sarah was unable to hide her delight at the prospect of parties and dances. Maddie felt betrayed by her joy. "See what your idea has got me into, Sarah?" she stormed, carefully out of hearing of her parents. "That is what comes of acting what one is not."

"You are not in England, Cousin Maddie. That was our goal."

"You're right and I should be grateful. But next the captain will expect husbands to come of it, for both of us. A suitable match may be pleasing to *you*. You can at least expect to be married for your beauty, which is part of yourself. I shall be a good bargain only because I am wealthy and the daughter of Captain Rathrock."

"Don't be so cynical, Maddie. It's entirely possible you might fall in love. I, myself, have determined to marry for love."

She gave a laugh. "So, it's love you must find on Hazard Island, Sarah. I wish you luck. As for me, if I were to fall in love, it would be with someone utterly unacceptable. That would be my style."

That was as close as she came to the confidence Sarah had hoped she might give. If Maddie were in love with the man who had been involved in her escapade, he was someone her father would not approve of. But Sarah had already guessed that.

Maddie's reaction to Sarah's ambition to marry for love had been more unexpected. It had seemed to amuse her unduly, as though she knew something Sarah didn't. It left Sarah with an uneasiness that lessened her enjoyment as she helped with Maddie's ball.

With her experience of a recent London season, Sarah found herself in the role of consultant, constantly called on for ideas of entertainment and details of decor; and happily absorbed, she could hardly remember the time when she had been bored on Hazard Island.

An additional pleasure was that Lucy had decided that Sarah might drop her half-mourning for the event. "It is really too soon, but Caroline would have liked it," Lucy told her. So she was to have the opportunity to shine. Better still, she was to have someone to shine for.

One warm day she had strolled down to a pebble beach and stopped to watch two young seals at play in the beryl-green water, turning on their backs, their black snouts in the air. As she basked there, the sun-heated rocks pleasant against her back, she heard the crunch of hooves and looked up to see the officer she had met at church, Desmond Crandell, dismounting.

"May I join you, Miss Ashton?" he said. His well-planed but unextraordinary face was made attractive by his tentative smile. There was no wit about him, none of the disregard for manners she had become accustomed to in Brye. She thought the change refreshing.

"I cannot refuse you, sir. It's a beautiful beach and a beautiful day."

He lowered himself to a rock beside her. "You are watching the baby seals, aren't you? And there are eider ducklings over near the shore. Everything young on Hazard Island is at play today." He smiled more securely, his eyes looking into hers.

"The weather is perfect," she said.

"Yes, as perfect as anything ever gets on this island. It's a lonely place, don't you think, Miss Ashton? Do you miss England?"

"Oh, indeed I do!"

"I, too. We have something in common."

"You! But your life must be full of excitement!"

"Excitement is not what I want. I am here because of a tradition of naval service in my family. It would have broken my father's heart had I not done it."

"But you have aptitude, Lt. Crandell," Sarah said. "I have it on good authority that you will be an admiral someday."

He flushed, making Sarah laugh with delight. "I apply myself, Miss Ashton, so that someday I may have my pick of assignments that keep me home in England."

"Ah, then you have a sweetheart who waits for you," she teased.

"No. No one. I have been wanting for feminine companionship. Duty has kept me in Halifax lately, but I have an invitation to the ball at South Cottage and you must promise to save me a dance."

She promised, and when he had ridden away the ball had taken on more importance. Desmond Crandell was altogether pleasing. He was perfect—wasn't he?

A skin of thin clouds drifted over the sun, dulling the sparkle of the waves. They sounded emptier, echoing her unacknowledged discontent.

Lt. Crandell was what she had been waiting for, hoping for. He was a way off Hazard Island, home to England. She could love him, she told herself. She must!

As the day grew nearer, Maddie became more and more impossible. She complained constantly, venting on Sarah the feelings she was afraid to voice to her parents. Worse, she grew openly jealous.

"I thought you were going to help me," she wailed. "You are no help at all! You're concerned with nothing but your own pretty face. The men will look at no one but you, and I shall be a complete failure. The captain will see the absurdity of it and send me to England!"

"Nonsense!" Under stress Sarah had adopted Maddie's favorite word. She was irritable, too, thinking of Lt. Crandell. She did not know why the idea of him made her feel that way instead of only happy or relieved. "You will not be a failure unless you think yourself one, Maddie," she said. "You are attractive and very interesting in conversation. And the captain will not go back on his word."

"Attractive!" Maddie cried, rolling her eyes. "Interesting! Men do not like women who are attractive and interesting. They like women who are beautiful and flirtatious!" She limped fiercely out of the room.

Still, on the night of the ball, Maddie looked very well in a chatelaine of oxydized silver and a simple trained gown of yellow grenadine that Sarah had designed for her. The captain noticed, to his credit, and Maddie pleased him further by blushing prettily. After receiving her father's approval, she held her head higher, and Sarah had every expectation that she would make a success of the evening.

The captain certainly did not seem to be worried. His laughter roared and he would take a turn with his concertina or lead groups of gentlemen away to the library to indulge in some game of chance.

Candlelight shimmered on Susan Treadway's heavy, jet-spangled gown as she flirted from behind her immense dagger fan. She was to be the competition, Sarah saw. Young men swarmed around her, and though she did not have the family Sarah did, she had a fortune. Among her admirers was Brye, who Sarah saw cajol her again and again for another dance.

Once he came to waltz with Sarah. He was a wonderful dancer, and she was sorry when it was over and his grin and his "Good luck, Sarah," sent her back to the business of the night. He went off to find his sister to make her the same wish. When Sarah saw him again after a long while, Susan was dancing in his arms.

Meanwhile Sarah was having a difficult time, for it seemed if any young man danced with her twice, he was siphoned off to Captain Rathrock's card game. It was a frustration to have them drawn away just as her efforts might have been rewarded. She had never worked so hard at being charming. In fact she had never worked much at it at all. In London, she had simply let her looks speak for themselves, so that all the work was done upstairs beforehand, much of it by maids who pressed and pinned.

Josh Treadway danced with her, twirling her gaily. "You look lovely, Cousin Sarah," he said, his eyes twinkling.

"You must not call me that, Mr. Treadway! I am not your cousin."

"Oh, but I can't call you Miss Ashton anymore. You're

too good a sport! Lucky Brye! He got off easy as a weasel raiding a beaver trap."

"You sound as if you're sorry, Josh."

"Well, I am in a way. I love Brye as if he were my brother who died at birth, but Brye stands to have everything I should have had. The North of Hazard Island belonged to my family long before the Rathrocks ever heard of it. I do not mind causing Brye discomfort when I can. It's part of our relationship. His dear mama thinks I lead him astray."

"And don't you?"

"No. If Brye is astray, it is only because he is Brye."

She wondered if Josh would cause Brye "discomfort" tonight, but the wildness he had shown that night at Shipwreck was not evident. Tonight he seemed almost gentle, a quality he might have inherited from his mother or which might represent the tender side she had glimpsed in Fitch in his attitude toward Polly in church. Later she saw him dancing with Maddie, talking earnestly all the while.

Then someone trod heavily on the hem of her green tulle gown, and fuming at the time she must take, she went upstairs to find Annie to help her mend a tear in one of its velvet-bordered flounces. When she came down again, a voice said at her elbow, "I'm sorry to be late, Miss Ashton." She turned and looked into the face of Desmond Crandell.

He danced with her once; he danced with her twice. "Pardon me if I seem to monopolize you, Miss Ashton. I have wanted to become acquainted for so long, and there is so little time."

"The captain is coming for you," Sarah said, after they had had three dances in a row.

"He shall not find me, but if he does, I shall tell him I am interested in something far more compelling than cards," said the lieutenant and led her out onto a deserted veranda.

The evening air was chill, and Sarah began to shiver in her thin dress. Then suddenly what he was saying made her forget the cold.

"I have been transferred, Miss Ashton. I am to have a position in Jamaica. It is a long way off, but a beginning, a promotion, and my fortunes will take me back to civilization soon, I am determined. Jamaica is always warm at least and there are palm trees. Do you suppose you could endure Jamaica, Miss Ashton?"

"I should find it interesting, I'm sure, Lieutenant, should I ever have the chance to go there. It would not be the first time I have gone to a far-off place, of course. It would not frighten me to go."

Lt. Crandell's face lighted. "I have a month, Miss Ashton. May I call on you tomorrow?"

"I would enjoy that, Lieutenant," she said. As easily as that she had found a way off the island, a man who could be her husband. A queer mixture of joy and triumph charged her as she went back to the dance.

She lay awake for a long time that night, thinking. How little she knew of Desmond Crandell, and yet she must love him. She let herself believe she would, that she already was beginning to do so. The glory of it—a whirlwind romance, a suitor with no time to spare for conventional courtship, who would carry her away with him, first to the far reaches of the globe and then, adventure done, home safely to England! What could be better?

Married! Within a month! How was a wedding to be accomplished in so short a time? Oh, the island would talk. Sarah would be delightful gossip for everyone, but it was the kind of gossip the Rathrock family could withstand. It was almost a page from Lucy's book, and when Sarah was far away from Hazard Island, she would no longer have to worry about her dreadful knowledge of Lucy and Galen Le Blanc.

As she lay planning it all, she became aware that Maddie, in the next room, was sobbing into her pillow. Sarah, in a generous mood, went in to her. The evening had been a disaster for her, though Sarah had not even noticed.

"The trouble is I am not talented at all in that direction," Maddie said. "Worse, I do not even want to be. It is all such a stupid game. Empty-headed girls fluttering their lashes and looking as if they have wonderful secrets about them, and men knowing so little about women they believe it is so."

"Don't worry, Maddie. All men are not so easily deceived. You shall be all the happier for having one who is wise."

"Oh hush, you don't really believe that! It is not that I want any of those creatures anyway. All I want is not to go to England."

Sarah sighed. If only Maddie would confide about the

man she loved, the one who was so unsuitable, they could be more honest with each other. "Well, anyway, be happy that I shall no longer give you competition. I believe I am to be wed."

Maddie stared at her, astonished out of her tears. "You have settled on someone in one night? Tell me who? Did you fall in love on the instant? You swore to your grandmother, Sarah!"

"I suppose I did. He is going to call on me tomorrow."

They sat together until dawn planning gowns and flowers, a wedding supper for the unmade match, and in the unflattering light of day Sarah's cheeks were too pale and her eyes were overbright. Morning was somehow borne, then luncheon. Tea time when she had expected him, came and slid past into dusk.

He had never come at all.

She took to her bed and wept more inconsolably than Maddie had the night before. At last Lily slipped into her room to try to comfort her. "It's not that he didn't care for you, Sarah," she said. "He's been sent away."

"Sent away!" Sarah was surprised enough to stop crying and sit up to stare at her. "But he had a month!"

"Father has taken care of it. He has all kinds of influence. Mother and Father had a terrible row about it this morning. Mother was furious, but she didn't get her way."

"But I understood that Desmond Crandell was entirely suitable. Why has the captain—"

She looked at Sarah, all smug delight, to watch the impact of her knowledge on her. "Father has decided you shall marry Brye."

Chapter 7

Sarah was aghast. The captain with his unbending will had cut off her only hope of escape from Hazard Island. There was no use looking further for a husband. Anyone she found would suffer the same fate as poor Lt. Crandell.

Marry Brye! Remain not only on the island but be drawn into the heart of the family!

Everything began to fall into place. She knew now why the captain had insisted she come to the island. He had not been satisfied with any of the marriageable girls of Hazard. Then had come the opportunity to import a bride for Brye, like a case of fine champagne, Miss Sarah Ashton, a belle of the London season. And the blood lines, impeccable!

What would Brye do? He did not love her, but Sarah could not imagine that he would stand up to the captain. He would try to weather the storm, she predicted, procrastinating until his father's patience was worn through like eroding rock. Could he do it?

The next day her judgment was borne out when she went out for a breath of air among the rugosa roses and blue flag in the garden. Brye, who was walking there with an unusually serious mien, turned when he saw her and abruptly went away. She came to a decision then. Brye must become engaged to someone else and set her free.

It would have to be Susan Treadway. He was fonder of her than of any girl, except Alyce, who was out of the question. Susan with her ripe beauty and sensual nature was the only one who might overcome Brye's love for Alyce.

Alyce would be her confidant. She would see the necessity; she had said herself that Brye must forget her. Sarah put on her walking costume of navy blue serge with its long, braided polonaise jacket and alpaca underskirt and set off across the island, waylaying Alyce as she walked toward the spit from school.

"Alyce!"

Sarah's friend turned and smiled, the wind tossing her hair as she paused near a pond fringed with great clusters of yellow brandy bottle. "I was hoping you would come to tell me about the ball, Sarah. Let's sit here. Was it marvelous? Tell me everything. I'm not in a hurry."

"It was a disaster!"

"With you wearing your green tulle? I don't see how!"

"It was. In every way. First my plan for Maddie went all wrong. I had her dressed to be herself, but I had her act someone else, with blushes and such. That was a disaster, and she may never forgive me. If Captain Rathrock sends her to England after this it will be my fault."

"It will not, Sarah. The captain would have sent her before this, if it had not been for you. How else was it a disaster?"

A smile fluttered at the edges of her sunrise-pink mouth. She had never been subject to the stress of monumental social events. She could not take this seriously.

"Captain Rathrock has decided to marry me to Brye." Sarah delivered the news and was satisfied to see Alyce's face go blank and pale.

Then as she recovered from the surprise, she threw her arms around Sarah. "How lucky you are! He is the catch of the island, of course. Yes, I believe it will work! I wish I had thought of it myself. You have spirit, but you will not overpower him like his mother. You will lean on the man you marry and that will make him strong. You are what Brye needs."

"But I don't love him!" cried Sarah in exasperation.

"You would come to. He is witty and sensitive and you would make him a good wife. He will need one more than most men. His responsibilities will be heavier than the captain's. The island will become more complex; it will all be different before his lifetime has finished. And the day of the clippers he loves as much as his father will be only a memory. Brye is a part of the island as it is. He is a part of its nature like the dolphins and the herring gulls, and that is the way he wants it.

"But Hazard Island will change. Civilization will have its way, and Brye will have to fight for his island in ways his father never dreamed of. He will need a wife who is both gentle and wise. I am glad the captain had the good sense to choose you."

"Wise! I am certainly not wise, Alyce!"

"No, but you can become so. It is in you."

Sarah drew a deep breath. "I can't marry Brye!"

Alyce's eyes fixed on her friend. "There is another reason, isn't there, why you will not consider this match? It's because you know something—Lucy Rathrock and my father are in love."

Sarah nodded, confused, thinking of the captain and Lucy embracing in the moonlight.

"It upsets you. It makes you more eager than ever to leave Hazard Island. Mrs. Rathrock isn't in favor of the marriage, either, is she?"

"No. Though I would never tell her secret."

"You are afraid you can never be sure, Sarah. And Mrs. Rathrock is afraid of the same thing. You might blurt it in illness or in childbirth. Or even in a dream, with Brye beside you in bed. Ah! It would pain Mrs. Rathrock more for Brye to learn of it than the captain himself. But if Mrs. Rathrock cannot sway the captain, it is impossible. Accept his decision gracefully as I do—though it might mean my father's life if the secret slipped out. You shall be a spinster otherwise!"

"I will *not* accept it! I am not from Hazard Island, and I do not bow to the omnipotence of Captain Rathrock. I shall play at his game too. I, myself, have a candidate to be Brye's wife."

Sarah paused to draw in a ragged breath, and Alyce, her fingers tightening over a book she carried, said fearfully, "Who?"

"Susan Treadway," replied Sarah firmly.

"Susan! But the captain and—"

"Oh, I know. The captain and Fitch Treadway are sworn enemies. But a man like Captain Rathrock does not have an enemy he does no respect. Those he crushes all around him with as little thought as a servant girl swatting flies. When the captain meets a man he cannot destroy, that is different. Captain Rathrock needs Fitch Treadway like other men need good chess partners.

"And Susan has more spirit than any of the other girls. I daresay the captain would approve at once if her name were not Treadway. Brye seems fond of her, and I don't think it would displease the captain if Brye stood up to him. It would please him to think he had a son as strong as himself."

"Oh, Sarah," Alyce begged, "give up this wild idea. Some other girl if you must, but not Susan. Susan is not the right woman for Brye. It would be dreadful if he married her!"

"That," Sarah said coldly, "will be Brye's lookout. He shall marry her only because he wants to. I can't marry Brye, and I can think of nothing else. I must try, Alyce. I must try!"

Sarah did try, almost immediately. She began by pleading loneliness and asking if they might call on Mrs. Treadway and Susan. She was indulged, for it was believed that she had a broken heart. In truth, she was too busy scheming to brood much on Lt. Crandell.

She thought of him only in odd, wistful moments, remembering how happy she had been when she had fancied herself in love with him. She knew she had imagined she might love him only because she had needed him and that he had been, not her great love, but only a pleasant young man. She would wonder to what far-flung post he might have been sent and regret the damage she feared she had done to his career.

One day about tea time Lucy, Maddie and Sarah drove off to North Pines. Polly Treadway, sunk almost into a stupor, slumped in a japanned beechwood chair in her drawing room. Her eyes were wild and strands of graying hair flew from beneath her mob cap like the edges of rain clouds, ragged and heavy. Though a warm breeze fluttered the muslin curtains, she clutched at a quilt and seemed to shiver. The sight frightened Sarah, and even Lucy seemed to have trouble going forward to take her friend by the hand.

"Polly!" she called gently.

At length she stirred, and her fingers tightened over Lucy's. "It's you. Who have you brought? That girl with the pedigree, who cut such a figure at Maddie's ball?"

"Sarah. She has quite a social flair." Lucy's neutral tone seemed to indicate that whatever other qualities Sarah might have were in doubt.

"Susan said that Jonathan would not allow anyone to dance with her more than twice. What is he saving her for, Lucy?"

"I am sure I am no master of understanding Jonathan, Polly. Have you eaten today? Let me ring for some tea. We have brought spice cakes with butternuts in the icing, exactly the kind you love."

Susan Treadway sighed, her dark eyes dull with the

tedium of her existence with this mother of hers. It was easy for Sarah to get her to leave the drawing room for somewhere more private. A mention of her trips to Paris, a hint of tales she could not tell in front of mothers and fortyish cousins and they were quickly away to Susan's bedroom.

At first it appeared that Maddie would spoil Sarah's chance by coming with them, but before five minutes had passed, Maddie said she felt ill and went to lie down in another room.

"What luck!" cried Susan, surprising Sarah by echoing her own thought. "Now you can tell me what it is like to live at South Cottage. Tell me about the Rathrocks! About the captain! Forceful men are fascinating, don't you think? Do he and Mrs. Rathrock sleep in the same bed? I have always wondered."

"Have you? You could ask Maddie." Sarah blushed at Sarah's bawdy turn of mind.

"Oh no! She is a Rathrock. I wouldn't want her to know that her family interests me. But you are not a Rathrock. You can tell me all the tittle-tattle."

Briefly Sarah reflected on her choice. She remembered Alyce's warning. But Susan was only uninhibited, she decided. She was not stuffy. She would be fun for the madcap Brye and would give him free rein. She drew a deep breath and said, "I saw them kissing in the hall in the moonlight, once, when she came out to meet him in her nightdress."

"Really! She did not wear a dressing robe? I wonder what it would be like to be kissed by him. I would faint away, I think!"

"*Brye* might kiss you," Sarah said tentatively.

"Do you think so?" Susan's merry laughter told Sarah he already had.

"Perhaps he will make you an offer," she said, thus encouraged.

"Oh, Sarah, you know so little of Hazard Island! There is not a chance of it. My father and the captain—"

"I know little of Hazard Island, but in *other* places, when a man loves a girl as beautiful as you, a way is found," Sarah said, twisting Susan's hair into a new style, letting her take stock of her lovely face in the mirror.

"Think of it, Susan. If you married Brye, you could hand your father Hazard Island on a silver platter. You would be queen of it someday, like Lucy."

Susan shook her head. "I would like that, but my father would never agree to it—not when the silver platter was engraved with the Rathrock crest. He thinks his rights to the island should have been recognized in court, but he would not like to have them simply because he had bred his daughter like a mare to Bryan Rathrock." Susan shuddered at the thought of her father much the way Maddie did as the thought of hers.

"Ah, so much the better!" Sarah cried. "What could infuriate the captain more than to have his son spurned, and on Hazard Island at that? Soon he would be shouting to the heavens that Brye might marry anyone he pleased. You know that when the captain has made up his mind, he sweeps away everything in his path."

"Sarah, you are mad! Do you really think I could marry Brye?" Susan's dark eyes, grown larger, stared at Sarah from the mirror. Sarah knew she had said enough. Soon Brye, his arms about Susan in some tête-a-tête, would hear of it. He would feel the pressure.

Sarah was pleased with herself as they went back to the drawing room. She could not guess what havoc would be wrought by her unleashing Susan Treadway. She could not know how much darker and more treacherous Susan's mind was than hers. What was to happen would be Susan's fault, yet for a long time to come, Sarah was to blame herself for the ideas she gave Susan that day.

Polly's hand trembled and made an abortive gesture toward the drawer of an enameled French cottage table as they entered the drawing room. Everyone's eyes fastened on the table. Inside must be the opium, the sweet smell of which lingered, despite the fresh breeze.

"We must go," said Lucy quickly. Sarah saw that she had given up hope of saving her friend. They would withdraw so that she would not weaken in front of them and reach for the drug.

"You cannot go without Maddie," Polly said with surprising strength. "I am not too ill to see you, Lucy. I will never be until I am dead. Now, tell me about Maddie. What will you do with her, Lucy? She was a disaster at her own ball. No, don't deny it. You and I are old friends, and if we cannot be honest, then no two human beings can. We have shared our lives since you were a bride and I was little more. Will Jonathan send her to England now?"

Sarah and Susan waited on tenterhooks to hear the answer.

"Jonathan is in favor of it, but I am not. Maddie is of fine stuff. I am willing to let her find her own way—on Hazard Island as she wishes."

"Ah, Lucy. It will not be easy for her."

"No. But if she succeeds, the results will be worthwhile. If she is sent to London or Paris, we will most likely only have more episodes like the one at the school in St. John—or worse. When I was in school—" Lucy did not finish the sentence, but her eyes had a sudden faraway look, and Sarah caught her breath. Cousin Lucy must be remembering the Frenchman she had loved and lost so many years ago. No one in the room, except Sarah, could guess that thought.

"Go and fetch Maddie," Lucy said, and Sarah, glad to be away, retreated up the stairs.

She thought at first that she was in the wrong bedroom. No one was there. The fourposter bed was perfectly neat; it had not been lain upon. Then, as she was about to go, she caught sight of the ivory handle of Maddie's brocaded pagoda-shaped parasol underneath the bed. She must have put it there—hidden it, Sarah thought with a gasp. Maddie had been going somewhere where it would only have been an encumbrance. She rushed to the window and peered out, wondering what she expected to see on the green, alder-fringed lawn beyond the white Priscilla curtains. She whirled about to the empty room again. What was she to do?

"Please hurry, Sarah," called Lucy's voice from the foot of the stairs.

Sarah went out into the hall. "Maddie is—asleep," she said, the lie springing to her lips before she was aware she had thought of it. "There's no need to wake her. I'll stay and we can walk home together."

"Oh, do wake her," Lucy said impatiently. "It is a very long walk."

Sarah's heart thudded. Why had she done it? Lucy would come in now and discover the lie. But incredibly, Polly was interceding. "Do let Sarah stay longer. I want to talk to her. I will send them home in my carriage."

Lucy gave in to Polly's whim. It was of no importance. When she had gone, Mrs. Treadway turned on Sarah. "Sit down, young woman!" Her eyes focused, and the effort of it made her gaze terrible. Polly sank, quaking, into a squeaky basket chair. Polly seemed to find new energy. She seemed to have forgotten the drawer of the enameled table.

"Now! *You* tell me what Lucy would not! That is why I've kept you. With whom are you to be matched? It will be someone desirable with your breeding. Will it be that Lt. Crandell who Susan tells me monopolized you so at the ball?"

"No," said Sarah weakly. "He has been transferred."

"Aha! That will be Jonathan's doing! He *does* have plans for you! Is it to be the governor's son?"

"Mama, do not pester Sarah so!" said Susan. "It's quite embarrassing." Sarah looked at Susan gratefully, but the girl's eyes shone with such interest that Sarah realized that the protest had been only a matter of form.

"Bosh!" said Polly. "The captain has selected someone, and we must know who. We must not waste *our* time on whomever he has picked!"

"Mama!" Susan jumped to her feet, blushing, truly distraught this time.

"I have not the time for niceties, Susan. I will be dead in a year. I want to see you married. If only your father would give you a season as Jonathan has done for Maddie! I suppose it is because of me he doesn't. If only *you* would go abroad!"

"I do not want to leave Hazard Island, and Papa doesn't want me to. He needs me to be mistress here. Besides, on Hazard Island, I am the daughter of Fitch Treadway of North Pines. I would be no one aboard."

"You will always live in the shadow of the Rathrocks on Hazard Island. It is bad enough that Josh must do it. Well, Sarah, *is* it to be the governor's son?"

"I—do not know the governor's son."

"Then it is not he." Suddenly a brutish light flashed into Polly's clouded eyes. Sarah started as though there had been an explosion. She had never suspected such a side to Polly's nature, the raw, ugly desperation she had glimpsed.

"It's Brye!" Polly rasped triumphantly. "You are to marry Brye!"

Sarah, too stunned to reply, jumped up and without a by-your-leave, ran for the stairs.

In the bedroom stood Maddie, flushed and out of breath. Her face paled as she saw Sarah.

"You came in the window—how—?"

"There is a trellis, and I am good at climbing. Did you—?"

"I told everyone you were asleep."

Maddie retrieved her parasol, offering no explanation in exchange for the trouble Sarah had been to.

"Thank you, Sarah," was all she said. "Why you took such a risk, I'll never know."

Why? It was only, Sarah thought, that she seemed to have a proclivity for keeping Rathrock secrets. She had kept Brye's secrets and Lucy's. Now she was keeping Maddie's, too, though she did not even know what it was.

Chapter 8

Within a week Brye left Hazard Island. It was a blow to Sarah's campaign for him to become engaged to Susan. Sarah supposed it was an equal blow to the captain's campaign for Brye to become engaged to her. Brye had continued to avoid her in the days following Maddie's ball, and Sarah was sure he was resisting the captain's plan.

The captain, used to recalcitrants, whether children or islanders, was taking measures. If Brye insisted on leaving, the captain would make sure he did not enjoy the trip. He was sending his son to Florida with a shipload of cod liver oil. The boat was slow and dull, the cargo, unglamorous. The port of call was insignificant; and, though the weather would be hot, it had not even a good beach for swimming.

Brye's forlorn description made it seem that he had been reprimanded this way before. Worse, Brye was not sailing as mate, as he was accustomed. He was to be only third in command.

The affair was accurately calculated to strike at Brye's pride, as well as his appetite for fun and adventure. He complained about it all over South Cottage, especially to his sister, Maddie.

"Well, Brye," Sarah heard her say, "you know you will never have your command until you do as the captain wishes."

"Oh, but I am not interested in marrying anyone! It was all right until Sarah came; Father thought no one good enough. *She* has made this problem for me."

"It was bound to happen, Brye. The captain cannot permit you to remain a bachelor, you know. You must have a son to carry on the name."

"Rubbish! I care what happens to me, not my name. If another Rathrock never walked the face of the earth, I do not think the world would suffer. I think it could do without this family. I wish you were in my shoes, Maddie. You would like having a son and running Hazard Island."

"Yes," said Maddie with a sigh.

Listening, Sarah was oddly hurt by Brye's blame. Why should she care what he thought of her? But suddenly all the problems of South Cottage, all questions of Brye and Maddie and Sarah were shoved rudely to the background.

The door of South Cottage crashed open. A pane of rose-colored glass shivered and fell from one of the sidelights. Captain Rathrock sent the silver card dish on the marble-topped table clattering with the tip of his walking stick and bellowed for Lucy.

His gaze fell on Sarah, who had the bad luck to be passing through the drawing room. She felt herself blown aside by the hurricane force of his eyes. She fell back out of his way, as though her feet moved of his accord instead of her own. Lily, who had been playing on the Aubusson carpet, scooped up a handful of her blue Canton doll's china and saved it before the toes of his boots unseeingly shattered the rest.

"Lucy!"

If Sarah had been the captain's wife, she could never have answered the call. Even now she wished she could run and hide in the pie chest as she had as a child on the captain's visits to Grandemas. Perhaps most women would have felt the same. But Lucy was not like most women; it was the reason she was the right wife for the captain.

Lucy stepped out of the library, her fingers splotched with ink, a "fig leaf" apron tied over her skirts to protect them from spotting. Into the center of the maelstrom she walked as collected as Joan of Arc going to her funeral pyre.

"What is wrong, Jonathan?"

"Wrong! It is more than wrong! It is outrageous! I have just been to Halifax to collect renewal of our lumbering contracts. Can you guess what has happened?"

"No, Jonathan." Her face had gone very pale, and from where Sarah and Lily had taken refuge on the stairs, her voice was barely audible. It seemed to Sarah that Lucy could very well guess what had happened, but it was too terrible for her to say.

"To the last one, they have all signed with a steamship line! The idiots! They say that the steamships are more dependable. If they are more dependable, why do they have auxiliary sails? Because the failures of wind, unlike those of engines, are always temporary. Because there is but one way that man is intended to sail, and that is by wind, which God has given us for that purpose! It is a third of our income, Lucy!"

"I warned you, Jonathan. We had a steamship, once."

"You are as bad as the rest of them. You do not understand at all. Hazard Island does not need steamships. They will wind up having to bind their lumber into rafts and float it to England before it is over."

"Jonathan, it is not the first contract we have lost to steamships," she persisted. "It is only the largest. We must sell the clippers now and buy steamships before it is too late. As it is we cannot purchase enough. We can only hope they will produce the revenue to—"

"And our shipbuilders, Lucy," he said bitterly. "What shall we do with them?"

"We shall have to convert, Jonathan," she said bravely. "You know very well that orders have been falling off for years."

"Desert our artisans, the finest in the Dominion? You know I will not stand for it! I will not stand for steamships! There will never be a steamship that can outsail *The Lucy Maid!*"

"No, Jonathan," Lucy said, almost gently, "but *The Lucy Maid* is at the bottom of Charleston Harbor."

"We will put our shipwrights to building a ship that is even faster," cried Jonathan, "and when we have the design, we will copy it—"

"You cannot, Jonathan," she cried, a note of command in her voice for the first time. "We will go bankrupt!"

He stared at her. "I can and I will, Lucy! Do not expect me home tonight. Do not bother to warm a place in your bed for me!"

Captain Rathrock stormed out of the house and was not seen until morning. Even then he looked as fierce as before. The liquor he had obviously consumed had not made him beaten or haggard. Instead, whatever wild night he had spent at Shipwreck had given him a fiery unpredictability, so that no one could tell what slight noise or movement might bring a blast of retribution.

Everyone left him quite alone. Lucy had all their meals

sent upstairs to the nursery, where they ate with Lily, leaving him alone in the dining room.

"What will happen, Mama?" Maddie asked. "Will we lose everything?"

"In time, if your father does not change his ways."

"You will not let that happen, will you, Mama?"

Lucy gave a wry smile. "How strange that you think I can stop it, Maddie. I am only a woman."

"I remember the night that the Americans tried to annex us," Maddie said. "You saved Hazard Island then. There was no way to put out the light, and yet you did it. You went out with the gun, but you didn't shoot out the light. It was shining the very next night. It wasn't broken. I have never known how you accomplished it, but ever since then, I have thought that there was nothing that you could not do for Hazard Island."

"I should not mind if we lost the island," said Lily. "I should like to live in England and go to London and all the cities that Sarah has told me about."

Lucy shot Sarah a look of cold resignation. "Well, Maddie," she said, "Perhaps I can think of something."

"I wish Brye were here," Maddie said.

"It is just as well he is not," said Lucy. "Brye has no business sense. He would probably side with his father."

That same afternoon Lucy rode off across the island, kicking clouds of dust as high as the bowler of her riding habit. When she returned just before dark, she had a new tenseness about her. Quickly everyone else at South Cottage adopted it. They were all waiting for a tempest, though only Lucy knew the nature of it.

At ten the next morning Fitch Treadway dropped the reins of his horse around the iron lion's head hitching post and asked to see Captain Rathrock.

Fitch had about him the same air of tenseness as Lucy. Ill at ease, but expectant, he stood and listened while the servant took word to the captain, and the captain's voice bellowed that he would see no one, especially Fitch Treadway.

Fitch might have been expected to turn and go at that. Jonathan Rathrock was, after all, the master of Hazard Island. But Fitch was not the subservient fisherman he had been when the Rathrocks had arrived on Hazard Island. He hooked his thumbs in the pockets of his white marseilles waistcoat and pushing past, roared back, "It's important, Jonathan! Pour me a rum; I'm coming in!"

The library door slammed shut with Fitch inside. Lucy went upstairs and sat in her bedroom, rocking and rocking in her new bentwood rocker. There could be no doubt that the expectancy of Lucy Rathrock and Fitch Treadway was the same.

A few minutes later the library door opened. Loud, angry voices moved onto the veranda as Fitch Treadway took his leave. "Captain, think it over. It's the only way to keep your clippers. You're a damn fool if you don't do it!'

"The Devil take you!" Jonathan boomed back. Lucy's rocker hung suspended as he mounted the stairs, his boots hammering down on every third step or so, as if the hot breath of his rage gave him wings to skip the rest. Lucy leaned forward, and Sarah thought she was about to pitch from the chair in a faint. Quickly she unfastened her locket vinaigrette and offered it to her cousin.

Lucy took it. Her eyes had a vacant look as if her mind were as profoundly occupied as at the moment of death. "Go quickly, Sarah," she whispered. "Go, Maddie."

They did not go quickly enough. The captain was in the doorway, and his expression made his previous choler seem but a thunder squall. Sarah's brain numbed. Her fingertips tingled with a reasonless fear. She saw Maddie throw a wild, helpless glance of sympathy at her mother. Then the captain moved and with an imperious gesture, motioned them by.

Maddie grabbed Sarah's hand and pulled her into the next room, where Lily's bisque and wax dolls sat in a line on her bureau. "Shh! Don't make a sound. Lily's room shares a wall. We can hear, if we put our ears to it."

"I won't do such a thing, Maddie. Why is it that everyone is always eavesdropping here?"

"It is the way of South Cottage, Sarah. It pays to be well-informed in this family. It cushions rough surprises."

Maddie pressed her cheek against the pink rosebuds of the French wallpaper. Sarah sat stubbornly for a moment on Lily's flounced bedspread. Then, unable to bear the rapt expression on Maddie's face, she decided that niceties she had learned at Grandemas were impractical at South Cottage, and she scrambled down to listen, too.

"Your idea, Lucy!" Jonathan Rathrock was saying in a strangled voice.

"Yes, mine." Lucy's voice sounded hollow. Was it because of the wall or because the tones were formed from the shell of her will, strong even when substance had gone?

"You ask me to sell part of Hazard Island to Fitch Treadway. I cannot believe it!" Jonathan did not sound exactly angry, after all. He seemed mortally wounded.

"It is that or the clippers. You cannot have them both, Jonathan. If you sell part of the island we will have enough money to begin a steamship line. Fitch Treadway's offer is generous. We are lucky he is so wealthy. Which do you love more, Jonathan, your clippers of being king?"

"We will raise rents, and we will buy steamships since you are so determined."

"It will not work, Jonathan."

"The island is my domain and meant to produce revenue. Everyone on Hazard Island prospers when I do, even Fitch Treadway."

"Yes. But there is a limit to what the island can give. The people will not stand for it."

"And you think I should simply bow to that?"

"I think they can work their will if they are determined. Remember how set you were against Confederation, and yet they voted for it."

"Because of Galen Le Blanc!"

"Yes. Because of Galen Le Blanc. He has become the voice of the people on Hazard Island. He has made things different for us."

"Are you saying that Galen Le Blanc, a fugitive I hired to keep the light, has become master of my island?" Jonathan demanded.

"It was his genius for upsetting authority that made him a fugitive, Jonathan. Perhaps we should have thought of that."

Suddenly Maddie and Sarah did not need their ears to the wall. They drew back, looking at each other wide-eyed as the captain went on.

"When I married you, Lucy, I thought Hazard Island was your dream, too. I thought you would devote your life to it, that you would stand by it and me forever. And now because of a damned steamship you have deserted me, asked of me things which my soul cannot bear. You have betrayed your marriage vows, Lucy Rathrock, as much as if you had taken another man as a lover! Think of me from this day as no longer your husband—"

"Jonathan!" Her voice was only a whisper, more felt than heard by the listening girls.

"I shall show Fitch Treadway and Galen Le Blanc who is master of Hazard Island!"

The girls cowered as his footsteps banged past Lily's door. They heard the clatter of hoofbeats, and running together to the window, saw him gallop away down the lane of tall sweet birches.

When they ran into Lucy's room, she was where they had left her, Sarah's vinaigrette in her lap, her head lolling over the smooth, round arm of the chair.

She had fainted dead away.

Chapter 9

They got Lucy to bed. "We will lose it all," she murmured distractedly when she revived. "He will do that rather than lose part."

"No, no, Mama," said Maddie. "He said he would show Fitch Treadway who was master of the island."

Lucy looked at her dully and turned her head away.

The captain did not come back that night or the next morning. When darkness fell a second time he still had not returned. Lucy remained cloistered in her room, as though with her plan for Fitch Treadway to buy part of the island, she had exhausted years of effort.

"How will the captain show Fitch Treadway?" Sarah asked Maddie.

"I don't know. But he will do it." Maddie was too restless to bother much with Sarah. On the third night of the captain's absence, she did not sleep at all.

A gale wind had come swooping in from the sea with a suddenness that took South Cottage by surprise, windows ajar in the pleasant night. The ruffles of Sarah's bed canopy whipped like tattletails on a mizzen, and an earthenware flowerhorn, top heavy with fresh roses, smashed to the floor, sending scarlet petals whirling before Sarah could rush to the window to slam it down.

She heard the bangings of other windows and Annie's footsteps muttering in the hall. Then silence again, with only the scream of the wind and Maddie's heavy clumps, a muted percussion accompaniment to the crazed string harmony of the gale. The thumping kept Sara wakeful. Finally she pulled on a dressing gown and knocked on the door.

There was no answer, though she could hear movement behind it. She knocked again. "It's Sarah. I can't sleep; the wind upsets me. Let's talk."

Now the door opened. "I don't want company tonight," Maddie said and shut it again. Sarah was dazed for a moment by her abruptness. Then her mind assimilated something she had seen when the door had been open. Maddie had been wearing a dressing robe, but it had not quite hidden the hem of a walking skirt beneath it. Maddie was fully dressed. She was going out! At this hour it could mean only one thing—Maddie was running away again!

Sarah beat on the door. "Maddie! Let me in! Let me in at once or I shall arouse the entire house!"

The door opened. "Sarah, whatever is wrong with you? Have you had a nightmare? You are acting like someone insane!"

"You are the one who is acting insanely, Maddie. You are running away."

"That's right, Cousin Sarah, you clever thing. And I shall get by with it, too, this time if you will keep your mouth shut! Think of it—it's a perfect time. Everyone is distracted. The captain is away, perhaps ravishing every young thing in Shipwreck to prove he is lord and master. Mama has taken to her bed and is not to be disturbed. So if you will go away, you can keep out of it. No one will blame you for whatever happens to me."

"But I will blame myself, Maddie."

"Well, you will have nothing to blame yourself for except my happiness, if you will only go away."

"Who is this man? What a scoundrel he must be not to stand up to your father and demand your hand. That is what you must make him do, Maddie!"

"I cannot, Sarah."

"You must. Otherwise you will lose respect for him, and he for himself."

Maddie gave a great sigh of impatience. Suddenly the door of Maddie's wardrobe burst open, kicked by a boot. Josh Treadway unfolded himself from amid the skirts and petticoats, his tall frame out of proportion with the spindly feminine furniture of the room.

He favored Sarah with his infectious grin and pushed a heavy shock of blond hair away from his eyes. "I am the scoundrel, Cousin Sarah. Do prove yourself a friend again as you did that first night with Brye!"

Sarah gasped and sank down in the rush-bottomed chair beside the glowing mortar candle that was the only light. "If Captain Rathrock catches you—" she breathed.

Josh sobered. The rapscallion who had climbed from the wardrobe was replaced by someone more mature. The old Josh had been charming; this one was compelling. The old Josh had seemed to gallivant on an endless holiday; this one had embarked on an earnest adventure. The blue eyes gleamed; the features, which had the same earthy strength as his father's, cemented with purpose. "This time I shall not be so careless as when I tried to take Maddie from school," he said. "But I am prepared to die for her, if need be."

He looked at Maddie, and Sarah saw the flash of something between them. She knew with a pang of envy that the ill-favored Maddie had found a love as great as any of her mother's.

"But if you do escape you will be cut off from Hazard Island, from all else you love!"

"We will come back to Hazard Island, Sarah, someday. It will belong to the Treadways, then."

"Maddie! Can you say such a thing against your own family?"

"I am only saying what is true. Father can hold it together, perhaps by the sheer force of being who he is. The captain will be master here as long as he lives. But Brye is not the captain. Brye is a poetic boy who likes a rudder in his hand and the wind in his hair. He cares nothing for the price of sugar."

"While I," said Josh, with another grin, "have been raised in a cannery where the smell of fish strips away everything that is not basic. I love Hazard Island and I love Maddie who is more like me than she is her brother, for whom everything has always been easy. We have the same vision for Hazard Island."

Sarah thought of Brye, sweltering his way to Florida, fighting marriage to a woman he did not love, and she questioned Josh's assessment. "Josh, does your father know of this?" she demanded.

He laughed. "My father will be as angry as the captain that I have made this match. But I have managed to commandeer a small sloop belonging to him without his knowledge, and someday he will be reconciled to his grandsons being half Rathrock."

"You are going to sail! In this wind?"

Both runaways burst out laughing then. "There is no other way to leave an island, Sarah," Maddie said, taking a reticule from under the bed and shoving Sarah gently into the hall.

"Maddie! Maddie!" Sarah whispered urgently.

"Good night, Sarah. Put a pillow over your head, and you will not hear the wind so much."

She did hear the wind. She heard everything. The screech of storm petrels, the bass echo of the mammoth breakers crumbling around emptiness, the slicing of gusts among the leafed limbs of beech and birch, the quiet rhythm of Maddie's limping gait, the almost indistinguishable squeak of Josh's boots as they crept away down the hall.

Sarah stood in the center of her room, her fists clenched tightly, almost afraid to breathe for fear of betraying them. She heard horses, a grind of carriage wheels, and running to the window, caught a shadowy glimpse of their departure.

They would be a good match, Sarah thought, if it were not for their fathers. They did both love Hazard Island. They loved it because it was their heritage, and they would do well by it, if it came to them. But something would be missing—something that the captain, for all his brashness, had brought to it. Something that Brye, for all his daydreaming, possessed as well. The captain had given Hazard Island an identity, an almost human soul, that it must have lacked before. And Brye could do likewise. In a way it would be a larger contribution than increases in tonnages of salt and sugar.

A rifle-like crack brought Sarah from her reverie, her heart pumping fear down to her buckling knees. "They have been caught!" she thought, before a broken tree limb dived darkly toward the earth. Suddenly she knew that she could not take the responsibility. She was too young, too inexperienced. If the captain killed Josh, if they were both drowned at sea, she would be to blame. She knew she could not live with that for the rest of her life. She must talk to Lucy. Lucy Rathrock would know what to do. Lucy always did.

She slipped out of her room and rapped on Lucy's door. It cracked open, and there was Annie's petulant face, formidable beneath a ribboned nightcap.

"Haven't you a whit of sense? It is past midnight, and my lady is sleeping."

"It's very important, Annie."

"Mrs. Rathrock will see no one!" Annie bristled, a large, well-armed battleship protecting the door.

"I must—"

Annie moved a firm hand to push the door shut. Sarah,

not as strong, but driven by her need pushed back. The door slipped from Annie's hand and swung open. With a grunt of horror, the maid threw her weight against it and slammed it.

But not in time.

Sarah had seen beyond. The old half-tester bed was neat and empty!

Lucy was gone—to the light tower, of course. How long since anyone at South Cottage had seen her? She might have been gone for days, and in a way it was no more than the captain deserved for telling her to consider him no longer her husband.

Sarah was alone with her knowledge. Aside from little Lily, she was the only member of the family in the house. She almost considered going to the child, for Lily had an uncanny sensibility. Instead Sarah lay tense on her bed, listening to the racket of the wind, imagining screams, gunfire, splinterings masts. Then, amid the universe-enclosing roar, she heard a sound she did not imagine, a sound that had frightened her the first time she had heard it in the night and which now terrified her even more.

It was the tap, tap of the captain's ivory-headed walking stick.

Briskly, purposefully, it came. To her very room, she thought! But no. It went on past. Sarah was just drawing a shuddery sigh of relief when the tapping stopped and a fist pounded on Maddie's door with such force that the panels rattled.

"Maddie!" he yelled, with no effort to keep his voice down. Sarah quailed and thrust her hand against her teeth.

"Maddie!" Sarah heard the door crash open. There was a curse, so foul as to be meaningless to Sarah's ears. More crashes, drawers being heaved onto the floor, the wardrobe ransacked to confirm that some of Maddie's belongings had gone with her.

The tapping resumed, going out of Maddie's room with furious hurry. She thought he was leaving South Cottage then, that he was on his way to intercept the lovers. She could think of nothing she could do.

Suddenly she realized it was worse! He was not leaving the house! He was going to his wife, like any man in trouble! Sarah sat up in bed as the voices reached her ears.

"Captain, my lady is not well."

"I am the master, Annie! Stand aside!"

Annie was loyal; Annie was brave, but Annie was a mere servant. She could no more stand down the captain than a birch leaf the gale! He would be inside in a moment. He would discover all!

Sarah did not think what she was going to do. She was out of her room, not stopping for robe or slippers, racing down the hall in her muslin gown. He stood silhouetted before the door, his walking stick half-raised as though he would strike Annie.

She flung herself between them, seized the stick in both hands and brought it down to impotence. "Sir! Have you no shame! Inflict yourself on your wife who is ill! And made ill by you! Look at you! You have been drinking! You reek like a swillpot! And your clothes—they are all dirty and rumpled, and two buttons are missing off your waistcoat! How did *that* happen, sir? And you would go before a lady in such condition!"

Sarah paused, gasping. She had never in her life spoken in such a manner. And she had done so to the captain! Surely the walking stick would be raised over *her* next!

He was looking at her strangely. She saw his gaze take in her bare shoulders, and she blushed, furiously trembling, but not relinquishing her stance. There was in his eyes a peculiar recognition. He was reminded of another girl, long ago, who had confronted him in her nightdress at Charles Ashton's bedside and, like Sarah, had refused to go away.

But Sarah could not guess what made his rage shrink to a more manageable proportion. She could not imagine that this vindication of her as his choice for Brye had made him half-pleased with himself, even at this moment.

"Cousin Sarah, I have it on good authority that my daughter has run off with that Treadway good-for-naught. Do not deny it, only tell me where they have gone, and I shall not trouble you or my wife further."

She drew a deep breath, knowing that if she did not tell him something, he would burst on into Lucy's room. She chose Maddie's own words. "There is only one way off an island, Captain. Surely that is obvious to you."

He blanched. "A ship. Not one of mine, but one of Treadway's, of course. No ship's master of mine would dare. A Treadway ship—in this gale and not a decent sailor in his pay! My daughter going to the bottom on a Treadway ship! They'll not get away! And when I catch up with Josh Treadway, I will rattle lose his every bone. I will—"

Captain Rathrock stormed away down the stairs, without elucidating the mayhem further. His locks, the color of hot coals, sank into the duskiness like fury incarnate on the wind.

Sarah and Annie looked at each other wordlessly. Nothing needed to be said to cement the bond between them. The world stopped moving for the time it took to draw a long breath, then everything began to pitch forward again at the same break-neck pace.

"Go and have someone saddle me a horse," she commanded Annie, and gown swirling, she raced to put on her riding habit. She had given Josh and Maddie away. Now she must right it if she could.

The roan gelding was too big for her—sixteen hands—she thought, and too spirited; but it was fast, and speed was all that mattered. She clung to its back insignificant as a flea in its mane as the animal went pounding down Tory Road toward Shipwreck. How convenient it was that the road led exactly where she wanted to go, for a heavy cream of mist flowed over the island. She would soon be lost if she turned from the road, but suddenly she realized that was exactly what she must do. She must take a shortcut if she were to beat the captain.

A jagged white cedar loomed in her path, its trunk split in some long-ago storm. She reined in the horse swiftly and turned, remembering that Maddie had once taken her this way to Shipwreck. The cedar was her last landmark. She pushed forward through the mist only hoping that she hove to the road. Once a clump of alders, rising before her told her her mistake. She turned back and went on, less sure than before.

Far off came a gleam from the light tower, and that was her only guide. She was still heading northeast as she should be. It was only a matter of degree, but degree could make all the difference. She must find her way down to the bay where the town and harbor lay, and all about the bay there were cliffs.

Her speed slowed. The way became rough, and she knew she had gone astray. She heard the queer whistle of wind in the hollows of the rocks. She was on the cliffs.

Her fear for her own life overwhelmed her concern for Maddie. She slipped down from her mount, half-expecting as she did so to slide straight down an escarpment. Instead solid earth was beneath her feet, and as she touched down, a light miraculously appeared. A light in the harbor, she thought, for it moved as though tossed on waves.

She followed it. It seemed to beckon with its diffused, rainbow-ringed glow. How close it seemed! She wondered that she did not see some other light in the town, but it was late, and in Shipwreck, the fishermen would all be sleeping, ready to rise before dawn.

She clambered across rock, thinking the incline would become gentle, leading to the round, grassy slopes behind the town. The light bobbed, as if motioning her to come ahead. She went confidently, utterly in its thrall.

Then the wind soughed in with a quick change of direction, and the air was rent with awful moans, rising and falling, wailing and sobbing, one over the other, a chorus of witches ululating a dirge. She knew where she was then, and she dropped on her face, prostrate, unable to move again.

In the dawn Bryan Rathrock found her there, her eyes wild and uncomprehending, her fingers tangled in the grass, inches from the edge of Wailing Widow Cliff.

He knelt and took her head into his lap, running his fingers through her fair hair, straightening it where it had fallen from its chignon, laying its soft, warm waves across his knees. "Sarah, it is all right now."

"Brye! It can never be all right! What has happened? Has the captain killed Josh?"

"No, of course not. Josh is too clever for that. Maddie did not have an easy night, though. She sacrificed herself for Josh, detaining the captain while he escaped. There is no telling what Father may do with her now. What a state the household was in an hour ago, when I arrived home! Father was breaking breakfast dishes as fast as they could be put on the table, and even Mother could do nothing with him!"

She began to shiver with uncontrollable relief. "Mother," Brye had said. So Lucy was home, and Maddie and Josh both still alive.

"Oh Brye, I am so glad to see you! I am so glad you are home!" she sobbed, her arms clasped about his waist.

It startled her that she was grateful that he had found her and not some other. His hand rested on her head, and, for the first time since she had come to the island, she felt comforted.

"I saw a light," she whispered.

"Yes. The ghost light. The light that wrecked the American ship when I was a child. I heard it was abroad last night, and I knew you might have seen it from these cliffs. I thought to find you at its bottom, Sarah!"

She noticed then that he was trembling, too. She lay looking up into his eyes, realizing for the first time what beautiful color they had, beryl-blue like the captain's, but hung in shadow with the glare of the captain's removed. Like rowing on a lake on an overcast day, she thought, and having your gaze drawn deep, instead of deflected by sunlight shimmer.

"Brye, what is to become of us? Of me? I do not belong on Hazard Island."

"Father thinks you do. He is not even especially angry that you tried to save Josh and Maddie. Whatever have you done to the captain, little Sarah? We cannot understand it, Mother, Maddie, Lily, and I."

"I don't know. I have tried everyway to fall afoul of him, it seems. You would think he would ship me back to England, now."

"He is more determined than ever for us to marry," said Brye.

Sarah sat up and began to cry, brushing her tear-dampened hair from her cheeks.

"There now, don't. I shall not marry you against your will. I am in love with another, if that is any comfort."

"You are in love with Alyce Cory, and you cannot marry *her!*"

"No matter. I will not marry anyone."

"You will have to marry someone. Could you not think of Susan Treadway?" Sarah's chest heaved with great sobs.

"Align myself with the Treadways? I should not care to! Besides, I cannot abide Susan!"

Sarah was brought up short with astonishment. "But you *kiss* her, Brye!"

He laughed. "Oh indeed. She is fun to kiss, but little else. It's an amusement. Susan wears men like prizes, and I treat her the same. But I would not marry a woman like that. Well, do not worry so, Sarah. If Father keeps on as he has, we shall all have to leave Hazard Island. Sometimes I think I don't care. I think it would be worth it to lose everything."

She looked at him, shocked, and saw that his eyes had become morose. He did not like the future that he saw for himself. He was not meant to be master of Hazard Island, yet he seemed to fit there on the cliff with the sea to his back and the hawkweed springing up around him. She saw the dreadful conflict in his face: his love of the island, his hatred of his role on it.

"I should care, Brye," she said softly.

"Sweet Sarah," he said unexpectedly, and pulled her into his arms and kissed her. "Your hair is almost as long and beautiful as Alyce's," he mused wonderingly as though to himself.

"Do not compare me to *her*," she cried, struggling to her feet, her sobs unceasing. Poor Brye, he had more to contend with than ever, she thought. For suddenly everything he did and said mattered terribly; and her heart, traitor that it was, conspired with the captain for their marriage.

Chapter 10

How had the captain known? Who could have told him about Josh and Maddie? Maddie herself could not guess.

When the captain's first anger had cooled, Lucy had declared herself in favor of the marriage and had sent him off on another tirade. He would look at Maddie warily, not knowing how to deal with her or what to make of her. Obviously he was too fond of her to visit upon her all the harshness at his command.

"You may send me to England, now, Captain, if you wish," she said one morning. "I am ready to go."

He thought about it, his brow knitting as he blew ashes from his clay pipe. "No, Maddie. For I would not be able to keep an eye on you. Young Treadway would find you and spirit you away. He would not fail a third time."

Her disappointed sigh told him it was exactly what she had had in mind.

"Ah, Maddie, the scandal about you has spread even to Halifax, I'm sure. It will do you no good to show your face at any of the balls you have been invited to."

"That is a relief, Captain."

"Thunderation, Maddie! Do you care nothing for your future? I do not know how we shall make a match for you now, especially since the lumberers and their idiotic steamship contracts may run us bankrupt."

"You shall not make me a match, sir. Don't add that to your other worries. I am determined to remain a spinster unless I marry Josh Treadway."

Captain Rathrock knew she meant it. It did not keep him from visiting Fitch Treadway and informing him that Josh was to be exiled forever from Hazard Island.

"It is not within your right, Captain," Fitch had said.

"That is your opinion. If the blackguard sets foot on Hazard Island again, I shall shoot him, and then we will take it to court, if you like. I know you are fond of courts."

But Fitch Treadway was disillusioned with courts. Courts had not served him well. Galen Le Blanc had taught him about one kind of power. Now, when Fitch made his way to Lighthouse Head, he taught him of another that was more direct, more to Fitch's liking.

One blue and gold day every vessel of the captain's own fishing fleet rocked in the bice-colored water, forming a line across the harbor entrance.

"It's the way the herring are swimming," their captains said, but the fisherman carried muskets.

"It's a damned blockade!" cried Captain Rathrock, viewing the scene from the cupola of South Cottage.

They had come from generations of independent men, and they had been forced to dependence that first winter of the captain's proprietorship, when their boats had been smashed in a storm. They had never forgiven the captain his negligence or the way he had brought them to heel by replacing their boats with his own. They had thought of themselves as helpless, doing what they must for their families. Until now.

Fitch Treadway was one of them, and in Josh's banishment, each of them saw the banishment of his own son. Fitch Treadway had made them see it. He had told them they must show the captain that his arrogance would be no longer tolerated.

"Hazard Island has come of age," he had told them with an eloquence learned from his friendship with Galen Le Blanc. They had believed him.

Day after day the necklace of boats hung across the throat of the harbor. In the soft nights women would row out with provisions. The mood would turn festive, and there would be dancing on board. The sounds of fiddles and concertinas mingling their various melodies would waft in distantly over the wharves where the Rathrock clippers sat idle.

Captain Rathrock was beside himself. It was not that he could not destroy the blockade. The fishermen were ridiculously armed, and *he* had vessels he could mount with cannon.

"What am I to do, Lucy?" he would cry. "I would be destroying my own fleet!"

"You cannot afford to do that, Jonathan," she would say, rocking gently in the drawing room. She would scarcely look up from whatever book she was reading. Sarah would marvel at her unconcern.

"And I cannot afford not to!" he would rail. "I am losing money every day my clippers do not sail. And with those steamships smoking and spewing at my heel!"

"I can think of nothing, Jonathan," she would say.

She let him figure it out himself. He rode away from South Cottage, and when he returned, he looked tired and old. He went to the library, all alone, and slumped in a great leather chair and ordered brandy sent to him.

Maddie, peeping through the door, was stricken at the sight of him. He seemed not so large as before, she remarked to Sarah. "I suppose it must only be the way he is sitting in that chair, of course."

But in a few moments she had slipped into the library with him. "Captain, I have decided to give up Josh Treadway. You have won, sir. You may let Josh return, and I will never see him again. Next spring I will go to England with you where my infamy will not have spread. And you shall arrange for me any match you like."

He did not look at the mixture of pain and devotion in her eyes. He only stroked her hand and sighed, "Not now, Maddie. It is not necessary now."

The next morning the trawlers had disappeared from the harbor. The draggers were far away after cod, haddock and pollock. The smaller boats worked the weirs, followed by clouds of herring gulls and terns.

"How did he do it?" Sarah asked of Maddie.

"It doesn't matter. He has had his way, as always. I was foolish to think him beaten." The day was fine, but Maddie did not want to go out. "Stay and play whist with me," she begged Sarah.

"But the blackberries are ripe, and Lily would like me to go with her—"

"Please stay, Sarah. I am too humiliated to show my face outside perhaps ever again. Anyway, Brye is going with Lily. You'll not be needed."

Sarah sighed. It was exactly the reason she had been so eager to go. When she heard the sound of hoofbeats in the drive, she looked up with only the mildest interest, unable to think of anyone who might break her mood of disheartenment. Maddie started with alarm, dropped her cards and lifted her skirts to run away.

"Where are you going, Maddie?" said Lucy, coming in from another room.

"Upstairs, where I shall not be stared at!"

"Well, make haste, then," said a masculine voice behind them. "If you do not, I shall stare at you forever."

Josh Treadway strode boldly across the room and took her in his arms.

Captain Rathrock had not had his way after all. He sold Josh and Maddie the North of Hazard Island as part of the wedding settlement. That he did not have to surrender his land to Fitch Treadway was something of a salve to his wounded pride—even if he had had to surrender his daughter to Fitch's son.

"You buy the damned steamships," he told Lucy, handing over Josh's draft.

"You will want to see the plans, of course, Jonathan."

"No. You are the expert on steamships. It is all in your hands. I wish I never had to lay eyes on the wretched things."

She paled with the enormity of the responsibility, but her hand did not tremble as she carried the paper away. "Yes, Jonathan," was all she said. The steamships were to be her domain, and Captain Rathrock would be perhaps even less likely to interfere than he had when that domain had been only the nursery.

The Rathrock empire, though diluted, was on solid ground once more. Sarah, seeing the captain's tired face take light from Maddie's glowing eyes, thought that he had accommodated the Treadways as much for her as because he was bested. Maddie thought so, too. It was evident from the way she would bring a needlework footstool to sit with her embroidery at his elbow each evening.

"I thought you hated embroidery, Maddie," he said once.

"I do, Captain. But this is different. It is a pillowcase, and the flowers are beautiful beard. Brye drew them on the cloth for me. They are my favorite of all the island flowers, and no one shall see except Josh. If the stitching is irregular he will not mind." And then she blushed uncharacteristically at the implication of what she had said.

That night she awakened Sarah from a sound sleep, and flouncing heavily onto the bed, demanded worriedly, "What am I to do, Sarah? I do not know anything about being a bride."

"I am a strange one for you to consult," said Sarah, yawning. "You should ask your mother."

"Do you think she has the answer, Sarah?"

"Well, she has been married for more than twenty years."

"Yes, but has she done it all the right way? Oh, I know that the captain depends on her, but does he love her the way he did when they were wed? And does *she* still love him as she must have to come out here with him? The island was different then. The town of Hazard was not even built, and she had scarcely a cultured woman to talk to. And she angered the captain right away by making a friend of Mrs. Treadway."

Sarah thought of the empty half-tester bed. She thought of Lucy in her nightgown being folded into the captain's embrace. "I don't know. I will never understand your mother, Maddie. There is too much I will never perceive."

"Nor I either," said Maddie. "The captain does not sleep in her room now. I think he cannot bring himself to. It is as if he blames her for the invention of the steamboat."

"He blames her for accepting progress," Sarah said. "I suppose that seems as bad. Shall you ask her, Maddie?"

"I think not. I think I shall rely on instinct. I shall do whatever I feel like doing when Josh and I reach that mysterious encounter everyone whispers of. I am always a failure at pretending what I am not, so perhaps it is better that this time at least I do not even know what I am expected to be." And her decision made, Maddie went resolutely off to bed, leaving Sarah wide awake to wonder in her turn about men.

"It is one thing I should have no fear of," she told herself. "I shall never find out, since Brye does not love me."

She saw more of Brye these days. He did less adventuring for some reason. Was it because his friend Josh was becoming a settled man? Brye would be about South Cottage in the evenings, sitting with his feet propped insouciantly on the great veranda. He might take out a harmonica and accompany his father's concertina; and when the captain had gone off to smoke his pipe, the rollicking chanties would give way to the haunting, a lament for impossible love, Sarah would think, as the notes hung like dew in the quiet moonlight.

When the night turned chill, they would play cards

together—Maddie, Josh, Brye, and Sarah. The two young men would taunt and tease one another and their companions until they all ached from laughing and Sarah, going to bed, would have a sense of the beauty and satisfaction of life.

It was a fleeting thing. All the more so because Brye told her he was going away.

He had taken her walking on a pebble beach bounded by a great spruce-topped headland. They were looking for seashells with Lily. The child had run on ahead, gathering green, yellow and pink stones.

The afternoon sun lay, a crimped apricot ribbon, on the filigreed tresses of the water. Small gray and white birds circled together, rose-colored coronas refracting from their bodies like light behind storm clouds. Brye had stopped, hands in the pockets of his Norfolk jacket.

"Brye? Here is the shell of a horned sculpin. Would Lily like that?"

He did not answer.

"Brye? Lily is getting too far away from us. What are you thinking about?"

He heaved a great sigh. "The birds. They are Northern Phalaropes and hardly ever seen. They look so soft and playful—like little gray kittens. I imagine I will never see them again."

"Why? Will they go away for the winter?"

He looked at her then and flashed his grin. "I, not the birds, will be going away."

She was stricken both in heart and conscience. "Poor Brye," she said. "Has the captain assigned you another torture voyage because of me? Would you like me to tell him how hopeless—"

He stood very close to her. The clean brisk air accented some male aroma about him sharp and exciting like pine or fresh-cut grass. She thought for a moment he was going to kiss her again, and a wave of dizziness swept over her. Then instead, he seized the turned-up brim of her Rubens hat, and pulled its flower pot crown teasingly over her forehead. "I am not going away because of you, little Sarah."

"Why, then?" she demanded, rearranging the hat with a gesture of severity.

"Why because I am a sailor, and there are many ports to see."

"That is not the reason, Bryan Rathrock! Winter is the time to stay at home, away from the storms."

He kicked the bright pebbles with the toe of his boot. "Ah, well, if you must know, it is because I have decided that I cannot make my life on Hazard Island. I do not wish to live out my existence accepting tribute and ordering people about. I have always thought it would be necessary, but now it isn't."

"Why isn't it? You are the captain's only son. When the island is yours, you can change whatever—"

He cut her off again. "I am not needed now that Maddie is marrying Josh. They will take good care of Hazard Island, and the captain will learn to accept it. In a way he is fonder of Maddie than of me."

"Brye—is it because of Alyce you have decided to forsake your birthright?"

He smiled again, wryly, not at her, but at the stony beach. "Perhaps. I cannot stand to go on being petted like a darling little brother. I am a man now, and I need to be loved differently."

"It is a bit confusing, Brye."

"Very confusing, little Sarah. Look, Lily has found a conch. We shall have no peace until we've listened to the sea through it a dozen times, as though we did not hear the ocean enough already! And Mother will be waiting tea."

Sarah said nothing to Maddie about Brye's impending departure. She did not want the worry to spoil Maddie's wedding day, though perhaps it was spoiled already, since the captain had decreed that it be a grand affair.

"It's the least I can do for him," Maddie moaned, dreading it.

Everyone on the entire island wished to be present at the joining of its two leading families. There had been nothing remotely like it since the wedding of Jonathan and Lucy. The church was not large enough, and one disagreement followed another about the guest list. Susan Treadway, taking the place of her invalid mother, would come breezing into South Cottage, strident with her demands, reeling with the sense of her new social position as a potential member of the family.

Alyce would be matron of honor. That was the one thing Maddie had insisted on. To all other plans she had been unresisting. Sarah would be bridesmaid, and Lily would walk before them and scatter daisies.

"I shall be ridiculous," said Maddie, the night before the event. "Can't you see it, Sarah? I shall look like a misplaced Hallowe'en ghost, limping through those silly daisies in my covering of veils."

But she was not ridiculous. In her trained gown of stamped velvet, blossoms wreathed about a simple chignon, Maddie looked as beautiful as any woman in love. And when the captain, with fierce pride on his face, gave her his arm, the hated limp was barely noticeable.

Sarah glimpsed familiar faces on either side of the aisle, cataloguing their expressions as the vows were read. Fitch looked solemn, Susan triumphant and Polly Treadway, blank. Did Polly even realize what was happening? She seemed very far gone with the opium. On the other side were Lucy, whose features were composed and matter of fact, and Brye, whose look alone of all of them was impossible to read.

The ceremony over, Josh and Maddie turned beaming from their marriage kiss. In the tumult outside the church Sarah saw Brye give Maddie a hug. A moment later he was gone. Instinctively, Sarah gave a wounded cry.

"What's wrong?" said Alyce at her side. "Are you faint? You must lie down. These corsets—what nonsense that people say they are evidence of well-disciplined minds!"

"It is not the corsets, Alyce."

"What, then?"

"Brye is gone."

"He will turn up again in a minute, when all this congratulating is over. Wait until the dancing starts. Brye loves dancing."

"He is leaving Hazard Island forever!"

"Sarah! Why!" Her cerulean eyes darkened, like a lowering sky over the sea green of her gown.

"I think he is going because he is in love with you," Sarah said, unable to keep a trace of bitterness from her voice. "It's a shame he must go because of you, when he could so easily stay because of me."

Alyce gave Sarah a sharp look. "You are in love with him?" she whispered. "You who plotted for him to marry Susan!"

"It seems so!"

"Oh, but he cannot go!" cried Alyce. "Hazard Island is the only place for Brye."

"I could not tell him," Sarah said. "Perhaps *you* could."

Alyce seemed to be listening to something far away. "There *is* something I must tell him before he leaves Hazard Island. Something he must know if he is ever to be at peace with himself. Yes, I must tell him. There's no other way." She whirled and ran down the flower-strewn hill toward the line of carriages waiting at the bottom.

"Alyce, wait!" Sarah was after her plummeting down the incline, her tied-down skirts and satin slippers impeding her progress. Behind them everyone must be staring. She heard Maddie's cry and paid it no mind. Alyce had slipped into the driver's seat of one of the Rathrock vehicles, unerringly choosing Brye's four-in-hand for speed. Hoisting her skirts Sarah clambered up beside her, clinging for her life as the carriage leaped away.

"You care that much, do you?" said Alyce. "Everyone will know that you do, now."

"I don't mind, so long as what you tell Brye is not that he must love me."

"I will not tell him that."

Alyce drove with a terrible skill, her entire body thrown into the task. Her hair whipped free of its simple catagan gathering and blew about her in a golden shower. What a picture they made from the height of the church, the horses stretched out in a full run, two wheels of the coach swinging free on turn after turn of curving Tory Road! Sarah, bouncing helplessly, thought Alyce had never looked more beautiful. It was a sort of beauty that was not at advantage in a parlor, but, like a field flower, needed the wind and grasses of its natural habitat.

"If I were a man, I should love her, too," thought Sarah with a heavy heart. Any man would be lucky to have her love. Was that what Alyce would tell Brye? That she would love him the way he wanted to be loved? And then what of the loyal Tom Cory? And their small son, Adam?

They reached Shipwreck and careened through the rows of smokehouses to the wharves. Alyce jumped down.

"What ship is leaving?" she cried to a fisherman who sat mending a net.

"The Mary Ann."

"Where bound?"

"Malaya."

"I've got to catch her!" A note of hysteria was in Alyce's voice, for clearly the ship was too far away to catch. Its anchor weighed, it was already passing the harbor's mouth.

"He's gone, Alyce," said Sarah. But Alyce was no longer staring at the sea. She was running back to the carriage, and once again Sarah had to dash to avoid being left behind.

"Where are we going?" she said as the carriage sped off.

"To Lighthouse Head. The ship will go around the headland, close in where the channel is deep. I can call to him there."

Sarah thought of the wind, the ever-present wailing of gulls and gannets about the head. "Will he hear you?" she asked.

"Perhaps not. But he will see me. He will be looking." He would be watching and the last glimpse he would have of the island would be of the woman he loved. The road ended at the precipice of the gut between the island and the head. Alyce jumped down and ran for the ladder. "Stay there, Sarah," she said. "I have not the time to help you."

Sarah stayed for only a minute. Suddenly she was desperately sick of her own helplessness. Brye might sail away with the sight of the windblown Alyce locked in his heart, but Sarah, who loved him, too, must have one last look for her memory. She slid down from the carriage and took off her shoes and her white stockings. Catching up her skirt by a loop around her wrist, she went down the ladder and stumbling and slipping made her way across the cut. When she reached the far side, her dress was ruined, a matter that usually would have distressed her with her love of pretty clothes. Now she did not give the wet silk a second thought as she scrambled across the rock and the yellow-flowered cinquefoil.

Sails were the first thing she saw as she gained the far edge of the head. And then Alyce, her hands cupped about her mouth, her hair waving like a signal flag.

"Brye!" Alyce's cry mingled with the screaming of birds.

Sarah was not looking any more at Alyce. Every fiber of her attention was focused on the deck of *The Mary Ann*. Suddenly a shriek reached her ears that was not that of gannets.

The spot Alyce had occupied was as empty as though she had taken wing to follow Brye's ship like the sea birds.

She had been leaning out too far in her desperation to stop him. The rock had crumbled, and Alyce lay a small green and gold patch on the brown kelp at the foot of the cliff.

Sarah got to the bottom of the cliff without knowing how she did it. She hurt from a hundred cuts and bruises before she reached Alyce's side over the coarse spongy kelp. As she did so Brye jumped from a skiff and splashed in, horror stamped on his features.

Alyce lay without moving, her eyes closed. Both of them called her name. It must have been Brye's voice that she heard, for she stirred as if remembering the thing she had so wanted to finish in the world of the living. Her eyes flicked open and met Brye's.

"Don't worry, the ship's doctor is coming," he said.

"Be quiet, Brye," she said softly. "It is especially important that I tell you now. Your memory of me must not be false."

"Nothing about you could be untrue. I will love you forever!" he choked.

"Do not love me like that, Brye."

"I cannot help it," he replied his voice catching in a sob. "Don't tell me not to."

"I loved you as a brother and it pained you. But I loved you so because you are my brother. Lucy is my mother, too." She gasped and her voice became faint. "Love me as your sister in your memory, Brye. Promise."

He promised, stunned and wretched, and her eyes went shut forever on the island that had been her life.

A boat carried her away from her beloved lighthouse home, and Brye and Sarah wept together.

Chapter 11

Alyce had accomplished at least part of what she had hoped. Brye did not leave Hazard Island. He had lost heart for that—and for everything else. He was far from free of his devotion. He seemed fevered, in the grip of an illness for which there was no cure but time. Could there ever be time enough to cure Brye?

The sharing of the tragedy made Brye and Sarah close, but not, Sarah thought, in the way she would have liked to be close. She would find him sitting in the conservatory, where he had managed to grow hay-scented fern and meadowsweet among his mother's more exotic plants. To remind him of summer on the winter-dead island? To remind him of Alyce, who had always had about her the fresh aroma of the fields?

Sarah would creep in and sit in the basket chair in the corner. Sometimes he would talk to her. Sometimes, when he heard the creaking of the chair, he would only turn and smile at her, letting her know he was glad she was there. No one but Sarah could understand what had happened to him. And no one could know the secret they shared.

Other times he took no note of her, and she would grow cold and frightened.

Brye regarded his mother in a new light. He had seen her all his life as simply a Rathrock, pushing him toward a life he was unsuited for. He had thought that she valued power and money and Hazard Island beyond all else. Now he had to change those ideas.

"Her life must have run very deep," he said to Sarah. "It is unsettling how little I know of her."

"Galen Le Blanc must be the Frenchman she loved when she was a girl in Paris. And she thought he was dead."

"I never heard that story."

"No, you would not have. It was quite a scandal when she did not marry my father, Charles Ashton."

"And the captain knew all about that and chose her anyway? He knew she was the right one. He is wiser than I ever gave him credit for being."

He was tender toward Lucy, and Sarah thought that this alone kept Lucy from collapse. Though she did not understand its source, it comforted her as little else could have.

Sarah would remember forever the moment in the Hazard Church, when Galen Le Blanc had bent over his daughter's coffin to give her a last kiss before it was sealed shut. He had hesitated; then his hand had gone to her white throat, slipping behind the spread of golden hair to unfasten the emerald locket Alyce wore.

He brought it away with him and placed it in Lucy's hand. Lucy had started as though the touch of the cold metal were painful, then she had drawn it close to her breast, her gaze and Galen's meeting.

Their love was illuminated in that instant as though lightning had flashed on it. Sarah could not believe that everyone in the congregation did not see. Its depth, its endurance were breathtaking. It would become the model for what Sarah longed for for herself and Brye.

After the funeral Galen began to come openly to South Cottage. He would arrive about tea time and sit near Lucy saying almost nothing; and when Sarah and Brye left them alone together, they spoke little more, the desultory conversation drifting out from the open door of the drawing room—talk of the island, of politics, of the future of Canada.

Captain Rathrock knew of the visits. They irritated him, but only because he still blamed Galen for the island's vote in favor of Confederation. He thought, like everyone, that Galen came to Lucy only because she had always been a friend to Alyce. He would tease her about Galen's visits.

"Well, so the savior of Canada has been here again. Have you had the silver counted? I would not put it past that old rabble-rouser to make off with a piece or so for his campaign funds. He does not forgive us our wealth."

"He is not campaigning, Jonathan. He does not have to on Hazard Island. He is returned easily each election."

"Ah, I meant for prime minister, Lucy. *There* one must oil the hinges of the doors. He will be prime minister someday, I think. It's in his blood. Well, do you know, I think I will make him a contribution. I should like having a prime minister from my island."

Then one day Galen was not alone when he came to

South Cottage. He had with him a boy of eight or nine with a valise and Alyce's special shade of golden hair.

"I have brought you young Adam Cory," said Galen. "His father has agreed with me that he should not grow up on Lighthouse Head as Alyce did. You shall look to him, now, Lucy."

She clasped her grandson in her arms. And her joy and her grief poured forth in a torrent of tears.

Lily liked having another child in the nursery, and their screams of merriment brightened the gloomth. The captain did not object to this philanthropy of Lucy's, and the days stretched on until the terrible fruit of Sarah's plot for Brye to marry Susan came to bear.

Fitch Treadway arrived at South Cottage, wearing on his earthy features an angry, dangerous expression Sarah had never seen on the face of any man. The captain was not at home, but Lucy received him.

Fitch was not certain he wanted to see Lucy. "I am looking for the captain," he said. "My business is with him."

"The captain is away for a week, sir. Come, we can deal with each other. We have done it before."

"And it was never easy. This is not a thing for a lady."

"Ah! I should have thought you would have forgotten such ideas about me long ago."

She took him into the library and emerged looking as angry and dangerous as Fitch. When they had left, she charged through the house calling for Brye. She found him in the conservatory with Sarah.

"Sarah, please go. I must speak to Brye alone."

She rose to leave, but Brye put out a hand to stop her. She had the feeling that, sensing trouble, he wanted her at his side. The idea made her glow.

"Sarah can hear anything, Mother. I have no secerts from her."

Lucy gave Sarah a long look and acquiesed. "Well, then, she shall hear that Fitch Treadway accuses you of having got Susan with child."

Brye gaped and looked as though he would fall out of his beechwood chair. "But I never! It is not mine!"

"Oh, Brye," cried Lucy in anguish, "are you certain? You would always flirt with that girl!"

"Flirting does not get babies. I swear to you that I have

never so much as seen the flounces of her petticoats, though I daresay I might have seen anything I wished."

"You will not marry her, then?" said Lucy.

"My word! What an idea!"

Lucy drew a shuddering breath. "I will go and send your reply, then, Brye."

Brye seemed to recover himself after she had left, and a smile played at his mouth. "I am sorry I asked you to stay, Sarah. It must have been very embarrassing for you."

Sarah, her head bent over her needlework, could not answer. She did not doubt Brye's innocence.

She had underestimated Susan Treadway. She had been stupid and naive when she had first come to the island, and she was overcome with guilt. *She* had suggested to Susan that she could marry Brye. *She* had made Susan think that if only she were clever, it could be arranged.

"What will happen, Brye?" she asked in a small voice.

"Oh, I suppose that now Susan will have to tell her father who the culprit really is," he said. "Let's play cards, Sarah. I do not want to think about it anymore."

They played, but the game did not divert Sarah's mind. She did not think the matter would be so simply resolved. Fitch Treadway had put his pride on the line in accusing Brye. He would not let it drop so easily.

The next day a letter came demanding an immediate marriage. Brye himself wrote the refusal. South Cottage tensed. The children, sensing the atmosphere, whined and fought. Lucy did not eat her dinner.

"Cousin Lucy, what is going to happen?" said Sarah with a dreadful sickness inside her.

"We must wait and see, Sarah."

Sarah was almost glad Lucy did not tell her. She was afraid to know.

Fitch Treadway demanded "satisfaction."

"A duel! It means a duel, doesn't it, Brye?" Sarah cried.

"Don't worry, Cousin. I am not going to fight a duel."

"You shall be called a coward. Won't you mind?"

"Yes, but not so much as I'd mind getting shot. I can think of nothing more ignominious than dying over a twit like Susan."

"What does your mother say?"

"She thinks I should leave Hazard Island until it has all blown over."

Sarah drew in her breath, thinking what a short time ago

it had been her dearest wish that he stay. "That might be a good solution, Brye."

He snorted. "Then *I* should have to call myself a coward. Father will be home tomorrow." And he sounded more afraid of the captain's arrival than of Fitch Treadway's dueling pistols.

Sarah lay wakeful that night, listening for the tap of the captain's walking stick in the hall. What would the captain say about the matter? If anyone could make Brye duel, it would be the captain. Would he risk the continuity of the dynasty against a smirch on its name?

She dozed, then jerked awake, drawing a deep breath of the cold night air that chilled her in the depth of her being. He was coming! She heard his footsteps banging with unusual haste.

Sarah crept to her door and cracked it just in time to see Brye come out yawning and tousle-headed in a paisley Berlin wool dressing gown.

"I have heard of this duel, Brye. Well, it is all arranged. At dawn, on Wailing Widow Cliff."

"Father—"

The captain waved a hand. "I do not expect you to fight, Brye. You shall be my second."

Brye had come fully awake. Suddenly Sarah wondered why she had ever thought his eyes, the set of his jaw, any different from his father's. *"You* defend *my* honor! Oh, no, sir! If you insist on that, I shall have to fight myself."

Sarah could not stand it any longer. With a cry she ran into the hall and between the two astonished men. Then, her legs unable to bear her weight, she crumpled to her knees, her face buried in her hands. For a moment she thought she would not have the courage to say what she had to. But she could feel Brye's presence—his wonder, his concern—and her voice came out clearly.

"Captain, you must not let Brye fight a duel! It is all my fault! I am the cause of it!"

"You, Sarah!" They chorused in helpless male disbelief. It was not the way things happened. They could not assimilate it.

"It began, Captain, when you sent away that young Lieutenant Crandell who was so interested in me. I learned I was supposed to marry Brye, and I couldn't because I had promised my grandmother to marry for love. And Brye didn't love me either. So I planned for him to marry

Susan, of whom I thought him fond. I convinced her such a marriage was possible. We women have ways that men do not suspect, but even I did not suspect what Susan's would be! Brye is innocent, Captain."

Brye was looking at her all agape, but the captain, lifting her gently to her feet, said only, "You have a penchant for running about halls in your nightdress, Cousin Sarah. I am aware of Brye's innocence."

"Then why—?" she breathed.

"Because when Susan's baby is born, it will have Rathrock features."

It was Sarah's turn to be confused, but Brye, understanding, leaned against the wall with a groan.

"So you see, I must give Fitch Treadway a chance to shoot me. Honor requires it. Susan is a comely lass, but that is not why I took her. I did it because she was Fitch's daughter, and he was threatening me by trying to buy part of the island. So I took something precious of his, trying to show him who was master here. I had drunk far too much—it was the night that Josh and Maddie ran away."

"*She* told you about them!" Sarah cried.

"Yes. In retrospect it is easy to see that she wanted to be the first Treadway to marry a Rathrock. She wanted to be queen of Hazard Island. She plotted to get herself in this condition. How delighted she must be! Since it will be a Rathrock child, she must think that I will make Brye marry her rather than let him duel or own up to the scandal myself. It has not been easy, owning up, but I have done it. Well, we must get some rest. Good night, Cousin Sarah. It was not fair of me to push you at Brye. I underestimated you as much as Susan. So my death, if it comes tomorrow, will not be your doing, but my own. I still wish you were to be mistress of my island."

She heard them leave in the darkness and watched from her window as the sky went lavender, then fiery with bloodstone hues. How macabre that the sunrise, the symbol of new beginnings, should be the harbinger of death.

She thought she heard shots, but it might have been only the crack of water over rock. They came back, both of them, the captain so gray that at first she thought he had been wounded.

He waved away the attentions of those who were trying to put him to bed. "I am not hurt," he said. "Fitch Treadway is dead."

Chapter 12

Captain Rathrock was not the same man. He had quelled Fitch Treadway forever, as he had always longed to, and it had made him anything but satisfied. Maddie came every day from her new home in Shipwreck to try to cheer him up.

"It's no use, Mama," she said finally. "It is quite hopeless."

"I know of one thing that may make the difference, Maddie. I have had a letter from a corporation that wishes to buy a section of the island for resort hotels."

"Hotels! On Hazard Island!"

"It seems that fashionable people will come by steam packet from New York and Boston. They say it will be very profitable, and we would make money on passenger traffic."

"Tear up the letter!"

"No indeed! I am going to let the captain do it. It will restore him to himself. Brace yourself. I am going in to show it to him."

But the expected outburst did not come. He said only, "Well, do as you like, Lucy."

"We could use the money, Jonathan," she said.

"For a larger fleet of steamships, I suppose."

"Yes, they are our future, our fortune far more than the land."

He sighed. "Sell them if you like. I will sign the papers. It will be only a small loss of land. Nothing like what I sold to Josh Treadway."

Early in the spring, before the birches had budded, while ice still floated in the quieter island inlets, Captain Rathrock went to sea.

Brye went at the same time in command of a clipper. He glowed with eagerness, and the captain, looking at him, smiled ruefully. "Enjoy it, Brye, while you may. The clippers are doomed."

"I shall always keep clippers, sir!"

"You are a true son of mine, Bryan Rathrock. Remember that. I am proud of you."

Brye could not help a happy flush.

Sarah, unable to contain her misery at his departure, wept in her room. How could he be so gay, so unfeeling! "He has his clipper and that is all that matters," she thought. "He has even forgotten Alyce, since he has his command."

At dawn there was a knock on her door. He stood before her, ready to travel, an inverness cloak around his shoulders. "Sarah, will you come for a walk with me?"

She dressed hurriedly and met him on the front lawn. The day was wonderously private. The air was chill and swirling with an airy fog. The cold, undisturbed dew soaked the hem of her cashmere skirt. They walked away from the house toward the wood where the violets had just begun to bloom, and a hermit thrush trilled its song.

He walked so far that she was growing breathless. She wondered if he were planning something to say. She was tense with waiting.

Finally he stopped by a clump of alders overlooking the sea. "Sarah, when you plotted for me to marry Susan, I did not love you, and you did not love me. But things do not always stay the same."

She shook her head and stared at the ground.

"Perhaps it is only the tragedy we have shared. Perhaps it is more. That is why I am going away. To be away from my grief, to sort out what is the truth and what I must do. And you must sort out your feelings, too, here on Hazard Island. May I have a kiss to take with me, Sarah, so I may think on that as well?"

Her blush gave consent, and he bent and kissed her softly. The touch of his lips told her beyond doubt that *she* had no sorting to do, and when he went away she was lightheaded with hope.

By the time the blue flag bloomed Susan Treadway had given birth to a baby girl. It seemed that Polly had only been waiting for the child's cry before she let go of life.

"What will you do now, Susan?" she asked, creeping in to her daughter's bedside.

"Go away and pretend to be a widow, I suppose," said Susan. "Don't worry about me, Mama. The world is full of young men. With my looks and wealth, I shall have my choice."

When Polly collapsed in a hallway, the servants sent for Lucy. "I shall come, too," said Sarah, throwing on her shawl mantle.

There could be no doubt that Polly Treadway lay on her death bed. Her breath rattled, reminding Sarah of winter wind through ice-laden tamarack limbs. Her gentle eyes were horrible with fear, and her fingers, clutching the coverlet, were as colorless as though they were already bones.

"Lucy," she whispered.

"Yes, Polly."

"Look out for Susan. She may need someone to turn to."

"I will, Polly. But capability is in Susan's nature. Motherhood will bring it out. Susan will take care of herself."

"Yes. She shall learn from this foolish start and make better of her life than I of mine."

Lucy's warm fingers closed around her friend's cold ones. She was embarrassed, not knowing what to say. No one could deny that Polly had wrecked her life.

"You were a good wife, Polly. Fitch always loved you. Perhaps if it had not been for the cannery—if he had remained a fisherman—"

"No, no, it was not that. I preferred a simpler life, but wealth itself did not destroy me. It was that it was founded on blood."

"Blood, Polly?"

"I must tell someone before I die, Lucy. Someone on this earth, on this island, must know. I loved Fitch so that I could not bear for him to lose his chance to win the North of Hazard Island in court. The night the American ship came, when we thought they might loot and burn and annex us, it was I who carried the light. I sent a shipload of sailors to their deaths. That is why I turned to opium—because it was the only way I could forget."

"*You* saved Hazard Island, Polly!"

"I am not glad that I did. I am afraid, Lucy. There will be no opium where I am going." She gave a long shudder, as though her soul were shaking free of her ruined body, and the light of terror in her eyes grew intense. Then abruptly it was gone, and Polly was dead.

She was buried in Shipwreck beside her husband and the infant son she had lost at birth. "She was strong in her own way," Lucy said. "To think I thought her simple and weak! Well, we have seen the last of the phantom light, at least."

Sarah, remembering the look in Polly's eyes, was not so sure that the weird light that had led her to the edge of Wailing Widow Cliff would not be seen again.

But Sarah had difficulty keeping her mind on the funeral. She was young, and the first warm breezes of the year were stirring her crape veil. The sweet scent it brought from the white blossoms of wild calla on the coffin reminded her of something other than death.

Brye would be coming home. She took to walking the cliffs, following the sheep trails among the wind-stunted alders, studying the bice-colored sea for that first hazy touch of white on the horizon.

"Sarah, you are blooming," Lucy said.

"Am I? It must be the weather."

"No. You are in love with Brye. Well, I am glad of it. Once I objected. You knew about Galen and me and it made me afraid. But you have proved your worth, Sarah Ashton. You proved it that night you stood up to the captain and would not let him disturb me, when you knew I was not there. Do not look so astonished that I know of that, Sarah. The captain told me. He would always tell me of things that impressed him."

"I hope Brye will be glad of it, too," she said.

"He will," Lucy said, and directed Sarah's glance out across the green, summery island. Far off came the cry of gulls; the sweet aromas of the smokehouses drifted up on the salty breezes, mingling with the odor of roses and canterbury bells in the garden.

"You shall be mistress of it all, someday, and bear its heir. You will be what Brye needs—someone steady and gentle who loves Hazard Island as he does."

Sarah thought about it wonderingly as she walked in the summer wind. She had come to love the island. Was it because she loved Brye, and in loving him she had seen Hazard Island as it was in his heart?

She saw the sails at last, and her heart crashed against her breast like the green tide over the shaggy cliffs. She started to run to Shipwreck to meet him; then, courage failing, she raced in panic to South Cottage.

He found her trembling in the basket chair of the conservatory. He took her hands in his, and turning the palms up, put into them a scrimshaw sailor's valentine he had made her. "And now, little Sarah, you shall marry me, without breaking any promises to your old grandmother."

"Yes, Brye," she said obediently.

He swept her into his arms and kissed her.

They were married within a month, Sarah wearing Lucy's wedding dress and blossoms in her hair. They had not waited for the captain's return.

"He is not coming back," Lucy said. "I have known it ever since he set sail. The captain is aware that his day is over. He will find some tempest to sail into—or there will be an uncharted reef. He will not plan it, but it will be there, and in his heart he will be sailing toward it. Let the marriage be at once, before we are in mourning. I wish to leave Sarah in charge of South Cottage. I am going back to England."

"Do you mean forever?" Sarah cried.

"Of course not. I only want to see my old Aunt Madeliene before she dies, and I want to see Callow Hill where it all began." She might even go to see if Pauline still ran that little bookshop in Paris, she thought—

Lucy Rathrock looked out toward the churchyard, toward the monument she had erected for Jonathan, which he would never lie beneath. Then she turned her gaze to the distant, gannet-circled tower of the Hazard Light, and the fervor of her youth gleamed in her eyes.

While Galen Le Blanc lived on Hazard Island, she would always come home.